Critical Acclaim for
New York Times *Bestselling* Author Winston Groom's
AS SUMMERS DIE

"Mr. Groom has invented any number of lively touches. . . . But more than these touches, it is Mr. Groom's endorsement of the American Dream that is appealing. . . . *AS SUMMERS DIE* is a kind of fairy tale . . . and before too long we find ourselves hissing the villains as they figuratively twirl their black mustaches, and cheering for Willie as he champions the underdogs and cats."

—Christopher Lehmann-Haupt, *The New York Times*

"*AS SUMMERS DIE* becomes a classic, palpable account of prejudice, the tyranny of class and the terror of underdogs, much like *To Kill a Mockingbird*. The story is more complex than that, however. . . . The plot . . . is eminently well paced. . . . And the descriptions, together with the sparse sections of Creole dialect, are hauntingly realistic."

—Nancy Webb Hatton, *Detroit News*

"*AS SUMMERS DIE* is amusing and ironic and touched with moments of genuine depth and impressive details . . . intense . . . a fast-moving story."

—Carol Donsky Newell, *Washington Star*

"The roster of novelists who have written about the Deep South is infinite. . . . But the fine novels are rare, and *AS SUMMERS DIE* certainly is one of them. . . . Groom has written a red-blooded novel with plenty of credible action and sharp insights that only an expatriate Southerner could delineate with such authority. . . . *AS SUMMERS DIE* also presents the unforgettable Willie Croft, whose sterling probity and wisdom bring him vividly to life."

—Charles Be

"AS SUMMERS DIE is an interesting, entertaining story; it is also a novel written with perception and feeling of a time and place many readers will recognize."
—*Dallas Morning News*

"AS SUMMERS DIE is a hearty yarn, well told and well rooted in place and time, possessing much style. . . . Winston Groom writes cleanly, but his prose also brims with detail and decoration. The hunting passages are vivid. . . . The characters, too, are vivid and well imagined."
—John Paul Newport, Jr., *Fort Worth Star-Telegram*

"AS SUMMERS DIE is a work of considerable talent, feeling and thought, deserving a mint julep toast."
—Alan Hodge, *The Charlotte Observer*

"AS SUMMERS DIE evokes the nostalgia of the South at the time when political upheavals were changing man's social status and his sense of his own fate and history. . . . Groom's descriptions of nature are breathtaking in their beauty and precision."
—*Best Sellers*

"Groom has composed a wonderfully romantic novel in which the underdog wins for a change. . . . The novel's vitality and rich characterizations help turn potentially melodramatic fiction into tense, realistic drama with an upbeat, acceptable finale."
—*Booklist*

"Vibrant and powerful . . . *AS SUMMERS DIE* is an entertaining look at the South's struggle to change at the beginning of the last half of the 20th century."

—Gracie Gregg, *Wichita Falls Times* (TX)

"With racist vigilantes riding, a Black Muslim banker dropping in from Chicago, and Willie falling in love with an unconventional lady . . . there's a lot happening in this entertaining novel."

—*Publishers Weekly*

"*AS SUMMERS DIE* is a wonderful, leisurely story of good versus bad, of rich against poor that examines the typical American notion that one can overcome adversity, find good fortune and insinuate himself into the upper reaches of society. . . . It is an engaging bit of whimsy and fantasy that Groom has created."

—Robert L. Hedgepath, *Chattanooga Times*

"This splendidly written and intensely human story is well worth reading and keeping for a second reading."

—Larry Waddell, *Asbury Park Press*

Books by Winston Groom

Forrest Gump
Gumpisms: The Wit and Wisdom of Forrest Gump
Better Times Than These
As Summers Die
Conversations with the Enemy (with Duncan Spencer)
Only
Gone the Sun

As Summers Die

Winston Groom

POCKET BOOKS

New York   London   Toronto   Sydney   Tokyo   Singapore

This book is a work of fiction. Names, characters, places and incidents are products of the author's imagination or are used fictitiously. Any resemblance to actual events or locales or persons, living or dead, is entirely coincidental.

POCKET BOOKS, a division of Simon & Schuster Inc.
1230 Avenue of the Americas, New York, NY 10020

ISBN: 0-671-52265-5

First Pocket Books printing July 1995

10 9 8 7 6 5 4 3 2 1

POCKET and colophon are registered trademarks of Simon & Schuster Inc.

Cover art by Dominick Finelle

Printed in the U.S.A.

To Baba

In a Wonderland they lie,
Dreaming as the days go by,
Dreaming as the summers die:

Ever drifting down the stream—
Lingering in the golden gleam—
Life, what is it but a dream?

LEWIS CARROLL, *Through the Looking-Glass*

I returned, and saw under the sun, that the race is not to the swift, nor the battle to the strong, neither yet bread to the wise, nor yet riches to men of understanding, nor yet favor to men of skill; but time and chance happeneth to them all.

ECCLESIASTES

As
Summers
Die

Prologue

THE LAND, LOOKING FROM ITS HIGHEST POINT, STRETCHED westward and south, rolling fields of broom grass and blackjack oak that glistened in the autumn dew, and a few scrubby pines and thistle bushes, and except in the draws where narrow swampy streams gurgled and tall hardwoods rose from the thickets, it was a harsh, unyielding place, long since timbered out and farmed out—aside from some truck vegetable patches that had been kept by the Negro families. Forty miles to the south, if it had been possible to see that far, lay the great blue-green Gulf of Mexico and the brackish waters of Mississippi Sound through which the original Holt ancestor sailed, took notice of the shoreline, landed and in time established himself as a functionary for the Spanish king, collecting taxes and tariffs.

Years later he was rewarded for this service with these very same acres and many more through a custom of the time called a thumb grant—that being the amount of land a man could cover with his thumb on a map of the day.

This Holt ancestor, Don Miguel Estaban, apparently was blessed either with an exceptionally large thumb or a very small map to put it on, since his gratuity extended westward clear into what is now the state of Louisiana, and east to the edge of the great forbidding swamp, and southward to the shores of the Gulf, passing through most of the present riverport-seaport of Bienville.

Even then it was of little use, this land; dry, alkaline, hard-pitched, sandy-soiled; inhabited by quail, opossum, deer, rabbits, possibly a bear or two and a few thousand Indians who were uninformed of the change in ownership. Realizing that the worth of the land rested solely in its trading or sale value, the original Holt ancestor continued to make a prosperous living in town, having entered the export and mercantile business, until he died, and afterward his sons and daughters continued the practice of selling off, as did their own offspring.

Midway through the nineteenth century, thanks to the inventions of Fulton and Whitney, a great cotton boom had swept the South, but the fertile cotton-growing soil stopped abruptly a hundred or so miles north in the rich, swaying deposits of the Tombigbee and Black Warrior rivers. While in the outside world, a senator from Kentucky named Henry Clay was delivering passionate states' rights speeches before Congress, European philosophers were tinkering with the innovative Hegelian *absolute* and the Light Brigade was preparing to annihilate itself in the Crimea, the land remained as worthless and unused as ever.

In the year 1860, as the nation trembled on the verge of civil war, the last of the Estabans had died or gone off someplace else and the first of the Holts came into possession of the property through marriage. At that time its value was still put at less than fifty cents an acre, and the Holts, also townspeople by inclination, continued to divest themselves of it, piece by piece, parcel by parcel, throughout the war and its aftermath, acre by acre, for taxes and debts and profits, through good and bad generations, assisted by crooked lawyers and greedy entrepreneurs until, in the 1880s, an enterprising crew of Holts emerged and prospered in the cotton brokerage business and the selling off stopped temporarily.

In subsequent generations, however, the cotton business failed and the selling began again and continued until after the turn of the century, when the first Johnathan Holt launched his own small stevedoring company and the money stayed in the family again and the land did also. By then, the original hundred thousand acres had been whittled down to some 1165, give or take, but even this, at the paltry price of fifty dollars an acre, was worth far more than the whole hundred thousand when it was first presented to the Spaniard.

Johnathan Holt the elder was a sturdy, religious man and a man of vision, who knew the value of land and money and stevedoring and did his utmost to instill this in his two children, Johnathan II and Hannah, and eventually he divided the land between them in his will. Hannah Holt, a graceful belle of the 1900s, married a man called Loftin, who owned a string of sawmills north of the city, and she and her husband selected a spot of high ground on her part of the property and built their home there. Johnathan II remained in the stevedoring business in Bienville but made frequent trips up to the property, which by this time had come to be known as Creoletown. There he would hunt and fish and walk around and sometimes look in on the lone Negro family who attended it and ultimately he bequeathed a substantial chunk of it to them before he died, dividing the rest among his own four children.

His first son, Johnathan III, was ingrained with the same love of the land as his father and spent not only his youth but much of his early adulthood hunting it and fishing it and subsequently he found his vocation as a guide for out-of-state hunters and fishermen who visited the city.

The second and third sons, Brevard and Percy, ran the stevedoring company, while their sister, Marci, lived a dissolute life in between husbands. Of these four, none but Johnathan III ever used the land and he only rarely in recent years since there was better hunting and fishing to be had elsewhere.

During all this time, unbeknownst to any of the generations of Estabans or Holts or the Indians who preceded them, a dark and silent geologic process was taking place, and in fact *had* been taking place long before the first

Estaban and Holt progenitors began hauling themselves up out of the primordial mud.

The billions of living organisms of the Paleozoic era, having long since died and sunk into the ground, were slowly pressed into a warm, decayed and gaseous loam. Eventually, by the fierce quashing weight of the earth itself, this loam was squeezed, fermented, pressed and boiled into a thick, black, gooey substance called oil.

The oil lay in limestone beneath layers of rock and dirt at various levels, and although petroleum companies had occasionally test-drilled the area for years, nothing was actually confirmed until the last week of November, nineteen hundred fifty-nine. Several days later, approximately the week of Thanksgiving, Brevard Holt received a telephone call in his office at Holt Stevedoring from Mr. Augustus X. Tompkins, the Holt family attorney. Tompkins's information was that samples taken from the Holt property, as well as from other properties surrounding, indicated that Creoletown and it environs were possibly sitting atop the largest oil and natural gas field since the famous Spindletop discovery near Beaumont, Texas, in nineteen hundred and one.

This news Brevard Holt received with his typically cool and collected manner, after which he experienced a stunned and delirious surprise and indulged himself by taking a small drink from a bottle of Jamaica rum he kept in a desk drawer.

But he kept the information to himself for almost a week, realizing its delicate and momentous import which, handled properly, could make millionaires of himself and his brothers and sister. Then, on the Monday after Thanksgiving, Brevard Holt called them all in to make his announcement and thereby set into motion a series of events which would gnash and claw at the Holt family and in the end threaten to bring it to ruin.

I

The Discovery

1

On the Monday after Thanksgiving, P. Willis Croft had, as he always did on Mondays, many things to do. As usual, he would not go to his office first thing, but instead, after two cups of coffee and grits and fried bologna at Swampman Charley's Diner, he drove straight to the county courthouse wherein a certain number of his clientele had been incarcerated for various antisocial behavior during the previous weekend. Since it was a longer-than-usual holiday because of Thanksgiving, there would be more of them to get out of jail (which fact he already knew for certain because of the phone calls received from distressed wives, mothers, friends and relatives or in some cases from the miscreants themselves).

In seventeen years of practicing law, Willie Croft had learned to deal with the weekend phone calls in a prompt and expedient fashion.

As soon as he ascertained the nature of the call he immediately interrupted the breathless voice at the other end and asked three questions: first, the name, address and occupation of the accused, second, the charges against him, or her, and third, the name, address and phone number of the caller—all of which information he wrote down in a notebook by his phone; then he would make the following speech:

"Please listen carefully. The courts are not open on weekends and holidays so there is no way to get him out of jail until they are. Meet me at nine A.M. Monday in the arraignment court on the first floor of the county courthouse building. Do not be late. Bring with you as much cash as you can, and all the identification you have. Also bring a blank check. The judge will set bail in the morning and after the hearing we will go either to the bail office at the courthouse or the bondsman across the street if you don't have enough cash on hand."

The cellblock itself was on the second floor of the once-elegant Grecian courthouse building—one story above the ground and freedom. And on Monday mornings Willie Croft was the Groundman.

This Monday, however, something else had occurred to occupy Willie's thoughts as he sipped his coffee and waited for Swampman Charley's grits and fried bologna. Priscilla, his cleaning woman, had arrived at the apartment an hour earlier than usual because, she said, she wanted to speak with him. Priscilla was a large, good-natured, light-skinned Negro whom he had employed two days a week for nearly five years. Willie had not actually seen her in at least six months because she ordinarily arrived at nine in the morning and left in time to catch the three o'clock bus, so he would simply leave her wages, five dollars plus carfare, on the kitchen table along with any special instructions he had, and these sometimes included asking Priscilla to prepare whatever food he had purchased—such as pot roast or ham and cabbage or meat loaf ingredients—and he would eat off this for a couple of days until she came again, and thereby avoid having to cook for himself, an art he had still not mastered at the age of forty-two.

But this particular November morning, with the kitchen windows steamed up from the coffeepot and Willie still in his bathrobe watching the morning newscast on television, Priscilla had knocked at his back door and told him she came early to ask his legal advice about something. He sat her down at the kitchen table and over a cup of coffee she told him a curious story.

Two days before, the day after Thanksgiving, a Mr. Brevard Holt had shown up at the door of Priscilla's mother's house up in Creoletown and offered her twenty-five thousand dollars in hard cash if she would leave the house and her property and move someplace else.

Mr. Holt, Priscilla said, had carried the money in a briefcase, along with a paper he asked her mother to sign, quitting all claims to the property. According to Priscilla, Mr. Holt had told her mother, Mrs. Elvira Backus, firmly, that while he realized the Holt family had taken care of her people for several generations, they now wished to develop the property and the twenty-five thousand was a fair price, which she could use to purchase a nice modern house elsewhere, and still have money left to spend.

Priscilla said her mother was deeply disturbed by Mr. Holt's visit, because she was a seventy-eight-year-old woman and this was her home, "where she had lived all her life, and in fact had been born in, and where she intended to die, God willing, peacefully, in her sleep, and furthermore, she did not need no twenty-five thousand dollars to do it with."

Willie poured them more coffee. He knew who the Holts were, of course, but did not know them personally. Everyone in Bienville knew who the Holts were. There was the Holt Bank Building, the Holt Stadium and Holt Boulevard, a broad, oak-lined street in an older section of town. From time to time Willie had sprung a few Holt Stevedoring Company longshoremen from jail, after Saturday-night brawls around the wharf area.

Priscilla said her mother had informed Mr. Brevard Holt, nicely, but just as firmly as he had her, that she was not interested in giving up her place, at least until after she was gone; then perhaps her son and daughter might sell it, since none of them lived there anymore. Whereupon, Priscilla said indignantly, Mr. Brevard Holt had announced that if need be, he and his family would take her mother to court and forcibly evict her without the twenty-five thousand dollars and put her right out, bag and baggage, on Route 23,

South, and so she had better take his money and sign the papers now, while she still had the chance.

At that point, Priscilla said, her mother produced a deed given to her by Mr. Johnathan Holt, Mr. Brevard Holt's father, just before he died, and which was signed in ink by Mr. Johnathan Holt himself, giving her the land. Priscilla said Mr. Brevard Holt had glanced at the paper and declared that it was completely worthless since he and his brothers and sister had sole legal title to the property and the courts were likely to look upon their claim more favorably than they would an almost twenty-year-old scrap of paper signed by a man who had died a few months afterward. Subsequently, Mr. Brevard Holt had departed, telling Priscilla's mother to think this over carefully and that he would be back in a few days to have her decision.

At this point, Willie stopped Priscilla, saying that he had to shave and shower and dress for the office and they could talk about it further when he had finished. Priscilla began to do the previous night's dishes in the meantime.

In the bathroom, Willie took off his robe and hung it on a hook. He examined himself closely in the mirror, and ran his fingers under his eyes, pulling back the little crow's-feet wrinkles. He parted his lips and examined his teeth. Thank God, he thought, I've always had good teeth: straight, white, very few cavities. There was a full-length mirror on the door and he turned in front of it, looking over his shoulder at his naked backside. Not bad either, he thought. He hadn't put on any weight to speak of since college, and he had been fairly trim then. He ran his fingers through his dishwater-colored hair and reminded himself to get a haircut. He turned his face from side to side, examining the profile. Sometimes he wished he had been born really handsome, but since that had not been in the cards, he had satisfied himself with being grateful that he was not ugly either.

As the hot water tingled over his scalp, Willie pondered the story. On its face, it had the markings of a routine kick in the pants for a colored woman.

Only the week before, he had sat through part of a case in

which a more or less respectable citizen of the community had been brought to trial for fraud on grounds that he had bought up several hundred shanties in the bleak Negro section of town, resold them to the Negroes at exorbitant prices (providing the financing himself when no bank would lend money), and then foreclosed the instant a payment was missed. The defendant turned over some of the houses three and four times a year for an immense profit, but as expected, he was acquitted, the juries in Bienville not being disposed toward loan defaulters or deadbeats, especially when they were Negroes, and when the creditor was a white man.

But Priscilla's story had a different ring to it.

The Holt family did not seem the sort to trifle in petty swindles, and what Willie found out from Priscilla when he returned to the breakfast table proved this assumption to be correct.

The day after Holt's visit, Priscilla said, her mother had been called upon by two representatives from the Union Oil Corp., who asked if she was the owner of her property. When she replied that she was, the oilmen told her their company would be interested in acquiring the opportunity to drill there and asked if she would be willing to sell them the mineral rights. However, after the encounter with Mr. Brevard Holt, Mrs. Backus's suspicions were sufficiently aroused to decline any offers whatsoever, and the oil company men thanked her politely and got into their car and drove away. Later that morning, Mrs. Backus had phoned her son Daniel, a high-school teacher, and related what had happened. Daniel in turn had called Priscilla and this, she said, was why she had come to work early: to ask if Willie, being a lawyer, could give them any advice about what to do.

Willie was mulling it all over when Swampman Charley's food arrived at his table.

So there was oil up there. He hadn't seen that part of the county in years—not since his college days when sometimes on Sunday afternoons he would take a shortcut through the stark, desolate roads near Creoletown on his way back to the university. Oil, he thought, would change a lot of things up there. He wished he knew how much oil they were talking about, and how the Holts were involved in it, because oil and the Holts together sounded like The Big Time.

One case like this could set a man up for life. Still, property rights, oil, mineral leases—they were far afield from what he'd been doing all these years. The last time he'd had a big case—any kind of big case—had been nine years before, in 1950. He'd thought *that* was The Big One: a police and firemen's benefit suit in which he'd won a three-million-dollar judgment against the city from a lower court and had it upheld by a higher court, and finally it got all the way to the State Supreme Court where, at age thirty-three, he was on the verge of collecting a cool three hundred thousand dollars in legal fees . . . and then, like practically everything else big in Willie's life, something went wrong at precisely the wrong moment: war broke out in Korea and his National Guard unit was called up and Willie Croft, the lawyer, became Sergeant Croft, of the Dixie Division, and he was forced to turn over the brief to someone else and the Supreme Court threw out the earlier rulings and the three-hundred-thousand-dollar legal fee vanished along with the three million in back benefits for the police and firemen.

When he returned from Korea, Willie hung out his shingle in a small, seedy office building near the courthouse and began taking on cheap criminal cases that none of the other lawyers wanted to bother with. In time he built his entire practice around them, and none of it had changed very much, except that the office building had gotten seedier in the nine years.

Willie was crossing the street from the parking lot to the courthouse when the murmuring began.

It began that way every Monday morning, a low humming from the second floor of the courthouse where the barred-up windows of the cellblock caught the first glimpse of the sun rising over Bienville Bay: slow, deep murmuring as Willie crossed the street, growing, as he approached, to a kind of basso chant and the barred windows filled with dark,

12

expectant faces. Willie figured it was his tan poplin raincoat they recognized first.

Today the voices seemed more intense than usual:

"Groun'man heah! Groun'man heah! Groun'man heah . . ."

It provided him with a feeling of dubious satisfaction.

At the entranceway to the courthouse Willie the Groundman passed Burt, the bailiff, half asleep as usual against a massive Corinthian column.

Willie leaned over so that his mouth almost touched Burt's ear.

"Hello, Burt!" he shouted.

Startled, flustered, his cap askew on his head, Burt scrambled up and tried to compose himself.

"Morning, Mr. Croft," he said, but Willie had already gone by. He acknowledged Burt with a wave of his hand.

"There's a lot of 'em up there today," Burt called after him. Willie continued on, straight down the hall, nodding occasionally to familiar faces, past the entrance to the arraignment court.

He put the raincoat over his arm and turned into the small side door theoretically used only by judges, which led directly to the courtroom. In the tiny foyer he straightened his tie and, looking into the mirror, worked into his face the sternest official expression possible.

It was exactly five minutes before nine when Willie marched into the arraignment court. Instantly two dozen anxious eyes were upon him as he came to an abrupt halt behind the dock beneath the judges' bench.

"All rise!" he commanded sternly.

Slowly, but as one, the group rose to attention.

"We will now sing 'America, the Beautiful,'" Willie announced, and began himself in a deep, solemn voice:

> "O beautiful for spacious skies,
> for amber waves of grain . . ."

Most began to join in and the few who did not stood reverently. They sang on:

13

". . . And crown thy good with
brotherhood
From sea to shining sea!"

At the end of the song a silence engulfed the room.
"Seats!" Willie said majestically.
Everyone sat down in a hush.
"Anyone wishing to see Attorney Croft," Willie said,
"please go out into the hallway. He will be there presently."
A dozen or so rose to leave. Willie watched them file out
and then marched out the side door he had come through,
retrieved his raincoat and briefcase and proceeded down the
hall to conduct his business.

In the following hours Willie stood up for an automobile
thief, two wife beaters, a slow-footed crapshooter, a suspected rapist and a man who had used a razor on a former
friend. All were set free on bail except the crapshooter, who
had had previous difficulties with the law. From the families
and friends of these malefactors Willie collected fees of two
hundred and twenty-five dollars cash, a fifty-dollar check
and promises to pay two hundred and seventy-five dollars
more before trial. Shortly before noon, Willie went to the
seedy office building, collected a few messages from the
answering service, read his mail and set out across the town
square, which was called The Parade, for lunch at Traylor's
Oyster Bar.

It was a perfect autumn day. The big live oaks spread their
limbs over the grassy Parade like a roof, allowing little
beams of sunlight to filter down on the bums and vagrants
lying on the benches, or onto the backs of people feeding
peanuts to squirrels and pigeons. But as luck would have it,
as he walked down St. Raymond's Street toward Traylor's,
Willie saw approaching him from the opposite side of the
street, wearing a dark three-piece suit and carrying a newspaper under his arm, the tall, austere figure of the Holt
family lawyer, Augustus X. Tompkins.

Good a time as any, Willie thought. Maybe better. Catching Augustus Tompkins on neutral ground was no mean feat

since Tompkins himself rarely appeared at the courthouse, and Willie knew there was little chance of getting him up to his own little office. It was a stroke of blind luck to catch him like this on the street.

But just as Willie started over the curb, Tompkins stopped, looked around furtively, then disappeared quickly into the town's only dirty movie theater.

Willie stopped almost in midstep, a puzzled look on his face. The marquee announced that the film that day was entitled innocently enough *Schoolgirls at Play,* but the art on the billing poster gave a far more sophisticated indication of what might be expected inside.

Willie hurried across the street, paid his two dollars and followed Tompkins into the theater. He found a seat near the rear and in the dim light could make out a dozen or so men engrossed in watching a thoroughly illegal, not to mention immoral, sexual performance take place on the screen. Far down the aisle and off to his right Willie recognized the head and shoulders of Augustus Tompkins. He waited until the precise culmination of the scene, a panting, heaving trio writhing and moaning on a bed, then, in his deepest, most authoritative disguised voice, cried:

"Paging Mr. Augustus Tompkins!"

Several men turned their heads nervously. Most did not, and the figure of Augustus Tompkins did not move at all, but instead seemed to freeze and stare straight ahead. Willie waited another minute or so, until a dark scene dimmed the light in the theater. He then repeated the call.

This time some faces turned angrily toward him but Tompkins was not among them. Moments later, however, Augustus Tompkins rose quickly out of his seat and hurried up the aisle and out of the theater, his chin tucked tightly onto his chest.

Willie caught up with him on the street outside.

"Goddamn it, Willie Croft! Was that you did that in there!" Tompkins blustered.

Willie grinned. "I need to talk to you," he said innocently.

"For godsakes, man," Tompkins cried, "you realize what would happen if this got out? If there was anybody in there

15

who knew who I was. It could . . ." He let the words trail off. "It's not funny," he said.

"I've got to talk to you," Willie repeated.

"What about?" Tompkins said sourly.

"About the oil on the Holt property up in Creoletown."

Tompkins, who had been edging steadily away from the movie house, stopped dead on the sidewalk and looked at Willie.

"What's this about oil on the Holt property?" he said. His mouth was pursed and he eyed Willie suspiciously.

"About the Holts trying to buy the old colored woman off her property for twenty-five thousand dollars when the oil companies are interested in her land," Willie said.

Augustus Tompkins shook his head deliberately and started to walk away, "Don't know anything about it," he said.

"Come on, Augustus," Willie said coolly, "a client of yours is into oil property and you don't know about it? Surely you jest."

"I know very little," Tompkins said, regaining some of his composure. "I understand there's been some talk of oil up there, but they've been drilling test wells for years. Anyhow, what's your interest in this? You're a little far afield from your kind of practice, aren't you, Willie?"

"My ah . . ." Willie didn't want to use the word "client" because he didn't know if he had a client or not. And if he did, was it Priscilla? Or her mother? Or brother? Or who? And he still wasn't certain he wanted to represent a bunch of Negroes who couldn't pay anything in the way of a fee except on contingency. And against the Holts at that, who could hold you up a dozen ways with writs and stays and continuances and make you file a hundred kinds of papers. . . .

"My interest," Willie said cautiously, "is that I've been asked to look into it by a member of the colored family up there—a daughter."

Tompkins shook his head again. "That family," he said, "has no claim at all to that property. Out of the kindness of their hearts the Holts have let them live up there, but they've got no title, Willie, simple as that."

"That's not the way I heard it," Willie said. "I'm told there is a paper bearing the signature of the old man—the Holts's father—deeding several hundred acres to Mrs. Backus, the woman, and her children."

Augustus Tompkins looked at Willie with keen, steel-blue eyes, but said nothing for a moment, apparently having decided it was the best way to find out how much Willie knew without giving away anything himself. And Willie, quickly realizing this, decided to let on that he knew more than he did.

He looked down at the pavement.

"If what I hear about the oil up there is true, there's an awful lot of money at stake, Augustus, and your people aren't going to be able to buy the colored woman off for any twenty-five thousand. From what I know so far, I think she's got a pretty solid claim—both from the standpoint of the paper and, if nothing else, squatter's rights—popular sovereignty. She isn't going to give it up that easily, and neither are her children. But it might be possible to work out some kind of accommodation." Willie was fishing and knew it.

Tompkins sighed deeply and shook his head for the third time.

"Listen, Willie, first off, nobody's trying to buy that woman off. As I understand it—and I don't know the whole story—Brevard Holt, at the request of the rest of the family owners, offered to give the colored woman enough to buy a nice place somewhere else. So far as I know the oil thing is just speculation—pure and simple, nothing more. Like I said, they've been drilling around there for years."

They eyed each other for a few moments, the aristocratic, senior partner in the city's largest law firm and Willie the Groundman in his soiled tan raincoat.

"Listen, I've got an appointment—some people coming in," Tompkins said. He smiled and then leaned over to Willie in a fatherly sort of way.

"If I were you I wouldn't get mixed up with this thing. I'll tell you what it is, Willie, it's a *nigger deal,* that's all. There isn't a court in this state that's going to rule against a legal title—and the Holts have one. That land's been in their family over two hundred fifty years. If you start meddling in this it would cost the old woman her twenty-five thousand to boot."

Willie Croft looked over at The Parade. The bums and vagrants had shifted to the northwest benches to catch the warmth of the afternoon sun. Several blocks away on the waterfront an unseen cargo ship sounded its horn.

"Maybe so, Augustus, we'll see," Willie said.

They walked side by side, silently, until Tompkins reached the street where his office was located.

"That was a hell of a thing to do to a man—in that movie theater," Tompkins said crossly.

Willie put on his most ponderous expression.

"I know," he said.

The two men parted without shaking hands.

When Willie got home that evening there was the pungent aroma of pot roast in his apartment. He put down his raincoat on a kitchen chair and lifted the lid of the big roasting pan on the stove. All he had left was the roast and some potatoes and onions, but Priscilla evidently had gone to the store herself and bought carrots and celery and a turnip to add flavor, and also, cooling on the kitchen table, was a freshly baked apple pie. Willie took off his jacket in the living room, loosened his tie and unfolded the late edition of the afternoon newspaper. A giant banner headline screamed out at him. The Union Oil Corp. had just announced that it had located a major oil field, possibly one of the nation's largest, in the Creoletown area.

The story went on to say that it was potentially the largest oil find in twenty-five years and almost certain to bring dramatic economic change to Bienville and the county and even the entire state. By the end of the hour Willie had polished off two glasses of Early Times bourbon, his old standby drink. His mind was racing and drumming and he felt the need for some fresh air. Leaving the newspaper on the floor, he stepped out into the brisk November twilight and, in the warm, exhilarating glow of the whiskey, started across the street toward the little neighborhood park that was surrounded on all sides with elegant old houses.

2

─────────────

Bienville, then, was neither a small town nor a big city. Two main streets, named for Catholic saints, ran past an oak-lined square—with a cannon and a bandstand from the old days—and this was The Parade. There were two five-and-dimes, a bank and a brokerage house, dealerships for the three major automobile companies and a pre–Civil War hospital. No building in town was higher than ten stories.

The nearest big city was New Orleans, which was where most of Bienville went when it wanted to indulge in culture or in sin. There was one good hotel in Bienville and three bad ones. There was a white section of town and a Negro section, which had formerly been a historic white section until the whites expanded the city south and westward. There were several antebellum mansions open to public tours run by the Daughters of the Confederacy, whose ranks were thinning quickly now to granddaughters. Suburbs were only beginning to sprout, and there were no shopping centers. People did their shopping in town.

There was a newspaper and a chamber of commerce and it was commonly said that between the two of them they had managed to wreck any hopes for a decent economy in the town. The newspaper was put out by smug conservative men whose politics were somewhere to the right of the Dixiecrats. The chamber of commerce was controlled by a dozen or so owners of the largest businesses, and engaged in a long-standing, overt conspiracy to keep out any new business that might be incompatible or in competition with their own.

Many of the people were Catholic, a legacy from the days of the Spanish and French, but there were Episcopalians and Presbyterians too, and Fundamentalists who had come to Bienville from remote places in the countryside. There was a Masonic hall and a country club and a seamen's mission.

The Frenchman who founded the place might have selected a more agreeable spot.

It was true that the tropical climate enabled the inhabitants to develop lush gardens and the lawns were green and the trees magnificent. But since the town had been located at the edge of a great swamp, flies and mosquitoes bred in grand profusion and it got so hot every summer that an annual event for the newspaper was to send a photographer out to take a picture of a child frying an egg on a sidewalk. Old ladies sitting on porches beneath ceiling fans and sipping iced tea would talk of this for entire evenings, watching the fireflies and shooting stars. Winters were more temperate, but whenever the thermometer dropped below fifty degrees these same old ladies would hurry to wrap rags and gunnysacks around their shrubs and complain fearfully of the bitter cold.

The commerce of Bienville revolved around its port. Ships arrived from the Caribbean, South America and West Africa and unloaded into railroad cars, then stocked their holds with goods from Bienville and other parts of the state. A few Bienvilleans were rich, and many were poor, but most were somewhere in between. The whites, middle class and poor alike, identified with the rich even though there was little hope that they would ever become rich themselves, and they knew it. But there was little despair among them either, for they were believers in the great American dream that someday, with a little luck and hard work, it was always possible. The Negroes identified with nothing and no one except themselves, for their hard work barely, if at all, paid for day-to-day needs, and luck was something that had long been trodden out of them. True prosperity, in any case, was something Bienville had yet to know, except for these few older, wealthy families, and the Holts were, of course, among them.

"What I have to tell you," Brevard Holt said in a reassuring, businesslike voice, "is about the Creoletown property." In his hand was the afternoon paper, containing the story about the oil discovery. He was standing beside the fireplace in the library of his home, before a large beveled-glass mirror that reflected the late November sunlight streaming through French doors and onto the faces of the Holt clan. Outside, a dozen or so Holt offspring and neighborhood children had organized a game of touch football on the lawn, and the noise of their play was all that disturbed an otherwise perfect silence.

"I might as well tell you now," Brevard said, "that I knew about this before the newspaper got hold of it. Augustus Tompkins called me about a week ago. We already have offers from oil companies to buy mineral rights for fifteen hundred dollars an acre, plus an eighth of whatever they find."

He let that sink in for a moment. The faces before him were intent and expectant. Johnathan III, Brevard's older brother, sat awkwardly in a chair too small for his large frame, hunched forward, fingering a can of beer. Percy Holt, ten years younger, wiry and intense, was drumming on a Parsons table with his fingers, and their sister Marci was seated on the sofa with her legs crossed, smoking a cigarette. Seated next to her was Whitsey Loftin, their cousin through marriage, who was there because of her close relationship with their aunt, Mrs. Hannah Holt Loftin, who, under the terms of their father's will, controlled not only her share of the undivided Creoletown property, but theirs as well.

"I don't have to tell you that there is a great deal of money at stake here," Brevard continued. "Just how much depends on a number of things, but at worst it will be a comfortable amount for each of us, and at best it could make us millionaires many times over."

"Well, if you knew a week ago, why in the world didn't you tell us?" Marci Holt said stiffly. "Don't you think we have any right to know?" Percy coughed and clenched his teeth on a pencil-thin cigar. Big Johnathan leaned even farther forward and studied his shoes. All of them seemed motionless, as if frozen in a snapshot, while Brevard measured his words carefully.

"It was my opinion that some very fast and direct inquiry be made before we all sat down to decide what to do. I thought I could best do it alone. There are some problems. Let me explain."

Marci Holt crossed and uncrossed her legs, took a swallow from her drink and stubbed out her cigarette impatiently.

"As you know, there are two separate parcels of land up there—the four hundred eighty acres off the blacktop road and the eighteen hundred around Aunt Hannah's place, of which we own an undivided one-half." Brevard looked at Whitsey Loftin.

"Now Aunt Hannah is a very stubborn woman. A few years ago when we tried to get her to divide our share so we could do what we wished with it, she refused. When the oil companies wanted to try a few test wells last year, she refused that too—even though we are all owners. I drove up there to see her a week ago, to tell her about this, and she didn't even recognize me—or at least she played like she didn't. Wouldn't discuss it—wouldn't even let me inside."

"It's because she's nuts," Marci said coldly; "we all know that." Whitsey Loftin started to say something; there was a frown of hurt on her brow, but Brevard cut her off.

"The situation with Aunt Hannah is very delicate. We want to avoid a fight. Her mental state is, ah, a little unpredictable, but Whitsey has usually been able to deal with her. Now, Whitsey, I've got to ask you to help us persuade her to sell these leases—or at least to let us divide our interest so we can sell what's ours. If you can't, I'm afraid we might have to take legal steps, and that won't be very pleasant."

Whitsey leaned forward on the sofa and ran her fingers through her full mane of blond hair. Brevard recalled how, even ten years before, people had sometimes confused Marci and Whitsey. They had had the same blue eyes, and blond hair, and shape of face, but while Marci's face and figure had hardened with time and drink, Whitsey's had almost softened, and her figure had become voluptuous and remained so.

"I'll try, Brev. I suppose I could go up there sometime this week."

"Good," he said. "I'll talk to you about what we want you to do."

"Why don't you talk to her now?" Marci said crossly. "Or aren't we supposed to hear?"

"Of course you are," Brevard sighed deeply. "I just want to get on with this so . . ."

"Why is it that *you* are always trying to get on with something that has to do with all of us?" Marci snapped. "You kept all of this to yourself for a week or something." She looked around at the others. "You seem to think you're running this whole family."

Brevard rubbed his forehead in exasperation. "Look, I'm sorry if I seem to be dictatorial—maybe I seem like that sometimes—but we're talking about serious money now. All this is complicated, and we're going to have to make some hard decisions."

"Well, it just makes me furious," Marci said sullenly. "You seem to think you've got to make the decisions for all of us. You act like Augustus Tompkins is just *your* lawyer. I'll bet you told him not to call us, didn't you?"

"I did no such thing," Brevard lied. "I simply wanted a couple of days to . . ."

"Oh, for God's sake!" Marci said. "I'm going to get another drink."

He shook his head slowly and watched her leave the room.

"All right," he said, "there's another problem. It's with that colored woman up there on the property off the blacktop road."

* * *

Unaware of the discussion taking place in the Holt household, Willie had been sitting on a bench in the park for nearly an hour, watching the sunset, nursing his drink and smoking Picayune cigarettes. And contemplating.

An orange moon that had risen over the Bay loomed enormous above the rooftops and the great gnarled, mossy oaks in the park. Lights glowed cozily through French windows and beveled-glass doors of the stately residences where pots of ferns and other dripping and drooping semitropical plants hung from expansive porches; palmetto and date palms and azaleas and occasional banana trees grew on lawns of thick Saint Augustine grass, all of it bathed now in the ocher moonglow. In the morning, just after sunrise, a milk truck driver would lay out the bottles of fresh milk and cream and cottage cheese at the back steps of these houses. And later, while the dew still glistened on grass and flowers, the white-bearded Negro would come up in his wagon from the wharf, singing, "Oh-st-ers, s'rimps, cr-abs, viggg-e-tables," and mothers and cooks would gather around to inspect and buy while their children gawked at the moth-eaten mule with blinders, even more moth-eaten than the previous mule, who had died a few weeks before. And later would come the tinkers and the yardmen, to grind knives and glue broken china and manicure the gardens and lawns and put everything in a perfect way.

Willie had never been invited inside any of these houses, and sometimes, walking past, he looked through the windows and wondered briefly what it was like in the elegant formal dining rooms and high-ceilinged parlors and hallways. The people who lived here were old Bienville.

Old, old Bienville.

They had lineage to French and Spanish settlers; they belonged to secret and exclusive mystic societies and to the fashionable country club; they had palatial summer homes across Bienville Bay; they were quiet, conservative people not as yet disposed to accept into their living rooms the son of a service station owner and a beauty parlor operator who had worked his way through college and law school by operating a campus laundry pickup service.

Never, since the day he moved into the little garage apartment in their neighborhood, had Willie Croft received an invitation from any of them, for anything.

It wasn't that Willie was poor, for he wasn't. Or that his family had been poor, which it was; it was the *name,* or lack of it; for in Bienville the name of Croft meant next to nothing for people with names like André, Wellington, Galtoire, Arneaux and Holt.

Willie crossed to the center of the park where the old Iron Deer statue stood. He regarded its broken antlers and withers worn smooth over the years by the bottoms of countless children brought by mothers and nurses to sit astride it.

Crazy, sad old feller, he thought. Pretty damned worn out, aren't you?

Willie circled the Iron Deer and gave it an affectionate pat on the rump and for an instant he had an urge to climb astride it himself and sit there for a while. Instead, he drained the last swallow of bourbon and as it went down, warm and sweet and good, felt a faint stirring of youthful dreams and sweet hopes so long forgotten they were as fragmentary now as the reflexive glint of lust in an old bull elephant's eye.

Willie no longer aspired to the things most men want in life—love, wealth, fame and such.

Or in any case he had long since reshaped them downward so as to protect himself against the rage and hurt of disappointment. Once he had seen a girl and wanted her. He had been seventeen.

It had been carnival and he was standing in the crowd as she passed by on the queen's float. A pretty blond girl, not the queen, but one of her "ladies-in-waiting." He was surrounded on the sidewalk by big, raw-boned farmboys from up-country, pushing and shoving their way forward, and sailors off the ships and women screaming and holding up children to receive the trinkets and candy thrown by the maskers, when suddenly she saw him and tossed him a tinsel-wrapped candy kiss and smiled. He caught it and waved back at her and then the parade went on and she passed into the distance to her fancy parties and balls and he was alone on the street and drifted away with the crowd.

And there had been the times he envisioned himself the hero of battles, a captain of infantry or officer of the deck of a great battleship, or a pilot in a fast combat fighter. But the captain of infantry and officer of the deck and red-hot cockpit jockey had gone on to become a sergeant of supply in the Dixie Division, handing out towels and washcloths and soap to deskbound GIs far behind the front at Inchon.

And once, he had seen himself as a college football star making the perfect block or game-saving tackle on a clear, fall afternoon, with the stands on their feet and roaring in his ears. But the closest he had actually come was second-string guard on a losing team in high school with only the coach's parting remark, that while Willie "didn't have much to work with, he always hung in there," to show for it.

Other times his dream had been to own one of the big lapstrake Dauber-built boats for fishing out in the Gulf or Bay, going after red snapper or pompano on a warm Saturday afternoon with a cooler full of icy beer and fresh turkey sandwiches; he saw himself at the helm, one hand on the powerful throttle, able to outrun ferocious line squalls or speed to the spot where gulls circled the water. But in fact he now contented himself by sometimes renting a beat-up fishing skiff and heading northward to the dark marshes to try his luck at speckled trout or bass.

And so, with his youthful visions of becoming another Darrow or Holmes now reduced to the defense of petty felons, and the girl with the pretty face on the float evaporated into an occasional woman on a weekend fling, Willie Croft organized his life the best way he could: he was able to go out and eat fresh oysters and big Gulf shrimp and drink beer whenever he wanted or spend his Saturday afternoons on a stand in a dove field listening to the university's football games on a portable radio, and occasionally go to the horse track at the fairgrounds in New Orleans. He had managed to put a little money aside for later in life, and carved out, thusly, a niche for himself, in which he had been perfectly, if not blissfully happy up till now, having learned, as most men do, to ride his failure gently and not rail against it, so that day by day it really did not seem like failure at all.

Willie moved around to face the Iron Deer head-on.

It seemed melancholy and peculiar with its missing antlers and wide, frozen, metal eyes. He had read in the newspaper a few weeks before that the city was planning to restore it to its old self: to weld over the rusted-out holes and replace the broken antlers and sand away the obscene scratchings of teenagers and give it a new coat of paint. The article had also pointed out that the Iron Deer was forty-two years old, coincidentally the same age as he was, which just went to show you, he thought wryly, that even if you were dilapidated and wrecked, it was still possible to get fixed up again.

Deep in his breast the old hopes and plans stirred but Willie checked them automatically in his mind. Success in a case like this, for a lawyer like himself, would be just poor, dumb luck. If there was actually a case at all. How could he know? If the Holt family said they owned something, they probably did.

Still, there was something he thought he caught in Augustus Tompkins's face—or voice—something nervous and uneven, something he had seen before in certain witnesses he was trying to break down, and when he sensed there was more to tell, he was usually right. He rattled the ice around in his empty glass and tossed it out on the ground. He was beginning to feel the chill in the air and he started back for his apartment to pour one more glass of bourbon, maybe even build a fire, then heat up Priscilla's pot roast on the stove.

"What kind of problem?" Percy Holt demanded.

"Maybe a big one," said Brevard. "Do you remember Dad telling us a few months before he died that he wanted to give that land to those colored people? Well, it looks like he might have actually done it."

"What!" Percy shouted. "Give it to them! That old . . ."

"Now hold on a minute," Brevard said. "It might not be

as bad as it seems. But let me back up for a minute and tell you everything I know. Maybe it's good Marci isn't here right now, because I don't think she's going to like what I'm about to tell you."

Percy let out a thin blue cloud of smoke from the cigar and leaned back in his chair.

"I went through Dad's papers the night I heard about the oil, and found a little notation in the file on the Creoletown property that said 'deeded Sawmill Creek acreage to Elvira Backus.' It wasn't even dated—and there's no trace of any deed or anything. But it bothered me. I wanted to avoid problems. It occurred to me that maybe he stuck a deed somewhere we don't know about. That maybe he didn't even tell her about it. Hell, I don't know, could be anything. In any case, it seemed to me—and I discussed this with Augustus—that the best thing would be to just get them out of there lock, stock and barrel, and that the best way to do that, considering the money involved, would be to buy them out."

Marci appeared in the doorway with one of her hands on her hip, sipping from a whiskey glass.

"So I went to the bank and got twenty-five thousand dollars from our joint account—in cash—twenties and fifties—and put it in a briefcase and went to see the old colored woman after I'd seen Aunt Hannah.

"I told her that we wanted the property for other things, and that she could take the money and buy herself a house someplace else."

"You did what!" Percy yelled. "Twenty-five thousand out of our account!"

"Listen, damnit," Brevard said, "it would have been worth it if she'd gone along. But she didn't. She's got the damned deed, signed by Dad and everything. She showed it to me."

"I don't care what she's got," Percy said savagely. "Dad wouldn't have either. You know what he would have done? I'll tell you. He'd of kicked their black asses right off that place! He might have wanted to give them a little piece of land to live on, but not if he'd known about any oil up there. They're just niggers, for godsakes."

This attitude of Percy Holt toward his Negro brethren was by no means exemplary of the feelings of all white citizens in the community at that time. Many were far more charitable, for these were the days before the infamous Stand in the Schoolhouse Door, the Voting Rights Act and the Public Accommodations laws, the Selma March, or the Battle of Old Miss; when every public toilet and water fountain bore the secure label of White and Colored, and the buses said Colored Take Rear Seats, and the restaurants said White Only.

In fact, quite a large segment of cultured and enlightened Bienvilleans were offended by the epithet "nigger" and when they thought of the Negroes at all, they thought of them fondly: smiling, watermelon-eating children swinging on old tires suspended by ropes from tree limbs, or happily listening to the radio while ironing clothes, or mowing lawns, or scrubbing floors, collecting garbage, making beds, serving food and drink, opening doors or cleaning fish— content at heart and damned grateful for the opportunity to do an honest day's work.

These were years when each town's chapter of the Daughters of the Confederacy carefully selected deserving Negro families to receive Thanksgiving and Christmas baskets, filled with turkey, bread, tangerines, apples, cranberry sauce, candy and canned goods (in which were also thoughtfully included such household necessities as toilet paper, facial tissues, sanitary napkins, soap, deodorant and toothpaste) and delivered them to the door, generously and benevolently, to a grateful mammy with a dozen bawling offspring at her back, and came away satisfied at having fulfilled their sacred duty to care for the less fortunate; stopping, no doubt, somewhere along the way home to shed a tear at the omnipresent statue of the Confederate Soldier (who, naturally, *always* faced south), and nevertheless, deep in their hearts blaming those selfsame Negroes for the woes and plights their fathers and grandfathers fought against in vain in the Gallant Cause.

These enlightened people were, of course, thoroughly unlike the Percy Holts, who actually hated and despised the Negroes with some deep, unexplained, uncontrolled, personal sense of outrage bred by three hundred years of deep, secret, unexplained, uncontrolled fear and suspicion; whose servants were constantly stealing from them, despite the fact that the only actual theft in Percy's household had occurred some years before when the only white woman ever in his employ had relieved the silver cabinet of a set of sterling coasters; or whose handymen were so inherently lazy and inept that they constantly had to be poked and prodded, neverminding that that very week Percy Holt's fifteen-year-old son had dawdled so flagrantly at raking up a pile of autumn leaves that Percy finally had to go out and finish the job himself.

It was between these two factions that the Negroes existed this Thanksgiving season, as they had for many Thanksgivings past, in little pocket niggertowns sandwiched in between white subdivisions or in the teeming, brawling, giant niggertown near the shipyards, bounded by the broad moat of an avenue which, for all its thirty yards in width, might have represented the quantum distances between galaxies. But there they lived nonetheless, more often despised than beatified, bearing the burden of the white man's opinion as well as his munificence in the form of holiday baskets and the opportunity to mow his lawns and make his beds and swab out his toilets.

Such was the state of race relations to which Percy Holt was now addressing himself—

Marci had reseated herself on the sofa and had lit up another cigarette. Percy turned to her.

"You see what it is now, sis? The niggers up there are claiming the land is theirs. And now Brev says we have to pay them off." Marci looked disgusted.

Brevard waved his hands in frustration. "I'm just trying

to head off trouble before it starts," he said. "Hell, even without the deed, they've been there so long they might have some kind of squatter's rights. We are talking about hundreds of thousands—millions of dollars. Now, I learned today from Augustus that the colored woman has hired some shyster lawyer to handle the case. I was trying to do it the easy way!"

"The easy way," Percy said, "is just to go up there and clear them out."

3

Two days later Willie was driving through the outskirts of the city, headed for Creoletown to see Mrs. Elvira Backus. Earlier in the morning he had visited Judge McCormack to cancel his court appearances for the afternoon, and received a stern admonishment from the old white-haired judge concerning the anthem-singing episode in the courtroom two days before.

"Willie, for seventeen years you have been doing these things and for seventeen years I have been telling you patiently to stop them," the judge said crossly. "This is *my* courthouse and I make it my business to know everything that goes on here."

The judge had then produced a coffee-stained business card from his desk. "I suppose you thought that I wouldn't find out about this either." He held out the card, which said this:

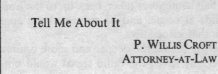

Tell Me About It

P. Willis Croft
Attorney-at-Law

Willie sheepishly accepted the card.

"If I believed for an instant that you were seriously using this thing I would have you up before the bar association. Then you would be in serious trouble. Willie, sometimes you go too far." The judge was becoming more agitated.

"And about that singing you started the other morning. I heard it all the way up in my chambers. I didn't even have to ask the bailiff to find out who it was. I knew who it was. When are you going to start behaving like an officer of the court instead of the court jester?"

Willie had been appropriately repentant and the judge had let it pass, and also agreed to postpone a probation hearing and a sentencing scheduled for the afternoon. They had had these conversations before, Willie and the judge, and both of them knew there would be a next time. Willie suspected Judge McCormack secretly enjoyed learning about his stunts as much as he himself enjoyed pulling them. And pulling them was one of the things that kept him from going nuts.

When Willie reached Route 23 the clusters of houses had thinned to an occasional shack or run-down store, between which were flat, brown fields, some planted, some barren, all somehow depressing beneath a gray, lowering sky. Farther on, even these vestiges of civilization disappeared into deep pine thickets that loomed along both sides of the road. Willie stubbed his cigarette out in the ashtray of his eight-year-old Nash convertible and reached irritatedly for the dial on the radio to retrieve a fading country music station.

He hadn't driven this road in years and going along it now gave him a slight but uncomfortable angst. It was the old shortcut he had sometimes taken back up to the university after weekends at home, and he suspected the angst was residue from that association.

The farther he drove, the deeper and more ominous the landscape became. Even the radio signal would not reach out here, but it wasn't a particularly good radio in the old Nash anyway. He looked at the odometer. He had driven forty-three miles, and it was just past 11:00 A.M., but the road seemed dark and lonely. The thickets were not composed of tall, straight trees, but gnarled, dwarfed slash pine growing densely all the way to the sides of the road; so thick, in fact, it was said that a man could walk in less than ten yards and become hopelessly disoriented and lost.

And underneath all of it, he thought, the oil.

In a matter of weeks or perhaps even days this land was going to come alive with buying, selling, trading; millions of dollars would change hands, and he, Willie Croft, might possibly be smack in the middle of it. The thought gave him a chill. Ahead, the unrelenting forests drew up tightly on both sides of the road. It didn't seem like the kind of place for oil.

Ten minutes later Willie turned off Route 23, onto a flat, unmarked blacktop road and, following Priscilla's directions, continued until he reached a ramshackle country store, opposite which was the rutted dirt road that led to the house of Mrs. Elvira Backus.

In the bare dirt yard half a dozen chickens were aimlessly poking and pecking about and a dilapidated cow tied to a tree by a rope gazed at Willie with a wan face.

The house itself was better than the unpainted, tar-papered hovels where most of the country Negroes dwelled. It was painted white, at least a few seasons ago. There was a little porch running the length of the house, upon which sat three crude wooden chairs and a small table. A wisp of white smoke curled from a brick chimney and floated lazily into the sky.

Willie was halfway out of his car when a Negro woman appeared in the doorway. From her weathered face, she might have been a hundred years old. When he reached the bottom of the steps, he announced himself.

"I'm Willie Croft, the lawyer. Your daughter Priscilla said she told you I was coming up here."

The old woman regarded him suspiciously, but if she felt anxiety it was hidden in her wrinkled skin, as she had probably hidden it from others of Willie's race, which for three hundred years had despised and tormented and exploited and generally kept its feet securely planted on the necks of the people of her race. The two of them stood that way for a few moments, then she said to him, in the rich dialect of country Creole Negroes, "Won'ts you come inside?" and Willie, who had dealt with countless black people over the years, in courtrooms, and jail cells, and hallways, and over the telephone, stepped for the first time in his life into a Negro home.

The room was dim, but surprisingly, to him, neat and clean, and there was a pungent smell of cooking food he could not immediately identify. On a table in the corner was a collection of glass and plastic animals, souvenir dishes and other odds and ends put out for display. Mrs. Backus motioned for him to seat himself at the dining table in the center of the room. "Woulds you want a cup of tea?" she asked.

Willie said that a cup of tea would be fine, and as she prepared it at the big woodburning stove in a corner, Mrs. Backus said, in a very matter-of-fact way (as though she had prepared all her life for this inevitable indignity), that she was afraid the Holt family was going to take away her home.

"Why do you think that?" Willie asked.

"'Cause his chu'rens, I guess they think they needs it now," she replied. He took out a pad and laid it on the table in front of him while Mrs. Backus gave him an account of the events of the past week which was more or less what Priscilla had related to him several days before.

Willie was careful to take down the exact times and dates. He learned that after the visit from Brevard Holt, and the arrival of the oil company men the following day, two other people had appeared at Mrs. Backus's door and offered to buy the mineral rights to her property. One was the owner of a small automobile tire store in a little town ten miles away and the other was a country doctor who had an office off Route 23. She had turned them both away.

"Well now, Mrs. Backus," Willie began, "let me tell you what's going on—at least what I think is going on. They have discovered oil up here and there is a good chance that some of it will be found right here on your place. If that is so, then it would become very valuable. It would make you a rich woman."

Mrs. Backus put a cup of tea in front of Willie and sat herself down at the other side of the table. Her expression did not change at all with the news Willie brought her. She simply stared at him across the table, her face placid and moodless, like a wrinkled old prune. Willie continued.

"As a lawyer, I would advise you this way. First, you should do exactly what you are doing, which is not to sign anything. Nothing, no matter what it is. The next thing, and this is most important, you must establish a claim to this land. First off, how much land are you talking about—I mean, how much do you own?"

She hesitated for a moment. "Alls the way up from the road, wheres you came up on, downs to the creek where the sawmill was, and up to the deer skinnin' station." She said this authoritatively, sweeping her arm in a descriptive arc that meant nothing to Willie.

"Well, about how many acres is that?" he asked.

"I don'ts know," she said. "I jest knows where it stops and starts."

"Your daughter said you have some kind of paper signed by Mr. Holt, giving you the land."

"I do," she said.

"May I take a look at it," Willie asked carefully.

"It put away," she said, and he sensed her suspicion.

"Well, it would help if I could see it. I mean, to establish ownership, you've got to have something a judge in court can look at, if it ever comes to that."

The old woman's eyes had dropped to the table and she was twisting her hands, as though trying to decide if she should let him, a perfect stranger, intrude on the thing most private and valuable in her life. The silence continued for a minute and then two, and Willie did not press it. Instead he rose and walked to the corner of the room where the little collection of animals and bric-a-brac was set out on a table. It was carefully arranged, each piece spaced to stand alone and not be overshadowed by any other: a lion, a dog and a mouse larger than both of them; a clear glass spray of flowers, petals painted red; a glass basket and a glass harp. In the center was a small square dish, in the bottom of which lay two gold medallions. Each bore an inscription: To Elvira—with love, and two separate dates but no signature or further indication of the giver. Willie had an impulse to pick them up and examine the other sides when the old woman spoke.

"I'll git it for you," she said, and went into the other room.

When she returned, Mrs. Backus had in her hand a faded white envelope which she put down on the table in front of Willie. For an instant their eyes met but no words were spoken. He opened the envelope and found a single sheet of yellowed paper, folded thrice, appearing thusly:

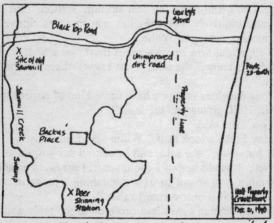

I Jonathan Holt I, hereby assign and convey the property described above to Elvira Backus, without reservation or exception.

Jonathan Holt   witness: *Hannah Holt Loften*

Willie studied the document for a while. It was crude, but the drawing looked as though it had been traced from an original plat, with the landmarks written in over. It had been witnessed by a Mrs. Hannah Loftin, and if the signatures could be authenticated it would have some legal force. How much, exactly, was of course uncertain. A nineteen-year-old scrap of paper, unrecorded, and millions might hang in the balance. . . .

"When did he give you this?" Willie asked.

"Christmas Day, in nineteen forty," the old woman replied. "He died the spring next year. He come up here hisself and give it to me and walked me around to take me exactly to where my property ended."

"Did he say why he wanted you to have it?"

"Uh-uh," she said. "He jes say, 'Elvira, I want you and your chu'rens to have dis place.' He was gentmanly but I think he kind of nervous."

"Why was he nervous?" Willie asked curiously.

"Don't know," she said.

"How did you know he was, then?"

"He jest acted it."

"Did he come up here much?"

"No, not for a long time before that. He used to comes up all the time, and he's always send things for Christmas, big baskets with a turkey and fruits and things and toys for the chu'rens." She paused for a moment, and seemed on the verge of stopping entirely, then added, "He stopped coming when the chu'rens got older." Willie was puzzled and had an inexplicable impulse to delve further. Every little bit might help if it ever got to court.

"Did the children bother him or something?" Willie inquired tentatively.

"They didn't bothers nobody. My chu'rens is good chu'rens," the old woman said defensively.

"Then why would he stop coming?"

"I don't know. He don'ts tell me nothing," Mrs. Backus said. There was a look of defiance in her face, and a hint of the memory of something long since past. "I jest thinks it 'cause he don'ts want to see them anymore," she said.

Willie was leaning back, studying the wrinkled face and

obsidian eyes now looking beyond him, through the little window, out onto the corn patch, and beyond it too, to the dark stand of trees, and past that, if possible, to the point where the land stretched out to rolling fields and meadows all the way to the green Gulf of Mexico, and far beyond that too. . . .

She drew a deep breath, and sighed.

"I s'pose because they his," the old woman said. "Priscilla and Daniel." She said it as though she assumed Willie knew all the while. . . . "Both them chu'rens is his chu'rens," she said, quietly rocking in the chair.

Can you beat it! Willie thought. Can you beat it!

He was bounding along at the wheel of the old Nash down the rutted two-track path toward the unnamed blacktop road. If there was a question of Mrs. Backus's claim to the land before, this certainly put a new complexion on it. She had even named the children after him. Priscilla *Holt!* Daniel *Holt!* He'd never even known Priscilla's maiden name . . . never asked her. But even if he had, he probably wouldn't have made the connection. It was simply too preposterous to believe. He wondered if Augustus Tompkins and the Holt family knew.

"Can you beat it!" He said it aloud this time. "Can you beat it!"

Before he left, he had tried to persuade her to let him take Johnathan Holt's paper back with him to town and photostat it and put the original in a bank vault. But she wouldn't allow it. For nineteen years she'd held on to that scrap of paper, she said, and would hold on nineteen more if necessary.

The other connection—the witness to the deed—Mrs. . . . Hannah *Holt* Loftin, was the sister to old man Holt, and she still lived up there, not far away.

"She a old lady now," Mrs. Backus had said. "I used to work for her, but she old and tired now."

Willie decided it was worth a chance to pay her a visit. He wondered what kind of reception he'd get.

* * *

An autumn sun burst suddenly from behind a cloud as Willie turned onto a winding gravel lane that led to Mrs. Loftin's place. In its grand explosion of warmth and brilliance the sunshine chased the pall of cold, gray gloom from the landscape. Goldenrod waved gaily in the open fields, maple and sycamore trees flamed against the clearing sky and Willie had an urge to stop and put the convertible top down on the old Nash; then he saw the entrance to the house.

Two brick pillars marked a driveway which led to the top of a tree-covered knoll, upon which was nestled the Loftin place. It was not an expansive house, and certainly not a plantation, but rather a large cottage with aging charm and grace. Ivy grew on tall twin chimneys at either end, and late-blooming roses climbed trellises against the white frame siding. Willie got out of the car and knocked at the front door. He waited and knocked again, but no one answered. Inside, several lights were burning so he walked around back and found himself in a small, but neatly tended boxwood garden. There, beneath a wisteria arbor, asleep in a lawn chair with a plaid robe covering her lap, was Mrs. Hannah Loftin.

He paused a moment, then coughed loudly, and when the old woman stirred he stepped forward and announced himself.

"Mrs. Loftin . . . my name is Willie Croft. I am an attorney."

The old woman had raised herself on the chair but did not seem particularly surprised or disturbed by his presence.

"I hate to bother you, ma'am, but if you have a minute, I'd like to talk to you."

"I was taking a nap, Mr. . . . ."

"Croft," Willie said.

"Croft," she repeated. "Forgive me. Did you say you're a lawyer?"

"Yes, ma'am, I am looking into some things for Elvira Backus."

Mrs. Loftin's eyes seemed to brighten. "Elvira, yes, Mr. . . . ."

"Croft."

"Elvira, yes, she was here yesterday. She does my cooking." A few brown wisteria leaves fluttered onto the damp bricks beneath the arbor. Willie stood awkwardly, still a few yards away, a puzzled look on his face.

"You . . . saw her . . . yesterday?" he said. "She was here yesterday?"

"Oh, yes, she only comes three days a week now. She used to come every day, but . . . I'm old now . . . and since Mr. Loftin's been gone . . . I don't need help as much, anymore. . . ." She stared distantly past the boxwoods toward a dark stand of trees at the edge of the back lawn. "Elvira's not in trouble, is she?"

"Oh, no, ma'am, not at all—at least, not exactly," Willie said. "I didn't quite understand, though. You said she was here yesterday?"

"Why, yes." The blue eyes sparkled. "Yesterday was Monday, wasn't it? She comes Mondays, Wednesdays and Fridays. So she was here yesterday."

Willie began to say something but caught himself.

"Would you like to sit down, Mr. . . . ."

"Croft."

"Yes," she said. "Would you like a cup of tea, or a cup of coffee?" She started to rise.

"Please," Willie said, "no, no, thank you. What I came for was to talk to you about Mrs. Backus's—ah, Elvira's . . . property, the land your brother gave her."

"What?" Mrs. Loftin said, almost startled. "What would I know about it? It's just land, isn't it?"

"Well, yes," Willie said. "But Mrs. Backus . . . Elvira . . . has a paper drawn up by Mr. Johnathan Holt, before he died, giving the property to her, and your name appeared as a witness."

Mrs. Loftin looked at Willie with her head cocked to the side, reminding him of a quizzical parakeet. "Oh, yes, I know, down there where her little cabin is. I remember when Johnathan came up here and said he was going to give her that cabin. I remember now. . . ."

"And he asked you to sign a paper as a witness, didn't he?" Willie said.

"Sign a paper? Oh, my, I don't remember anything about a paper. He might have. Let me see."

"Do you recall when he came, Mrs. Loftin—I mean the year?"

"Why, of course I do," she said. "But it wasn't a year. It was . . . it was just a few weeks ago. I remember the day very well; it was raining and it was cold."

Willie pursed his lips together. Something in him sagged a little. "But, Mrs. Loftin, your brother died in nineteen forty-one. It would have to have been before that."

"Oh, no," she said, "oh, my, no. Why, he was out here only . . . let's see . . . a few weeks ago. I remember exactly. It was cold and raining, and I said, John, you come in here and sit by the fire. And I made him take off his shoes and gave him a cup of hot tea. . . ."

A car ground to a stop in the gravel drive; its door slammed, followed shortly by a knock at the front door.

The old woman's ears perked up. "We're around back," Mrs. Loftin shouted cheerfully, and moments later, Whitsey Loftin, radiant as the autumn day in tan slacks and a red cashmere sweater, appeared at the corner of the boxwood garden.

"Oh, hello, darling," Mrs. Loftin purred, "I'm so glad to see you. This is Mr. . . . ."

"Croft," Willie said, already on his feet.

"Mr. Croft is a lawyer, dear. He is helping out Elvira with her property."

"How do you do, Mr. Croft?" Whitsey said. Her face had a curious look that combined suspicion and recognition. "Haven't I seen you in my store? I took over the Black Star Bookshop in Bienville a few months ago."

"Oh, ah, well, I guess you have, then," Willie said, startled. He suddenly remembered seeing her behind the counter, but she had always worn glasses and had her hair pulled back. He hadn't thought of her as being pretty then.

Whitsey moved to her aunt and kissed her lightly on the

cheek. "Aren't you chilly out here? It's not really warm. How long have you been outside?"

"Only for a minute, darling," the old woman said. "I just came out to talk to Mr. . . . ."

"Croft," Willie supplied dejectedly.

"Would you like to go inside? We could have some tea."

Whitsey Loftin gave Willie another brief, curious glance that might have smacked of disapproval. "Well, perhaps we should," she said, "if Mr. Croft is going to be staying."

The three of them went into the large, comfortable living room. Mrs. Loftin seated herself in a fat morris chair and Willie plopped down on a couch. Whitsey went into the kitchen to put on water for the tea. She could hear them talking in the other room, her aunt going on about something, and Willie occasionally laughing, or concurring. By the time she returned with the tray of cups and pot of tea, Willie had steered the conversation back around to Elvira and Johnathan Holt and the property.

"I know it was a long time ago, Mrs. Loftin," he said, "but don't you remember anything about witnessing a deed that Mr. Holt had drawn up for Mrs. Backus?"

The old lady looked thoughtfully at the empty fireplace. "I dried out his shoes and his coat right there," she said. "He was soaking wet."

"And he had a paper with him, didn't he? He wanted you to sign it. . . ."

"He had . . . oh . . . I think maybe something . . ." For an instant there was a flicker in her eyes, as though she were plunging across the years, hearing voices. . . . "He had something . . . he wanted to tell me. That was why he came," she said.

Whitsey poured a cup of tea, added cream and sugar, stirred it and handed it to her aunt.

"Oh, Mr. Croft," Whitsey said suddenly, and with a sharpness in her voice, "would you help me for a minute in the kitchen? There's something I can't get open."

"Of course," Willie said. As he rose, Mrs. Loftin put the

cup to her lips, took a sip and put it back on the saucer. In the doorway Willie heard the old woman make a sound, very faint, something between a moan and a sigh. He turned and she was staring vacantly again at the empty fireplace.

"Mr. Croft," Whitsey said when they were out of earshot, "I suppose you can see my aunt isn't exactly, ah, in possession of all her faculties."

"Yes, I know," Willie said.

"Well, then, I don't see what purpose it can serve for you to question her like this. Maybe you should come back when she's better."

"Do you think she'll get better?" Willie asked.

"She has good days and bad ones."

"I thought for a minute she was on the verge of something," Willie said.

He was backed against the kitchen counter. Whitsey looked at him carefully. He was drawn to her clear blue eyes, which somehow managed to seem sleepy and half-closed even while they were open.

"Listen, Mr. Croft," she said softly, "this isn't easy for me—or for any of us. I'm not sure you belong here at all."

She stepped back for a moment and drew herself up as though to emphasize authority. The intention of the gesture was not entirely lost on Willie, but he took a more immediate interest in her full breasts beneath the red cashmere sweater.

Whitsey said, "If I understand correctly, you must be representing the colored people living on Uncle John's place. Is that right?"

"Well," Willie said, "I don't know. I am not retained yet, but I might be."

"But you're here in their interests, aren't you—which would be against the interests of my family?"

"I guess I'd have to say so, yes," he said.

Whitsey continued to eye him firmly. She understood something about lawyers, having known two of them intimately, the first while she was living in Atlanta and the second during her two years in Washington, and also she

45

had been acquainted with others casually and had formed
the opinion that they were mostly tedious men who spent
their days creating or unraveling mumbo jumbo and practicing verbal legerdemain.

Yet she could not immediately toss Willie into this
category, mainly because she remembered him from the
times he had come into her bookstore and she had been
curious about him then, always wearing the frayed tan
raincoat, carrying a cheap plastic briefcase that seemed to
be falling apart. And the books he bought were a strange sort
of grab bag. She had seen him every few weeks; he would
come in around closing time and pick out six or eight books,
usually paperbacks. An odd assortment: two or three Hem-
ingway novels, perhaps, and a detective story or two. One
day he had acquired Descartes' *Principia Philosophiae,*
Shakespeare's *Richard III* with notes and seven cheap pulp
sex novels. She remembered wondering how in the world he
read them—did he get started with Descartes and then put
it down for one of the sex books? Or did he read the sex
books straight through and then tackle the heavier stuff? In
any case it interested her, Willie's reading habits, and by
connection, Willie himself interested her. Mildly.

Whitsey had made the rounds during the past ten years.
Lived in three cities and traveled in foreign lands, attended
nice parties, had her share of affairs. A year ago, she had
come back to Bienville, back to the close-ordered, provin-
cial, tight-minded place of her ancestors where the name
Holt meant something besides just another new skirt to
chase in town—and she was already tired of it again. Tired
of the foppish bachelors and their overstated attempts at
courtliness; of the conversation at dinner parties which
inevitably revolved around money, babies and "the niggers"; even tired of her old childhood friends, simultaneously, most of them now, on their second pregnancy and second
home.

Somehow, although she didn't know him well, Willie
seemed a relief from all that. She felt a kind of attraction for
him, but in a backhanded way. He wasn't handsome, but he

wasn't plain either. He was really kind of nondescript. He wasn't tall, but he wasn't short either; he wasn't fat, but he wasn't thin. He had a rounded, cherubic face, slightly freckled, and his hair was of a color almost impossible to identify except that it was lighter than it was dark. But she liked his broad, easy grin and his offhand manner. She wasn't sure if he was the kind of man she could manipulate or not. It was hard to tell. There was something about him that she hadn't been able to put her finger on before. Something about his eyes, or maybe his whole face—the look of some terrible hurt from the past, a woman perhaps, or possibly his whole life. It intrigued her—it always did. She liked to take in stray dogs. Had all of her life. Usually she would tire of them after a while, but she kept on doing it.

"I don't want to seem inhospitable," Whitsey found herself saying, "but I really don't think you should be here. My aunt isn't quite herself today. My cousins would be positively furious if they knew you came to see her about this. It's one thing for a person in her right mind, but . . ."

Willie put up his hands to stop her. "You're absolutely right, Miss Loftin. To tell the truth, I knew I wasn't doing any good as soon as . . . as soon as it became apparent to me that your aunt was having a . . . *spell.* I'll leave now."

Whitsey said nothing for a moment. There was something touching about Willie—after Atlanta and Washington and New York—perhaps especially after them. She suddenly felt she might have seemed rude.

"Well, why don't you come back in and have your tea first," she said impulsively, "and we can talk about other things."

They sat and talked, the three of them, for nearly half an hour. Willie told animated stories about his cases and clients and Whitsey and her aunt listened and laughed. There were moments when it seemed as if the old lady was clearheaded, then she would lapse back into incoherence. When Willie rose to leave, Whitsey accompanied him outside.

"I'm sorry, Mr. Croft," she said. "I mean about my aunt and . . ."

"Call me *Willie*—please," he said, "and there isn't anything to be sorry about. You were nice to let me stay at all."

"Well, it was nice to see you—to meet you, I mean." She looked at the sunset. "Beautiful afternoon, isn't it? You'll have a nice drive back to town."

"Yes," Willie said. "Are you going to stay over?"

"No, I'll come in later. I think I'll have supper here."

"I guess I'll see you in town, then. I'm getting low on things to read."

"Come by anytime," Whitsey said. "We've got a lot of new stock."

Willie nodded, and backed away toward his car. He wanted her to ask him to stay and have supper with them—but it was his infernal luck that the very thing responsible for his having met her was the same thing that would probably put them forever on opposite sides of the fence. And after what he had learned today, he guessed that a range war lay ahead.

When he got back to the city, Willie stopped by his office and read his messages. Augustus Tompkins had phoned twice and left word for Willie to call him. There was an office number and a home number and a club number where he might be reached.

Willie tried the office first and to his surprise Tompkins himself answered the phone. It was past 6:00 P.M. and Willie wondered if he had been waiting there for him to call.

"We need to get together about this Creoletown thing," Tompkins said offhandedly. "Why don't you meet me at the Raphael House, in the bar?"

"Now?" Willie asked. Bienville had never been the kind of town for after-work business over cocktails.

"The sooner the better," said Tompkins, and Willie thought he recognized a speck of anxiety beyond the booming confidence in his voice.

"All right," Willie said. After they hung up he gathered some work he needed to take home, left a note for the girl who worked for him half-days, put on his tan raincoat and went down to the street. Crossing over, he entered the elegant lobby of the old Raphael House Hotel, paused as he always did to admire the enormous stained-glass dome skylight, tossed a penny in the goldfish fountain for luck and started for the bar. Augustus Tompkins was waiting for him.

"What'll you drink, Willie?" Tompkins motioned authoritatively for the waiter.

"Bourbon," Willie said, and the waiter disappeared. "What's on your mind, Augustus?"

"You and those damned colored people up there." Willie sensed that Tompkins had budgeted a certain amount of time for this conversation and intended not to exceed it.

"What about them?" Willie asked.

"Are you representing them or not?"

"Not—well, not formally yet, but I think I probably will be soon," Willie said cagily.

"Hummmmm," Tompkins growled. "Then I guess we should proceed on the assumption that you are." He paused, regarded Willie sternly.

"My clients, the Holts, are anxious to have this matter resolved so they can proceed with their own plans."

"Which are?" Willie said.

"You know goddamn well what they are, Willie." There was no animosity in Tompkins's voice. He just spoke that way. A flat voice, dull and deep, like the growl of a jungle cat. Willie had heard him use that tone in court, a driving, hypnotic grumble that left the impression of evenness and right, backed up by authority.

"Now," Tompkins continued, "I have looked into this thing, and had my people research the law pretty carefully, and your people don't stand a snowball's chance in hell. Of course if you want to you can tie the thing up for a while and every day is money going down the drain for my people. As you know, they've made the old woman an offer—a very generous one, I might add—of twenty-five thousand dollars to get her off that place. They are now prepared to add to it just to avoid a squabble. Do you think she will take thirty-five thousand dollars to quit her claim?"

"We've got a paper, Augustus." Willie decided to play cat and mouse, feeling that for the moment the cards were stacked in favor of the mouse.

"I know all about that paper," Tompkins rasped. "It's worthless. Mortmain statute, Willie—it was drawn less than a year before the old man died, and we can prove he wasn't in good mental health."

Willie sipped his bourbon. He bet they could, too, and drag in every doctor for forty miles to testify old man Holt had been crazy as a loon when he drew the deed. But Willie still had his trump card to play.

"Listen," Tompkins said, "suppose you can get her to take the thirty-five thousand cash. It would save you a lot of headaches in the end. You know damned good and well if this thing goes to litigation we'll be filing ten papers a day. You'll have to chuck the rest of your practice just to handle it. And from what I hear you are on the verge of some very lucrative cases." There was a devilish smirk on Tompkins's face and he began packing a blunt, round-bowled pipe with tobacco from a monogrammed leather pouch.

Willie was puzzled. He knew that Tompkins was not unaware of the quality of cases he handled—and that the last way they could be described was "lucrative."

"What do you mean by that?" Willie asked.

"Only this," Tompkins said, fingering the pipe. "There are a few young lawyers in this city that don't get the kinds of cases they probably should be getting. Maybe it's because they like practicing alone, or that they enjoy courtroom work, or whatever. But I know it doesn't pay very well. Now I'm sure you're aware that my firm does a lot of business, and even as large as we are, sometimes we have trouble handling all of it."

Tompkins lit a match to the pipe and sucked on it. Through the smoke he looked at Willie.

"So, when our load gets too heavy I occasionally steer some of these cases out to those young lawyers—men much like yourself, Willie. Maybe only one or two a year, mind you—but these are the kinds of cases a man can make a very comfortable fee from."

"Are you saying that if I get the old woman to take the thirty-five thousand dollars you will hand out some of those cases to me?" Willie asked.

Tompkins removed the pipe from his mouth, looking askance. "Why, I'm not saying anything of the sort, Willie. It has nothing to do, of course, with any of that. As I said, I've been doing this for years, and I've been thinking on and off about parceling out some cases to you. You've got a reputation as a good, hardworking attorney, and frankly, Willie, I like your style."

Willie took a swig of bourbon, put the glass down, then leaned forward and looked Augustus Tompkins in the eye.

"You old bastard," he said evenly, "you ought to be put in jail."

Tompkins's face swelled indignantly and he drew himself up like an adder. "Now just a minute, Willie, I wasn't . . ."

"I know just what you are trying to do, Augustus," Willie interrupted. "Suppose I had a tape recorder in my coat and played this conversation for the bar ethics committee?"

Tompkins let out an exasperated sigh. "I see you misunderstand me entirely."

"Perhaps," Willie said sarcastically. "I guess you have just now decided that you like me."

"Listen, Willie," Tompkins said. The growl had returned. "I'm just trying to save everyone a lot of time and trouble and fix it so the colored people get something out of this too. What's wrong with that?"

"I'll tell you what's wrong with it," Willie snapped. "It's bullshit. That woman and her children have a rightful claim to that place and you and the Holts know it. And if I can, I'm going to see that she establishes it."

"Impossible," Tompkins declared haughtily. "I told you before, Willie, we can show old man Holt was out of his head."

"Doesn't make any difference," Willie said triumphantly. He had already decided to spring the trap. "You know those children she had, the old woman? Do you know what their surname is? I'll tell you. It is *Holt*. And do you know why?"

Tompkins sucked on the pipe and a puzzled, impatient frown crossed his face. "I don't see what . . ."

Willie cut him off. "Okay, let me tell you, then. Those children are the product of a union between Mrs. Elvira Backus and your clients' father, Mr. Johnathan Holt. Both of them. So the fact is, Augustus, your clients have got a bunch of pickaninny half brothers and sisters running around up-county."

Tompkins reared back as though someone had dangled a snake in his face.

"What!" he bellowed.

As he said it, Tompkins's pipe suddenly slipped from between his teeth and clattered to the table, dumping a wad of burning ashes into his lap, and he leaped up with a flood of horrible profanity, brushing furiously at his trousers. The oaths were evenly divided between the smoldering pants and the hot news Willie had delivered to him.

4

GODDAMNIT! DON'T YOU DARE EVEN SUGGEST ANYTHING LIKE that!" Percy Holt bawled. He was leaning forward in the chair, his face a contorted mask of beet-red fury.

"I am simply telling you what you might expect, Percy—all of you," Augustus Tompkins said hoarsely.

"Percy, for heaven's sake, let him finish," Brevard said.

"Finish my ass! Finish my ass!" Percy howled. He began pounding himself furiously on the leg. "He isn't going to talk that way about this goddamn family! Nobody in this goddamn family would have ever done anything like that! I'm not going to listen to it. It's . . . it's . . ." He searched for the words. "It's *disgraceful—*"

"I don't believe it," Marci said disgustedly. "Father wasn't that kind of person. He wouldn't have done that with *anybody,* let alone . . . some . . ." She let the words trail off.

"I am just trying to tell you what to expect," Tompkins repeated, "exactly what their lawyer told me. Now there are ways of establishing such things—or rather, of disproving them—blood tests, that kind of thing. I'm sure in due time . . ."

"Due time my ass!" cried Percy Holt. "There isn't going to be any *due time!* If that sonofabitch hack lawyer so much

53

as breathes a suggestion to anybody about Father and that nigger woman I'll . . . I'll kill his ass! I swear it!"

It was midevening and a wet, chilling wind was blowing down from the northeast. It swept across the flat, fertile black belt to the north, rattling dried cornstalks and cotton bolls in the fields. Closer to the city, in the tangled Delta swamp, it rippled the surface of dark shallow sloughs and streams, causing the wild ducks—canvasbacks, mallard, teal—and other waterfowl to shiver in their protected potholes. As it gusted across the great shallow bay, huge rafts of coot squawked bitterly and drew closer together. This wind groaned in the superstructures of ships in their docks, rustled the leaves of the giant oaks on The Parade and muttered around the eaves and windows of a large turn-of-the-century house, where the Holts, Brevard, Percy, Johnathan III, Marci and their cousin, Whitsey Loftin, had gathered for the second time in a week to discuss their newfound fortune.

Brevard had opened the proceedings standing before the mirror of his library with almost precisely the same pose he'd struck on the last occasion.

"I think it's best," he said, "if I simply turn things over to Augustus." It was a statement Brevard could have made seated, or not at all, but by announcing Tompkins formally, he felt he had asserted himself as the head of the clan.

Tompkins took the floor with an air of showmanship of his own and assumed a position at center stage. He wasted no time getting to the point.

"I know you are anxious to know about the Creoletown property," he rasped. "I should tell you now, some of the news is good and some is not so good, but let's start with the good news first."

Tompkins said that the oil companies were now willing to offer as much as eighteen hundred dollars an acre for mineral rights—an increase of nearly twenty percent over previous offers. Furthermore, he explained that he had worked out a financing scheme for a joint "cartel" to purchase rights from surrounding property owners. "However," he said, "a few wrinkles have developed in other areas.

"Whitsey has been to see her aunt and reports that she is firm about not dividing the property at this time, or allowing the sale of oil leases. The gist of her response, as I understand it from Whitsey, is that after she is dead and gone you may do what you like with the place, but not before."

There were audible groans from Percy and Marci Holt. Big Johnathan simply frowned, and Brevard and Whitsey, who knew this already, looked at each other.

"The problem," Tompkins said, "is that by the terms of your father's will, she remains in control of the entire estate." He continued talking as he packed his pipe. "So, here's how it stands: either you are going to have to forget it for the time being and hope that Whitsey or some of the rest of you can change her mind later, or you'll have to get some court to override her. If it were a simple case of joint, undivided ownership it might be easier, but your father provided Mrs. Loftin to be sole executrix of that property, so the only course I can see would be to challenge her, er . . . *stability* . . . to continue in that role. These kinds of things, unfortunately, tend to be nasty affairs. An attorney would have to be appointed in her behalf, and it would become, in effect, an, er, *adversary* proceeding."

"May I say something?" Whitsey asked.

"Of course," Tompkins replied in a courtly way.

"When I went up there she was having one of her 'days.' I know her better than anyone here, and I know that a lot of the time she's completely reasonable. All it takes, I think, is to catch her in one of those times. . . ." She did not mention Willie Croft.

Marci crushed her cigarette in the ashtray and began fumbling for another. "Oh, Whitsey," she said, "let's don't kid ourselves. Everybody knows she's a fruitcake. We can't just let her ruin this for all of us."

Whitsey turned to reply but Brevard also cut in.

"None of us wants to hurt her, Whitsey, but timing is

everything now. We can't wait and wait, with her in that *condition.*" Brevard rose to his feet, taking the floor from Augustus Tompkins.

"We've got to decide something, and we can't dally, so let me make this suggestion: Whitsey, if you think you can get her to sign the papers, go ahead. If you can, fine. But meantime, let's do this. . . ." He turned to Tompkins.

"Augustus, why don't you begin whatever process is necessary to have her . . . ah . . . to do whatever is necessary. Don't file anything until you hear from us, but get the papers ready so we can act quickly if the situation demands it." He turned back to Whitsey.

"I think that a week or so more won't hurt. If you think you can do it. Otherwise, I suppose we'll probably have to let Augustus go ahead. . . ."

Whitsey nodded balefully.

It was then that Augustus Tompkins took up the subject of the Backus situation and his conversation with Willie Croft. It took a full five minutes for the initial shock to wear off and it was, as Brevard commented later, "Like we had just been told we had been adopted or something, or that our parents —our father, at least—had never even existed."

A few days later, Willie stood in the open doorway of a small cluttered office. Assistant Principal was stenciled on the door. "Daniel Holt?" he asked.

The lean man at the desk laid aside a book and peeked up at Willie over thick, horn-rimmed spectacles.

"Mr. Croft—please, come in," he said, rising, and motioned Willie to a straight wooden chair beside the desk. As Willie sat down the man pulled his own chair away from the desk to face him.

"Thank you for coming to the school," the man said pleasantly. "I know you must be busy, but as I said on the telephone, with the two jobs, I simply go from one to the other. Would you like a cup of coffee, or some ice water?"

"No, thank you," Willie said. Outside in the schoolyard there was the clamor of children at play, and the smells of an autumn afternoon filtered in through the half-open window.

The long hallway Willie had just walked through was quiet and the classrooms filled with students. He had not been in any kind of high school—white or Negro—since his own graduation nearly twenty-five years before. Weird nostalgia needled his mind.

Daniel Holt was remarkably the kind of man he'd expected: light-skinned Negro, thinnish, with close-cropped hair, dressed in a white shirt and tie and black trousers and shoes. He appeared to be a few years older than Willie. Willie had learned from Priscilla that he worked as a short-order cook at night to supplement his income. He did not defer in his mannerisms; this much was obvious to Willie despite their brief exchange of words—he sensed it instinctively, as an animal might sense the demeanor of another without lengthy or formal discussion.

"Well," Daniel Holt said, "you have seen my mother. What do you think? Will they be able to take the property?"

Willie did not expect to be asked questions, he expected to be the one asking them, and he hesitated a moment before answering.

"Frankly, I don't know," he said cautiously. "This is a fairly complicated matter, ah . . . Daniel. . . ." He had already made the split-second decision to address Daniel Holt in the customary way one addressed Negroes, by his first name rather than *Mister* Holt, and in that same instant he had seen, or thought he'd seen, his own troublesome decision-making process register in Daniel's face, the recognition of his decision and acceptance of it, but he couldn't tell if the acceptance was with disapproval or not.

"You see," Willie continued, "the Holt family has retained title to the property because your mother has never registered her claim. The Holts have also been paying taxes on it all these years. Legally, even with the deed she probably wouldn't stand much of a chance except for the, ah . . . except for the matter of Mr. Johnathan Holt and their relations together. . . ."

"You mean my father," said Daniel.

"Your father?" Willie repeated. "Oh, yes, your father, yes."

Daniel Holt leaned back in the chair and closed his eyes. "'Wherefore base?'" he proclaimed in a deep, theatrical voice. "'When my dimensions are as well compact,/My mind as generous, and my shape as true,/ . . . Why brand they us/With base? . . . /Now, gods, stand up for bastards!'"

"Wha . . . ahm . . ." Willie stammered.

Daniel Holt smiled broadly. *"King Lear,"* he said. "Edmund was the Earl of Gloucester's bastard son. He's wondering in that scene why he's treated differently from the others."

"Oh," Willie said.

"He finally takes power over his legitimate brother—but in the end he's killed."

"He is?" Willie said, slightly astonished.

"Yes, in the end," Daniel said softly, "but for a while he has his day."

Willie returned to the original conversation.

"Like I was saying, this is a complicated case, and unless we can bluff somebody out or buy them off it's probably going to have to be settled in court. It could be expensive, and the Holt family has, ah, many assets."

"My mother," Daniel said, "never had a thing in her life to call her own until my . . . father . . . gave her that place up there. I remember the day he did it. I was up there visiting mother—Priscilla and I. It was Christmas Day, and . . ."

"Oh, you remember it?" Willie cut in. "That's very good. Were you there when he came?"

"No," Daniel said. "We were down to the highway, Priscilla and me, picking up chestnuts. There was a big tree at the edge of a pasture and nobody minded if we took the nuts. I remember very well, it was a kind of a rainy day and we took two paper sacks and filled them both full—just like we did as children. What we'd do, Thanksgiving and Christmas, is put a couple of rows of them up by the fire and they'd heat up and pop open. Then we'd put two more rows until we'd opened them all and spend all night eating them."

"Sounds pretty good," Willie said.

"Good, yes. They were fine chestnuts," Daniel said.

"That tree's still there; you can see it from the road just before you turn off to Mother's place. I've thought about stopping off sometimes. . . ."

Willie pressed on.

"But when you and your sister came back, your mother had the paper then?"

"Yes. He'd gone and she was sitting by the fire in that big rocking chair my grandfather had built—you must have seen it. She was holding the paper in her hand—just looking at it. She can't read, you know, but she was staring at it and she handed it to Priscilla and asked her to read it to her. As she did, Mother just sat back in the chair and listened and smiled, and tears came into her eyes. She said, 'Children, praise the Lord, our troubles are over, praise the Lord.'"

"When was the last time you actually saw Mist . . . your father?"

"It was about a year before that. On a Thanksgiving, I think. He'd been hunting. What I remember is his big muddy boots. He left a basket with a turkey and some food. I had driven up for the day. I don't think he expected to see me there. He never sat down. He and Mother talked for a while and then he drove off. That was the last time."

"When did you, you and your sister," Willie asked carefully, "learn that he was your father?"

Daniel leaned back contemplatively. "I don't remember exactly when it was. I think I was about to start grade school. It had something to do with that. When my name came up somehow, I asked my mother and she told me. It didn't seem strange at the time."

"Did Mr. Holt ever acknowledge to you or your sister, that you know of, that he was your father?"

A shaft of sunlight from the open window was beaming down on the head of Daniel Holt. In the hallway a school bell rang and there was a clamor of activity.

"No, he never did."

Willie continued to probe and turn Daniel for anything that might be usable in court or for bargaining. He took copious notes. He tried to imagine the Holt family's counteroffensive. Finally they came to the subject of money.

"From what I can tell," Willie said, "the leases on your mother's land would be worth nearly half a million to the oil companies. The Holts aren't going to give up that kind of money easily. If it gets into court I imagine they're going to use everything in their means to dispute not only the legitimacy of the deed but your parentage and your sister's as well, and they'll probably attack your mother. I expect it would be very nasty."

Daniel Holt placed his hand on his knee and again declared in a great basso voice: "'Well, sir; by this you cannot get my land:/Your tale must be how he employ'd my mother.'"

"King Lear?" Willie said.

"King John," Daniel said thoughtfully. "The speaker is Philip the Bastard, son of Richard Coeur de Lion, in defense of his rightful claim to property."

"What happened to him?" Willie asked.

"He was knighted Richard Plantagenet and later assumed the English throne."

"Did that really happen?" Willie asked, fascinated.

"Only in the Shakespearean version," Daniel said.

Before Willie left, he and Daniel discussed the matter of tactics. The most immediate step was to have Daniel's mother register her deed with the county assessor's office, then begin negotiations with the oil companies. It would be better, he argued, than waiting for the Holts to take action.

"I think," Willie said, "that in this kind of fight, he who strikes first stands a better chance of winning. From what I've heard, some people are already forming syndicates to buy up all the leases in the area. There's going to be a big stampede pretty soon, and people are going to be running around filing claims like in a gold rush."

"I suppose the people who've lived up there all their lives won't stand much of a chance," Daniel said mournfully. "The Negroes, I mean, like us."

"Well, they will probably get something out of it," Willie offered.

"Like what they promised my mother, I suppose."

"Your mother's case is different," Willie said. "She has a claim to that property."

"So do most of the other people up there," Daniel said. "Somebody's going to get awful rich out of this and you can bet it won't be the people who live there. It'll be the white folks."

Willie shrugged his shoulders. "It's a dog-eat-dog world," he said, "and I guess the bone goes to the big dog."

"I believe that is what de Tocqueville calls the 'tyranny of the majority,'" Daniel observed.

"Whatever," Willie said. "Anyway, I think we'd better worry about your family's property now, not all these other things."

"Perhaps," Daniel said thoughtfully, "perhaps. But something else has occurred to me."

"What's that?" Willie asked.

"Perhaps nothing," Daniel said. "I'm going to think about it. I'd like to talk to some people before I say."

5

WILLIE'S NOTION OF THE FIRST STRIKE EVAPORATED TWO days later. A near-hysterical Priscilla Holt phoned to tell him that a process server had delivered an eviction notice to her mother that morning, giving her two weeks to vacate the property.

"Tell her not to worry and not to do anything," Willie said reassuringly. "I'll counterfile in a day or so and that will tie them up until we go to court to settle it."

After he hung up, Willie gathered up the mass of papers he had been working on and laid them aside on his desk. This maneuver by the Holts had put a new complexion on things and he had to decide what strategy to use now— namely: how much of the cat to let out of the bag and to whom. Since it was a major decision he decided to ponder it over a cup of coffee and a slice of pie down at the corner drugstore.

It was a wet and windy afternoon with low banks of clouds billowing up from the mouth of Bienville Bay and a thin, needling rain driving in from the direction of the ship docks. The Parade was deserted except for a few pigeons poking the ground beneath the dripping oaks. Willie clutched his raincoat at the neck and lowered his head to the wind. As he turned the corner a female voice addressed him from beneath a huge umbrella.

"Mr. Croft . . . Willie . . ."

He leaned forward to see who it was.

"Oh, Miss Loftin, how are you?"

"Soaking," she said. "Don't you have an umbrella?"

"I lost it someplace," Willie said. A gust of wind drove at him vengefully and he turned his back to it.

"You ought to have a hat," Whitsey said. "You're getting drenched."

"I was just going in here to have some coffee. Would you like to join me?" he said.

She hesitated for a second and a second gust caught them, lifting her umbrella. "Yes," she said. "Maybe the rain will let up a little."

They sat in a booth near a window and watched the rain slanting at it in a crazy, sideways angle.

"A couple of books came in today that you might enjoy," she said. "The new paperback of *Some Came Running* and an Agatha Christie mystery."

Willie sipped his coffee. "Days like this are good for reading," he said wistfully, "not much else."

They talked for a while, of books and the weather, and then Willie learned that the Holts were moving quickly in matters other than the Backus property.

"How is your aunt?" he asked.

"She's . . . fine," Whitsey said.

"She's a kick. I enjoyed meeting her."

"She's . . . oh, hell," Whitsey said. She pursed her lips in exasperation. "I'm so upset. I don't know what to do. I've just come from Augustus Tompkins's office. He asked me to come over. My cousins, it seems, have filed in court to have her declared insane."

Willie frowned. "Insane or incompetent?" he asked gently.

"What's the difference—incompetent, I suppose. The point is that it's going to kill her." Then she poured out to Willie the story of the old lady's refusal to divide the property despite everyone's efforts to persuade her.

63

"She just doesn't want to," Whitsey said. "She's in her eighties and she doesn't need the money. She's been living up there for forty or fifty years. They say she doesn't understand the importance of it, but I think she does. It's just that it isn't important to her."

"I'm sure from their point of view she's being pretty stubborn," Willie said.

"If I had had more time," Whitsey said, "it might have made a difference. They told me they weren't going to do this for a while. When a person's that old, they need time for things to sink in. They need to adjust to new ideas."

"Who's her lawyer?" Willie asked. "What does he say?"

"She doesn't have one," Whitsey said. "Augustus Tompkins always handled things for the whole family, but now he's on the other side. He told me she'll have to get one of her own or the court will appoint one. Now he wants me to go up there and tell her about all this and see if she'll change her mind."

"Do you think she will?"

"I think just the opposite. I think she'll get so mad she'll never change it."

"Hmmmm . . ." Willie said, "this is certainly shaking up people's lives."

"I'd like to ask you, Mr. Croft . . . Willie . . . would you . . . would you like to be her lawyer?"

Willie was stunned. "Would *I*? Ah . . . why me?"

"Because she knows you—and she seemed to like you. And, well, all the lawyers I know are friends with Augustus, and you seem to be in on all this oil business anyway . . . I don't know—but would you?"

"Certainly," Willie said, "if she wants to retain me."

"I'll suggest it to her. I'm going up there tomorrow. I'll have to tell her. It's going to break her heart; I know it. She'll think her family has turned against her."

"Are you coming back early or late?" Willie asked.

"Am I, ah . . . early, I guess. Probably before dark. Why?"

"Because I was wondering if I could take you to supper tomorrow night?" he said.

"I think I can manage that," she said demurely. "I'd like to very much."

From the fifth-floor window in his office, Willie gazed out into the gloom. He was barely able to make out a few swatches of the muddy, rain-swept river over other buildings. The clouds rolled ominously out of the south. He took out a legal pad and began to draw up his petition for Mrs. Backus. Might as well shoot for the moon, he thought, and let the rough end drag.

It was nearly eight o'clock before he finished. First thing in the morning his part-time secretary would type it up and he could file it in the afternoon and wait for the explosion. A childhood vulgarity came to mind:

> There you stand
> So spic and span;
> Where was you
> When the shit hit the fan?

He put the pad aside and straightened up his desk, picked up his raincoat and switched off the lights. He stood for a moment in the darkened room, then put everything down and sank back in his chair. Below him, and beyond, the city glowed like a deserted carnival ground; neon signs advertised sleazy waterfront dives. During all these years he had been in his office, he thought, nothing had changed, but now, in just one week . . .

He was suddenly possessed by a reluctant feeling of hope. It came mistlike, slowly filling the chambers of his brain, white, consuming, comfortable, satisfying, euphoric, some of it to do with the oil and some of it with Whitsey Loftin. Perhaps more with her, he thought. The oil was still a vague, chancy bet. Why, he wondered, in all this time, had he never met someone like her?

Old girlfriends came to mind.

There had been Gladys Parker, the vegetarian nurse, nondrinker and nonsmoker, and that had lasted nearly a year, on and off again, until he couldn't stand her non-ness any longer despite the regular screwing which she somehow managed to view as healthy exercise and, so far as he could tell, nothing more.

There was Wanda Beasley, the nonscrewer, religious nut, who lived with her mother and didn't kiss well either.

"I never learned how," she had explained one night, but finally after six months he had gotten her to bed—or rather, on the couch—and to his astonishment was rewarded with the best piece of ass he had ever had. But the next morning, a Sunday, she had dressed and gone before he woke up, back to her mother, and when he phoned her later she informed him coolly that she had spent the entire day in church begging forgiveness for the sinful thing she had done. For six more months he relentlessly pursued her and she denied him steadfastly. He spent a small fortune taking her to suppers until finally one day Willie learned from colleagues that she had done it with half the males in town, and cut them all off after the first time with the same excuse.

In between those two there had been a depressing assortment of others: secretaries, waitresses, elevator operators and divorcées, some of whom Willie had slept with and some he hadn't. And now there was Whitsey Loftin.

The warm, hopeful feeling soared and still Willie did not try to stifle it.

She was beautiful to him, an earthy, robust beauty with a certain warmth and firm independence. He'd never met anyone like her. He let himself picture the two of them spending weekends together, rising late on Saturday or Sunday mornings to read the newspaper and have breakfast, and make love. . . .

Wouldn't it be grand if it happened, he thought; then the impact of that proposition suddenly struck him with the force of an ax handle, and he methodically began to deflate the hope the way someone lets air from a tire. Because if you let hope take hold of your senses—as he had often done before—the hoped-for thing almost surely would fail to materialize. That was the harsh lesson Willie Croft had learned in the last fifteen or twenty years. He stood, picked up the umbrella and briefcase and went down into the rain.

Late the next afternoon Willie filed his pleadings in the matter of Mrs. Elvira Backus. Later the same afternoon he received an icy telephone call from Judge McCormack's secretary.

"The judge would like to see you right away, Mr. Croft," she said.

Half an hour later Willie was ascending the steps of the courthouse and Burt, the bailiff, greeted him at the entrance.

"You musta done something awful wild this time, Mr. Croft. I never saw him this way before."

"Just called a spade a spade, Burt, that's all," Willie said knowingly. As he stepped into the anteroom a bark issued from the judge's chambers.

"Where the hell is he!"

"He just walked in," the secretary said, looking Willie up and down disapprovingly.

"Send his ass in here," the judge growled.

Judge McCormack was a short, rotund man in his early sixties and he was standing stiffly behind the desk, holding in his hand the papers Willie had filed. The judge's countenance was consumed in a black scowl.

"Good morning, Your Honor," Willie said courteously.

"It is not!" the judge declared violently. "You have really done it this time, Mr. Croft. I have tolerated all I am going to tolerate of your foolishness."

Willie looked puzzled. "I'm not sure what Your Honor means. What have I done?"

"You know goddamned well what I'm talking about, Croft!" the judge burst out. He was beginning to wave the papers across the desk into Willie's face. His fat, flabby neck strained at the collar.

"If you believed I would find this amusing," he growled, glaring at the sheaf of papers, "you are sadly mistaken. I have had to put up with just about every imaginable prank from you, Willie Croft—the damned poo-poo cushion in the district attorney's chair, the phony business cards, the fireflies let loose during the power company case, the fake signs on the water fountains, that goddamned singing in the courtroom . . . but this . . . this . . ." He searched for words. "This . . . *atrocity!* This is the limit. I have always told you someday you would go too far. Now you have," Judge McCormack seethed.

"Your Honor," Willie protested, "that is a serious pleading on behalf of my client. I did not mean it as a joke."

The judge squinted at Willie in total disbelief.

"Do you mean to tell me you are *seriously filing* this thing?" he said contemptuously.

"Very seriously," Willie replied.

The judge collapsed into his chair and the papers dropped to his lap. He swung around to face the window and after a few moments' silence he began glancing over Willie's brief.

"Preposterous," he said finally, shaking his head.

Willie said nothing. The silence endured for long agonizing seconds, and then the judge leaped to his feet again and confronted Willie like a maddened dog.

"You must be insane!" he cried. "Out of your head! Do you know what you have said here? Do you know what you imply? You have accused perhaps the most prominent family of this city of . . . of . . . goddamned *miscegenation!"* the judge said, waving his hands. "And in this state miscegenation is a crime. You have accused them of a *crime!"*

"I'm not accusing anybody of anything, Your Honor," Willie said politely. "I am simply trying to set forth the facts of the case. It only involves the elder Mr. Johnathan Holt. And he is dead."

"This is pure slander, Willie Croft," the judge hissed. "Pure slander."

"You can't slander a dead man," Willie reminded him.

"The hell you can't!" Judge McCormack said with renewed fury. "I'm not talking about law, I'm talking about good, honest citizens!" He flung the offending papers onto his desk and pointed at them. "You are accusing the Holt family—a family of good, decent Christian people—of having goddamn nigger brothers and sisters. If that isn't slander in this day and age, I don't know what is!"

"Your Honor," Willie said, "facts are facts and I sincerely believe my clients are telling the truth. And I . . ."

"Truth!" the judge howled. "Shit on truth! Do you have any idea what this would do to that poor family? Those young children? The scandal? The abuse they would suffer if something like this is even hinted at?"

"Sir, with all respect, the Holt family is not exactly *poor*. And what about the abuse they are heaping on my client? A seventy-eight-year-old woman, being evicted from her life-long home?"

"Good Lord, good Lord." The judge sat down again and buried his head in his hands. "Johnathan Holt was a close friend of mine. You have stained his memory."

"I don't want to stain anyone's memory," Willie said contritely. "I simply want to represent my client the best way I can."

The judge raised his head and peered up at Willie as though he were looking at some unbelievable freak. Then he slammed his fist on the desk, upsetting an ashtray.

"Well, goddamnit! You are not going to get away with this shit, Willie Croft." He began waving his arms again wildly. "I'll tell you what I'm going to do. I'm going to seal those goddamned records as of right now. I am going to seal the whole goddamned case and if it ever gets to this court I am going to hear it in closed session. And if you breathe so much as a word of this to anybody else I will have you in contempt of court! I will throw your ass in jail!"

The judge paused to catch his breath.

"And," he said, raising a stern finger into the air, "you had better start thinking about a new defense for this woman because . . . because . . . this is *indefensible!*" the judge stammered.

Willie nodded. "Will there be anything else, Your Honor?"

"No," the judge said scathingly, "that is all."

* * *

That evening Willie picked up Whitsey Loftin at her apartment, a small, neatly restored cottage behind one of the antebellum mansions in the Garden District. He headed the old Nash southward out of town. There was a small café on the Bayou aux Oeils called Beaudreux's Place, which served the best seafood on the Gulf Coast, or so its patrons, Willie included, were fond of saying.

It was a splendid evening for a drive. The sun was only a faint glow in the west as they drove past flat farmlands of harvested corn, soybeans and potatoes, crossed rickety bridges over murky streams which poured into the Bay. He assured Whitsey repeatedly that the eighteen-mile trip would be worth it when they were fed. They did not speak of the oil.

Beaudreux's Place was basically a shack perched on stilt pilings above the salt marshes beside the bayou. A wharf led from the road to the screen-door entrance. The dining area was a single large room with windows all around and in a corner a potbellied stove radiated heat against the chilly night. Smelling of shellfish and the swamp, Beaudreux, an enormous Acadian with huge beefy hands, the son of the original Beaudreux, greeted Willie with an embrace.

"Ah, Mistair Croff—well-comb, well-comb—and you luvely frond!"

He escorted them to a table in the corner with a view of the salt marshes, a vast sea of tall reedy grass that stretched toward the Mississippi Sound, illuminated brown and gold by a half-moon already high in the sky. Across the dark, musky bayou they could make out the booms and nets of a shrimp boat tied to a pier. Without being asked, Beaudreux brought them two glasses, a bowl of ice and a pitcher of water. Willie placed the bottle of Early Times bourbon he had brought on top of the table, wrapped in a paper bag, opened the top and poured a healthy finger of whiskey in both glasses.

"Dame Bap-tist arn bootliggers," Beaudreux complained sourly. "Pas dis dame law. Be the ruin of us wis dis whiskey beezness. Used to be a mon could have a drink any-pless. No more! De ought to be shot."

"Ho," Willie said, "that's strong medicine, Beaudreux. Democratic process, you know."

"Ha!" Beaudreux said darkly. "Democratic process would be de find themselves float facedown in Bayou aux Oeils. De try to keep a mon from his whiskey—dat's democratic process enuf for me!" Then he grinned broadly. "Wait," he said, "I get you a lamp."

"He's a character," Whitsey said.

"He's a cook too," Willie said.

Beaudreux returned with a small kerosene lamp and placed it on the table between them. "Dame electricity," he grumbled. "Too dame expensive—but this is nicer too—eh?" He disappeared into the kitchen.

"Doesn't he have any electricity here?" Whitsey asked.

"Nope. He does it all with kerosene and coal and wood stoves. He gets ice from the shrimp boats for his icebox. Quaint, isn't it?"

"My goodness," Whitsey said, "it certainly is. By the way, I'm starved. Where's the menu?"

"Isn't any," he said. "Beaudreux will tell us what he has."

They were halfway through their drinks when Beaudreux returned.

"Tonight," he said, "I have a red snapper I got from the boat dis after-nun; and a coupla flounder caught dis mornin'; an' some Bon Secours oyster Charlie Antoine took dis mornin' an' day so fresh an' sweet I almos' ate up ta last but I save some for you; an' I got s'rimp creole but you gotta tell me if you want dat now so I can be goin' over to Arnaux's wharf an' get some of dose s'rimps. An' I also got some crawfish come in hea about three hour ago still live."

Willie looked at Whitsey. "You ever had crawfish?" he asked.

"No," she said dubiously.

"Beaudreux, we'll start with them."

"How many you want? Platter?"

"Half a platter," Willie said.

"Okay—half. I put 'em in a steam pot now, okay?"

"Fine," Willie said. He poured them another glass of bourbon. "How did it go with your aunt?"

"All right, I suppose," she said. "She was having one of her 'days.' I told her what has happened but it didn't seem to sink in."

"That's too bad."

"Well, I just don't know," she said. "I mean, she seemed to understand it well enough, but not . . . not really. She just said her mind was made up and they weren't going to do anything with the property while she's still alive and that's that."

"Did you explain that she's going to have to deal with their lawsuit?"

"Yes, of course. I told her she had to get a lawyer or the court would appoint one for her. She just said that was all nonsense, what do I need with a lawyer?"

Beaudreux burst through the kitchen door and set down a platter of dark-red boiled crawfish and dishes with melted butter and sliced lemon.

"Bon appétit," he said.

Willie demonstrated the peeling of crawfish and handed the first succulent tail to Whitsey.

"Ummmm—this is incredible," she said. Willie smiled.

"The thing with your aunt," he said, "is that more than likely they are going to be able to win it in court. I think you should know that. It seems to me the best move at this point is to get her to work out some kind of compromise beforehand. Something that would leave everybody reasonably happy."

"Well, that's what I've been trying to do," she said. "She's so stubborn she won't listen to anybody. You know, sometimes I think she understands everything completely, and then other times, maybe not at all."

"Maybe if I talk to her," he offered.

"Maybe so," Whitsey said.

After the crawfish, they ate between them a dozen or so Bon Secours oysters and afterward Beaudreux brought them steaming red snapper topped with a powerful spicy sauce and steamed rice. Willie was in wonderful spirits. Looking across the table at Whitsey, seeing her face soft and smiling in the lamplight, he felt blissfully comfortable—something he had not felt with a woman in many years, if ever he had.

They had not discussed the subject of the oil and the Holt family—outside of Whitsey's aunt. He wanted to bring it up, to tell her himself and spare her the shock of hearing it from the Holts, but Judge McCormack's edict prevented him from doing so. From what little he knew of her, he hoped she would take it well, but naturally he couldn't be certain. She might decide never to speak to him again. But it was too late to do anything about it anyway.

On the ride back they did not talk much. The half-moon that had shone above the marshes when they arrived was now comfortably settling in the west. He tuned the radio to a soft big-band music station out of New Orleans and for most of the drive Whitsey was asleep, with her head resting between the window and the seat of the car. When they reached her apartment Willie got out first and opened the door for her.

"Let me ask you something," she said. They were walking up the steps.

"Okay," he said.

"There's a dance next Saturday. The Azalea Ball. It's the opening of the season for debutantes."

"There's an open season on debutantes?" he said.

"You know what I mean."

"I've heard about it."

"Will you take me?"

They had reached the door. Willie hesitated a moment before answering. He suddenly worried about the impact the Backus papers would have on this invitation. Then he decided, Oh, what the hell.

"Sure," he said, "if you want to be seen with a clod like me."

"It's formal," she said.

"Well, I've got an old tux I've had since college. I think it still fits."

She looked at him. "It's full formal, I mean. White tie."

"Oh," Willie said. "I guess I'll have to find one of those, then."

6

TWO DAYS BEFORE THE AZALEA BALL, WILLIE PHONED
Whitsey Loftin. He figured that by this time she would have
heard about his pleadings in the Backus case and decided he
might as well find out if she still wanted him to take her to
the dance. It took him three shots of bourbon to screw up
the courage to dial her number.

"Hello."

"Whitsey, this is Willie Croft."

"Oh, Willie, hi. I was just going to call you."

A knot tightened in his stomach.

"You were?"

"Yes," she said, "about the dance. Can you pick me up at
nine instead of nine thirty? They lock the doors until the
tableau is over and I don't want us to be late. Is that all
right?"

"All . . . right," he stammered. "It's . . . it's fine."

"Good," she said. "By the way, you sure did set off a
bomb with my cousins. That suit you filed, I mean. They're
having a fit."

"Well," he said, more composed, "I was wondering about
that. I thought maybe when you found out you'd be,
ah . . . upset. And I couldn't tell you before because the
judge ordered the papers sealed and I . . ."

"I think it's kind of funny," she interrupted. "You should have heard them. I never knew Uncle John—he died when I was a child—but I'm not really surprised. Not by anything that happens in this family."

"Well, that's one way to look at it," he said.

"I think you'll like the dance. Lots of champagne and that sort of thing."

"Maybe I can bag a debutante or two," Willie said. He put down the phone. The palms of his hands were damp.

The following morning Daniel Holt called and asked if Willie could come to the school again. He said he preferred not to discuss the matter over the phone. Willie drove over in the afternoon.

"I think what you have done, this lawsuit with my mother, could have repercussions," Daniel said.

"It may," Willie said. "It is not going to be a popular case in court."

"I am willing to bear the brunt, and my mother and sister will, too," Daniel said. "But I'm a little bit concerned. Do you think there is a chance for harm to come to them?"

Willie thought for a moment. "No," he said, "I don't think there'll be any harm—physical harm, I mean. The Holts aren't that sort of people. But they are very, ah, proud. I think they will use all of their means to discredit what we allege in the suit."

"That is to be expected," Daniel Holt said. "I think we can all stand that, so long as there is no violence."

"I don't think that's in the cards," Willie said.

Daniel Holt seemed to be studying Willie. He leaned back. "There is something else," he said. "It's why I wanted to talk to you. Something I've been thinking about and discussing with some other people. Are you a gambling man, Mr. Croft? I mean, willing to take a gamble?"

Willie looked puzzled. "Sometimes I've taken a few," he said.

"What would you say, then, if I suggested to you that there are people, friends of mine, who would like to put up money—and property—to buy oil leases in Creoletown? In effect, to form our own syndicate. And get in on the financial part of this thing?"

Willie frowned and pursed his lips. "I would say, how much money and how much land? And then I would say—not knowing any more than I do now—that it would be very risky, because from what I have heard you would be dealing against very wealthy, experienced people with a great many connections."

"There wouldn't be a lot of money at first," Daniel Holt said, "but I think it would come. Property, there is a great deal of. There are a great many colored people up there who own their own places. And everybody's trying to buy them out—to make deals. The people are afraid. I have talked to some of them. The money is good, and they're afraid if they don't agree somebody will take their property away."

"It's probably true," Willie said.

"However," Daniel continued, "what if we went to them? I have a dozen or so friends, doctors, businessmen who have saved some money over the years, myself included. We would offer to support their leases if they throw in with us. The plan would be to form a corporation. The lease values seem to rise by the day. The newspaper said they started out offering fifteen hundred dollars an acre—now it's up to around two thousand dollars. If we control large chunks of that land, we can make our own deals with the oil companies."

"Like I said," Willie countered, "you're dealing against big money. I hear there are six or seven syndicates formed already and I suspect there will be many others."

"Ah," Daniel said majestically, "but there is a difference —they don't *own* the land."

"All I know," Willie said, "is what I hear around the courthouse. But if it is only half true, then those deeds—the ones the, ah, colored people have—will be in dispute, just like your mother's—except that she probably stands a better chance. Most of the colored people are just living on land some white people said they could live on years ago and then forgot about—until now. There are going to be a lot of battles fought in court."

"But we could tie it up there," Daniel Holt said. "If everyone gets together and we pool our money and don't get picked off piecemeal. What I'm saying, Mr. Croft, asking, is . . . will you consider representing us, and set this thing up?"

"But why me?" Willie asked curiously. "For something like this you'd be better off with a corporation-type lawyer. I think I can handle your mother's case, but when you are talking about something so complex as a . . ."

Daniel interrupted him.

"Because, Mr. Croft, you are the only lawyer connected with this thing that we know. There are no Negro lawyers in this city. Now there are Negro doctors, and Negro undertakers, because the white folks don't want to fool with sick Negroes or dead Negroes, and there are Negro motel owners and restauranters, because the white folks don't want to sleep and eat in the same places with us. But did you know that there isn't one single Negro law school in the South? Because if there were, the Negro lawyer would have to deal with the white lawyers and white judges and they don't want that either."

Willie had not really thought about that, although he guessed it was true. He did not answer Daniel Holt immediately, but looked away through the window to the playground.

"What do you think?" Daniel asked.

"I still don't know how much money you're talking about," he said hedgingly.

"Between the twelve of us perhaps half a million dollars," Daniel Holt said. "Some have more, some less. And whatever we can raise from the banks."

"You can probably forget banks," Willie said. "They'll be on the other side."

"How about out-of-state banks? How about banks in Chicago, or New York, or Washington? I have heard that there are even some banks owned by Negroes—up North."

That had not occurred to Willie. "They might," he said, "but I wouldn't count on it. How much land are you talking about?"

"We can't be sure," Daniel said, "but as much as four or five thousand acres. Perhaps less. Eb Hooper, who owns the funeral home up there, knows about all the families in the area. We sat down the other night and made a list. There are at least forty colored families working hundred-or-so-acre plots."

Willie shook his head. "I don't know," he said. "Even assuming you can get the people to throw in with you or sell you their leases, you've still got the question of ownership. I don't even know what I can do for your mother."

Daniel looked at him painfully. "The point is, Mr. Croft, are you interested or not? We don't know either if we can get this thing off the ground. But we would like to try."

"All right," Willie said, "I'll tell you what. Get me the names and addresses of your people. Phone numbers, ages, all that sort of thing—and exactly how much each is willing to put up and in what form: cash, stocks, bonds. When I have that I'll draft an incorporation paper and get back to you. By the way, you'll have to have a name, and elect officers."

"Obsidian," Daniel said.

"Obsidian?" Willie repeated.

"That is the name we picked. It is the name of a black rock. The Obsidian Oil Corporation," Daniel Holt said.

The venerable old hotel glowed like a liner on the ocean at night. Dark-colored Buicks, Chryslers, Oldsmobiles and Cadillacs waited their turn to arrive beneath the marble-columned portico, disgorging long-gowned women and men in formal attire. Willie's Nash sputtered and coughed in line. When they reached the portico an attendant opened Whitsey's door and Willie caught a glimpse of the hotel foyer, packed with people. The attendant, a young Negro dressed in a white jacket, took the car, giving Willie a cursory and possibly condescending glance as he took the wheel.

Whitsey took him by the arm as they reached the steps and the soft warmth of her breast gently pressing his elbow was reassuring. Two enormous bouquets of flowers stood on either side of the doorway. She took the lead, pulling him along into the crowd. This revived his discomfort since he could not remember having a woman take him by the arm before and lead him around. Several people on the fringes of the throng called out to Whitsey, but she merely smiled at them and pushed her way through. This made Willie wonder if it was because she did not want to introduce him to her friends.

"I was hoping they would have let people into the ballroom by now," she said.

He nodded and smiled. The noise of conversation was ear-shattering.

Just when it seemed they had mired themselves totally in the mob, he caught sight of an open space in the main lobby near the marble goldfish fountain. Whitsey saw it too.

"I thought we were going to be mobbed," he said.

"They always gang up like that. Everybody wants to see who's coming in next."

He took a coin from his pocket, a dime, and tossed it into the fountain. Ordinarily, when he came into the lobby he threw in a penny, but the occasion seemed to call for a more extravagant donation.

"It's supposed to be good luck," he said.

"Yes, I know," Whitsey said, "for both of us."

"Maybe I ought to put in fifty cents, then," he said.

"Maybe *I* should put in fifty cents," she said.

They stood there for five or ten minutes, alone in the crowd. Willie's discomfort slid away in the gaiety and laughter. He recognized a few of the faces, silver-haired men, lawyers from the large ponderous firms whose clients were the shipping lines and railroad companies and paper mills. Though he knew most of them slightly from around the courthouse, he was seeing them now on their home turf, another, very different side of the town in which he had been raised. Here tonight was the power, the Driving Force, the buck, and where it stopped. Here was the mysterious *they* to whom everyone referred, without whose express advice and consent no one was elected to public office, new industry was not allowed into the county, buildings were not built and newspapers did not print. It was as though all his life Willie had ridden in the coach section of a train, then for a brief moment got to come forward and visit the engine compartment with its connectors, rods and sprockets, power plant, generators and wiring.

"Say," he said, "can we have a drink?"

"I'm afraid not yet," she said. "Tradition, I suppose; they never serve until after the call-outs—and then it's just champagne. Oh," she remembered, "but you can get one at the hotel bar."

"Do you want to come with me?"

"I think I'll stay here," she said. "It looks crowded in there."

Willie had sandwiched himself in the third row at the bar and was waving a five-dollar bill when a hand took him at the wrist and thrust a drink at him.

"Here, I've ordered two," a voice said. It was Augustus Tompkins.

"Thank you," Willie said hesitantly. "I still have one to go, though."

"Well, have this one too, then," Tompkins said. His croaking voice rose above the noise. "The bartenders here know me. I can get another."

"That's okay, I wanted a Scotch," Willie said.

"Give me a Scotch!" Tompkins roared. Moments later the Scotch appeared and was handed back through the mob.

"We need to talk, Willie," Tompkins said.

"I have to get back to my date."

"Just for a second, it's important."

"All right, what's up?"

"It's about that paper you filed," Tompkins said. He bent toward Willie secretively.

"What about it?"

"It was a reprehensible thing to do—to a fine old family of this city."

"It's the truth," Willie said. "Besides, I gave you fair warning."

"It's not the truth!" Tompkins said indignantly. "Anyhow, it's beside the point now."

They were standing in the doorway to the foyer and people were pressing past them.

"The truth is never beside the point, Augustus," Willie said piously, and with a smile.

"All right," Tompkins hissed, "let's stop farting around. My people will deal. They'd rather pay than have this kind of scandal. How much will she take?"

"She only wants her property," Willie said. "Clear title and hands off by the Holt family."

"That's too much," Tompkins snorted. "We're willing to make concessions—but not to give the damned land away lock, stock and barrel." Tompkins took out his pipe and began to pack it. "Let me make this proposal," he said. "Suppose we do give her clear title—but with an agreement as to the mineral rights. We would retain seventy percent of her share."

"Nope," Willie said.

"All right, then—how about this: she gets clear title but agrees to sell the mineral rights back to us for five hundred an acre, and we retain the royalties."

"I don't think so, Augustus," Willie said.

"Good God, man!" Tompkins seethed. "That damned woman never in her life had a pot to piss in or a window to throw it out of before now. I'm talking about giving her four hundred eighty acres free plus nearly a quarter million cash and you're standing there saying no!"

"You can't give somebody what they already own, Augustus," Willie said calmly. "Besides, you know as well as I do that the oil people are paying two thousand dollars an acre now—and if just a couple of acres come in on that land it'll make that quarter million look like chicken feed."

"Damnit, Willie! You don't listen to reason. You've got to give my people some shred. They're not going to just roll over and play dead on this. There's a limit to everything. I'll guarantee you this—if you push this with them they'll fight it with everything they've got. And some people are liable to get hurt—maybe you too, Willie."

"Are you threatening me?" Willie said.

"No, I'm not threatening you," Tompkins said in frustration. "You know what I mean. Hurt in reputation. The Holts have powerful friends in this town. A lawyer's reputation is his most important asset."

Before Willie could answer, Whitsey Loftin appeared, unsandwiched herself from between several people and came up to them.

"Well," she said, "I bet I know what you two are talking about."

"Hello, my dear," Tompkins said graciously. He kissed her on the cheek. "Do you know Mr. Willie Croft?"

"I should hope to say," she gushed, taking Willie by the arm, "he's my date."

"Huh!" Tompkins exclaimed. "Your, your . . . *date?*" From the expression on Augustus Tompkins's face, he might have suddenly been jabbed in the seat with a hat pin.

"Oh, there's the fanfare," Whitsey said breezily. "We should go in." She tugged at Willie's arm and led him away.

An electric sense of mirth and gaiety filled the huge ballroom. Expectant parents of new debutantes, envious parents of debutantes from previous years—and years to come—young men, tanned or pink-cheeked, in formal regalia, waiting to screen the new crop of eligibles, grandparents, friends and out-of-town guests, all mingled intensely among the white-covered tables and enormous bouquets of flowers.

Willie had never known anything like it before.

Elaborate white trellises ran from floor to ceiling on all four corners of the dance floor, and entwined on them were thousands of roses and camellias. The stage itself, draped in a white bunting sheet, was awash with azaleas, reds and whites and pinks and purples, and an enormous arrangement spelled out Azalea Ball, 1959. The orchestra was playing "The Most Beautiful Girl in the World."

The tables were filling quickly, especially the ones nearest the dance floor. Willie and Whitsey were walking past these when a voice shouted Whitsey's name. It was Brevard Holt. She gave Willie a cautionary glance and led him to the table.

"Hi, Brev," Whitsey said as the men at the table rose to their feet.

"Whitsey dear," he said. She leaned forward so he could kiss her cheek. "You know Evan Walker and Pooka, and these are their friends from New Orleans, the Hawthorns." Whitsey nodded and smiled. On the far side of the table was Marci with her escort, Donald Savage, whom everyone called Wah-whoo.

"And I'd like all of you to meet Willie Croft," Whitsey said brightly.

Brevard Holt's hand was already extended and Willie grasped it. "Pleasure to meet you," he said.

The expression on Brevard's face turned much like the one Augustus Tompkins had had a while earlier, a squint of utter shock, but Brevard quickly got it under control.

"Oh, Mr. Croft," Brevard said. "Well, we have *certainly* heard a lot about you."

"My God! Is *he* the *one?*" Marci asked loudly. "The one who . . . I don't believe it." She was looking up and down at Willie and then Whitsey. "And he's here . . . with you? Why . . . the *nerve!*"

"Well, we'd better find ourselves a table before the tableau," Whitsey said. She took Willie by the arm. "See y'all later," she smiled.

They found a table near the back of the room. Neither Willie nor Whitsey knew the two younger couples already seated, but Whitsey knew their older brothers and sisters and parents. She did, however, know Hamilton ("Ham") Bledsole, a tanned, handsome redhead who had graduated from the University of Virginia Medical School, where he had been a better-than-average tennis player and an excellent bridge player. He started a cheerful conversation with Willie about state politics until the orchestra struck up the fanfare again and the master of ceremonies began announcing the call-outs. As their names were called, the debutantes appeared from the wings one by one and descended the stairs to the dance floor, where they formed in a line facing the crowd. Each wore an elaborate white ball gown and carried a bouquet. They smiled rapaciously on the biggest evening of their lives. There was applause, then their fathers greeted them for the first dance, a rendition of "Beale Street Blues."

Ham Bledsole leaned into Willie's ear. "Crockashit, huh?" and Willie, still slightly awestruck, smiled politely and nodded.

"Been coming to these things for ten years," Ham Bledsole said. "Their mothers think they're getting them introduced to polite society, but all they're doing is waving their asses on a stick. There ain't any polite society anymore."

The band was still playing and the young girls were whirling about the floor. Spotlights from the balconies played upon them in shades of red and silver.

"Maybe they're just looking for an excuse to have a party, or a good time," Willie offered. He was older than Ham Bledsole by perhaps ten years and felt qualified to give a more generous assessment.

Bledsole peered at him over steel-rimmed glasses. "They would all have a better time in the back of somebody's car or on the couch of an apartment. This just ruins 'em," he said. "All the guys start crawling around so they can get invited to the parties. They think the guys are really interested in *them*. Look out there; most of 'em are dogs anyway."

Willie surveyed the swirling dance floor. The faces, from a distance, looked pleasant and pretty. Close up might be different, but from here it was a gay and impressive sight. "I don't know," he said. "I've never been to one of these before."

"Really?" Bledsole said. "Well, I guess it's different for you, then. I suppose I've been to too many—maybe that's the problem. My wife likes to come, but she's not feeling well tonight."

"Why'd you come, then?" Willie asked.

"It's the only game in town," Ham Bledsole said.

Timed to perfection as the first dance ended, Negro

waiters, in starched white jackets with frayed cuffs and collars, came to the tables with champagne bottles. During the next hour the champagne flowed like a strong Gulf tide and couples whirled about on the dance floor to the big-band music of the forties. Then the beat began to quicken and some of the older guests began to drift off. Willie and Whitsey danced twice, he stepping on her feet several times, with profound apologies. The sweet scent of flowers filled the room.

"Is Ham Bledsole any kin to the Bledsole Oil Distributors?" Willie asked.

"It's his father—and uncles too, I think," she said. "Why?"

"Just curious," he said. "My father used to order from them."

"Well, that's who he is." They finished the dance and walked off the floor. "We're invited to a room," she said.

"What for?" he asked.

"Well, there are sort of private parties. To get away from the crowd and get something besides champagne. I'd like you to meet some of my friends."

"All right," he said reluctantly. He was just beginning to feel comfortable.

They left the ballroom and walked down a corridor, passing several rooms filled with revelry, their doors ajar and large letters of the alphabet taped on them. Finally they came to the last room.

"This is it, room J," she said.

Room J was less crowded than the others. Several people sat in overstuffed chairs and sofas, or stood in groups talking quietly. Most of them were older than Willie. Tables of hors d'oeuvres had been laid out, along with a fully stocked bar, tended by an elderly Negro barman with shaking hands.

"Oh, there's John," she said brightly. "I didn't think he was coming." She led Willie up to Johnathan Holt, who shifted awkwardly in his stiff white collar.

"Hiya, Whitsey," he said, leaning down to kiss her cheek.

"John, you came, didn't you?" she said brightly. "I want you to meet Willie Croft."

"Hiya," Johnathan said, extending a large meaty paw.

"I'm pleased to meet you," Willie said. Obviously, he thought, it hadn't yet occurred to Johnathan who Willie was. Whitsey suddenly thought it her duty to explain it.

"Mr. Croft is the lawyer for the colored people on the Creoletown property," she said.

"No kidding," Johnathan said. His brow furrowed as though he were trying to comprehend what he had just been told. He looked at Willie, then at Whitsey.

"You mean—he's the one who . . ."

"He's the one," she smiled. She took Willie's arm. "But he's just doing his job. I like him."

Johnathan nodded. "Well, I guess if you do, it's okay." He took a sip of whiskey and said to Willie, "That's a nice place up there, isn't it?"

"Very nice," Willie said.

"You know, there're still a few birds up there. Used to be more," he shrugged, "but they've been thinned out some, I guess."

"I'm pretty much a duck man, myself," Willie said. "Grew up with it."

"I just got back myself," Johnathan said.

"Where'd you go."

"Coon Lake—you know, up the river."

Ham Bledsole walked into the room and joined Willie's party.

"Have enough of the hoopla?" he asked.

"Whitsey brought me in here for a breather," Willie said. "Do you know Whitsey's cousin, Johnathan Holt?"

"Of course I do. How're you doin', John?"

"Just talking about ducks," Johnathan said. "I just got back from up the river."

"How'd you do?" Ham asked.

Whitsey gave Willie's arm a squeeze. "I'll let you men talk about ducks. I see somebody I want to say hello to." She went over to a younger couple who had just walked through the door.

"I got one canvasback," Johnathan said, "and a couple of black mallards. Goddamn redheads are all over the place since they put 'em out of season last year. I could of brought back a dozen if it wasn't for the law."

"It's a damned good eating duck, a redhead," Willie said. "How do you fix them?"

"Roast it on a grill," Johnathan said. "About the only way I know. Rub it down with a little red wine and salt and pepper and just lay it over the fire for about fifteen minutes a side. Meat falls right off on your fork."

"You don't stuff them with anything?" Ham said.

"Nah, ruins it, I always thought, especially if you're barbecuing."

Willie glanced over at Whitsey, who was in conversation with the young couple. He noticed a short, wiry man who had come to the doorway and begun looking around apprehensively, then strode over to Whitsey and took her by the arm, almost spinning her around. Willie could not tell what he was saying to her, but from the look of it, it was serious.

"Now a wood duck I like to bake," Johnathan was saying. "And there's one you can stuff because he doesn't have so much fat to drip down and ruin the stuffing. I guess of all of them, wood ducks are my favorite."

"They're damned delicious," Willie said. "I got two last Saturday."

"On the river, or what?"

"No, up by Maleux Bayou," Willie said. He again glanced at the conversation between Whitsey and the wiry man. It seemed to be growing more intense.

"You got a place up there?" Ham asked.

"Just a shack near there," Willie said. "It belonged to my father." Although he was talking, mostly he was watching Whitsey and her friend.

"There's a lot of ducks on Maleux Bayou," Johnathan continued. "That's usually where I take my people. There's some potholes back around Hammer Bend where you can jump mallards too. . . ." Johnathan stopped in midsentence. "Uh, oh," he said, nodding toward Whitsey and the man, "that's *Percy*. I guess he heard about you being here with her or something. He's pretty mad about all this."

Ham Bledsole seemed to sense something was happening

and decided to excuse himself. He turned to Willie. "If you need company up the river sometime, let me know," he said. "I went out a couple of days last year on the Bay but I'd like to see what it's like up there."

"I'll give you a call," Willie said.

"Great," Ham said. "If I'm not in the office, my number's in the book. See you, John." He walked back outside, toward the dance floor.

Percy Holt was glancing back and forth between Whitsey and the end of the room where Willie was standing. He took a step in that direction and Whitsey grabbed him by the arm, but he shook free and stalked up to Willie.

"I don't know what's going on here," Percy said, "but I'll tell you one thing, mister, you've got a lot of nerve coming here. This isn't a place for your sort of people."

Whitsey, who had followed on her cousin's heels, stepped between them, facing Percy.

"Please, Percy, don't make a scene. He's with me. He's got a right to . . ."

"Right, hell!" Percy snapped, still glaring at Willie. "He doesn't have a right to come anywhere near this family. He doesn't even have a right to live in this town, so far as I'm concerned." Percy edged closer to Willie, and Willie could feel his breath on his face as he spoke.

"Let's go back out on the dance floor," Willie said to Whitsey. He looked at Johnathan. "Nice talking to you."

"You're just a shit," Percy spat, "a lying, nigger-loving shit!"

"Now hold on a minute," Willie said. He began to feel flushed, the temper welling in him like steam in a riser pipe. "There's no call to talk that way. I'm a lawyer, I'm . . ."

"You're not a lawyer," Percy raged. "You're a little shyster crook. You ought to have your ass kicked."

"Aw, Percy, cool it off, huh?" Johnathan said nervously.

"Stay the hell out of this," Percy barked. "You—you big dumb bastard—were standing here talking to him!"

"Come on, Willie, let's go," Whitsey said. She had him by the hand, and they started off, but Percy stepped up beside him.

"Just remember one thing," he said. "You don't belong here, around decent people. You're just a no-good little shit!"

Willie stopped. "Listen, you've said your piece already. Why don't you just buzz off, now, huh?" He stared at Percy for a moment, then turned to go, but as he did Percy's fist caught him on the side of the face.

Willie felt himself stumbling sidewise from the force of the blow, and he caught himself on the chair of a surprised old dowager who leaped up shrieking and gasping as the drink on the chair arm fell into her lap. He turned to see Percy Holt coming at him, fists raised.

Percy swung again, his right hand grazing Willie's cheekbone as he snapped his head back to avoid it, then, reflexively, Willie threw a left hook that caught Percy flush on the mouth and straightened him up long enough for Willie to lash out and catch him full force on the nose with a right of his own.

Percy went down on the seat of his pants, the black tails of his formal suit splaying out crazily behind him. Both of his hands were at his nose and a trickle of blood was beginning to run down around both corners of his mouth and drip into the penguin-white vest and shirt. He did not try to rise.

It had happened instantaneously. Ten or fifteen seconds at most. Four blows. Everyone was stunned. There was bewildered silence in the room. Johnathan had moved to stop the fight when he saw what was happening, but there had been no time, and now no need. He was kneeling beside his brother, trying to examine the nose, while Percy cursed and swore repeatedly through his cupped hands. Willie stood with his arms by his sides looking at Whitsey, who was pale and frightened. A few people were beginning to murmur and drift closer to see what had happened. Johnathan yelled at the Negro barman to bring him some towels. Whitsey recovered and tugged at Willie's sleeve.

"There's a way to the street through here," she said. "Let's go home." Outside, in the chill of the autumn night, Willie felt unusually aware of the damp smell of the Bay, a few blocks distant. His senses of smell and sight and hearing seemed brilliantly illuminated, and his heart pounded within his chest, animal-like. Whitsey stopped beneath a streetlamp.

"You're hurt," she said. "Your cheek."

He put his finger to his cheekbone and winced. It was sticky and burned.

"It's all right," he said. "Let's get the car."

Neither of them spoke for a while. Willie wasn't exactly sure what she meant when she said, "Let's go home," so he took her to her own house. He stopped in the gravel driveway and walked her to the porch, but she said, "Come inside, I'll put something on that for you."

"It's okay," he told her, "it's just a scratch."

"Then come inside and I'll give you a drink."

"That sounds like a better idea."

He sat on a sofa in the living room while she went into the kitchen.

Over the fireplace was a full-sized portrait of a young man, presumably a Holt ancestor, dressed in the frock coat and boots of a gentleman of the early 1800s. He was standing beside an oak tree on a bluff overlooking a river and there was a hammer gun in his hand and a hunting dog at his feet. The foliage around him reflected the pale greens and golds of autumn.

Willie studied the face. The young man's expression was placid and unsmiling, yet bold, as though even in his youth (he might have been twenty) he was determined to carve out of the wilderness around him a place for himself and his descendants—which, in fact, he had—decade after decade; while Willie's own people eked along in small fishing boats in the British Channel Islands, this youthful ancestor became a Southern planter, attended dances, had his portrait painted and gave his sons to the Civil War—as officers—and they in turn came home and rebuilt and prospered, while Willie's people had remained in their longboats or in the fields for however many hundreds of years, fishing and tilling for someone else until the fish ran out and the soil became barren and they were forced to emigrate out of sheer necessity—certainly not out of any sense of grand adventure—to America, probably in the hold of a steamer, and immediately went to work for someone else, because the idea of self-employment went against the grain of three or four or five hundred years of serfdom . . . and when they finally did break away, as his father had, it was to open a gasoline filling station, and now he, Willie Croft, was the first—at least that he was aware of—of these generations of Crofts to pull himself up even with the kind of respectable and genteel job that this Holt ancestor had held one hundred fifty years before; and even so, the Holt family could continue to look down on him and call him names and spit on him—as they had tonight—to let him know that he was no more in their social class now than his great-great-grandfather would have been in the same class with the man here in the painting. . . .

"Here," Whitsey said. She handed him a tumbler of bourbon whiskey and sat down beside him with a wad of cotton and a bottle of alcohol.

"I'm sorry, Willie," she said. "I never thought anything like that would happen." She dabbed some alcohol onto the cotton and reached toward his cheek. "I'm so embarrassed," she said.

He felt the cold sting against his face and forced himself not to wince. "It isn't your fault," he said. "You couldn't know."

"Oh, I should have! I should have!" she said. Suddenly she choked up and buried her head in her hands.

"Hey, it's all right." He put his arm on her shoulder. "It was just one of those crazy kind of things that happen."

"It's more than that," she sobbed. She turned her face up to him, eyes brimming with tears, and he kissed her softly on her lips. For a moment she didn't respond, then she was kissing him back and pressing against him. After a while they separated and she was breathing heavily, looking at him in a bewildered way, as though somehow he had gotten hold of her and touched her innermost feelings. She ran her fingers through his hair and put her cheek next to his chest.

"I like the way you kiss," he said, sneaking an elbow below her breast and pushing up with slight pressure.

She snuggled closer to him. "You too," she said.

Willie reached over and turned off a table lamp beside the sofa, pulling her with him as he did so she was nearly prone, then he swung his feet up, nudging hers, and they were lying down. He could feel her heart beating and he kissed her again and this time moved his hand up to her large breast, rubbing his palm over it, and she squirmed against him. After that he lost track of time. They made out like crazy high-school kids, probing and rubbing and kissing and nuzzling and squeezing and panting and writhing until finally she said, to his surprise and utmost elation, "Do you want to go into the other room?" Dumbfounded, all he could say was, "Uh-huh," but it was enough, and she got up and straightened herself and led him into the bedroom, both of them stripping as they went, and lay on the bed, she naked except for a half-slip and he in his undershorts, and in a few minutes' time they had divested themselves of these and he spread her legs and put himself in her and the joy of it was unlike anything he had ever felt before; he was not just screwing for screwing's sake, but giving something of himself, something undefinable, to her, and for her, until she interrupted his bliss, saying, "Oh, Willie, I'm not wearing anything, be careful," whereupon he immediately withdrew himself, like a gentleman, not really disappointed, merely concerned for her welfare, and lay beside her, kissing and caressing. Then she said, "Let me help you," and moved down on him, trailing her breasts and nipples across his chest and stomach—deliberately, it seemed to him—and took him in her hands, and then into her mouth, and brought him to glorious and wonderful climax, which was also the first time anyone had done *that* to him.

They lay cuddled together for a while afterward and he fumbled in the darkness for a cigarette, and lay back watching the glow of the ash in the dark, her head resting on his chest.

"That was so good. That was beautiful," he said.

She didn't say anything for a while, so he ran his finger across her cheek. "You all right?" he asked.

"I guess so," she said. She seemed to sigh. "I'm just upset

about what happened at the dance. It was so awful, so humiliating."

Willie took a deep drag on the cigarette and let the smoke out slowly. He felt on top of the world.

"It's not so bad," he said. "After all, I guess I won the fight."

7

THE FOLLOWING MONDAY TWO MEETINGS TOOK PLACE. BOTH were highly secret and highly important to those involved.

The first was in the massive Holt Stevedoring Building near the riverside docks. Visible from a window in the third-floor office of Percy Holt, senior vice-president and comptroller, two large white-hulled ships of the United Fruit Company strained at a pier with their enormous lines. There was little activity outside, though, for the stevedores and longshoremen had stopped their unloading of dollies at exactly 4:00 P.M. and gone home to their wives and beer halls—except for two of them, and these were men who had no families, or even friends, except an occasional acquaintance at a dockside saloon. They were called "Snake" Crenshaw and "The Roller," for reasons known principally to those who had encountered them in waterfront brawls, and they were standing now, sweaty and grime-covered, in front of a large desk behind which sat Percy Holt, with a large metal splint taped over his nose, obscuring it.

"They tell me you fellows like to do a little extra work sometimes," Percy said.

The Roller and Snake Crenshaw exchanged glances. Neither of them commented on or inquired about the nose.

"Depends on what it is, Mr. Holt," The Roller said. He was an enormous man with a hatchet face and crew-cut hair. As he stood he continuously flexed the muscles of his forearms by opening and closing his fists.

"It is a private thing," Percy said, eyeing them harshly. "Very private. It concerns a piece of paper an old nigger woman up the country has. I want that paper back."

The Roller looked at Snake Crenshaw, who was gazing out of the window, obviously fascinated by the view.

"Don't sound too hard to me, Mr. Holt, unless she don't live by herself."

"She lives alone," Percy said.

"Then it don't sound too hard," said The Roller. "All it is is a piece of paper, huh?"

"That's all," Percy said, "but I want it, and I don't want you coming back here saying you can't find it. You may have to tear the house down, or burn it up, but I want that paper in my hands—or I want to know that it doesn't exist anymore. No ifs, ands or buts—you know what I mean?"

"I believe we get what you mean, Mr. Holt," said The Roller. Snake Crenshaw had listened to the last part and he nodded.

"Good," Percy said. "Now let me tell you exactly what I'm talking about."

An hour later Willie pulled his car into the dirt parking lot of Booker T. Washington High School. On a rough practice field before him the football team was running a scrimmage. The quarterback's barking signals resounded across the field in the chilly afternoon and pricked him with nostalgia.

He walked down the deserted first-floor hallway to the office of Daniel Holt, Assistant Principal. Finding the door closed, Willie knocked. A moment later Daniel opened it and ushered him inside, shutting the door behind him. The slapping of leather pads and other sounds of the football team were audible through the half-open window.

"Sit down," Daniel said. "Sit down, please."

As he turned to sit, Willie noticed the other man. He was a

thin black man, dressed in a dark suit and wearing impenetrable sunglasses, a white shirt and black tie. His hair was close-cropped and on his lap was a black leather briefcase.

"This is Mr. Croft," Daniel said to the man.

He turned to Willie. "This is Suliman Bey from Chicago."

"Hello, how are you?" Willie said awkwardly.

Suliman Bey of Chicago nodded, did not smile and did not extend his hand, for which gesture—or lack of it—Willie was mildly relieved.

"He is connected with a bank in Chicago that might lend us some money," Daniel said. "He wants to talk to you."

"Well, ah, fine," Willie said uncomfortably. What he had heard about colored people who had taken up names like Suliman Bey was not especially good.

Suliman Bey was looking at Willie through the sunglasses. He sat ramrod straight in the chair, hands folded in his lap over the briefcase as though he might actually have money in it.

"I would like to know what you think of this venture, Mr. Croft," he said somberly.

Willie cleared his throat and glanced disapprovingly at Daniel, who had seated himself at his swivel desk chair. As a lawyer, he did not like having these kinds of situations sprung on him without warning. He turned to Suliman Bey.

"Ah, you mean about trying to get the leases up there—the oil leases, I mean? Ah, well, what I think is that, if you could do it, you would, ah, make a lot of money." He realized that what he had said sounded stupid.

"How difficult do you think it would be to acquire this property?" asked Suliman Bey.

"Well, again," Willie said falteringly, "that depends. I mean, what Daniel and I have discussed is to get the people who are property owners, or who might have claim to the property, together and not sell right now, and then, with whatever money can be raised, to begin buying up leases. But there are going to be big problems with deeds and such, you see, because most of those people, I suppose, will not have proper titles to the land they are on, and so it may have to go to court."

"What will happen then?" said Suliman Bey.

"Well, I don't know. No way to tell really," Willie said. "There are going to be questions of law and also questions of equity, but I would expect that the courts here will not be, ah, particularly receptive to the people up there."

"Because they are black people?" Suliman Bey asked.

"To be realistic, yes," Willie said. He glanced again at Daniel Holt, who was leaning back listening. "And there will be other problems—the title problems I mentioned earlier. A lot of the black people will not have proper title and other people do."

"White people, you mean?" Suliman Bey said.

"Yes, white people," Willie said. "You see, for many years that land was almost worthless. You could buy an acre for a hundred dollars or less, and so the white people who owned it, they let the Negroes live on it. In some cases, like with Daniel's mother, they gave it to them, but now it's become very valuable, and I expect they're going to try to get it back."

"The white people?" Suliman Bey said.

"The white people," Willie answered. Suliman Bey made him very uncomfortable, even frightened him slightly.

There was silence for a moment, then Suliman Bey spoke again.

"Do you propose to represent Mr. Holt here, and the others, if they decided to go ahead and start buying up the mineral leases?"

"Well, yes, I said I would," Willie replied. "I have already drawn up a preliminary paper of incorporation that they have to look at and sign and all."

"This is for the Obsidian Oil Corporation?" Suliman Bey said.

"That's right," Willie said; "that's what we're going to call it." He looked again at Daniel Holt and saw the faint trace of a smile.

"Good," said Suliman Bey, "that is a name we like."

Three days later a chalklike fog floated in over the salt marsh and bayous and hung quickly across the blacktop road that turned off to Beaudreux's Place. Willie drove slowly through the rolling mist and parked in the oystershell drive. As he escorted Whitsey Loftin down the wharf toward the restaurant, the only discernible noise was the lone sounding of a waterman's horn, the weary and forlorn voice of honest toil.

Beaudreaux met them with the customary fanfare and led them to a lamplit table already set up with ice and glasses.

"For you, the best table," Beaudreux crowed, "right on the Bayou aux Oeils."

"It's foggy," Willie chided. "You can't see anything."

Beaudreux feigned a scowl and spun sharply toward the window. "Ah, so it is, so it is. But why should I know this? There is no window in Beaudreux's kitchen. Anyhow, here you get a great view of the fog," he added cheerfully. "You have a drink, I come back."

Willie took his bourbon bottle from the paper bag and poured two drinks over crackling ice. He lifted his in a toast.

"Here's to you, Miss Loftin," he said.

"Here's to you, Mr. Croft." She smiled and clinked her glass with his, and for a moment he felt the same surging connection to her he had the night of the dance—or the night of the fight—or the night they made love, as he now thought of it.

He hadn't seen her since then, but had called the next day and made tonight's date, and in the car, driving down, she'd been gay and animated but he sensed a certain coolness, a nervous distance, or thought he did, and at one point said, "This is kind of crazy."

"You mean us going out together?" she said.

"What else?"

"It doesn't bother me if it doesn't bother you," she said.

"It doesn't bother me."

"Then it doesn't bother me either."

But he still thought he sensed a coolness.

Willie took a deep swallow of the bourbon and put the glass on the table.

"This is crazy," he said.

"You said that before."

"I know I did," he said. He reached across the table and took her hand and she seemed slightly surprised and although she did not withdraw it, neither did she respond exactly as he had hoped. "I really like you," he said. "I suppose you know that by now, don't you?" He tried to fix her in a gaze but she looked away; accidentally his eyes strayed downward to his chest, where he noticed a large soup stain on his necktie, which, ordinarily, wouldn't have bothered him.

When he looked up again, there was pained ambiguity in her face. She swept back a curl of blond hair that had drooped over her left eye and drew herself up in a way that suggested resolution.

"Listen, Willie, I like you too. It hasn't anything to do with my family. You're sweet and fun to be with . . ." But she let the rest of the sentence hang and took a sip of her drink. He let go of her hand.

"What's that supposed to mean?" he asked.

"Nothing, really," she said, "it's just . . ." And again she let the sentence trail off and he knew something was wrong.

"Just what?" he said.

"Just, oh, nothing. . . ." She looked away from him.

"Well, it doesn't sound like 'nothing,'" he said. "I wish you'd say whatever it is."

She was still looking away and when she turned back to him there was a compassionate determination in her face.

"All right, I will say it. I guess I ought to now, instead of later. Willie, I don't want you to make too much of us. Do you know what I mean?"

"I'm not sure—go on," he said. He felt himself flush a little. Something sagged inside him.

"Well, I mean about the other night. It was great and wonderful and all, but I just don't want you to make too much of it."

"You mean you don't want to do it again?" he blurted out, instantly wishing he hadn't said it. "I mean, you don't want to see me anymore or something. Is that it?"

"No, no. It's not. It's just that . . . well, I don't want you to get hurt, that's all."

"You're saying you just want to be *friends?*"

"Willie, nothing's really happened between us," she sighed. "I'd still like to see you, but . . . yes, I do want to be your friend. I don't want it to get complicated."

He felt as though his heart had suddenly become smaller, quickened its beat and fluttered into his stomach. Nothing's happened! he thought—what the hell did she think that was the other night? That was . . . that was . . . *beautiful.* It meant something. To him! Friends, he thought—friends! He wanted to ask—no, he wanted to demand—why. He felt he deserved an explanation, but his dignity wouldn't permit him to say it, so he tapped out a Picayune from the pack and lit it, and said quietly, "No, it won't get complicated."

She smiled and nodded and seemed relieved. Just then Beaudreux reappeared beside the table.

"Tonight I got some big flounder just took off Marshal's wharf and a oyster gumbo, and corn and fresh okra and some pole beans, and you don't like none of that, I fix you somethin' else."

"It all sounds good," Willie offered.

"It all *is* good," Beaudreux said. "Hey, what about t'is oil business, Mistair Croff? They say they might even find oil round here—maybe right under Beaudreux's Place, eh?"

Willie and Whitsey exchanged glances. "All the way down here?" Willie said wryly. "I didn't hear that, no."

"Yeah, it says so yesterday in the paper. It says maybe they have oil all the way down here. Wouldn't that be somethin', Beaudreux get rich on oil! Close t'is place and get a big won up in town, huh?"

Willie frowned. "You'd take the joy out of my life, Beaudreux. I wouldn't know what to do without being able to drive down here and eat this great food."

"Oh, 'at place in town would be better, eh? Big place with air condition. Beaudreux going to do that when they find the oil!"

"I don't think it would be the same, Beaudreux."

"Same!" Beaudreux shouted. "Who wants same! Beaudreux wants same as everybody else—lots of money, lots of women, a big car and air condition. How I'm gonna get t'is sellin' fish down here, huh? They find oil here, I'm gonna be rich, that's what. Now," he said, almost indignantly, "what *you* gonna have, pretty lady?"

After dinner Willie nursed his drink glumly while Whitsey told him about a book she was reading.

"You don't seem very interested," she said after a while.

"No, that isn't it. . . . I'm just thinking."

"What about?"

"About oil," he lied.

"What about it?"

"Well, it's going to make some people pretty rich."

"So I hear," she said. "Are you one of them?"

"I don't know," he said. "Maybe. I expect you'll be, though."

"Maybe," she said.

At that moment he wanted her badly, wanted to take her home, undress her and make love to her. He wanted to hold her, and even more he wanted her to hold him. He needed that just now, someone to hold him. His hopes had let him down again.

"You know, it's not important to me, really," she said. "The money. Not right now, anyway. A lot of money seems like, well, just a lot of money, I guess."

"That's what it is," he replied absently.

"I suppose it's because I know that eventually I'll get it. I mean because of Aunt Hannah. She's old and, well, I'm an heir, I guess."

Willie wasn't really listening. He wanted to answer that what she really needed was *him*. That they should go back right now and make love or at least be alone. Perhaps she hadn't understood what he was saying before. Perhaps he hadn't made it clear. Women were sometimes like that—obtuse.

He reconsidered. No, it wasn't that.

She had known. She had taken precise steps to head him off.

He looked at her again, longingly, then forced himself back into the conversation.

"I'll tell you something," he said; "no matter what we can do for her in court—and it's going to come to that, I think—I still feel she'd be better off to go ahead and divvy up that place and avoid all the mess. You know as well as I do she's not playing with a full deck anymore. Honestly, she ought to try to work something out with her relatives."

"You sound like Brevard Holt," Whitsey said testily.

"Maybe he's right."

"For God's sake, he wants to have her declared insane— his own father's sister."

"Incompetent," Willie said, "and he doesn't want to do it except to get his share of the land—for all of them."

"Incompetent—whatever," she said. "They'll get it all soon enough. You'd think they could let an old lady alone."

They said nothing for a few seconds, then she changed the subject.

"Listen, I'm thinking about playing tennis Saturday if the weather's nice. Would you like to play?"

"Where?" he asked.

"At the club."

"I'm not a member," he said sullenly.

"Oh, for heaven's sake, you'd be my guest."

"I don't play tennis either," he said.

"Not at all?"

"Well, I tried a few times years ago, and I wasn't any good then."

"I'm not either," she said, "but we could just hit some. I feel like exercise."

"I don't think so," he said. "Anyway, not Saturday. I forgot, I'm going duck shooting."

"Just by yourself?"

"No, your friend Ham Bledsole said he liked to shoot so I called him up yesterday—and old Guidre is coming down; he has the fishing camp on the causeway. He was a friend of my father."

"Well, why didn't you just say that in the first place, instead of getting so defensive about playing tennis?"

"Sometimes I don't know why I do anything I do," he said soberly. He looked out of the window into the fog. Damn, he thought. It was only a week or so till Christmas. A lonely time of the year. He really wanted to fall in love.

8

THERE WERE THREE OF THEM IN THE SKIFF, WILLIE, HAM Bledsole and Guidre, who was at the outboard motor. Near sunset the sky had cleared and it was cooling quickly. Gnarled, moss-draped cypress trees loomed along the banks of the river, casting ghostly reflections in the flat-calm water. Gear and provisions for two days were piled in the bottom of the boat and Ham Bledsole had his feet resting on some of them.

Willie surveyed his new shooting companion. He exuded a self-assurance that had once made Willie uncomfortable; still did, but not quite so much anymore. Ham was handsome in an impassive, casual way, with heavy-lidded scholarly eyes behind the steel-rimmed glasses. He was likable and easy to be around, but physicians had always fascinated Willie because of their strange, macabre knowledge.

There was also the prospect that Bledsole Oil might help him in some way—though he had no idea how. He realized he was going to need all the help he could get in this, very quickly, for in that morning's mail he had received a preliminary letter of credit from the Southside Chicago Bank and Trust Company, agreeing to lend up to three million dollars to the Obsidian Oil Corporation, provided they raised four hundred thousand capital of their own and could secure the loan with uncontested mineral rights for at least fifteen hundred acres in the oil-bearing area. Willie knew very little about title law, less about mineral rights and nothing about oil. But he was going to have to learn it now.

Willie looked back at Guidre, at the dark Acadian eyes beneath the wool cap and the wrinkled, brooding face. It gave him an odd, melancholy feeling and recalled memories of other trips when his father had been alive. Guidre smiled and gave him the high sign, and Willie smiled back, jaws clenched. Behind them the wake of the boat was true and clean in the flat-river twilight.

"I suppose you know you busted Percy's nose pretty good. I had to set it," said Ham.

Willie nodded but stared straight ahead at the closing riverbanks. Off to the right, a fish gurgled near the surface.

"What was that all about anyway? He say something to you?"

"Nope," Willie said.

"Was it over Whitsey or something? Percy wouldn't say what it was either. Everybody's wondering."

"I guess they'll just have to wonder," Willie said. The sun had dropped far behind the trees and the evening star was shining brilliantly in the Christmas heavens. The boat droned on.

"Were you ever a fighter, a boxer, I mean?"

"Nope," Willie said, "never was." They rode on in silence.

Darkness closed around them after a while and they proceeded by starlight and Guidre's sure sense of direction farther and farther into the tangled winter night. Frequently the little boat would turn into narrow sloughs which opened again onto a larger body of water which ultimately narrowed again into a slough.

Finally after half an hour on a winding creek overhung with cypress trees, they came into a larger, lakelike place and Guidre began to throttle down the motor. As they slowed, the wake of the boat rolled under the stern, lifting it high.

Before them, dimly visible against the sky, was a prepos-
terously constructed wharf that stretched fifty or sixty
yards over the water, then seemed to disappear into the
swamp.

"Here we are," Willie said.

"Where's the camp?" Ham asked, looking around furtively.

"Back up in the swamp," Willie said. "There are duckboards."

Guidre guided the skiff to the end of the wharf nearest the
land and cut the engine. There was an eerie silence, a sense
of utter isolation. Willie moved to the bow, seized a plank of
the wharf and tied a line around it.

"Jesus, it's quiet up here," Ham said.

"It's 'cause there ain't a road in twenty-five miles of the
place," Guidre said.

"Anybody else come up here?" Ham asked.

Willie had gotten up on the wharf and was pulling the
boat nearer the end of it. "Not many," he said.

"It's 'cause they afraid of snakes," Guidre said charming-
ly. He began handing gear up to Willie.

"You and Ham finish this while I go turn on the gas and
get some light inside," Willie said. He walked to the end of
the wharf, stepped down on the duckboards and opened a
wooden box on the side of the camp, reached in and turned
a knob. Then he went inside. Moments later the small
windows beamed with light from two overhead gas lanterns.

When the other two came in they found Willie hovering
over a black iron stove, filling it with coal.

"That's interesting," Ham said, indicating the stove.

"My old man bought it from the railroad. It's off a
caboose or something." The propane lanterns hissed and
glowed above them, casting stark shadows on the unfinished
walls. Ham Bledsole investigated the inside of the camp. It
was about twenty feet long and ten feet wide. There were
two crude bunk beds made up with blue woolen blankets,
their edges moth-eaten. The floors were of rough plywood.
In a corner was a sink the contents of which ran straight out
beneath the camp into the swampy mire; behind a curtain

106

was a wooden toilet which did likewise. There was a small card table and several large jugs of water.

"Who built this?" Ham asked passively.

"Used to be a houseboat," Willie said. "Some old guy put it together and floated it on some oil drums and when they rusted out it sank. My old man bought it for a hundred bucks and raised it and pulled it back in the swamp here. He spent about thirty years fixing it up before he drank himself to death. The last few years he worked on the wharf mostly."

"G'arantee you no sober man built that wharf," Guidre said. He was stowing his gear beneath a bunk. "Never seed a man could drink like your pappy. Quart-a-day man, and sometimes two. Anathang he could lay his hands on. One time I said to him, 'Tom, that goddamn wharf is all over the place, what you need it for anyway?' He laughs and says, 'I'm gonna keep building on it till it's clear to the other side of the lake. That's gonna be the world's longest wharf, so when I go, it's what they'll remember me by. I'll be the man that built the World's Longest Wharf.'"

"He fell a little short," Willie said unhappily.

"Your old man didn't fall short at nothin'," Guidre snapped. "That was one somebitch had real c'ar'ter—and a heart too. Knowed him thirty-seven years."

"I only said he fell short about the wharf," Willie said defensively. He went over to the propane stove and lit the burner and placed a pan on it.

"Know what you said; know what you mean too, Willie," Guidre said scornfully. "Knowed you since you was a baldheaded pup waitin' for a leg to pee on—and now you turned into a Bigass Pete!" He took a tug at the bourbon bottle. "After you growed up you decided your old man was a bum. You took off to that school and all of a sudden you was better than him. Don't you think he didn't know it too? He knowed it till the day he died."

"Maybe he shouldn't have sent me, then," Willie said. He reached into a brown bag and brought out a package wrapped in newspapers. He laid it on the counter and opened it, and laid out half a dozen fish, cleaned and scaled. "You catch these?" he asked.

"Nah, a guy brought 'em in to me," Guidre said. "Claimed he caught two dozen speckled trout up t'other side of the causeway. Say, ain't you gonna grease that pan?"

Willie glanced at him reproachfully.

"Hell, let me do that," Guidre said. "I been cooking up here twenty-five, thirty years."

The old man commandeered the stove and spooned out large dollops of grease from a tin into the frying pan. Then he began to roll the fish in a mound of cornmeal he had poured onto the newspaper. "Gimme some salt 'n' pepper," he fussed. "I bet you ain't even got no salt 'n' pepper. Your old man wouldn't of run out of salt 'n' pepper."

"It's in the cabinet above you," Willie said. He looked over at Ham Bledsole, who was stretched out on the bottom bunk, the steel-rimmed glasses low on his nose, ignoring the conversation and reading a faded hunting magazine.

"What would you like with your fish, Doctor?" Willie asked.

Ham looked up. "Anything you do is fine with me. I will take a tug of that bourbon, though."

Willie handed him the bottle.

"Doctor!" the cook exclaimed. "You a doctor? What kind of doctor?"

"Internist," Ham said.

"You mean you're just starting out, huh?"

"No," Ham said patiently, "that's an intern. What I do is diagnose things—things that might be wrong with a person's insides."

"Why don't you look at old Willie there," Guidre said demonically. "He don't seem to have no heart. His old man had it for the both of them." He began laying the fish in the hot pan. "Hey, I see you got some beans up here; you want me to heat 'em up?"

"Go ahead," Willie said. He was becoming faintly embarrassed by Guidre's remarks. When it had just been the three of them—himself, Guidre and his father—it hadn't bothered him, but with Ham along, they became different—aggravating. He reached for the bourbon himself and took a stiff swallow.

"You might as well look at his brain, too," Guidre continued, unwilling to let the conversation drop, "if you can find it, that is. Maybe you could use a magnifyin' glass." He laughed uproariously at his joke.

"I suppose I could perform a lobotomy," Ham said casually. "Would you like one too?"

But Guidre by now was busy with the sizzling fish in the pan. "Hey, Willie," he said, "ain't you got no apron? There was always an apron up here before."

"It's at home; I took it home to wash it," Willie said.

"Jesus Christ, Jesus Christ," Guidre complained, "took it home and washed it. Hell, boy, why didn't you do what your old man would have done—just take them things out on the wharf and tie 'em in the water and let the tides do the cleaning?"

"My old man didn't have a washing machine," Willie said curtly, and regretting immediately that he'd said it. Guidre turned back to the stove, muttering to himself and shaking his head.

No one spoke much while they ate, and the long periods of silence were broken occasionally by the bark of a duck in the swamp. The little caboose stove gave off warmth for about ten feet or so, but no more, and after supper they pulled up around it. Guidre had placed the dishes in a grapefruit sack and tied them beneath the wharf for the currents to scour. Willie and Ham sat around the stove on the halves of a sawed-in-half stave barrel, and when Guidre returned he pulled up the only chair and began rolling a cigarette.

"You might want to shut down the lights and not waste the gas that way," he said piously.

Without a word Willie got up and put on his jacket and went outside. When he had shut off the handle, he stood by the window and watched the lamps dim, then sputter, and finally glow incandescently as their mantles died out, leaving only the illumination of the coal stove and the conversation around it as evidence of human presence inside the little camp. He looked up before going back in. The billions of hard, cold winter stars were spread thickly across the entire horizon, their reflections dancing in the still water.

Before him, the World's Longest Wharf snaked excessively across the lake, its planks uneven and rough cut, upwarped and twisted as if by a terrible earthquake. He walked out a little farther. The marsh was brownish-gray, bathed in the silvery starlight.

He remembered his old man, bent on his knees in the broiling sun, nailing planks—most of them culled from driftwood and flotsam—or standing in waist-deep muck, setting in a piling, or bolting timbers together, the concept of the World's Longest Wharf bright in his whiskey-soaked brain; never asking for help or advice, working alone in the heat of the day, every year adding ten or fifteen or twenty feet of wharf, his work shirt dripping sweat, beefy hands as red as his puffy face with its whiskey breath; and later would come inside and say, "Son, they'll be bitin' now!" and the two of them would go out and sit on the rough-cut wood, legs dangling over the water, and throw out lines as the afternoon cooled and the tepid, tea-colored water would remit a string of bull bream or an occasional green trout to fry for supper—or for breakfast with grits and eggs.

If Guidre was along—and he usually was—after sundown the two of them, Guidre and his father, would sit outside drinking and talking about things—just *things*—rolling cigarettes, while he would lie in his bunk and watch the glow of the cigarettes and listen to the ceaseless somnolence of the crickets and tree frogs until the mosquitoes drove them back inside, where they would continue the conversation there until they were too drunk to talk straight, while he lay in bed half in, half out of a dreamless, wondering sleep.

Willie unzipped his fly and began to urinate in the water. His mother, before she died, said to anyone who would listen that the old man had drunk himself to death—had not said it vindictively either, or even bitterly, but matter-of-factly, whenever the subject came up—"Drank himself to death!" and that was the end of it, as though such fate was utterly to be expected of the man building the World's Longest Wharf; who was only an owner of a service station that barely paid the family bills, and never aspired to be anything else, never wanted to own a string of service stations, or the oil supply companies that sold him the gas and oil, or to run for office, or even buy them a decent house to live in—so that the only appropriate epitaph was the one Guidre delivered a while earlier, in front of Ham Bledsole, whose father did, in fact, own the oil supply companies, and a lot more too: "I never seen a man could drink like your pappy," and his only memorial outside the gravestone was what Willie was standing on, one-half or one-fifth or one-tenth finished, while at the state docks the Holt family had recently erected what they billed to the newspapers as the World's Largest Crane, which actually *was* the World's Largest Crane—finished and operating, for anyone to see.

Willie zipped up his trousers and turned his collar against the cold. Heart, he thought savagely. Well, maybe you had to give him that. The old man would have given his last dime to a friend—while his family might have needed it more. All his life Willie had had to work, pumping gas at the station, or collecting laundry, busing dishes in college when everyone else was out falling in love and going to parties.

He'd never resented any of it, however, then or now, and knew he never would.

But what he *was* beginning to resent was the legacy of failure the old man had left him, which he was only now beginning to realize. He had made his life just as comfortable as he wanted it, and no more; had been satisfied to be a third-rate lawyer, and settle for third-rate women and third-rate everything, because he had believed—had grown up believing—it was the way things were.

Willie took a deep breath and the chill air made his lungs and throat ache. Somewhere in the distance there was a brief gabbling of ducks.

What if, he thought, what if? He felt lonely, and suddenly inadequate to the things that lay ahead.

The harsh bell of the windup alarm clock shattered the morning blackness of the camp until Guidre reached over and pushed its button.

"Chilly here," Willie said, sitting up. He looked over at

Ham, who was sleeping like a baby. The alarm clock said four thirty.

Guidre was at the stove pouring water from a jug into a battered coffeepot and also a grits boiler. Willie put on his boots and stepped outside to relieve himself. The sliver of moon was low, almost precisely tangent to the treetops. Nothing stirred across the lake, not the faintest breeze, and there was no sign of dawn. When he came back inside, Ham was sitting on the bed dressing himself and Guidre was fussing again.

"Hey, ain't you got no ketchup up here?"

"Might be some in the cupboard," Willie said wearily.

"Done looked. Ain't none. How you expect a man to eat his food without ketchup?"

Somehow they managed. Guidre fried more fish and they had them with Vienna sausage, eggs and grits and hot black coffee.

"Sunup's in forty-five minutes," Willie said. "How about it, Doc, you ready to shoot some ducks?"

"Bring 'em on," Ham said.

Guidre finished clearing the table. "How 'bout let's you and me get the canoe while the doc gets his gear ready?"

"Right," Willie said.

The two of them walked over the narrow, rickety duck-boards back into the swamp behind the camp, Guidre in the lead.

"These damn duckboards are all broke up; you ought to fix 'em," he said.

"This summer," Willie said. They came to the canoe, a long, ancient-looking, square-sterned vessel of canvas-covered wood, resting upside down on two cutoff cypress stumps.

"Watch when you turn it over," Guidre instructed, "might be a water moccasin or sompin' hole' up there."

"For God's sake, Guidre, will you take it easy on me? I'm not a kid," Willie snapped. The old man stopped and fixed Willie with a hawklike stare. His feelings were obviously hurt.

"I don't mean nothin'," he said quietly. "It's just I don't want to see this place go down. I want it to be like before." He turned and straddled the duckboards and put his hands beneath the gunnels of the overturned canoe.

"Yeah, I know," Willie said. "I do too."

They turned the big canoe upright and began to march it back toward the water.

"This doc friend of yours, he hunt?" Guidre asked.

"Says he does," Willie replied.

"Says he does! Ain't you never been with him?"

"Nope."

"Well, we best look out he don't shoot one of us by accident, or a goddamn hole in the boat."

They eased the canoe into the water just below the wharf and went back inside. Ham Bledsole was sitting on the bunk and beside him was an opened, leather-covered gun box, bound in brass and with a green felt interior.

"Great God Almighty!" Guidre exclaimed. "What you got there, Doc?" Willie had noticed the elegant gun case before they left but had not inquired about it.

Ham took out an intricately tooled set of barrels and fitted them into a hand-chequered rosewood stock. He snapped on the foregrip, looking a little embarrassed. He did not reply to Guidre's question.

"What in hell kind of gun is that!" the old man demanded.

"English," Ham said.

Willie, who had removed his old Winchester pump gun from a cloth case, stepped over for a closer look. Guidre was leaning forward, peering at the double gun as if it were something fashioned in outer space. "Can I see it?" the old man asked tentatively.

"Certainly," Ham said. He handed him the gun. "I picked it up in Scotland a few years back. It's a Purdy. Got two of them actually. One for birds and one for duck. It's an old one, made about nineteen thirty-seven, I think. They did marvelous work in those days."

Guidre ran his fingers over the unscratched blued-steel

barrels, turned it over and admired the gold inlaid engraving on the side locks.

"What's something like this cost?" the old man asked greedily. Ham again looked embarrassed but was about to answer when Willie cut him off.

"A lot," Willie said, "a whole lot."

They packed their gear into the square-sterned canoe and headed across the lake as the first rosy glow of dawn began to lighten the eastern tree line. Guidre, wearing an unimaginably moth-eaten green sweater, was in the stern with one paddle and Willie with another was in the bow. Ham Bledsole and the Purdy double gun were passengers. The water was flat and still with a layer of white mist rolling a foot or so above its surface. There was only the noise of the paddles gurgling, and also they heard ducks, but had not seen any so far. Guidre trailed the paddle and leaned forward to Ham in a whisper.

"Around that bend by the marsh there"—he pointed straight ahead—"we're prob'ly gonna jump a few. They'll prob'ly take off downstream, but we'll come up to the right there, and you'll have the light in front of you, though."

Ham nodded and broke open the breech of the Purdy, inserting two shells. Guidre resumed paddling toward the rapidly lightening sky.

Willie, in the bow, had taken a long, backward glance at the wharf his father had built; its mist-shrouded pilings and gnarled planking stood as a fantastic monument to a past he was beginning to feel himself slipping away from, here in the boat with a well-to-do society doctor and his Purdy shotgun.

The bow of the canoe rounded a clump of tall marsh grass and turned around a bend. Guidre backpaddled so as to enter the slough broadside, and they began to drift down.

There was now not a sound, not a bug or cricket or tree frog or fish. The three men remained as motionless as they could, almost rigid, eyes keen, taking in everything, scarcely breathing, like jungle beasts. Then the first notice: a startled *gawk!* at the reed's edge, followed by two or three more— still they could see nothing—suddenly an explosive flapping of wings on water as the ducks burst out a few feet above the slough in a supreme effort to get away, three or four at first, as Ham jerked the shotgun to his shoulder, then several more.

The blast of the big twelve-gauge shuddered the canoe.

"Canvasback!" Guidre shouted as Ham's gun roared again. Willie had jammed two shells into the pump gun as a flight of four swept back past them on their way to open water. He fired twice and two ducks tumbled into the water behind him. Guidre had loaded his automatic and was watching the reeds intently, although nothing could be seen. Suddenly two big ducks took off in the opposite direction and as they gained a few feet over the water and turned downstream he fired once and the nearest duck fell as if poleaxed.

Another pair came beating back high and over the swamp marsh. Ham tried a far-out shot and missed, then fired his second barrel, and the lead bird tumbled as though killed, only to recover just before it hit the swamp and glide low for a few hundred feet, and disappear into the marsh.

"Damn!" Willie said. "He's down. We'll have to go in and get that one." Ham said nothing and Guidre paddled in toward shore.

"I'll do it," Ham said. "I shouldn't have tried that shot, they were too far out."

"You'd better let me," Willie said. "I've got on waders. It's pretty deep in there in places."

"I'm sorry," Ham said, as Willie stepped out of the canoe into the marshy swamp.

"Don't worry about it. You and Guidre collect the ones down. I'll meet you here in a few minutes." He gave the bow of the canoe a small shove to get it back into deeper water and slogged in the direction he had seen the duck plummet.

The marsh grass was nearly as tall as Willie but there were little trails through it, padded down by raccoon and opossum, and he was able to follow them for a while. He had sighted the downed bird on a line between the canoe and the tall skeleton of a dead tree, but as he got farther into the marsh he realized he no longer had a reference point behind him because he couldn't see either the canoe or the slough from where he was. With muffled curses he thrashed on toward the tree. By dead reckoning the duck would have been about fifty yards in. The swamp was above his knee-caps now, dark, slimy water and muck beneath that seemed to suck him down. Fancy gun or no, he thought wryly, and with a slight satisfaction, Ham Bledsole had something to learn before he could consider himself a duck hunter.

The duck gave itself away. It was crippled, as Willie suspected, and made just the slightest sound against the dry grass stalks as he approached, but he still could not see it, so he stopped in his tracks.

It was a stroke of luck that he had actually found it, but he would have tried under any condition short of impossible, for to leave it dead or dying without trying to retrieve it would have been to repudiate the entire idea of the hunt that he had learned from his father and Guidre. There was game, and plenty of it up here, but a man took what he could eat and no more, and the killing itself was a solemn thing, done cleanly and skillfully, to put meat on the table, which it had when his father was alive. They did not waste or spoil.

Willie was motionless now, listening, bent over in a half crouch, waiting for the noise of the wounded duck. Seconds turned to minutes and while he waited he remembered the first time he had been taught about the hunt and what it meant—he had been scarcely nine years old. It was a Christmas Day and he had received a secondhand, single-shot twenty-gauge—unblued, the stock varnish scratched and pitted—but he had treasured it as if it had been the Purdy. Late in the afternoon his father had taken him to some open fields not far from their little rented house on the outskirts of town. Beyond it, the countryside was fairly open. He had walked with the old man for hours, expecting at any moment to raise a covey of quail, or a dove, or at least some game bird. When they had not, and the Christmas sun was low in the trees, they started back. His disappointment had been bitter and hard, as was his urge to fire the prized possession once, so that when he spied, low on a branch of a sallow, almost leafless oak tree a single tiny bird—some kind of finch, he recalled, or chee-chee—he raised the shotgun before the old man had a chance to restrain him, and even before the ringing in his ears had stopped, the old man had him and had the gun in his hands as well. The blast, at that range, had literally blown the bird to kingdom come. There had been nothing—nothing they could find anyway—except a few feathers and a claw, not even blood or entrails, and he had not seen that gun again until the following Christmas, when it was presented once more, that time with a stern warning against the destruction of things for the wanton sake of their destruction.

And there had been another time, when they had gone up-country to shoot doves, a cold and rainy afternoon—

Willie had begun to stalk again, hearing no sound from the wounded duck; it lay ahead of him somewhere, and off to the right, perhaps a few more yards.

They had returned, four of them—himself, his father, George Hart, the farmer, and Ben Crow, an old Negro who worked the farm—a dozen doves among them, already stiffening in their jacket pockets. Suddenly they had come across an opossum perched on a fence rail, its fur wet and matted and ruffled by the wind. "Go ahead, Ben," George Hart had said, knowing that neither they nor he himself had any use for an opossum, but Ben Crow had, and Ben Crow acknowledged the same by laying down his ancient shotgun and picking up a stick from the ground, and proceeding stealthily toward the opossum, which eyed him warily until the final steps of his approach, then sprang down into a cornfield and began to run. To Willie's surprise Ben Crow had vaulted the three-rail fence with the grace of a gazelle, brandishing the stick, and run the animal down in midfield and thrashed it to death, knowing that while it was not worth even the waste of a single shotgun shell, it was nevertheless the main ingredient for his evening stew; and returned, holding the limp animal by its tail, grinning at his unexpected bonanza. Willie, age thirteen, had watched that unsportsmanlike behavior with a sort of awestruck fascination, but it was not until years later that he would realize Ben Crow could no more have contemplated the rules of the shoot than he could have understood the theory of relativity, for his rightful interest lay in the filling of a pot; and that he had assigned to all birds and beasts in his domain an economic value, which he had demonstrated to the little hunting party that afternoon: the opossum might not have been worth much—not even a ten-cent shell—but it was at least worth something, at least the time and effort to pick up a stick and chase it down across a field of cut hog corn.

Willie saw Ham Bledsole's duck about the same time as the duck saw him. It was sitting in a clump of brambles surrounded by the marsh grass. It made one feeble attempt to fly, then settled back down and looked away impassively in the opposite direction as Willie came up. He reached down swiftly and wrung its neck, stuffed it into his bag and started back for the slough.

Guidre worked the canoe around the edge of the lake until they came to several large clumps of cane and marsh grass standing on a little island about ten feet from shore. He glided in and dropped off three battered wooden decoys, then maneuvered the boat behind the island and dug in the paddle to secure them in place. The sun was just beginning to rise over the trees and warm them, and they could make out several flights of duck against the brightening horizon.

"I'd give two ducks and a pack of cigarettes for a shot of Vinnie's shine right now," the old man said.

"Who's Vinnie?" Ham asked casually.

"An old black man who use to bring moonshine around to the camp," Willie said. "I remember Dad and Guidre talking about him."

"Did he live up here?" Ham asked.

"S'pose he did," Guidre said. "Nobody ever knew where, though—except Vinnie, and he wasn't saying."

"Dad and Guidre used to leave out a milk jug on the wharf with a dollar bill in it, and in the morning it'd be filled with whiskey," Willie said.

"That shine was smooth as a baby's bottom," Guidre declared. He was looking cannily through the marsh grass. "Got a pair headin' our way," he said.

Willie watched them flying low over the marsh, circling the edge of the lake, then suddenly veering south to disappear behind the trees.

"You ever see him?" Ham said.

"Vinnie? Nah," Guidre said. "We'd hear him now and again. Come around in an old rowboat. Never seed him—not'n twenty-odd years."

"What's happened to him?" Ham asked.

"Don't know. Came up one year an' he wasn't around."

"Probably made a bad batch and drank it himself," Ham suggested.

"Hellfire, for all I know he got rich an' went out an' bought hisself a plantation." Guidre was squinting again into the sun. "I lost 'em," he grumbled.

"Took off downriver," said Willie, who had been watching them too.

"I tell you one thing, though," Guidre said, "that was one good nigger, Vinnie. He didn't ask nothing of nobody."

"How do you know? You never talked to him," Ham said.

"That's why I know," Guidre said. "There was a nigger had his own business. Didn't want favors. Jus' made good whiskey and sold it at a fair price. Prob'ly poached a few alligators on the side."

"Maybe they caught him and put him in jail," Willie offered.

"Possible," the old man said. "Be a shame, though. That nigger was better'n a lot of white folks. Be just like them bastards to snatch him up and throw his ass in jail."

"He'd be with his friends anyway," Willie said.

"Hellfire, Willie"—Guidre was again squinting into the rising sun—"what'd you expect them pore devils to do? Cain't make no honest living here 'cept'n to clean people's houses. Fellow like Vinnie, what'd he gonna do? Be a damned dinin' car waiter or a yard cutter? Man who could make whiskey like that? Crime wouldn't be that he did it—it'd be that they *wouldn't* let him do it."

"I don't care if he made whiskey or not," Willie said. "I was just saying that every Monday morning I go down to the jail and try to spring ten or fifteen of them out of the jug who wouldn't have been there in the first place if they'd just behaved themselves."

"Behaved theirselves, my ass!" Guidre snorted. "Only difference 'tween them and most whites is the whites don't git caught. And when they do, they hire some smartass lawyer like yourself to get 'em off the hook. And a judge, he's gonna put a nigger in jail a lot quicker than he is a white man. You know that—Hey, we got four coming in, straight upriver!"

They sat motionless as the ducks appeared, flying low on the water. Suddenly they soared, exposing brown underbellies, barely out of range, then dived again, low over the marshes. Guidre cupped his hand over his mouth and began to call. He could make a duck call with his fingers better than any store-bought or man-made call ever invented. The ducks turned and again took altitude, the leader obviously judging the decoys, the call and the little island of marsh grass where the three men crouched in the canoe. Guidre called again, a low cackling. Willie was looking at Ham Bledsole, who was bent low, eyeing the ducks through the reeds, the Purdy double gun cradled in his arms. Willie wondered what he knew about oil, or at least what his father knew. Bledsole Oil only distributed to service stations, but they had to know something about it—more than he did anyway.

The ducks made another circle, lower this time, a good sign. The sun warmed them benevolently as Guidre called again and again. Then they turned, circling, wingbeats audible as they closed.

"Here they come," he whispered.

The ducks turned twice more before pitching in, the leader first slanting into the marsh clumps innocently, breast exposed, carelessly—even recklessly—a fatal mistake. At Guidre's sign, the hunters leaped into action. Willie fired first and his blast struck the leader chest-on. It tumbled forward and hit the water no more than ten feet from the blind. The other three soared but Guidre and Ham opened fire. The canoe shuddered from recoil shock. When it was over four ducks floated in the water; one flapped a wing spasmodically, then fell silent.

"Nice calling," Willie said to Guidre. He turned to Ham. "How'd you do?"

"They all belong to you guys," the doctor said dejectedly. The fancy double gun rested on his knees. "I guess I'd better go back to shooting skeet or something."

Guidre backpaddled the canoe into the open water and they picked up the dead birds—black mallard.

"I rec'on this is as good a spot as any," Guidre said.

"Good so far," said Willie.

"Damned straight," Ham said.

Guidre eased the boat back into the grass and resumed the conversation as though it had never been interrupted.

"I'll tell you about the niggers," he said. "I've knowed a few of them in my day and it seems to me they ain't no worse than most of the white people I know. Trouble is, they ain't never had a chance to make nothin' of themselves, 'cause somebody like you or me or the doc here is always waiting to take it away from 'em."

"Well, that might be so some of the time," Willie said, "but I'm not sure it is all of the time." He was thinking of Daniel Holt and his friends who were able and willing to put up nearly half a million dollars for the oil venture.

"Often as not it is," Guidre declared. "My granddaddy told me that when I was just a little kid. He carried a lead ball in his leg till the day he died after a Yankee shot him at Sharpsburg. Lived to be eighty-four, and I never heard him say a bad word about the nigger—an' they the ones caused him to use a cane the rest of his natural life." He lit a cigarette.

"I remember one time we'd been fishing down on Magnolia River, me and him and my Uncle Cary, and along come a nigger with a pair of *fine*-looking hosses—prob'ly Arabians or something—and Cary says, 'Now where would a nigger get a pair of hosses like that?' And Granddaddy says back, 'Where he gets 'em, boy, hit don't make any difference, 'cause the first white man he sees is gonna cheat him outta 'em first chance he gets and probably arrange for his ass to be hung for a hoss thief to boot—even if he raise 'em hisself.' An' I asked him why that was—I was just about eight or nine years old—and he says, ''Cause that's the lot of the nigger, boy, to be cheated and gypped and used and run down by the white man, and it's a damned shame,' he says, but it's the way things are, and he says that if it wasn't, he wouldn't be carryin' around that goddamn lead ball in his leg half his life.''

"What about now, though?" Willie said. "Times have changed—I mean with all this integration stuff and everything?"

"I doubt it," the old man said. His face looked hollow and cadaverous in the bright sunshine. "Prob'ly just make things worse. Least in this town. People in this town ain't gonna stand for such. They'll be runnin' around getting out shotguns and rifles and carrying on like a bunch of idiots, and they'll prob'ly scare the niggers so bad they'll go on back to doin' what they was doin' before."

"Well, suppose they don't?" Willie said. "It's coming. It's going to come, you know. The people in Washington decided it already. It's just a matter of time, they'll put the Army in here like they did at Little Rock, they'll . . ."

"Don't make no difference," Guidre said furiously. "Don't make no difference a-tall if the nigger goes to school with the white children or he gets to eat with 'em or ride in the bus. It'll just make 'em madder when they see what the white folks got and they don't. Hell, I prob'ly ain't got any more money of my own than most niggers I know, but I'm white, and that counts for a lot—especially in this town—it ain't right maybe, but that's the way it is, nonetheless."

"Suppose I told you," Willie said, "that it was possible, right here in this city, for them to be as rich as the white people. Even richer—a lot richer."

"What they fixin' to do, hold up the banks?" Guidre said.

"No, something else—nothing like that—something perfectly legal."

The old man looked at Willie, his face gray and dark. "Then I'd have to say you was crazy as hell," he said.

Ham said nothing.

Willie looked out across the lake to the tall trees on the other side, thought of them dying, rotting, pressed into the dark, swampy waters, so that sometime in the far-distant future they, too, might provide oil in this very spot.

He had hoped Ham would bring it up. Pursue it. He didn't.

"Well," Willie said, "I was just supposin', I guess."

Later that afternoon, as Willie's hunting party prepared to return to the camp, the sky broke frail and ragged gray, but the weather remained warmish and the sun had become a faint pastel halo above the small village of Creoletown.

A lone automobile, battered and rusted, turned off Route 23 onto the unnamed blacktop road, turned again slowly at Garley's country store down the two-track dirt road that led to the Backus place.

About a hundred yards from the house the car pulled off the road into a pine grove, stopped and The Roller and Snake Crenshaw got out.

"Ought to be right down this road a piece," The Roller said, "if Mr. Holt give us the right directions."

Snake Crenshaw hawked and spat. "I rec'on the man knows how to give directions on his own property."

Stealthily, they made their way through the waist-high broom grass, hiding along the edges of the pine grove, until they could see the cabin. Working their way around the edge of a clearing the two men approached from the back side, where there was a single small window. When they reached it, The Roller raised his large rawboned frame up on his toes and craned his neck to see inside.

"Don't think she's here," he said in a hoarse whisper.

Snake Crenshaw nodded and rounded the house in a weasel-like crouch until he reached the front porch. He did not bother with the steps but hoisted himself onto the bare-wooded porch in a sitting position, then stood and walked deliberately to the front door. There was no knob, so he pushed it open and stepped inside. The Roller waited until Snake Crenshaw poked his head out and said in a normal tone, "Yeah, she ain't here," and the two of them entered the living room.

"Where you s'pose a nigger would hide something?" Snake said, looking around darkly.

"Prob'ly under the bed," said The Roller. "They spend enough time in it." They lifted the mattress off the iron cot and, finding nothing, began to go through every drawer, cabinet, cushion, closet, chair and fixture they could find in search of what Percy Holt had sent them for. They dismantled the stove, and parts of the icebox, and were preparing to rip up the floors and ceilings when The Roller, who had been keeping an occasional watchful eye on the window that looked out across the dirt road, said, "Uh-oh, here she comes," and nodded toward a small lone figure walking head down, a shawl clutched around her shoulders, down the road toward the cabin.

"Shit," Snake Crenshaw spat, "we gonna have to set it up, I s'pose." He went over to a can of kerosene beside the stone fireplace, and unscrewed the top, and began pouring it on the floors and furniture in huge dollops, saving the last for a wad of papers used for starting fires.

"You want to do it, or me?" he said matter-of-factly. He had a box of matches in his hands.

The Roller was still at the window, watching the old woman approach. "C'mon, hurry it up, she's gonna be here in a second," he said nervously.

Snake took out a match, struck it against his shoe and tossed it into the wad of papers. There was a deep, gruntlike noise as the papers burst into a flame which quickly spread across the floor. The two men hurried out of the house and down the porch steps and ran into the woods barely in time to escape the eyes of the old Negro woman.

II

The Plan

9

THE SUN WAS LOW WHEN THEY REACHED CAMP. THEY STOWED their gear and went back onto the wharf where Willie had left three ducks. Each of them began to pluck and clean.

"I've never done anything like this before," Ham said appreciatively. "It's wonderful." Duck feathers by the thousands, some brightly colored, floated on the surface around the wharf.

"You guys finish this up, I'm goin' ta start the fire," Guidre said after a while. He walked back to the side of the cabin and pulled out a rusted, cut-in-half oil drum, and began filling the bottom with aged swamp logs.

Willie offered Ham a thin-honed, curved gutting knife. "Need this?" he asked.

Ham accepted the knife tentatively. His duck was thoroughly plucked but he had not attempted to eviscerate it. He looked curiously at Willie's gutted bird.

"You want some surgical gloves?" Willie said. "We might have some in the cabin. Don't think we have a scalpel, though—sorry."

Ham smiled. "I've really never done this, you know. Sounds silly, but all my life—I mean my duck hunting career—I've taken my birds over to Enmeyer's—that place

127

where they pluck and dress them for you. It just seemed easier."

"You might want to cut off the feet and head first," Willie said. "That way it don't look so bad."

"All right, all right," Ham said good-naturedly. "I take things apart that look a good deal worse than this every week." He seemed faintly embarrassed.

"I wanted to ask you something," Willie said.

"Shoot," said the doctor. He had inserted the knife and was working it through the duck in a gentle, professional way.

"I need to talk to somebody about oil. I'm sort of involved in that oil business up at Creoletown and I really don't know much about it. The technical and financial sides. I was thinking that your family is in the business and maybe somebody there could help me."

"Well, I'm sure they'd be glad to. But they're only distributors, you know. We don't produce anything. You might be better off going to one of the oil companies."

"I've thought of that," Willie said, "but I don't want to tip my hand. Oil companies are going to be at odds with my clients. I'd probably have to reveal things I don't want to at this point."

Ham screwed up his face in thought. "There's a guy I knew in college who might help you. He's kind of a nut, but brilliant, I hear, when it comes to oil and gas and those kinds of things. Name's Vernon Skinner—they call him V.D. 'cause his middle name's David. He's kind of a free-lance producer—knows everything about it, including what goes on at the bottom of the well. It's all he ever talks about. I haven't seen him in four years, but he's somewhere in Oklahoma right now because I got a card from him a few weeks ago."

"That's a thought," Willie said. "I'd appreciate it."

"I'll get the card when I get back. You shouldn't have any trouble tracking him down. Any place Skinner stays more than two days, the whole damned town'll know him."

* * *

Supper was splendid. They dined on delicious roast duck and wild rice and Guidre's special gravy, and washed it down with bourbon and coffee. There was lengthy discussion of shooting techniques with respect to angles and altitudes, camouflage, calls and the habits of different ducks. Willie's participation was not as enthusiastic as it might have been. Even more than the legal battle he would face in the coming weeks, Whitsey Loftin was needling his mind. He might have had a taste of love, though he wasn't sure that's what it was.

"Hey, Willie, you ain't *bored*, are you?" Guidre was leaning across the table, his whiskey glass out in front of him, squinting, the dark eyes deep and fathomless, and smiling with a crooked, broken-toothed grin.

"No, no," Willie said. "Not at all. A little warm, I guess; I think I'll step outside for a minute."

He rose and walked out. It was warmer than the night before and the sky was slightly overcast and flat. Embers glowed low in the oil drum grill and the smell of burned duck fat hung in the air. He had been standing there a few minutes when the cabin door opened and Guidre ambled onto the wharf.

"You wanta be alone or sompin'?"

"Nope, just came out for a second."

"Sompin's eatin' on you, Willie; I've knowed you long enough for that."

"What makes you say that?"

"You ain't yerself. Y'all balled up tight. Is it about yer job?"

"Nope, job's fine."

"Is it some woman?"

"No, not really."

"I shoulda known it. You done got yerself mixed up by some woman, ain't ya?"

"Nope, I sure haven't. If there's anything I'm not, it's mixed up with a woman. Not anymore."

"You are, then?"

"Are what?"

129

"Mixed up with a woman. I mean, it's about a woman, ain't it?"

"I don't know, Guidre. The whole thing's goddamn crazy." He sat down on the wharf and lit a Picayune. Guidre sat beside him.

"You wanta talk about it?"

"Not really," Willie said. "Isn't much to talk about. I met this girl. Saw her a few times. Soon as she found out I liked her, she backed off. Simple as that. Said she wanted to be 'friends.'" He pronounced the words as though he had a mouthful of dirt.

"How'd she find out?"

"Find out what?"

"That you liked her?"

"I told her."

"Shouldna done that, Willie; then they start trouble."

"I suppose."

"Secret is to find out if she means it," Guidre said.

"I think this one means it." He took a drag from the cigarette.

"How come? She any different from other women?"

"No—I mean yes—whatever. I just think she means what she says."

"Damn few of 'em mean what they say," Guidre said. "Damn few. Guess it's why I don't have much to do with 'em. It's a helluva lot easier to figure what a trout's gonna do than it is a woman."

"You can't fall in love with a trout," said Willie.

"Who says!" Guidre cried. "Trout'll give you a helluva lot more pleasure than a woman half the time. Anyway, is that what's raggin' at you? You done fallen in love?"

"Nah," Willie said unconvincingly, "never got the chance. Even if I had, it probably wouldn't have worked out anyway. Story of my life."

"Cum on, Willie. Who is she anyhow? One thang I learnt 'bout women a long time ago is they're like bugs. Lift up any rock and two or three of 'em 'll come crawling out." His dark skin crinkled at the edges of his eyes.

"You can't fall in love with a bug either," Willie said dejectedly.

"What is it, then? You wanta get married or sompin'?"

"Well, hell, yes I do," he burst out. "I'm forty-two goddamn years old. I'm tired of living by myself." He flicked the cigarette into the water savagely. "Everybody's married in this town . . . everybody my age anyway. Got kids and houses and something to do when they get home at night and on weekends."

"Well, for Chrissakes, Willie, there's plenty of women around. Why don't you find one of them?"

"What women!" he exploded. "Do you know the kinds of women I've been seeing the past ten years? Bunch of dumb bunnies that wait tables or run elevators or shuffle papers in somebody's office. It's not just that I'm lonely, it'd be nice to fall in love."

"What's wrong with takin' out somebody who waits tables and things! You too good for it now?" The old man was ruffled again. Willie stared out into the darkness.

"What's her name?"

"Whitsey Loftin."

"Loftin? Any kin to ole man Loftin owned the sawmills up-country?"

"He was her uncle."

"Jesus God, Willie. That's a high-pow'r'd family. Wasn't they kin to all the Holts and them people too?"

"Yup."

"Well, what in hellfire you doin' running around with them kinds of people? Them kinds of people ain't your kinds of people—jeezus, you really *are* gettin' to be a Bigass Pete!"

He could see the old man's eyes in the dark, wide with astonishment. Ever since Willie could remember, Guidre had used the expression "Bigass Pete" to characterize arrogance or snobbery. So had his father. Willie assumed there had actually been a Bigass Pete at some time. But he'd never asked.

"What's that supposed to mean? What's wrong with it? You've been living here too damned long."

"I mean," Guidre said, "why don't you find one of them nice girls like you used to go out with in high school? The one I saw a picture of one time at your old man's house? You don't have to get yersef set on the daughter of the king of France."

Willie looked at the old man reprovingly. "First off, there isn't any king of France. It's a republic. And second. I'm not *in* high school anymore. That was twenty-five years ago."

"Well, you sure in hell's got nothing in common with them people—the Holts and all—they ain't like everybody else, 'n' everybody else knows it. I seen ole man Holt horsewhip a man right out on St. Jude's Street once. Middle of the day. Took a whip out of his buggy and flailed the sonofabitch till he bled cause he didn't stand up and take off his hat when old Miz Holt got down out the buggy."

"When was this?" Willie asked curiously.

"I was jus' a little kid. Must of been 'bout nineteen hundred ten, I guess. The goddamn sheriff was standing there, watchin' the whole thing. Didn't lif' a finger. Them Holts ran the town, those days. Still do, I s'pose."

"Must have been the grandfather," Willie said. "Hell, the great-grandfather, maybe. How old was he—that Holt?"

"Old—fifties or sixties then, I suppose."

"Must of been the great-grandfather then. Doesn't make any difference anyway. Good grief, Guidre. I'm a damned attorney-at-law. There isn't any reason I can't see anybody I damn well please—including Whitsey Loftin."

The old man thought for a few moments, grappling with this alien suggestion. "Well, maybe not. Maybe not," he said. "But that may be where your problems are with this girl."

"She's not a girl really," he said. "She's over thirty," Willie said.

"Whatever she is. But if she's one of them Holts, you better look out. I don't do nothin' but work a ole fishin' camp, but I tell you this. I take a lot of people out, and I hear a lotta talk. The Holts are pow'rful people down here. You don't want to cross 'em. Far as I'm concerned, you don't want nothin' to do with 'em."

Willie stood up on the wharf. A breeze was blowing out of the south, warm and puffy, pushing aside the chill air, carrying the sweet smell of rotting wood from the swamp. "I think I'll go back inside and have another drink," he said.

"You ain't gonna take my advice, are you, son?" Guidre said.

"I don't think so," Willie said. "But I'll keep it in mind." The rotting wood from the swamp smelled sweet and good, and the ducks barked and gabbled in their coves and potholes.

10

It was nearly dark when Willie got home and he was tired and dirty and his arms and legs and back ached from the exertion. He tucked a bagful of ducks into the freezing compartment of his refrigerator and put down his gear and the morning paper—which he'd picked up at the bottom of the steps—on the kitchen table. Wearily, he shed his clothes and turned on the shower, then wrapped a towel around himself and sat down in his old leather chair with the paper, waiting for the shower to warm up.

He skimmed the front page, a bland hodgepodge of local, state and national news, and turned to the features section. He grimaced over how bad the paper was. Even the *New Orleans Times-Picayune* was better. In the back pages, sandwiched between the classified section and a supermarket advertisement, a small item caught his eye: CREOLETOWN WOMAN BURNED TO DEATH. He read on:

A 78-year-old Negro woman was burned to death yesterday when flames consumed her house near Route 23, Creoletown.

County fire officials said they have not yet been able to determine the cause of the blaze that reduced the two-room dwelling of Elvira Backus to rubble. The body was found in the bedroom, according to Asst. Fire Chief A. U. Comer. Comer said the blaze might have been the result of smoking in bed.

Willie's heart jumped. He read through again from the top, furious that there was so little information. Then the phone began ringing, and he answered it.

"Mr. Croft," the voice said, "this is Daniel Holt. I've been trying to reach you since late last night."

"Good God!" Willie said. "I've just seen the paper. What happened?"

"Somebody set that fire. I'm sure of it," Daniel said.

"But how? Christ, I'm sorry."

"I was afraid this might happen," Daniel continued. He sounded strangely calm under the circumstances.

"What makes you believe it was arson?"

"I know it was," Daniel said.

"Listen," Willie said, "I don't know what to say. I feel like it's my fault in a way. I mean your mother, she was such a nice person. She was . . . well . . . I really liked her. . . ."

There was a brief silence on the other end, then, in his deepest Shakespearean tone, Daniel declared, " 'Her voice was ever soft,/Gentle and low, an excellent thing in woman.' "

There was another silence, then Willie said, finally, "I really am sorry, Daniel."

"*King Lear*," he said.

"What about—God, I hate to bring this up—but the paper? The deed. I suppose it was burned too? . . ."

"Let us not worry about things like that now," Daniel said quietly.

"Will there be a service?" Willie asked.

"In three days. At the church on the blacktop just past the turnoff to her house. At eleven o'clock."

"Well, I'll be there, of course," Willie said, "and if there's anything I can do—anything at all . . ."

"Thank you, Mr. Croft. But I believe for the time being

everything is taken care of. We will talk later. I just didn't know if you'd heard."

"I'm sorry," Willie said, "terribly sorry. . . ."

Willie put the phone down and read through the newspaper story again. Arson. But how could you prove it? And without her, and without Johnathan Holt's deed, how in hell could they prove anything? Jesus, he wished he'd insisted that she let him take the deed that day and record it for her.

Still standing in the towel, Willie poured himself a tall glass of bourbon, threw in a few ice cubes from the refrigerator and took a long swallow. He almost gagged, shook his head and took the glass into the bathroom with him; the shower had steamed everything. He adjusted the water and stepped in, letting it run over the back of his head and neck and down his back. Had the Holts actually done *this?* It was a monstrous thing to think, but who else would have? If it *was* arson, it must have been them. He wished he'd thought to ask Daniel if he'd mentioned this to the fire department investigators. Surely he must have. He would have to find out. He saw his whole case slipping away. But *arson, murder,* it was terrible.

The chill winter sunshine filtered through the forest of oaks in the park into Willie's bedroom. The bourbon had helped a little, but he hadn't slept well. He finished dressing, picked up the phone and dialed Judge McCormack's chambers. The secretary answered.

"Is the judge in?" he asked.

"No, he's not. Who's calling, please?"

"It's me, Gladys—Willie Croft."

There was a sudden iciness in her voice.

"May I tell him what it's in reference to?"

"It's personal," Willie said.

"Mr. Croft, the judge has appointments this morning, and he goes on the bench at eleven thirty. If you could tell me what it's about, perhaps he might see you."

Willie felt his blood rise. "You tell Judge McCormack it's important. Damned important. And I would appreciate it if he could find time this morning to talk with me. He'll know what it's about."

"Well," the secretary said coldly, "I'll tell him. But I don't like to hear profanity, and without any idea of . . ."

"Just tell him," Willie said.

After he hung up he drove to his office. As soon as he turned the knob he knew something was wrong. It wasn't locked. He opened the door and looked around. The office had been ransacked.

Six blocks away, in the Holt Stevedoring Building, Brevard Holt sat behind his spacious desk, shaking his head bitterly. In front of him in one chair sat Augustus Tompkins and in the other was Percy Holt. The mood was dire and grim.

"I simply don't see how you could have done this!" Brevard said for the third time. "It is the wildest thing I have ever heard."

"Look, nobody had any way of knowing she was going to come back there just then," Percy said. "I've told you, it was just to get that goddamned paper."

"For Christ's sake, Percy!" Brevard exploded. "Couldn't you foresee something like that would happen! Why in the world you took this on yourself, without consulting me . . ." He let his voice dribble off.

Augustus Tompkins cleared his throat. "Where are these two, ah, *characters* now? Do you know?"

"Thugs," Brevard said angrily.

"Do you know, Percy?" Tompkins asked.

"Down on the docks, I guess. We're working the *Panamanian Rose* this morning."

"Well, I'd say, first of all, it might be a good idea to get them to lie low for a while. Perhaps someplace out of town. Any kind of loose talk from them, and everybody's cooked."

"Do you know that this is murder!" Brevard cried. "You could be charged with *murder!* That's what it is, isn't it, Augustus?"

"Well, possibly. But I don't think it will come down to

that. Manslaughter, perhaps. I'll take Percy at his word that they never meant to do anything like this. In any case, it will be very messy if it ever gets out—for all of us, at this point."

"So what do we do now?" Brevard said dejectedly.

Tompkins began packing his pipe. "As I said, I think the first thing is to call in these two men. Let Percy do it alone. Give them some money—enough for a few months—and tell them to get the hell out of town. Maybe even out of the country. Perhaps it could be arranged to have them shipped out on one of the boats.

"As for the rest of it, I don't know. They failed to find the deed or paper or whatever it is in either place, so we must still assume that the niggers have it. But—and I know this sounds horrible—without the old woman's testimony, I think they're not going to have much of a case. I think we can counter the deed, assuming it still exists, by showing that your father was non compos mentis when it was drawn. We can probably get them to deal before it goes to trial."

"I don't know, I don't know," Brevard said, waving his hands. "This is very serious business. I've never been in anything like this before. We could all go to jail."

"You only have two choices," Tompkins said placidly. "Percy can go to the police and tell everything, or we can keep quiet about it and let it blow over. I've had feelers out with the sheriff's office up there, and nobody seems to suspect anything. Nobody has come forward saying they saw a car or anything. Unless somebody talks, I don't think there's much to worry about."

"Not much to worry about!" Brevard gasped. "A woman is dead!"

"It was an accident," Percy said.

"Listen, Brevard, I feel as bad about this as you," said Tompkins. "And I've got more to lose in a way—I am an attorney. But it's done. Besides, the old woman was nearly eighty years old. She was going to die pretty soon anyway. I know it's a rough way to think about it, but what choice do you have?"

Brevard glared at his brother. "You are an idiot," he said.

"I don't think we'll ever be able to live with this on our consciences." Then he turned to Tompkins.

"All right. Percy can call in those two hoodlums and get them the hell out of town. You do what you have to about the property. Now I'm going to leave here and go play some golf when I can get a breath of fresh air."

Willie had nearly finished with the police when the phone rang. It was Judge McCormack's secretary. The judge would see him if he could come right away. Willie had not mentioned to the police anything of Mrs. Backus's death or a possible connection with the break-in.

"Good morning, Your Honor," Willie said. Judge McCormack was sitting behind his desk studying some documents. He motioned Willie to a chair. He did not stop studying the documents and he did not say good morning.

"Your Honor, something has come up in the Backus-Holt matter, and I would like to discuss it with you."

"What's that?" the judge said sourly. He leaned back in his chair, holding one of the papers in his hand, still reading it.

"Are you aware that Mrs. Backus burned to death on Saturday?"

The judge looked askance. "She did? How?"

"In a fire. Her house was burned down."

"What do you mean, 'was burned down'?" the judge said.

"It appears to have been arson," Willie said, "and furthermore, my office was broken into and ransacked sometime over the weekend."

"Have you told the police?"

"Of course," Willie said. The judge reached for a cigar.

"Well, I'm very sorry—about your client—and your office too. But what do you want me to do about it? It sounds like a police matter. I am only a judge."

"Your Honor," Willie said, "you have read the briefs in this case. It's coming up on a motion for dismissal in a few weeks. My best witness is now dead, and has taken whatever personal light she could have shed to the grave with her. But her heirs are still entitled to a hearing and the best way I can think of to prove my client's case is to have blood tests run—on my people as well as the Holt family. It seems like the only way to settle this matter."

"Blood tests!" the judge growled. "Are you still persisting in this insane accusation against the family?"

"Your Honor," Willie said, "I do not find my pleadings *insane*. And I am asking you if you would consider an order to have the Holt family tested. I am told that blood tests can indicate genealogical connections with some degree of accuracy."

The judge was wide-eyed. He leaned forward across the desk. "You *are* going to persist in this!" he screeched. The fat round his collar tensed and flapped.

"Your Honor," Willie said, "the blood tests are the only sensible way. They can . . ."

"Blood tests, my ass!" the judge roared. "I'm not ordering any blood tests for anybody. If the Holts want to have them to refute your shameful claim, then that's up to them. This is a civil proceeding, not a criminal trial! Croft," the judge said, his eyes narrowed, scowling, "you must be out of your mind!"

Willie walked out into the bright winter sunshine. From the second-floor cellblock someone yelled out, "Hey, Groundman!" He looked up and waved absently at a dark, obscure face behind the bars whose fingers were wrapped around the thick metal frame, and then he crossed the street. Four blocks away the enormous superstructure of a freighter glided slowly downriver, dwarfing the low tin warehouses at the dock. Gray smoke steamed from its funnels. Willie wondered momentarily where it was going, and where it had been.

When he got to The Parade a vendor sold him a ten-cent bag of peanuts and he sat on one of the benches, sharing the nuts with the squirrels and pigeons.

He felt churned up inside. For the past fifteen years or so things had gone smoothly. Smoothly, but not very well. Not many ups and downs, just a straight line with occasional blips. This he had become accustomed to, but now, in a few short weeks, everything seemed to have changed—beginning with that early morning when Priscilla had decided to confide in him about her mother. It had led to his meeting Whitsey Loftin, and if he was not in love with her, he badly wanted to be, which was worse. And the Obsidian Oil Corporation, and the Holts, and now a murder and the burglary of his office, and a fistfight in front of the most prominent people in Bienville and the promise—at least the outside promise—of his becoming the lawyer for a wealthy oil cabal—all of it just in the past few weeks.

Perhaps Guidre was right. Perhaps he shouldn't have gone up against the Holts. Everyone might have been better off if he'd taken Augustus Tompkins's offer of thirty-five thousand dollars and told Mrs. Backus it was the best they could do. She'd still be alive, anyway. And what now? No deed, no witness to testify. And what about the Negroes up there? After this, would any of them be willing to go along with Daniel Holt and his friends? He saw the situation turning bitter and mean and more perplexing.

Just as he was about to leave, Willie saw Augustus Tompkins crossing The Parade, walking toward his office building—he was coming from the direction of the river, where the Holt Stevedoring offices were. Willie got up and went across the grass to a point on the path where he would intersect Tompkins.

"I'd like to talk to you, Augustus," he said.

Tompkins flinched when he saw him, started, but he stopped. The pigeons and squirrels followed Willie, and gathered around his feet.

"Well, Willie, what can I do for you today?" Tompkins's steel-blue eyes gave away nothing. He was not smiling. Willie stood directly in front of him.

"Your people are playing rough, aren't they, Augustus?"

"I don't understand you, Willie. You'll forgive me."

"You understand all right," Willie said. "Killing an old woman and burning down her house—not to mention my office." Willie was planted firmly in front of Augustus Tompkins. There was no one else on the walkway. It was cool beneath the massive oaks and Willie felt a shiver in his spine as his eyes locked with those of the corporate lawyer.

"Willie, I really haven't any idea of what you're talking about, and I'm late for an appointment. I must be going," Tompkins said. He tried to sidestep around Willie.

"Yeah, I'll bet you don't," Willie said, turning with him. "You're in this thing up to your neck, Augustus. And I'm going to see you're found out too."

"What thing? What in hell are you talking about, man?" Tompkins said defensively. His voice was gravelly, but Willie thought he detected a slight waver.

"I mean that somebody went up to Mrs. Backus's at Creoletown and set it on fire and burned her to death on Saturday. And I mean that somebody—and I'll bet it was that same somebody—broke into my office and ransacked it looking for something—and I'll bet I know what that something was. And I'll also bet I know who is behind it, Augustus. And I'll bet you do too."

The beginnings of a sneer spread across Tompkins's face. He seemed on the verge of losing his composure.

"Now, I'm going to say this, and say it once, Willie. I don't know what in hell you're talking about. I haven't a clue. And I don't have all day to stand here listening to you. You had your chance, and you refused it. Anything you have to say to me about this matter, you can say in court, in front of a judge. Do I make myself clear?"

The two of them stood looking at each other like prize-fighters receiving instructions. Then Tompkins stepped away without a word and marched confidently toward his office. Willie remained on the walkway for a few moments watching him, the squirrels and pigeons scampering and pecking at his feet. Tompkins did not look back, but walked straight and quickly and disappeared into a doorway. At least, Willie thought, I've given him something to think about.

When Willie got back to his office the part-time secretary

was putting the last of the strewn-about file folders back in their place.

"You had a message from a Dr. Bledsole," she said. "It's on your desk."

Willie picked up the message. It said: "V. D. Skinner. Enid, Oklahoma, that's all I know."

He sat down and picked up the phone. The operator got him information for Enid, and he asked for the number of the main hotel in town. There were three, he was told, so he started with the first. Three calls later he located V. D. Skinner.

"I am a friend of Hamilton Bledsole, and he tells me you know something about oil," Willie said.

"I know *everything* about oil," the voice at the other end replied in a flat, South Carolina twang. "Favorite drink of mine's a glass of motor oil—thirty weight, nondetergent. What can I do for you?"

Willie sketched out his situation. He told Skinner about the property of Mrs. Backus, and the plan of her son and his friends to form their own company. "What I need from you, or from someone," Willie said, "is consultation. I'm not quite sure how these things work and we've got, or will be getting, some money. If my clients agree, could you possibly come down here for a few days and go over things with us?"

"Funny," V. D. Skinner said, "been wonderin' when somebody down there was going to call me up. Ever since I read about it in the paper. You're lucky, Croft, you got me first, 'cause I can tell you the best, the cheapest and the most profitable way to do whatever it is you're trying to do. Know every trick in the book. Hellfire, I wrote the book. Got to finish up a job here for the next few days. Be in touch with you after that." He hung up, leaving Willie staring into the receiver.

Willie sat at his desk thinking for a while. There was something about Skinner that made it more real. At least here was somebody who knew what he was doing. Or said he did. He tried to picture Skinner in his mind and he imagined a tall, burly man, tanned and tough; a handsome out-of-doors type, with shining teeth and shining confidence. He wondered briefly if he should have told him about the death of Mrs. Backus and the tentative status of the property. And also, he purposely had not mentioned that they were Negroes.

Two days later it was raining again, a slow, chilly drizzle that spattered against the windshield of Willie's Nash all through the outskirts of the city and on into the countryside. The funeral services for Mrs. Elvira Backus were at 11:00 A.M., and Willie calculated that he would arrive just about on time. The afternoon before, Daniel had called again to ask if he was coming, and Willie thought he seemed unusually anxious for him to be there.

He hummed past small farmhouses, gray and lonely in the rainy twilight, then he was in the deep woods where the gnarled and stunted trees grew savagely to the edges of the ribbonlike road.

There was something strangely determinate and fatal about this land: flat, ugly, untilled. Willie never had a sense of it the way people who had lived there might have had, because in spite of his affinity for the out-of-doors, his knowledge of the swamp and hunting and fishing, he was essentially a creature of the town, an urban animal who knew the land, but did not have that keen, undefinable *sense* of it that those who lived on it did.

Or rather *in* it.

They lived more *in* it than *on* it because it was the kind of place where everything closed in around you, a dark green creeping jungle of kudzu and pine and oak and ash and broom grass and thorn vines. You could cut it back, or burn it off, but in a few months' time it would be lapping at you again, encircling you, and finally growing over you and everything you had built.

Somewhere, out there, Willie knew there were cabins. Mostly Negro cabins, and a few white ones, many of these buried now beneath a forest so mean and dense a man would have to walk almost on top of them before he recognized that they were places where people once lived; where they were born, grew up, loved and hated and slept and ate, cried, laughed, argued and finally died, generation after generation until the forest claimed them back again after the last inhabitant gave up and left or died off.

Willie knew this, but had never been a part of it.

Black or white—and they were preponderantly black— the people up here were as foreign to the people of Bienville as inhabitants of the polar regions might have been. There were no fancy planters on this soil. There were no elegant plantations here whose owners might have traveled to town after laying by for a winter of gay socializing and debauchery with their city cousins. These were people who could feed whole families not on forty, but on ten acres or less and a couple of pigs and a handful of chickens and perhaps a cow. Ignorant people maybe, but not stupid or dumb; not worldly-wise, but land-wise, with different values, thoughts and dreams than the lawyers and stockbrokers and clerks and bus drivers and forklift operators forty miles to the south. In the city they would have been strangers, outlanders—but not here on their land. They were consumed by it, belonged on it and were creatures of it as much as the deer and squirrels and raccoons and foxes and snakes and lizards that inhabited it alongside them.

The church was about what he had expected. White, small, set off in a copse of beech trees near the road. A tiny steeple pinnacled above the front entrance. A dozen or so automobiles were parked around it and as many people stood outside in the gray, rainy morning beneath a small covered portico. Willie parked the Nash on the roadway and walked to the doors. Daniel Holt was waiting in the vestibule and he greeted Willie warmly and took him aside.

"I am happy you came, Mr. Croft; we all are." In a small pew near the front, Willie saw Priscilla and several other women. A closed casket stood beneath the pulpit and a fat Negro woman was playing "Abide With Me" on a battered upright piano near the altar.

"Please come in and sit down," Daniel said. "We're about ready to start." Given the circumstances, he seemed collected and undisturbed. It must be, Willie decided, that because Negroes are more accustomed to death, closer to it, they are less fearful or in awe of it than white people.

Just as Willie found a seat on one of the hard wooden pews in the back of the church, the preacher took the pulpit. He was a man in his early thirties, with close-cropped hair and no mustache, and he opened the service with "Rock of Ages, Cleft for Me." Willie stood and sang the first verse with the rest, but he did not know the second, and there were no hymnals. When they had finished and taken their seats again, the preacher spread his arms as though to embrace the casket before him. "Here," he said in a soft and trembling voice, "was a child of the flock, a creature of God."

He continued to describe Mrs. Backus in this vein, vague, glowing euphemisms, as though even in her life she only existed in a shadow world of the spirit, not of the flesh. When he finished, they sang another hymn, and the service was quickly closed. Willie waited on the steps until Daniel and Priscilla came out. He wanted to say something, but they walked immediately to an old, black Lincoln parked behind an aging hearse, and sat there until pallbearers brought out the casket and lifted it inside. The procession drove to a small cemetery less than a mile from the church where an open grave was waiting. The preacher gave an ashes-to-ashes intonation, then the little party of mourners drifted away to their cars. Willie, who had remained on the fringe of the group, was about to leave when Daniel Holt came up to him. He started to say again how sorry he was when Daniel spoke first. There was harsh calm in his voice.

"Could you follow us to a friend's house?" he asked. "I'd like to speak with you in private there."

Willie felt slightly uncomfortable somehow. It was the conduct of the services that had unsettled him. There was something cold, hard and nervous about it, as though no one really cared. Perhaps they were more concerned with the land and the oil and the money than the loss of a human life.

Well, maybe that was the way things were with Negroes. Willie was learning all the time.

"Uh, yes, certainly," he said. "I'll have to get back to my office this afternoon, though."

"It shouldn't take long," Daniel said. "You can follow Priscilla and me."

Willie drove behind the black Lincoln down bleak country roads. He noticed in the rearview mirror that several other cars from the funeral were behind him. There was something about the feel of it, something awry. After they had gone several miles, the Lincoln turned without warning down a two-track dirt road with no sign to mark it. Apprehensively, Willie followed and the two automobiles behind him closed him in.

A hundred yards down the road, beneath dark, dripping trees, they came upon a neat little frame house with a television antenna on the roof. At one time it had been a working farm; fields stretched behind it, untended for many seasons. Several other automobiles, at least two of them late models, were parked in front. Willie pulled up beside the Lincoln and got out before Daniel and Priscilla, and when they opened the door he was waiting for them. The scent of damp pine hung in the air.

"Listen, Daniel, I've got a lot of things to do back in town. Is this going to take long?" Willie asked nervously.

"Not at all," Daniel replied.

Other car doors were slamming behind them. Willie looked around. The preacher was getting out of one car, and several other men were getting out of another. Daniel escorted Willie up the steps and the front door suddenly opened. A large, bearded Negro wearing overalls appeared in the doorway. Unsmiling, he stepped back to let them through.

The room was dim because of the low-hanging weather. Willie glanced closely at his watch. The luminous dial told him it was just before 2:00 P.M. On a low couch three men sat silently and observed the newcomers. They were neatly dressed, but he did not recognize them as having attended the funeral. As his eyes slowly grew accustomed to the light, Willie began to scan the rest of the room. Behind him the door slammed shut and he turned quickly, then he felt his heart catch up.

In a rocking chair in a corner by the door, smiling, watching him, with dark, bright eyes, an old robe pulled over her lap, was the dead woman, Mrs. Elvira Backus.

11

"My God!" Willie cried. "What . . . ? What the devil's going on here? What the . . ."

"Mr. Croft, I think you'd better let me explain," said Daniel Holt. "Please," he said, "sit down." He motioned Willie to a chair.

Willie was too dumbfounded to do anything else. He sank down, looking back and forth between Mrs. Backus and Daniel and the others in the room.

"The woman we buried today was old Cassie Hacker," Daniel said. "She was crazy—had been for about fifteen years. Mama never was near that house when it burned. She was over to the Cruickshanks' place, canning tomatoes."

The others in the room seemed amused at the consternation that was painfully visible in Willie's face. The preacher had come in, as well as the man Willie assumed was the funeral director, and a few others who must have been in the cars behind him.

Daniel continued.

"All we can figure out is that Miss Cassie must have stopped down to Mama's place to visit. She did that every few weeks or so. Didn't have any family. We don't know if she was killed first by the people who did this, or she just

149

happened on the fire. It doesn't make any difference. She's dead now, either way."

Willie's brain was straining to make sense of this. It was revelation enough to see the dead woman sitting alive in a rocking chair after the funeral. Now there apparently was another person dead, who had to be accounted for.

He asked a lawyerly question. "Well, couldn't it have been that this woman—the one you just buried—Cassie, or whatever—that she started the fire somehow? You say she was crazy. What makes you think it was deliberate?"

Daniel glanced around the room. All eyes were on him. "Because," he said, "Mr. Garley here"—he gestured toward the large black man who had let them in—"saw an automobile turn off at Mama's place a little while before the fire must have begun, and leave shortly afterward. There were two or three white men in it. Now what else would they have been doing there? Nobody ever comes down that road. It was them that set that fire. Old Cassie just got caught in it, I'm sure of it," Daniel said. "We all are," he added.

"Well, it might have been they came for any number of reasons," Willie said. "Who knows who they are? Or what they wanted?"

"Right now, none of us," Daniel said somberly. "That's what we'd like you to find out."

"Me?" Willie said. "How would . . ."

"Because Mr. Garley took down the license number," said Daniel. "He takes down the license numbers of almost any car he doesn't know that passes his store. This is a small place, Mr. Croft. Not many cars come by these roads. If they're strangers, it could mean trouble. Garley takes down four, maybe five a week." He handed Willie a slip of paper upon which was penned:

1953–54 Chevy 2–3648–51

Willie stared at the paper as Daniel continued.

"Mr. Garley called me just after the fire broke out. He knew Mama was at the Cruickshanks' and I told them to keep her there, because I wasn't sure what was going on. When I got up to the house and found out about Cassie, I decided to let them go on thinking it was Mama, until we could find out what was going on." Daniel paused a moment and looked at the others in the room. They were middle-aged men, with serious, canny eyes. As Willie was to learn shortly, they would be the directors of Obsidian Oil.

"You see, Mr. Croft, during this past week things have been moving much more quickly than I anticipated. Mr. Hooper," he said, nodding toward one of the men, "who owns the funeral home, has spoken to quite a few of the property owners, as has Mr. Garley and the Reverend Clowers. Practically everyone we've talked to wants to throw in with us. The question now is exactly what do we do next?"

Willie was still reeling from shock. "Well, uh, how many—I mean how much land are we talking about?" he asked meekly.

"Several thousand acres right now," Daniel said, "and probably more. A lot depends on how far out the oil goes. So far we have only talked to the ones right here."

"Well," Willie said, "well."

It didn't seem possible. But if it was . . . If they had . . . He decided to tell them about V. D. Skinner.

"I think this fellow can help us," Willie said. "I didn't ask him how much he charges, but if he knows what I'm told he knows, it'll probably be worth it. Meantime, you'll have to get me the names of every one of those people, their addresses and a description of their property—titles, deeds, if they have them. I'll draw up some initial papers they'll have to sign. That should protect us for the time being. This thing seems to be moving awfully fast. We have to be careful. Once I get all of these titles, we should get in touch with Mr. Bey in Chicago, and see about getting some of that money started."

Then Willie turned to Daniel. "I think you are going to have to do something about your mother. About the fire. At some point go to the police."

Daniel shook his head. "I don't agree, Mr. Croft—not now, in any event. I think it's better if they believe she's dead."

"This is all very unusual," Willie said. "I'm a lawyer. I cannot operate outside the law."

"We're not asking you to," Daniel said. "But, perhaps just for a little while, you could neglect to mention the truth of what happened up here. By that time you should have found out whose car that was with the men in it."

Willie rubbed his forehead. "Well, I don't know. I suppose it wouldn't do any harm. Tracing the license ought to be easy enough." No *harm,* he thought. It could do a great deal of harm, at least to him. Concealing evidence of a possible murder was harm indeed for an officer of the court. Yet he also knew that this could be a very important hole card for him, if it turned out the way it might. Keeping it quiet for a while . . . well, the harm would have to be weighed against the possible advantages.

"You see, Mr. Croft," Daniel said, "you are a white man. But most of us up here, we know the sheriff. The sheriff doesn't give much of a damn about any of us. He may even be in cahoots with whoever did this to Mama's house—and I think both of us have a good idea who is behind it. Then we'd be sunk."

The argument was persuasive: the law might have to be bent a little for justice's sake. Willie was consciously trying to convince himself, and he didn't like to do that.

He nodded. "Maybe you're right."

Daniel drew himself up oratorically: " 'Hear not my steps, which way they walk, for fear/The very stones prate of my whereabout.' "

Willie watched the old woman rocking back and forth in her chair. She smiled at him. Yes, it was moving quickly. Very quickly indeed.

The drive back into town was even gloomier than the morning trip. Great scudding clouds out of the south blanketed the sky and the rain fell in torrents that often obscured the roadway. Willie's mood matched the weather.

There was something dark and gloomy about this affair. He wasn't sure he liked it, but neither was he all that sure he didn't like it. One thing was now certain: If the iron was to be pulled from the fire, he would have to be the one to do it.

All his life Willie had lived by a simple, homespun honesty. He had worked hard, learned his law and had a certain assurance in the way he applied his craft, such as it was. Nothing fancy. The chicanery of mock funerals and the prospect of murder that hung over the Backus-Holt case had no place in this. And yet he began to realize, during this storm-driven trip toward home, that he was now in a fight, an honest-to-goodness battle that was pushing him—or pulling him—toward pragmatic and possibly ruthless justifications. Much was at stake, and if there was ever a time to make the horses of his dreams work for him, it was now or coming soon. Even if he was uncomfortable with this thought, it overtook him just the same.

The part-time secretary had gone and the lights were turned off in Willie's office when he finally got back to town. It was late afternoon and rain was still pouring down. She had left a note on his desk—a Mr. V. D. Skinner had phoned long-distance and was flying in from Oklahoma at eight that evening and could Willie arrange for him to be picked up? As though he were some potentate, Willie thought. There was another message stating that Dr. Hamilton Bledsole would appreciate a call. He dialed Ham's number.

"Dr. Bledsole is in a conference with a patient," a secretary said. "May I tell him who's calling?" Willie gave his name. "Oh, yes, Mr. Croft," she said. "He wanted me to tell you that he is having a Christmas party Saturday night and would like for you to come. I'll give you the address."

Willie hesitated a second, wishing no repetition of the episode at the debutante ball, then quickly decided that Ham would have considered that, and wouldn't have invited him if there might be trouble. "Yes, tell him I'll be delighted," he said.

He sorted through the day's mail. There was a letter from

a client who, with Willie's assistance, had received a suspended sentence for running a street-corner numbers operation. The letter contained a well-worn ten-dollar bill and a handwritten note that said, "Now IOU $70." He started to leave the bill and the note on the secretary's desk, then decided to deal with it himself. He went to the file cabinet and pulled out the man's folder. In the account ledger, he wrote in the ten dollars, and scanned back through the inclusions. The original fee had been two hundred and fifty dollars—that was four years ago. Periodically a five-dollar or ten-dollar bill would show up in the mail. He looked at the right-hand margin and did some quick mathematics. Sure enough, the account now outstanding was seventy dollars. He tucked the ten dollars into his wallet and went into the other room. Three utility bills were also in the mail and he left them on the secretary's desk with a note, "Pay these please." Then he opened a letter from the clerk of court's office. It said that a preliminary hearing in the competency case of *Brevard Holt et al. vs. Mrs. Hannah Holt Loftin* had been scheduled in four weeks. His name was listed as counsel for Mrs. Loftin.

The rain had thinned to a slow, steady drizzle in the darkness as Willie pulled up in the airport parking lot. At the information counter he inquired about the flight arriving from Oklahoma at 8:00 P.M. It was on time, the clerk said, and as a matter of fact, she added, pointing through a glass window to a pair of headlights rushing toward them, just touching down. Willie watched the plane taxi, feather its propellers and come to a stop near a movable stairway that a ground crew had wheeled into place.

Three passengers got off, a mother and her small daughter and a portly man in a cream-colored suit, brown-and-white saddle oxfords, thick black eyeglasses, a wide-brimmed white hat with a thin blue band around it, carrying an enormous black umbrella. This had to be V. D. Skinner, Willie realized. More than anything else, he resembled a butterfly hunter.

Willie approached and was about to introduce himself,

but before he could the man called out, "Croft? Skinner here!"

Willie stuck out his hand and Skinner gave it a cursory squeeze, then breezed past him. "C'mon, man, get out of this here goddamn rain!" He sailed into the airport lobby and stopped up short. "My God," he cried, "what a Duckburg this place is." Hearing this comment, several bored-looking employees looked up from their tasks. "Where's our car?" Skinner demanded.

"It's outside," Willie said. "But don't you have to wait for your baggage?"

Skinner's umbrella remained open; the shaft looked as though it might have concealed a sword. He was peering around the room through the thick black spectacles which caused his eyes to seem large and menacing. His hair was longish and unkempt, giving him a slightly wild appearance.

"Don't have any baggage," Skinner said. "Forgot it in Oklahoma. Have to send for it in the morning. Say, is there someplace we can get a cheeseburger? I'm hungry."

"There's a place on the way to town," Willie said. "The car's this way."

They walked into the lot where Willie's Nash was parked sadly between a delivery truck and a large black Chrysler. Skinner went straight for the Chrysler and began to get in.

"No, over here," Willie said.

"Huh?" Skinner said. He had already folded his umbrella.

"I'm over here," Willie repeated.

"My Gawd!" Skinner exclaimed. "Ain't seen one of these in years." He opened the door and examined the inside of the Nash as though he expected to find spiders and cobwebs. It was the first time anyone had ever commented on Willie's car, and he had not thought much about it one way or the other until just now. Somewhat like himself, the old Nash was the hopeful product of another generation, now regarded as a failure. Still, so long as it drove all right, Willie had seen no reason to get rid of it.

"I'll need a car myself while I'm here," Skinner announced. "Where's the local Cadillac dealer?"

"Downtown," Willie said faintly, deciding that the services of V. D. Skinner were not going to come cheaply.

"There're a bunch of restaurants along here," Willie said as they drove along. "Any kind of place in particular you want to go?"

"How about a cheeseburger?" Skinner said. "Been thinking about one all the way down here on that plane. Worst ride I ever had. Worst damn plane too. Thing was dirty and the food tasted like shit. Stewardesses so ugly you didn't want to ride on the same plane with 'em."

"It wasn't the best airline you were on," Willie offered. Actually he didn't know, since he'd only been on a plane once in his life and that was in the Army. He pulled into a barbecue place. Through the plate-glass window they could see a waitress stacking chairs but there were still two or three people sitting in booths.

"Get a beer in here?" Skinner asked.

"Yeah, I think so," Willie said, noticing a beer advertisement in the window.

Inside, the harsh overhead lights played across the plump, wide-mouthed face of V. D. Skinner and illuminated a rapacity in the eyes, mouth and chin that spoke of brash vanity. If there were any signs of weakness, dishonesty, sloth or stupidity, they did not show up here.

As soon as they sat down Skinner called out to the waitress, a hatchet-faced woman in her mid-forties, "Hey, honey! We have a couple of beers?"

She stopped stacking the chairs on the tables and came over to them. "What kind of beer?" she said unenthusiastically.

"Heineken," Skinner said.

"We got Schlitz, Bud, Miller and Jax," she said.

"Okay, Schlitz," Skinner said. The waitress vanished and Skinner leaned forward conspiratorially.

"Okay, now tell me what you're up to, Croft."

Willie lit up a Picayune. "Well," he said, "like I told you, I have some people who've formed a syndicate—a corporation, actually—to deal in oil leases. Some of them have holdings in the field area outright. Others will have disputed claims. But what they want to do is acquire as much of the acreage up there as they can, and turn it around to the oil companies at as high a profit as possible. They've got a promise of bank financing up to three million dollars, maybe more provided certain criteria are met. And they have some capital of their own. That's it in a nutshell."

"The standard deal," Skinner said. "So what you want me to do is figure out how much land they should buy, where and at what price and how much to sell it back for—right?"

"I guess that's about it," Willie said.

The waitress came with two beers and a menu. "We close in twenty minutes," she said sullenly.

"I'll have a cheeseburger," Skinner said. "Lettuce and tomato and onion and pickle—and French fries."

"This here's a barbecue place," she said. "You don't want a barbecue?"

"Honey, when I want a cheeseburger, that's what I order. If I wanted a barbecue, I would have asked for it," Skinner replied with an autocratic smile.

Willie ordered a barbecue sandwich on a roll, outside cut.

"Now," Skinner said, "how much land are we talking about? I mean, how much do they own, and how much can they account for?"

Willie took a swallow of beer. "Well," he said, "that's a little hard to say just now. There's something I'd better tell you before we go on. There'll probably be some legal questions over a lot of the land up there. My people have claims, most of them have lived on it a long time, but there's going to be a wrangle, because my people are colored." He paused.

"Colored?" Skinner asked.

"Negroes," Willie said.

"Negroes?"

Willie nodded.

"Great God Almighty!" Skinner thundered. "All of them?"

"I think there's a good legal case for most of them," Willie said. "You'd have to see the country. They've been living up there—most of them—three, four, five generations. Some of them have deeds, some don't. But just about the whole area where the oil is, is colored, except for a few white farms and two or three little towns."

"Who in hell would lend coloreds that kind of money?" Skinner asked incredulously.

"Bank in Chicago," Willie said. "It's run by the Black Muslims."

"Muslims!" Skinner cried.

Willie glanced around. "We'd better keep our voices down. Yes, Muslims. I know—but they've got money. They've been down here. I've met with them. They're serious. Like you say, where else could my clients raise that kind of dough?"

"Christ," Skinner said, "Muslims are supposed to be dangerous people." His eyes were wide, so that the whites showed behind the thick lenses.

"They also have a bank," Willie said.

"How in hell did you put this together, Croft? It's amazing."

"I didn't really. It sort of fell in my lap. But it's kind of a weird story."

For the next half hour Willie told Skinner everything he knew about the Creoletown oil case, about Mrs. Backus and Daniel Holt and the Holt family and the burning of the house and the mock funeral and Mrs. Loftin and the potential oil leases and the Obsidian Oil Corporation. By the time he had finished, V. D. Skinner was on his second cheeseburger and his fourth beer.

"Croft, this is the damnedest thing I've ever heard," he declared, emitting a loud belch. "You actually got a bunch of coons who're trying to go into the oil business in a town like this, and against the old line too? It's crazy, it's insane."

"I believe they might do it," Willie said firmly, "with a little luck and some fast footwork."

V. D. Skinner fixed Willie, through his thick black glasses, with a wide, unblinking, eaglelike stare, but said nothing. It occurred to Willie that Skinner bore resemblance to various animals or objects, depending on the angle at which he was viewed. Walking behind him into the barbecue place, Willie had thought he looked something like a refrigerator.

Finally Skinner lifted the beer mug to his face and drained it, belched again loudly and slammed the mug onto the tabletop.

"Well, this *is* interesting, Croft. Give you that. It certainly is interesting!"

The first place Willie went next morning was the office of the Department of Motor Vehicles. In his wallet was the slip of paper with the license number of the car that was seen the day Mrs. Backus's house burned.

He had ensconced V. D. Skinner in the Raphael House Hotel, and arranged to meet with him later in the morning to go over a map of the oil-bearing area. But first, Skinner had wanted to go to the Cadillac dealer and arrange to rent a car. Also, he had to figure a way to get his luggage from Oklahoma.

"Hello, Strop," Willie said to the head clerk at the license plate office. He extended a tinfoil package he had brought with him. "I thought you and your wife might like these. Couple of ducks I got this weekend. I got more than I can use myself."

The clerk accepted the package gratefully. "Why, thank you, Mr. Croft."

"Listen, Strop, I've got a little favor to ask you," Willie said. "I need to find out the registration of this car." He handed the clerk the slip of paper.

"Don't s'pose that'd be too hard."

"I'd appreciate it too if you'd be discreet. I'd rather not have anyone know anything about this just yet."

"Wouldn't be too hard neither, Mr. Croft."

"Good," Willie said. "I'll call you later this afternoon."

"Good nuf," said the clerk. "Thanks for them ducks."

V. D. Skinner was waiting alone in the bar at the Raphael House when Willie arrived. He had a beer in his hand and was examining himself intently in the mirror behind the bar. He was as fat as a mole.

159

"How about it?" Skinner said cheerfully, standing up as Willie walked in.

"About what?" Willie asked.

"I mean, how *about it!*" Skinner said. "You ready to go to work?"

"I brought the map," Willie said. "I drew in the oil-field area myself from a map printed in the newspaper, but this map is better." He handed it to Skinner.

"Good Lord, man," Skinner cried, "this is a goddamn road map!"

"Well, it's better than the one the paper ran," Willie said, a little taken aback. "I mean it's bigger and . . ."

"Man, when I said do you have oil company maps, I mean geologic maps. Petroleum charts, they're called. Kind an oil company would use."

Willie was embarrassed and bewildered. "I don't have anything like that. I don't even know where I'd get one. I just thought you wanted to get a look at the area we're talking about."

"Yeah, okay," Skinner said brusquely. "Lay my hands on the other ones later." He looked at the Shell Oil road map Willie had brought him.

"This is one damn big field they're talking about here," Skinner said, "provided it comes in."

"Any reason why it shouldn't?" Willie asked.

"Hard to tell," Skinner said. "Depends on what they find down there—what kind of rock. How deep the oil is. Be various levels in a field this size. What they've hit already is just a tip of something, but there's no way to tell until you actually get down there and start pumping up stuff. Pretty encouraging, though. Heard it's high-gravity crude—good an' sweet—none of that fuel oil garbage. There'll be gas too, of course."

"How do they tell where to dig—drill, I mean?"

"Have to study the structure of the rock," Skinner said brightly. He seemed to be becoming more enthusiastic, talking about the oil.

"Sniff around for an outcropping someplace and see where it's likely to lead. See what the faults look like. Have to drill down a few times to make sure where it's going. This is mostly Paleozoic rock down here—unmetamorphized. You know what oil comes from, don't you?"

"Well, not really," Willie said. "Fossils and things, I guess."

"Tell you, then," Skinner declared exuberantly; "just a bunch of decayed bugs and plants and crap that was deposited at some time or other in the sea. Seas hardened it into rocks but the damned rocks got pores in 'em and by some process, don't guess anybody really knows what, the stuff in these pores transforms to oil and gas."

"That's it, huh?" Willie said.

"More or less," Skinner said. "Now, how 'bout your people? Show me on this . . . map . . . where their land is."

Willie began with the Backus property and outlined with a pencil the other plots that Daniel Holt had showed him. When he had finished, Skinner drew in a deep breath and let it whistle through his teeth.

"That is one hell of an operations area," he said, "smack in the middle, almost, from where the test well came in."

"That's if the courts don't take it away from them," Willie said.

"That'll be your job, Croft. But from what I can see here, if we can consolidate all your people and then buy up leases on a little more land in the area, we'd control more'n seventy percent of the field. Best part of it, too. By the way, I'm hungry; there someplace we can go for lunch?"

"They serve lunch in the dining room here," Willie said. "Pretty good too."

"Yeah, I looked at the menu," Skinner said. "Don't have hamburgers. Let's go someplace else."

Willie went to his office after lunch, leaving Skinner on his own to acquire the requisite petroleum charts. He was impressed by Skinner's resourcefulness, and, also, despite obvious peculiarities, he seemed easy to get along with.

The secretary had left a stack of mail on Willie's desk, including a fat manila envelope from the firm of Tompkins, Tompkins, Hastings and Blair. He opened it to find an avalanche of legal weaponry: writs, stays, interrogatories and demands, all designed to distract and confuse the lone issue in the Backus case—who was the legal owner of the property. He shuffled through the papers and replaced them in the envelope. Then he phoned Strop Clark at the license bureau.

"I got your information," Strop said.

"Great—shoot," Willie said.

"It belongs to a Hiram R. Crenshaw. You want his address?"

"Yeah."

"Twelve oh one and a half Foxe Street. And he's forty-three years old."

"How about where he works? Anything else too," Willie said.

"That's all I have, Mr. Croft. You'd have to go to the tax assessor's office or someplace for that kind of stuff. We just keep name, age and addresses here."

"Well, thanks, Strop," Willie said. He paused, then added, "Listen, you know those people over at the tax assessor's office, don't you? Could you make a call for me? Find out where he works?"

"Well," Strop said hesitantly, "I reckon I could, but I'd feel better about it if you could tell me why you're interested."

"It's kind of private," Willie said. "Has to do with one of my clients. A case I'm working on. That car might have been involved in it. I'd really rather not go into details right now, but I'd appreciate it if you could help."

"Okay, Mr. Croft. I'll do it. I'll give you a call."

Willie stood up and reached to the bookshelves behind him for the state code index. He ran his fingers down the titles until he found Mental Competency, then he sought out the volume and settled in his chair to read some cases. He had been reading for nearly two hours and jotting down notes when the door opened and V. D. Skinner sailed in, carrying under his arm a long cylindrical container.

"Say, Croft," he said, surveying the shabbiness of the

room, "I seen more luxurious lawyers' offices in my time. Trying to cut down on your overhead?"

"My practice is mostly in front of a judge and jury," Willie retorted. "Don't judge a book by its cover."

"You gonna crap when you see these charts," Skinner chortled wolfishly. He began removing the lid from the canister.

"My God, you got them!" Willie said in amazement. "That was quick. Where in the world did you go to . . ."

"Never ask such questions, my boy," Skinner said majestically. "Just you know that if there's something to do with oil, Vernon D. Skinner is all-knowing, all-seeing and all-doing." He lay one chart out on Willie's desk and smoothed its edges. It was a geological cross section of the terrain in the Creoletown area. With his fingers, Skinner described an arc across a section of the chart cluttered with numerous symbols and markings unfamiliar to Willie.

"Here's where most of your people's property is located," Skinner said. "Now, look at these." He pointed to half a dozen red arrows just outside the arc. "These are the test wells the oil companies have drilled. Right along the fault of this obsidian rock. Just look at that. I'm a sonofabitch if most of this oil ain't going to come smack in the middle of your niggers' land. Oil people know it too. I snooped around some today—talked with one guy says they're mad as a cat that's just been pissed on 'cause your people won't deal. Calling a lot of meetings, that kind of crap."

"You don't say," Willie said.

"Do say," Skinner replied. "What's more, a lot of other people are grousing around too. There're at least four or five syndicates here in town trying to buy up leases and they haven't gotten anywhere either. Puttin' out the word your people don't have titles that'll stand up in court."

"Like I said, that's a possibility," Willie said. He was privately fascinated at how Skinner might have come to acquire the charts and this other information.

"Listen, Croft, I been thinking. This is going to come to some kind of head at some point. Right now, all we know is that your people are on the land. That counts for a lot, in court, I mean, doesn't it?"

"Yes, I think it does," Willie said. The oilman had an impish grin on his face. Willie did not know what was in Skinner's mind but he was sure it was part of a greater plan.

"What I'm going to suggest now might sound extravagant to you, wild maybe. But, Croft, it could lead to something very big." Skinner peered at Willie through the thick, black-rimmed glasses. "I made my living as a wildcatter of sorts for nearly ten years. Oil consultant too. Know this business upside down. If your people hang fire together, they'll control one of the biggest oil fields in the country. Maybe even *the* biggest. We don't know what's going to happen in court, but there's a better-than-even chance they'll get clear title, right?"

Willie was about to answer, but Skinner pressed on.

"Now, with what I know and what they've got, I'll make you a suggestion. Why let the oil companies grab up everything? Sure, your niggers can make a few bucks selling the mineral rights, but there's a chance to go way beyond all that."

Willie noticed that Skinner was getting more excited as he spoke. The subject of oil seemed to consume him.

"You got this company, right, the Obsidian Oil Company or whatever you call it. On paper, that is. Why make it just a paper company? Why not do something real?"

Willie looked perplexed. Skinner was pacing up and down in front of the window. Outside, the low winter sun glinted off the flat-calm waters of Bienville Bay.

"Why not drill ourselves? What in hell do we need the majors for? I set up rigs for years. Probably know more about the whole goddamn process from beginning to end than any ten men in a major oil company. We can do it cheaper, without unions. Hell, we can probably get a lot of the labor from folks that live up there. It's the difference between making a tidy profit and a fortune," Skinner said.

Willie was flabbergasted. "I . . . I don't know," he stammered. "I mean, if we don't even know who has clear title to the property, how could we set up drilling on it? How could . . ."

"Exactly what I was talking about," Skinner said excitedly. "You see, two can play that game. I mean, the legal crap, right? Now instead of you pressing for a decision, you just delay—and delay and delay and delay. Just what they're doing to you now. Meantime, we're pumping oil. I can rent rigs and have them shipped here by the end of the month. A few at least, and it'll take another few weeks to set it up. But then we'll be drilling. In the end even if your people lose, we'll have wells in and can make a better deal with the majors."

"Well, I, ah, don't know," Willie said. "I mean, suppose you do—we do. What do we do with the oil?"

"Easy," Skinner said; "lease some tanker trucks first and ship it out. There're half a dozen small refineries within three hundred miles of here. They aren't connected with the majors and they'd be glad to get our crude. Run our trucks twenty-four hours a day. That way, we don't have to pay for storage and we can undersell everybody else. All we do is bring it up and sell it off while you stave off these bastards in court."

"What if I can't?" Willie said. His mind felt numb, as though he were recovering from a blow.

"Well, some days you eat the bear," Skinner declared grandly, "and some days the bear eats you."

12

HAM BLEDSOLE LIVED IN A LARGE ANTEBELLUM REPRODUCTION with spacious, planted grounds and a tall wrought-iron fence around them. Automobiles lined both sides of the street in front when Willie and V. D. Skinner arrived in Skinner's newly rented Cadillac convertible. An elderly black man in a tuxedo showed them inside and took their coats. The hallway was filled with young, talking faces, all of them unfamiliar to Willie; an enormous Christmas tree towered as high as the second-floor stair landing, surrounded by presents. Willie worried sheepishly whether he should have brought one.

The two of them funneled into the living room with several other guests and pressed their way to a bar lined three deep with men. As they waited for drinks Willie continued to be amazed to see so many young, attractive people—especially attractive women. In all the time he had lived in Bienville he could not remember seeing a single one of them before, and he regarded them distantly, and uncomfortably too. Furthermore, an atmosphere of camaraderie hung over the room, also threatening to make him feel like an outsider—then Ham saw Skinner and yelled at him from the other side of the room.

"You old scoundrel," he cried joyfully, pumping Skinner's hand. "He did it! He got you down here! Welcome! Welcome!"

"My Lord, Doc," Skinner said, surveying his surroundings with mock awe, "didn't know you could make this kind of money filling teeth."

"Damn," Ham said, "you haven't changed a bit." He feigned a close examination of Skinner's worn brown suit. "Say, isn't that the same suit you got from the Salvation Army in Ann Arbor?"

"Nah," Skinner replied hastily. "Had this suit for years. Saving the other for *nice* parties."

"Let me get you to meet some people," Ham said. He took them around the room and introduced them randomly to clusters of guests. Willie had wolfed down most of his first glass of bourbon and was about to go off to get another when he saw Whitsey Loftin. She was sandwiched between a printed silk drapery and a drunk-looking man in a greenvelvet jacket who was smoking a cigar and ogling her cleavage.

He hadn't seen or spoken to Whitsey since the night at Beaudreux's, but she had frequently worked her way into his thoughts. His immediate impulse was to turn away so she would not see him and to gather his thoughts so as to present himself in the best possible light when the opportunity arrived. Suddenly a Negro servant in a black uniform came up with a tray of hors d'oeuvres. Willie speared a tiny sausage on a toothpick, dipped it into mustard and popped it into his mouth. As it turned out, the sausage was extremely hot—made even more so by the mustard—and he was in the desperate process of spitting it into his hand when she started across the room toward him with an exuberant smile on her face. Damn, he thought, working his scorched tongue in the air, something like this is always happening to me.

"Willie!" she gushed, kissing him on the cheek. "I'm so glad you're here! I was hoping you would be. Ham told me you were invited." He was profoundly grateful she hadn't tried to shake hands since he was still holding the mushed remains of the sausage.

"Uh!" he replied, fanning his mouth. "I jus' ate hot sausage."

She suddenly noticed that his eyes were tearing.

"Oh, my goodness! Here, quick, drink something!" She tapped a man standing next to them on the arm, seized his half-empty glass and put it to Willie's lips. The man, a blond giant who might have been a former football star, spun around in astonishment, and unaware of the problem—though probably thinking Willie swallowed something wrong—slapped him hard on the back. The contents of the glass flew down the front of Whitsey's dress and she instinctively shrieked and threw her hands to her face.

All at once people were rushing from all sides of the room to see what had happened. The man who had slapped Willie on the back was apologizing and asking him if he was all right now, and he was nodding his head affirmatively and watching two other women wipe Whitsey dry with their handkerchiefs. She was laughing, almost hysterically.

"I'll be back in a minute," she said, and went off toward the bathroom.

"What happened?" said Ham Bledsole, who had rushed over himself when he saw the commotion. Skinner was behind him.

Willie was shaking his head. By now most people had returned to their conversations. Willie began explaining, then thought better of it and waved his hands. "Hell, forget it," he said crossly. "I shouldn't be let into places like this."

Ham began to chuckle. "Sounds like something I'd do," he said. "Listen, go get yourself another drink. I have to tend to some things."

"Sounds like a good idea," Skinner said. He and Willie made their way back to the bar.

"Just met a fellow who's involved in an oil syndicate up there," Skinner said. "Told me something very interesting."

"What's that?" Willie said.

"Says he's heard the majors are about ready to come out with a big offer to your people—real big."

"They are, huh?" Willie said.

"See what that means, don't you?" Skinner said. His eyes were wide and greedy behind the thick lenses.

"Not exactly . . ." Willie said.

"If they're going to make a move like that, it's a last-ditch gamble. And it's because they know damned good and well what they've got up there and are willing to pay a lot to get at it. Isn't just random speculation. They know."

"I don't see how they can make an offer," Willie said. "I mean, since our people don't even have clear titles yet. All that's to come."

"Look," Skinner said, "don't make any difference to them. If an oil company makes a deal, then they can start to drill right away, you see, and let the rough end drag. Don't matter to them if there's a court fight or not. In the end, whoever winds up with the title is bound to sell the rights to them anyway—meantime they've started pumping oil."

"So?" Willie said.

"So that's exactly what I want us to do. Tell the oil companies to go to hell and start drilling ourselves. Gives us a leg up."

"Hummmmmmm," Willie said, "I see what you mean." The barman gave him his drink and he noticed Whitsey returning through the door from the hallway, accompanied by a tall man in a pinstriped three-piece suit with a gold watch chain. He was tanned and clean-featured with dark hair, a lawyerly-looking man, but Willie had never seen him around before.

Willie watched from the corner of his eye as they joined some other guests. Skinner went off to intercept the hors d'oeuvres tray and Willie, after a minute or two alone, began to shrink back into a corner, all the while keeping an eye on Whitsey and the handsome young man. They seemed to be a couple now. He considered going over and apologizing again, but something kept him from it. He hoped she would come over to him, but she didn't, and, almost without noticing it, he shrank farther and farther back until he was standing alone in the corner. Time began to swim by without meaning and the conversation of the others faded into a dull, unharmonious blur.

He had been standing there for quite a while when a hand touched his arm and a voice asked, "Aren't you having a good time?" A tallish young woman in a black dress was at his side. She was tanned and athletic-looking, with long, wavy black hair and dark brown eyes and a lipstick smear on her prominent but well-formed and sparkling teeth.

"Wha . . . ?" he said, almost startled, then, "Oh, sure, I was just taking a breather."

"I'm Tallulah Bledsole," the girl said. "I don't think we've met."

"Oh," he said, "I'm Willie Croft. You're Ham's wife, then?" He was surprised because she couldn't have been more than twenty-five.

"His cousin," she said. "That's his wife over there." She pointed toward an older woman in a long green dress talking with other people.

"Why are you standing all by yourself?" Tallulah Bledsole asked.

"Just passing time," Willie said. "I don't know too many people here."

"Are you a friend of Ham's—you must be."

"Yeah, we hunt together sometimes."

"Oh, he loves that—oh!" she said brightly, with recognition, "you're not the one he talks about—he went with you a week or so ago, right?"

"Yeah, we did. Went up the river."

"He says you're great. You're a great shot. You're a lawyer, right—you're the one who had an argument with Percy Holt at the Azalea Ball. I remember now."

"Were you there?"

"No, I was out of town but everybody's talking about it. You hit him, or he hit you, or something, didn't he?"

"Something," Willie said.

"Well," she said, "just between you and me, I always thought he had it coming. He's so loud and obnoxious."

"Maybe so," Willie said. He was looking in Whitsey's direction again.

"Why don't you come over here with me and meet some

people," Tallulah said. "Bring your drink." She took him by the arm and led him to a group standing by the window. These people, Willie thought, are always taking you by the arm and leading you somewhere. But there wasn't much he could do about it.

It was a jovial group, three or four couples in their late twenties or early thirties; red-faced men with whiskey glasses and women who most likely spent their days on golf courses and tennis courts and driving children around in station wagons. Tallulah Bledsole, thank God, did not introduce him as the man who slugged Percy Holt, so the handshaking went off quickly and without comment. A horsey-looking girl with honey-blond hair had been telling a story and recapped the beginning for Willie.

"I was saying," she said, "about the time I went upstate for a wedding and at the rehearsal party one of the girls kept telling about how bad the cockroaches were in their apartment. So I spoke up and told them about the roaches here, that they got about *this* long"—she measured a length with her fingers of nearly three inches—"and," the girl cackled, "she said, 'Well, you people in Bienville *always* have got something *bigger* and *better* than anybody else in the state!' "

There were peals of laughter at this and Willie joined in, though he didn't really feel as though he belonged to the joke. He was distantly aware that Bienville, being older and presumably more sophisticated, had purposely and snobbishly separated itself from the other towns and cities, but he, himself, did not know about such things firsthand.

One of the men in the group began telling an anti-Semitic joke and Willie again stole a glance toward Whitsey. The lawyerly-looking man had his arm around her now, and Willie couldn't tell if he was merely holding her tightly or if she was snuggling close to him. This annoyed him immensely and he began to sweat. Tallulah Bledsole leaned close.

"You look like you need some fresh air," she said. "Want to go out back?"

"Yeah, that'd be nice," he said, grateful and a little relieved. She led the way through French doors that opened onto a terrace. It was a warm, misty night and the bricks were damp with deep-green mossy furrows between their cracks. A gaslight flickered at one end of the lawn, illuminating the gray Spanish moss that hung from the oaks. A stone path led through shrubbery toward what appeared in the darkness to be a pool. They walked down the path a little ways and the din of the party faded behind them.

"Are you still seeing Whitsey?" Tallulah asked.

"No, I guess not," he said miserably. "We just went out a couple of times."

"I heard you two were together at the Azalea Ball. I'd forgotten, but I remember now. Have you lived in Bienville long?"

"All my life," Willie said.

"Really?" she said. "That's funny. We've never met."

"I haven't met anyone here to speak of," he said. "It's a different world."

"From what?"

"From what I'm used to."

"Which is . . . ?" she asked. She had beautiful soft eyes and a lithe, elegant figure. She looked as though she'd be good in bed. Almost automatically he checked himself from such thoughts. They seemed dirty. Here was a dignified young girl—a woman, perhaps—but probably half his age and maybe less than half his age. It had been a long time since he had had so young a woman.

"It's just different, that's all," he said. "I grew up differently. My family, ah . . . well, I've just never been a part of this group."

"What group are you a part of?"

"Is there more than one?"

"I suppose there are," she said. "The different societies all have different people who belong to them. The yacht club crowd, and golf and all . . . sort of overlap. I guess in the end, though, it's just one big group."

"I didn't know that," he said. "Do you apply for membership?"

She looked at him strangely for an instant, then smiled. "All right, I'm sorry, I guess it sounded like I'm a snob."

"A little," he said, "but I'm getting used to it."

"How did you know Ham?" she asked.

"I met him at . . . the dance, through Whitsey."

"Nice, isn't he? He's my favorite cousin."

"He's very nice," Willie said.

Suddenly she stopped. "It's getting a little chilly; do you want to go back inside?"

"Sure." He walked behind her along the path toward the house. Inside the lights were warm and bright and the sounds of gaiety wafted across the lawn. Tallulah's backside jiggled invitingly ahead of him but he kept a lid on his desires. He had already decided she had only been checking him out, and that he'd probably failed the test.

Back inside, Willie saw Skinner engrossed in conversation. Whitsey was nowhere to be seen. He returned Tallulah to her group and excused himself to go to the bathroom. The Negro doorman pointed him up the stairs. He passed two closed doors and stopped at a room with the door open, thinking it might be the bathroom.

It was not.

It was a bedroom with a pile of coats on the bed, and one dim table lamp in a corner, and a man and a woman standing near the door with their arms twisted around each other. They both looked up as he stood silhouetted in the pale light, Whitsey Loftin and the lawyerly-looking man in the three-piece suit.

Willie was too stunned and embarrassed to say anything and had already begun to back out of the doorway when she called out, "Oh! Willie—come here."

Like a child obeying a command he stepped back into the room and felt his face begin to flush.

"I'd like you to meet Emile Montague—Emile, this is Willie Croft," she said.

173

The man extended his hand. "I think I've seen you around."

Willie tried not to look at her, afraid she might see hurt in his face. "Down at the courthouse, maybe; I spend a lot of time there."

"No, I don't think so—somewhere downtown—at Traylor's maybe?"

"That's probably it," Willie said. "I go to lunch there a lot."

"Are you all right—from that thing you ate?" Whitsey said. "I didn't see you when I came back. Where did you go?"

"I was around," he said. "I went outside for a while."

It's because you didn't look, he thought sourly.

"Emile and I grew up together," Whitsey said. "When we were children we used to go to all the same birthday parties. I haven't seen him in years—he's only been back for a few months. He's been living in New Orleans. . . ."

Willie felt a little better. At least she was attempting an explanation. Montague, he thought. New Orleans. The Montague Steamship Company.

"I was looking for the bathroom."

"Next door down," Montague said cheerfully.

Again, Willie turned to go, then said to Whitsey, "Can I see you a minute?"

She glanced at Emile Montague, then stepped outside the door into the hallway.

"I got a letter from the court that lists me as your aunt's attorney. Are you sure you still want that?"

"Of course," Whitsey said. "Why do you ask? Why wouldn't I?"

"Just wanted to make sure," he said. "It's coming up for a hearing in a few weeks."

"That soon?"

"Well, it's only a preliminary hearing. Each side makes arguments then. It's got a long way to go."

She nodded and glanced over her shoulder into the bedroom where Emile Montague was biding his time.

"Look, I'm sorry," she said. "I really wanted to see you. Can I call you next week?"

"Call me anytime," he said. "You know where I am."

She gave his hand a squeeze and went back into the bedroom, leaving him in the hallway to figure out what she meant.

13

CHRISTMAS NIGHT, WILLIE AND SKINNER WENT TO SEE DANIEL Holt, who had suggested they come over to his house and talk after Willie told him Skinner had a proposal that would require serious consideration. He had not gone into detail. That afternoon he and Skinner had Christmas dinner in the only downtown restaurant that was open. Bland turkey and dressing and mashed potatoes were the special of the day, and they had washed it down with red wine, and Skinner had also ordered beer.

They had discussed what approach to take when talking to Daniel Holt. Willie was more than a little skeptical of Skinner's plan, but it seemed so far-fetched it intrigued him, and it wouldn't hurt for Daniel to hear about it and go back to the others and let them make up their minds. Democracy.

In late afternoon, back home, he had watched the last quarter of a dull football game on television and when *The Bells of St. Mary's* came on afterward he turned off the set because he had watched that movie every Christmas for the past five years and it depressed him now.

He filled a glass with ice and Early Times and went down to the park across the street. On the sidewalks children were playing with Christmas toys and the streets were lined with the cars of people paying Christmas visits to friends and relatives. It was warm outside and he needed only a sweater. The sun was low and cast a burnished glow over the park, the light filtering down through the gnarled branches of the oaks. Willie sat on the bench across from the Iron Deer and sipped his whiskey.

Directly before him was a giant oak, larger than any other in the park, or for that matter on any of the surrounding streets so far as he knew. The great-granddaddy oak from which all the others had probably derived, spored about the time the first Holt ancestors arrived, spreading each decade with an irretrievable secondary growth, its long knotted limbs snaking out across the park, its bark grown tougher than the skin of any prehistoric beast, climbing for the light, shutting it out for the others.

Now, in its old age, the oak had fallen victim to its relentless greed for supremacy.

The huge branches, tentacled out twenty or thirty yards in every direction, were so heavy they had begun to fall under their own enormous weight, ripping gigantic gashes in the side of the ivy-covered trunk. The crotches of the limbs had now filled with green parasitic lichens, damp and rotting, the branches weighted even more with the clinging Spanish moss. The roots of the old oak had become barren as soil beneath it was washed away from lack of ground cover, for it had shut out the light even for that. As the other oaks began to grow it had extended itself still farther to get at the light until it had tilted its entire trunk westward, pulling up roots and earth; now it was merely a matter of time before it uprooted itself completely and died.

Willie reached for a Picayune. Well, he thought, maybe it had lived too long anyway, grown too big. Time to give the other trees a chance. He tried to imagine what would happen in Bienville if Skinner's plan actually worked. A far-fetched proposition, he thought, but it would shake a lot of things around here. Sure would. The big oak tree glowered over him like a sullen monster.

Two hours later Willie was riding in the passenger seat of Skinner's rented Cadillac, guiding him through narrow, empty streets of colored town, past bare and shabby row houses, some lit by strings of Christmas lights in green, red and blue. Occasionally they glimpsed a Christmas tree through a half-pulled shade. Toys had all been opened, dinner served and the relations gone home: the gloomy letdown of Christmas night, like a Sunday. Tomorrow would be a working day.

"Turn here," Willie said. He was looking at a set of directions Daniel Holt had given him over the telephone. Skinner eased the big car onto the wide avenue that was the main thoroughfare for this part of town. It was cluttered with pawnshops, storefronts and honky-tonks, most of them dark. Two white policemen were herding a party of brawlers into a precinct station, four men and two women. The women screamed obscenities at the men.

"All right," Willie said after they had gone another four or five blocks, "I think it's here; turn right." They went into an unpaved, darkened street lined with narrow, shotgun houses, and where the street came to a dead end they turned around. "Here it is: white house, blue Ford out front," he said.

Willie went to the door and knocked. He saw a curtain being drawn back. He waited a moment, then knocked again; this time the door opened a crack and a small, thin woman peered out at them.

"You Mr. Croft?" she asked.

"Yes, and this is Mr. Skinner."

The door opened and the woman let them in.

"You must be Mrs. Holt," Willie said.

She did not answer, but as she turned, Daniel Holt appeared in a doorway.

"Hello, Mr. Croft," he said, "please come in."

Willie introduced Skinner; Daniel nodded but did not offer his hand. He showed them into a small living room in the corner of which was a small Christmas tree. Wrapping papers from a half-dozen presents lay beneath it and from somewhere in the back of the house they heard children's laughter.

"Can I get you something to drink—a cup of coffee, or

some tea?" Daniel asked. Willie started to decline when Skinner boorishly requested a beer.

Daniel Holt's face showed a flash of embarrassed surprise from which he quickly recovered. "Beer, why, yes, of course, we can have a beer. Just a minute." He left the room and could be heard in discussion with his wife in low, whispering tones, after which they heard the back door slam. Then he returned.

"We will have some beer directly," he said, and offered Skinner and Willie seats on the sofa while he eased himself into a large chair.

"Daniel," Willie said, "Mr. Skinner has come up with an idea, a plan, that I think you should know about and perhaps put to the others." He looked at Skinner, who had picked up a small toy race car and was spinning its wheels in the palm of his hand.

"It's sort of daring," Willie continued, "but there's a possibility it might bring in a great deal more money than what we are trying to do now—if it works." Again he turned to Skinner. "You can explain it better than me," Willie said.

Skinner looked up at Daniel Holt, who was leaning back in his tattered chair packing his pipe. The demeanor in the room was formal and imposing. In other circumstances it might have been a board meeting of some large corporation.

"All right," Skinner said, leaning forward, "here's what I think you ought to do. You people ought to start pumping oil."

He let that statement sink in for a few moments, then began outlining his opinions of the situation and opportunities for direct exploration by the Obsidian Oil Corporation.

"What you got now, you see, isn't really an oil company, it's more a real-estate company," Skinner said. "All you're doing is trying to buy up and sell off leases. There's a gamble in what I'm suggesting, but life's a gamble. Want to make real money, then go into the oil business and stop pissing around. Otherwise, I'll tell you just what I told Croft here: hold out for a little bit longer—a few months maybe—then sell the leases to the majors. Won't make everybody millionaires, but it'll bring in some good money."

Daniel listened silently and attentively through Skinner's sales pitch, his pipe giving off clouds of blue smoke. When Skinner had finished, Daniel asked the question that had obviously been on his mind since the conversation began.

"What if it doesn't work, Mr. Skinner? What if there's not any oil up there, or the court says we can't drill, or if . . ."

"Listen," Skinner said masterfully, "life is filled with 'what ifs.' I've heard them since I was a kid. My old man was a 'what if' man, and all it ever got him was owning half of a second-rate dry goods store near Homer, South Carolina." Skinner paused, looking balefully sincere. "There's always a chance something can go wrong," he continued. "Everything for that matter: the court could issue some kind of injunction to keep us from starting, or the majors or somebody else'll figure some way to stop us from drilling, steal the damned equipment or foul it up—or there might not be any oil down there. Who in hell knows? But life's a gamble, Mr. Holt. You can walk out on the street tomorrow and get hit by a falling piano. What I'm saying is, do you want to gamble a little, or do you want to take the money and run?"

"Let me tell you," Daniel began, reaching for a match to relight his pipe, "that your idea has already been discussed. Not in detail, you understand, but Miller, who's got about sixty acres just below the school-board property, used to work on an oil platform off Louisiana. He suggested pretty much what you did one night a few weeks ago when we had a meeting up there in the church. The response at first was not unfavorable, but then, as we talked about it, it was evident nobody knew exactly how to go about it. Miller said he could maybe set up the rigs all right, and keep them working, but he wasn't sure how to get the equipment, or where to put it, or what to do with the oil. After a while, we just drifted away from the subject and on to something else."

Daniel leaned forward in his chair and put his pipe down.

"But you seem to me to know what you're talking about, Mr. Skinner. And Mr. Croft seems to trust you, because he brought you here. Quite honestly, I don't know what to think about it. We are not wealthy people, you know. Most of us just get by the best way we can, and the money we might get for selling the land would be more than we have ever known. Quite frankly, I have wondered many times if we have not already overstepped our bounds just by trying to set up this company." He stopped for a moment and gazed pensively at the little Christmas tree, its lights blinking on and off, some of them burned out. Willie and Skinner exchanged brief, uneasy glances.

"You know," Daniel continued, "times are beginning to change for the colored man down here. It's hard to see it now, but we notice it, just in little ways. We can sit down on the buses where there's a seat now, and we can get ourselves a sandwich or a Coca-Cola at a lunch counter, and our children can play in the public parks even if they can't get into the white people's schools. There are a few better jobs than there were ten years ago and I think we're not so afraid to do things as we used to be—but something like this . . ." His voice trailed off. There was a silence in the room. From somewhere in the back of the house the sound of children playing could be heard faintly. Daniel Holt seemed to be in deep contemplation for long, agonizing seconds, then resumed.

"I am not a pusher or a mover," he said, not in the manner of an apology, but as though they might better understand his position, "and I suppose I am basically ignorant of the business intricacies that might go into setting up something like Mr. Skinner is suggesting. However, we should put it to the others, and see what they say. It sounds like we could be taking a great chance, but then I suppose we are taking a chance merely by trying to stick together and not sell the leases off, 'every man for himself.'"

Willie lighted a Picayune and leaned forward. He had been debating whether or not to speak up, and finally decided that he must, for he was as ambivalent about Skinner's proposal as Daniel Holt, and possibly more so.

"I ought to tell you where I stand on this thing," he said.

"With all respect to Mr. Skinner, it's a new idea, and it strikes me, also, as being somewhat dangerous. I haven't had time to study it closely—the legal ramifications, I mean. What worries me is that anyone filing a claim for the land against any of your people might be able to walk in and get an injunction against drilling and setting up rigs. Then we'd be stuck with all this equipment and it could cost a fortune."

"Been working on that one," Skinner interrupted. "I know a guy who's about finished a job in Kansas. Got about twenty-five or thirty rigs that's about to be moved to storage. He's a pretty savvy fellow, name of Horner. Now he's got to get them rigs on trucks anyway, so suppose I call him and tell him just to bring 'em down here instead? Bet I can get him to work on a percentage or something, so it won't cost anything until the wells start coming in. We worry about the trucks and all that other crap later. Take things one step at a time."

Willie considered this for a moment. "That sounds pretty good," he said, "but I still think we'd be taking a bit of a chance."

"Could be the chance of a lifetime," Skinner said merrily.

In the car, as they made their way back toward the white side of town, Skinner said to Willie, "You think they'll go for it?"

"I don't have the faintest idea," Willie said. "And I'm not sure they should. This whole thing seems to be getting out of hand."

"Listen here," Skinner said firmly, "it was out of hand the second they found oil up there. One of two things are going to happen—either the goddamn court is going to award them titles or it isn't. If it does, then we'd be on firm ground to drill, right? If it doesn't, then it's all been a waste of time anyway. You got the damned Black Muslims bankrolling this, haven't you? Then use their money. I told you, it's the difference between making some tidy dough and getting out, or having more damned money than anybody's dreamed of."

"What do you expect to get out of all this?" Willie asked, remembering that he hadn't even inquired what Skinner was charging in the way of a fee.

"Not much," Skinner said. "Usual fee's a hundred bucks a day and expenses, including the car, and if it works, maybe a share or two. I don't give a shit about getting to be a millionaire. I got enough money already. Get things started up and going good, then I'll be moving on. Don't like sticking around a place too long. Besides, I been thinking that after this I might get into gold."

"Gold?" Willie said.

"Why not?" Skinner replied. "There's gold in the ground in this country nobody ever thought about. Someday it's going to be worth a lot more than anybody ever dreamed of. There's plenty of oil, too much. Hellfire, I'm getting tired of oil."

They rode in silence for a while. Then Willie said, "You know, I haven't told you this, but we haven't even cleared you with that bank yet. There wasn't any mention of a consultant. I'm not altogether positive they'll stand for paying your fee."

"Don't make any difference," Skinner said. "I'll work on spec for a while. Got confidence in this, Croft. I seen those charts. There's oil there and plenty of it, I'll bet. I ain't worried. You pay me when you can."

Everything about Skinner exuded reassurance. Willie was profoundly happy he was no longer in this alone.

Willie climbed the outside stairs to his garage apartment and turned on the light in the kitchen. It was just past 9:00 P.M. and he was feeling a little hungry. There wasn't much in the refrigerator; he considered a leftover stew that Priscilla had made about a week before, took off the lid of the bowl and put it back, making a mental note to tell Priscilla to throw it out in the morning. He decided to have a peanut butter sandwich, but after he had gotten out two slices of bread he discovered there was barely a small spoonful of peanut butter in the jar. The ducks he had shot were frozen solid and he didn't want to bother with them anyway. Meantime, he mixed himself a stiff bourbon and water and was contemplating what he might scrape up for supper when the phone rang. It was Tallulah Bledsole.

"Merry Christmas—I didn't call too late, did I?" she said apologetically.

"Certainly not," Willie said. "Merry Christmas to you."

"How was your day?" she asked. "Did you get a lot of presents?"

The purpose of this call baffled Willie. Furthermore, he did not know how to answer the last question without sounding maudlin or pathetic.

"Well," he said with required jocularity, "not *too* many." It occurred to him just then that he had not given any presents either, except a ten-dollar tip to Priscilla, which really didn't count. As a matter of fact, he had neither given nor received any presents for Christmas since his folks had died and probably wouldn't even have thought about it if Tallulah hadn't brought it up.

"Did you have a big Christmas dinner?" she asked. "I bet you're stuffed like a pig."

"Yes, it was nice," he said uneasily.

"With your family?" she persisted. "These things always go on forever."

"Actually I ate with my friend; you remember him, the one from the party—Ham's old pal from school, V. D. Skinner."

"Oh," she said, with an inflection of puzzled understanding, "well, I hope it was a nice dinner—all the trimmings."

"Yes," he said, "it was very nice." It began to dawn on Willie that Tallulah was making some kind of social call to him. His pulse suddenly fluttered with excitement. "How was your day?" he said.

"Really nice," she said. "We were all at Uncle Tommy's, and Ham and I talked about you a lot. He really likes you. He couldn't stop talking about that hunting trip y'all went on," Tallulah said sweetly.

"He was good to have along," Willie said. "We're going to have to do it again."

"Listen!" she said. "There's a New Year's Eve party at Serena and Jack Pierce's. Would you like to go with me?"

Willie's pulse raced again. The idea of *those* parties, like the Azalea Ball, and the party at Ham's, was uncomfortable agony in so many ways but, having had a taste, something in him now wanted to be a part of them too. And besides, he was flattered and excited that Tallulah had asked him, though he hadn't the slightest notion why she would, with all the eligible young guys around.

Without appreciable hesitation he said, "That sound's very nice," and made arrangements to firm up a time. After they hung up, he fixed himself another bourbon and water and decided to forgo supper. He had two more drinks before going to bed, and slept as peacefully as a baby.

Next morning Willie followed his Groundman schedule for after weekends and holidays. Finishing breakfast at Swampman Charley's Diner he went straight to the courthouse and secured the release of a depressing assortment of petty criminals, miscreants and drunken mischief-makers. Then he went to his office where several messages awaited him.

Daniel Holt had phoned, wondering if it would be possible for him to come up to Creoletown that evening for a meeting at the church. Also, Skinner had left a terse and unsatisfying message that he would be out of town for a few days, and Willie did not know what to make of that. And, Strop Clark at the city license bureau had phoned him. He immediately returned the call.

"Strop," he said, "what you got for me?"

"Got this off the tax bureau," Strop said. "Here it is: Crenshaw works as a longshoreman for Holt Stevedoring. Worked there about six years. No wife or children. Made seven thousand two hundred and seventy-six dollars last year."

"Anything else?"

"That's all they got, Mr. Croft."

"Thanks, Strop," Willie said. "I owe you one. By the way, how were those ducks?"

"Just great, Mr. Croft. We had one a couple of days ago. Guess we'll have the other this week."

Since he was going to Creoletown anyway to see Daniel Holt, Willie thought it would be a good time to visit Mrs. Loftin too. He decided not to phone her first, but simply to drive to her place, figuring she probably wouldn't remember who he was over the phone and that seeing him might jog her memory.

He had drawn up several documents to counter the Holts' incompetency proceedings and would need her signature on these. Actually, he held little hope for success once the matter came to court because any jury who got a look at her on the stand would swiftly conclude she was a nut. The papers he had with him were a stalling action to give them a little time, in case something providential might intervene.

It was a dry, graying day and the weather had turned cold again. This was the winter cycle in Bienville: rain one day, warm fog the next, warm sunshine the next, then cold, then rain again. Once out of town there was little traffic on the roads, only an occasional farmer's pickup or an empty school bus. Wind bent and waved the broomstraw in the open countryside and a flock of fat doves were scattered in a stubble field.

Willie, however, was preoccupied with the information he had received from Strop Clark. Even though he had suspected some kind of Holt involvement in the burning of Mrs. Backus's house, he was not fully prepared for this incontrovertible proof—incontrovertible for him, anyway, but perhaps not enough to stand up in a formal charge, unless of course this Crenshaw could be found and made to talk. But at the very least there was enough to connect the Holts with murder and arson.

How to use it? Willie wondered. It might be the key to his problem. The police had not been put on notice to look for an arsonist. Even so, and if they picked up Crenshaw, what would they have? The fact that his car was seen in the vicinity of the Backus place about the time it burned, and that he worked for the Holts, and that the Holts had much to gain by eliminating Mrs. Backus.

All circumstantial.

The Holts probably had somebody in the sheriff's office in their pocket anyhow, and after a few hours' interrogation, Crenshaw would reveal nothing and the matter would be forgotten. On the other hand, if Willie's information were to be brought before the Holts themselves, it might be all it would take to get them to lay off Mrs. Backus.

What he was considering at this very moment was an act that might cost him his professional career—concealing information of a felony, and possible blackmail.

Whatever failures or lack of accomplishment had marked his life thus far, he at least had been scrupulously ethical in his practice. In fact, the first and last crime he had committed had been at the age of eleven when he had stolen a sackful of kumquats off a neighbor's tree. It was an incident he would never forget. When the neighbor had come shrieking and complaining to his doorstep, his old man, whiskey glass in hand, had gone out and taken up for him, pointing out that people who maintained kumquat trees in their yards should not be surprised when little boys came around and picked them. The neighbor had been a squat, gray-haired woman of dour eccentricity, with a reputation for disliking children.

Even before Willie was born, she had installed around her house a special corrugated concrete sidewalk which resembled an enormous washboard—merely to prevent children from roller skating, the noise therefrom she claimed was disturbing. But so eloquent was his father's defense over the kumquat theft that the woman was forced to retire in embarrassment. Willie's elation, however, was short-lived. The old man had first lectured him, then beat him with a switch.

Of course it was not a bag of kumquats he was dealing with now but a deliberate plan of extortion to force the relinquishment of a claim by withholding possible evidence of arson and murder from the police.

It was a vague sort of crime, Willie knew, for no punishment, even if it could be inflicted, could bring back the life of the old crazy woman who burned to death, and the Holts' claim on the property would not be altered even if they were caught. On the other hand, he reasoned, it might be fitting justice if the Holts were forced to give up their claims in exchange for saving their family name from scandal and disgrace.

Yet this was not the law. The law said otherwise, justice or not. The law would require Willie to turn in his ace-high hand for two pairs and to draw again, possibly against a stacked deck. He knew damned well what Augustus Tompkins and the Holts would do under similar circumstances, but that did not relieve him of responsibility. He was an attorney-at-law, which he considered a respectable profession. All of this he would have to ponder in the coming days.

He turned off the main road and wound up the lane to Mrs. Loftin's house. The trees were bare and the garden bleak. The house looked shuttered and closed. He pulled into the gravel drive and honked the horn, then walked to the door and knocked. Moments passed, then he saw a drapery pulled back and a face peered out at him from a window. More moments passed, then there was the sound of a lock being turned and the door opened. Mrs. Loftin greeted him with a smile, dressed in a long velvet robe and a wide-brimmed hat with paper flowers sewn onto the brim. In this strange costume she looked gaily demented.

"Oh, hello, hello, Mr. . . . ."

"Croft," Willie said, as she ushered him inside.

"I was wondering when you were going to come back," she said. Willie was highly surprised that she even remembered him, let alone that he was due back.

"Have you had your lunch?" she asked.

"Oh, no, thank you, ma'am—I mean, yes, I have." It was a little past 1:00 P.M. but he had decided not to eat any lunch today.

"I was just having . . . a little drink." She giggled. "Would you like one—or some tea?"

Willie shifted uneasily as he looked at the glass in her

hand. It appeared to be straight, undiluted bourbon whiskey.

She must have noticed the look on his face, for she smiled and said, "It's just some sherry. Come into the sitting room and I'll get you a glass."

He stood while Mrs. Loftin went to a cabinet in the far corner and poured a generous glass of sherry from a decanter, handed it to him and motioned him into the big leather chair. She then curled herself up on a large sofa opposite him, looking, in the flowered hat and gown, like a weird imitation of Sarah Bernhardt.

"It's about that dreadful business of the oil and my niece and nephews, isn't it, Mr. Croft?"

"Well, yes," Willie said, further astonished that she understood why he had come.

"Oh!" she cried. "It gives me such pain. You know, before Johnathan died, he said to me, 'Sister, I am going to give you charge of my part of this property over my children because I know how you love it so. You're the only one who does.' I think that's in his will, too. Now see what they're trying to do. They want to have me put away! The nerve! The gall!"

Her eyes were bright and shining fiercely as she sipped her sherry. It occurred to Willie that this must be one of her "good" days.

"Well, Mr. Croft, what do you think I should do about it?"

Willie was not really prepared for this kind of conversation, but he managed. "I've brought you some papers to sign, Mrs. Loftin. Essentially, what they do is deny to the court that you can't control the property any longer, and ask the court to quash the motion for a certification of incompetence."

"Squash what?"

"Ah, quash, Mrs. Loftin—that means to throw out—your nephews' request that you be relieved of control of this property."

"And don't forget my niece—Marci's her name—a shrill girl—she's right in it with them."

"Yes, your niece too," Willie said.

"So they say I can't control this place anymore, do they?"

the old woman said with a cackle. "Well, I've controlled it for almost nineteen years, and I expect I'll control it nineteen more, if I don't die first."

"That's only the allegation in the court papers," Willie said. "You see, they believe—and I'll try to state their position for them—that you should allow the sale of oil leases up here and . . ."

"Yes, yes, I know what they say." She waved him off. "As if they all haven't got enough money already! Now they want more. Well, they'll get it soon enough, but not off this place in my lifetime. Not if I have anything to say about it." Her eyes were dark and piercing and her wrinkled face set in stern determination.

"Do you know when I first came up here?" she said. "It was in nineteen hundred and eighteen, just after the world war. Mr. Loftin had heard that one of the things they needed over there in Europe was lumber, and he had this little sawmill near Creoletown, and he arranged that the American ships going over empty to pick up our boys after the war could have free ballast of the lumber from this mill— dunnage, I think they called it. And he went into a partnership with a man in England, and when the ships got there, and put on the troops, they took off the lumber and they sold it over there. They made quite a bit of money in those days, and they began to buy up more of these sawmills. At one time I think he owned over a hundred of them."

The old woman's face was serene now, as though she were living the story as she told it.

"But all that was later," she continued. "When we first moved up here, we had to live in a tent, near one of the mills. Oh, it was a nice tent, with boards on the floor and mosquito netting, and the sides rolled up, and we even had some furniture. We lived here for a year, and then, when he was buying some of the other mills, we would move the tent nearer to them, until he could set things up.

"Finally, we got together enough money so we could start building this place right here, on a piece of my father's land that he had given to my brother Johnathan and me. It took nearly three years to get it finished and forty years of keeping it up and making it nice."

She turned and swept her arm across the broad French windows that overlooked the garden out back and the meadows and fields beyond them.

"Do you see those fields there, Mr. Croft? In the fall, they turn absolutely golden, and in the spring they're full of buttercups and daisies. And did you see the azaleas when you drove in? Aren't they big and tall? Well, I put in every one of those myself, and the japonica and the poinsettia too, and the jasmine. It's taken them forty years, forty years with my care, for them to grow that way. Did you know that before we had running water up here, I'd go out every single day in summer with a bucket and water them. Sometimes it took all afternoon!"

Willie nodded and sipped his sherry. He was afraid the old lady was working herself up.

"And on Sundays we would always go for a drive around the property, in the afternoons. And sometimes Mr. Loftin and I would get out of the car and walk down in the woods or to the little pond back off the blacktop road, and sit there, and he'd say, 'Oh, Hannah, this is such a nice place.' He wouldn't even allow them to timber on it.

"Forty years," she cried, "and now they want me to put those oil things up all over my lawn!"

Willie searched for a way to soften her a little. She seemed nearly lucid now, but he supposed she'd slip back into the fog in court.

"Well, Mrs. Loftin, I don't think they would actually be on your lawn. As an alternative, I could suggest that you might work out some scheme so the Holt family got their land divided but you get a cleared-away area round your house and for as much distance as you want where there would be no drilling. It might serve you better in the long run to compromise a little and avoid a rather nasty scene in court."

"I'll do no such a thing!" she barked. "I'm sick and tired of them. All of them. Brevard, coming up here so high-handed just like John Jacob Astor, and telling me what I have to do! I've lived on this place half of my life and very comfortably too, thank you. This is my home! Johnathan gave them all they could ever want—that company in Bienville, the other property in town, a good family name and upbringing. That's the trouble with the young these days. They all want too much money before they deserve it. Whatever land is up here is mine until I die and I'll be the one to decide what's done with it, and when!"

"Yes, ma'am," Willie said placatingly. He was more than a little impressed by the clarity of her argument.

"I don't often swear, Mr. Croft," she said, "but it's going to be a cold day in hell when they have me put away." She took a large gulp of the sherry.

"I don't think that's what they're after," Willie said. "I think all they want is to force you to split up the land now."

"Well, I'm not, and that's final. And if they want to have it out, then that's just what I'm going to do!"

"Well," he said, "then you'd better sign these papers so I can file them tomorrow."

She accepted the sheaf of papers and began examining them.

"Would you like me to read them to you?" Willie asked.

Mrs. Loftin regarded Willie over her nose, in an amused and faintly condescending manner. "Young man," she said, "I am perfectly capable of reading myself. However, since I expect this is just so much lawyer's mumbo jumbo I shall trust that you are doing the proper thing. Where do I sign?"

Willie indicated the spaces. "What will probably happen next," he said, "is that you will receive instructions to be interviewed by a psychiatrist appointed by the court. My advice would be for you to obtain a psychiatrist of our own, the sooner the better, and file his report first. Preferably someone from another town, who hasn't any possible interest in the matters at hand."

"A psychiatrist!" Mrs. Loftin said distastefully. "Some stranger to decide if I'm crazy? I won't stand for it!"

"Mrs. Loftin," Willie said, "I'm afraid you'll have to. I

mean, if you're bent at this point on fighting the allegations against you, I can only advise you in the strongest terms to follow my plan."

"What if I refuse? What if I simply say I won't talk to one of these . . . *psychiatrists?*" She pronounced the word as though it were a dirty thing.

"Then," Willie said, "they will probably order you into court and put you in the witness chair and then the court's own psychiatrist will be allowed to interview you. He would present his findings to the court and the jury. I think it would make your case much stronger if we could get a psychiatrist of our own to talk to beforehand and file his opinion with the court as well. The reason is that if our psychiatrist says you are all right and the court psychiatrist says you aren't, at least we've created a difference of opinion and then I've got something to argue about. Otherwise, it's going to be a very one-sided affair. If the jury had a doubt put in its minds, it might be much more likely to side with you than with your nephews."

"And the niece," she reminded him. "Don't forget her."

"And the niece," Willie said.

She put her signature on the papers. When she had finished she handed them back to Willie.

"That Augustus Tompkins makes me sick," she said bitterly. "For twenty-five years he handled my affairs, such as they were, and now he's turned coat."

"He makes me sort of sick too," Willie said. "By the way, the last time I was up here, a month or so ago, I asked if you remembered your brother asking you to witness a paper deeding over a piece of property to Elvira Backus. Do you remember that?"

She thought for a moment. "Oh, yes, a long time ago, before the second war, I think. He came by. I remember it was a cold day, and raining, and I made him come in and take off his boots and sit by the fire. I do remember that."

"And you remember witnessing the deed?"

"Yes, I guess that's what it was. He said to me, 'Sister,

would you sign this?' and as I recall it was a paper with a map on it and he said he was going to give that place where Elvira lived to her and to her children. I told him I thought it was a nice thing to do."

"You're sure," Willie said, astounded.

"Certainly I'm sure," she said. "I signed it, didn't I?"

14

THERE WAS AN HOUR'S TIME BEFORE WILLIE'S MEETING WITH Daniel at the church, so he drove into the little village of Creoletown and found a café where he sat in a booth and ordered a slice of apple pie and a cup of coffee.

The waitress, fortyish, with sun-hardened skin and dry red hair piled on her head, hovered above his table.

"You one of them *awl* people?" she asked, setting the pie in front of him. Her inflection almost made Willie want to examine his flesh to make sure it wasn't black or greasy. She might have asked the same question of a person stepping out of a flying saucer.

"No, not really," he said.

"Well, there's been a lot up here lately," the waitress said. "I s'pose you heard about the *awl* and everything."

"Some," Willie said.

"An' about the niggers? Some people are sayin' the niggers are gonna own the *awl.*"

"Are they?" Willie said.

"Can you imagine that?" she said disdainfully. "They might get to be *millionaires*. You ever heard of a nigger *millionaire?*"

Willie suddenly remembered the Chicago banker,

Suliman Bey, and wondered if he was a millionaire. He doubted it.

"Nope," he said. "Couldn't imagine that in a million years."

Some were there, the rest were coming, as Willie stood in front of the little church talking with Daniel Holt. He had passed a few of them on the road, most on foot, wearing faded overalls and worn boots and cheap flannel or denim shirts. Others came in battered pickups or rusted Fords and Chevys; they were poor men, dirt poor, who scratched out their lives on barren, wasted farmland or by working for the few white men in the area, walking or riding as many as twenty miles for eight- or ten-dollar-a-day jobs, and in the wintertime, damned glad to get even that much to feed and clothe the family. The faces filing into the church house were tired, lined by the sun, wind and cold and by worry and fear; calloused hands grasped pew fronts and lowered the men into their seats. Willie suddenly thought of old Ben Crow on the hunting trip with his father, his black face set in stern determination as he leaped over the rail fence to chase down the opossum with a stick because he couldn't afford to waste even a single shotgun shell on it. He studied the faces again, some close to his own age, many older, in their fifties and sixties, expectant, illiterate and hopeful, and he wondered how much they would understand of what he was going to try to tell to them.

He sat at a table in the front of the church with Daniel Holt and his partners: Garley, who ran the country store, Hooper of the funeral home, Brinson, a restaurant owner in the city, Brown, who owned the Ghana Motel. Daniel glanced at his watch, then stood ceremoniously and introduced Willie, who gazed at the sea of expectant faces before him and began trying to explain Skinner's plan and how it might affect them.

There was no reason under the sun, he thought, why they should trust him, but nevertheless he went ahead.

When he finished, he asked if there were any questions. He'd expected a great many, but there were none.

Either he'd put it all perfectly or they didn't understand a word of what he'd asked them—the gist of which was whether or not they wanted oil rigs drilling on their property as fast as Skinner could set them up, in exchange for shares in the Obsidian Oil Corporation. Willie had described it as a sort of cooperative venture, "like we were sharecropping your places and then taking the whole load to a market someplace else, except you're paid part in money and part in stock in the company."

"All I can tell you," he had said finally, "is that if it works, you're going to be rich as Croesus. If it doesn't, you're just back where you started. But the only way to make it go is for everybody to pull together. Otherwise everybody'll get picked off bits and pieces."

He felt as though he'd told it all without much enthusiasm. What he needed was Skinner's ebullient persuasiveness. He had picked a fine time to take off, Willie thought—and without any explanation either.

Daniel Holt took the floor again and addressed the little flock before him. Speaking for himself, he said, and the others on the board of Obsidian Oil, the plan was a good idea and he hoped they would consent to it. There were, of course, legal details to be worked out, papers to be signed, deeds and titles to be searched, but all of this could be done later with Mr. Croft. What was needed now was a show of hands either for or against the drilling plan.

"All for," Daniel said. There was an uneasy shifting in the pews, then one man raised his hand, followed by another, and quickly every hand was raised.

Lord, if it works . . . Willie thought. He remembered the red-haired waitress at the café. Seated here in front of him might just possibly be three dozen Negro millionaires, but he'd be damned if they looked it now.

The New Year's Eve party to which Tallulah had invited Willie turned out, to his surprise, to be in one of the big fashionable houses facing the park just across the street from his own little garage apartment, one of the many he'd never been invited into before. Drawing room, hallways and a library were awash with tinseled decorations, and balloons floated along eighteen-foot ceilings. In the main living room a three-piece ensemble of colored musicans, playing clarinet, trumpet and trombone, had broken into a gay and fast-paced version of "Bill Bailey, Won't You Please Come Home?" The rooms were crowded with Bienville's finest—women, young and old, in slinky gowns, and some of the men wore tuxedos; others were in suits or sport jackets.

In the dining room an enormous mahogany table and sideboard bore an extravagant buffet: smoked and glazed hams and turkey and roast beef; sterling silver chafing dishes contained creamed peas and creamed potatoes, cauliflower and broccoli. There were oysters Rockefeller, enormous boiled Gulf shrimp and crabmeat salad. There were several varieties of pies, and the pièce de résistance was a huge ice carving in the shape of a cotton boll that contained creamed strawberries to be dished out with a foot-long sterling silver ladle.

Tallulah wore a stunning emerald-colored velvet gown that swept to the floor and a pearl necklace and earrings which may or may not have been genuine; Willie was in no position to say. She was as tall as he was in her heels, and might have been a fashion model or a movie star, lithe and svelte. She led him from room to room, introducing him to people along the way, chatting briefly, taking him by the arm—always somebody taking him by the arm. He was slowly getting used to it.

He recognized some of the people from the party at Ham's and the debutante ball, but again he was astonished at how many new faces he saw, and how many beautiful and elegant-looking women were among them. It was as though he had never lived in the town he had grown up in, or that all the guests at these parties had been imported from someplace else. Suddenly, through the crowd, he saw V. D. Skinner, dressed in his same brown suit, talking and laughing in a group that included Ham Bledsole. Also, in another corner, was the silver-haired lawyer, Augustus Tompkins. Drink in hand, Willie left Tallulah with some friends and excused himself to join Ham and Skinner.

"Good God!" Skinner cried. "Look who's here!" The group turned and Ham's face brightened in delighted surprise. Whatever the topic of conversation had been, it now changed.

"I'd like to talk to you," Willie said to Skinner.

"Figured you would, figured you would!" he exclaimed confidently. "Let's get ourselves over to the bar."

"I was wondering what . . ." Willie began.

"Just got back a little while ago," Skinner interrupted joyfully. "Found a message from Ham to come over here. Damn fine party, huh? Yessir, you people in Bienville certainly know how to throw a party."

"Where in hell were you?" Willie demanded. "I needed you. I had to go . . ."

"Kansas City," Skinner cut him off. "Needed a good steak. Goddamn good steak. Thought that'd be the best place to get one."

"But damn," Willie said, "I thought the least you could have done was say where I could reach you, or how long you'd be gone. I had to go up there in front of all those people and try to explain this plan of yours for drilling oil on their places. I didn't know what I was talking about half the time. You might be pleased to know, however, that they've agreed."

"Knew they would, Croft," Skinner said, nonchalantly breezing past people on his way to the bar. "Wasn't no doubt in my mind you could get your niggers to go along."

"I don't know why in hell there wasn't," Willie said irritably. "It was damned tough, trying to explain all that. They might have had questions I couldn't answer."

"Doubt it," Skinner said. "Faith—that's what I've got in you! Everybody's gotta have faith. Never doubted it for a minute. Knew you'd get your niggers up to this."

"Stop calling them *my niggers,* for godsake," Willie said sourly; "after all, this is your scheme—and now you've got to come through with something . . ."

"Already have," Skinner declared. "That's another thing I was doing in Kansas City. After I had that steak, I went to see my buddy Horner—the guy I mentioned before—had a job 'bout sixty miles south that petered out a few weeks ago. He's on his way right now with twenty-eight drilling rigs. Be here with the first two or three in about a week or so. How's that for getting the show on the road?"

Willie was slightly stunned. "Jesus," he said, "that's . . . that's very fast. I mean, if it's going to cost money. I don't know how quickly . . ."

"Don't worry 'bout it," Skinner said grandly. "This guy'll work on spec, till we see what we've got. He don't have any more jobs for a while. Old-school wildcatter. Looking for a chance to make a buck or two, and he ain't afraid to try something new. Now let's get ourselves a drink."

Willie rejoined Tallulah with his fresh drink and she introduced him to a pair of tanned and athletic-looking young men with whom she'd been busily chatting. One was apparently a younger brother of a girl Tallulah's age, the other a law student at the university whose last name Willie did not immediately catch. Both had the aristocratic features of young scions: upward-pointed noses and sleepy eyes and hair that seemed never combed but fell naturally into place.

"Didn't you have that trouble with Percy Holt at the Azalea Ball?" the brother of Tallulah's friend suddenly asked.

Willie nodded, embarrassed. Tallulah seemed to sense his embarrassment and she tried to change the subject.

"He's a lawyer," she said to the other boy. "David, you're in what? Your first or second year up there?"

"Second," the student said, obviously more interested in what he had just heard about Willie and Percy Holt.

"I heard about that," the student said. "You punched him around pretty good." He had fixed his eyes on Willie's face and there was a faint trace of a smile on his lips that bespoke aloofness, or so Willie perceived it.

"It was an unfortunate incident," Willie said bluntly. He, too, tried to change the subject. "Are you planning to practice here—after you graduate?"

"Wouldn't make much sense not to," the boy said.

"His father's a lawyer," Tallulah said. "I thought you'd know him."

"I'm sorry," Willie said. "Who's your father?"

"Right over there," the boy said, pointing at the lean, silver-haired figure of Augustus Tompkins.

"Yes," Willie said, "I know him. We've had some dealings. As a matter of fact, I need to talk to him right now." He excused himself.

Augustus Tompkins, wearing a tuxedo with gold-set diamond studs, was in a group of three or four other men when Willie came up beside him.

"If you've got a minute," Willie said, "I'd like to see you."

A look of clammy surprise came over Tompkin's face when he saw Willie, but he immediately stepped back and bade Willie welcome into the group, saying in a voice that almost smacked of delight, "Well, well—Willie, how are you, young fellow? Come meet some people."

He introduced him to the others. One Willie knew by reputation and the fact that his photograph frequently appeared in the newspaper for chairing some cause or other. He was president of Bienville's largest bank. Another operated a citywide restaurant chain. The third owned a paper bag manufacturing plant. All were tanned and fit from weekly hours on golf and tennis courts. Prosperity seemed to ooze from the pores in their skin.

"Willie Croft," Tompkins explained, "is representing some of the colored folks up near Creoletown, the ones who say they own the land where they found oil."

The unanimous response from the others, as shown in their expressions, was, "Oh, really?"

"Willie and I," Tompkins continued, "have been having our problems working this thing out, because I'm representing the Holt family, you know. But I'm sure we'll sort something out pretty soon so everybody can get on with their business." There was a tone of confidence, even moral conviction, in Tompkins's statement.

"There might be something we can talk about now," Willie said. "It'll only take a minute." He motioned Tompkins into a corner.

What Willie had actually intended to say was that he was going to be counsel of record in the case of the Holts versus Mrs. Hannah Holt Loftin—if Tompkins didn't know already. Willie figured this would be surprise enough and he thought he might feel out Tompkins about the competency hearing and related matters.

But just as he sidled toward an empty space with Tompkins following behind, Whitsey Loftin swept into the room, arm in arm with Emile Montague, looking as beautiful as he had ever remembered her, and more and more like a woman in love. Something between desire and anger stirred in Willie's loins, rose quickly to his brain, then seemed to settle at the halfway point, in his stomach, as if he had received a sharp punch.

"Yes, Willie, what is it?" Augustus Tompkins said placatingly, as though he were sure now that Willie was ready to deal his way.

Willie felt his cheeks flush; hurt welled up in him. Nothing had happened between Whitsey Loftin and himself —*nothing*—that's what *she* said, but what about *him!* Something sure as hell happened to him! He'd let himself in for it, gone against his time-proven better judgment— somehow, without really knowing it, he'd let himself hope, and now he was paying the price. He fought against a rage that threatened to fan into meanness.

"You said you wanted to talk," Tompkins said impatiently, rattling the ice in his almost empty glass.

Willie spun around savagely. "I do, Augustus, I do," he snapped. "First off, I want to tell you I'm representing your clients' aunt, Mrs. Loftin, in the competency case, and that we are going to contest the hell out of it. Second, I think you should know that we are aware of Mr. Crenshaw and his activities on the day Mrs. Backus's house was burned down."

If this news had any noticeable effect on Augustus Tompkins it did not show in his face, and Willie was watching keenly for signs of dismay or weakness.

"I don't quite understand," the elderly lawyer said coolly; "something about representing Mrs. Loftin? And what was that other?"

He understands damned well, Willie thought.

"I *said,* I am representing Mrs. Loftin against your clients and that I also have knowledge of one of their employees, a Mr. Hiram Crenshaw, and his part in a certain fire that was set in which an old woman was killed and her house burned down."

Willie again glanced sharply at Whitsey Loftin and Emile Montague. His arm was around her waist and they were talking to another couple. Willie was boiling.

"Well," Tompkins said, "this certainly comes as a surprise—you getting involved in Mrs. Loftin's affairs. I don't know how that happened, but it really doesn't make much difference. I suppose she has to have *some* kind of lawyer," Tompkins said with marked disdain. He drew himself up. "If you want to get mixed up with trying to represent a poor old crazy lady, that's your business. I think we can handle that all right. As for this other thing, I have no idea what you're talking about." But just then, for a flickering instant, Willie saw a twitch in Tompkins's face.

"Think about it, Augustus," Willie said. "Think about it very carefully before you proceed in this matter." He nodded curtly and walked away, in the opposite direction from Whitsey and her beau.

Tallulah by this time was surrounded by no less than five admirers—and possibly one detractor in the form of a dumpy girl who seemed to be eyeing sourly the pearls around Tallulah's neck. Willie strode over with a mixed air of confidence and muted anger he could not remember having experienced before.

To his lights, what he had just done was daring and bold. The outcome of this case and his chance to become something more than a half-assed, cheap-case lawyer were now squarely on the line—not to mention his professional career, should the authorities learn that he was withholding evidence of a crime. You pay your money, you take your chances, he thought. Such was the creed of the Holts and the Tompkinses and probably every other sonofabitch in the room who had any power, or position, or money, unless he inherited it—and even then one of his ancestors had probably got where he was by utilizing similar philosophy.

In the moments it took him to cross the room, it occurred to Willie for the first time both in mind and spirit that he might for once wind up on top instead of second or third, where he usually was. It was a feeling of keen exhilaration and satisfaction and for the moment he suddenly felt in control of things. As a matter of fact, he felt as though he could rule the world.

"Tallulah," he said, entering the circle of admirers who surrounded her, "sorry I've been running around here. I had a little business to take care of. Do you want to eat? I think people are starting to." He gestured toward the dining room where a small line had begun to form. Then, before she could respond, he had her by the arm—for a change—and was leading her toward the buffet. He was now in charge.

They helped themselves to comfortable portions of the fabulous buffet, took glasses of chilled wine and found a place to sit in a brightly decorated sun-room with ferns suspended from the ceiling.

"Did you accomplish anything?" she asked.

"I suppose I did," Willie replied confidently. "I'm just starting to learn how business in this city is really conducted —and it ain't in somebody's office, or over the phone."

"I guess not," she said demurely. "I don't know. I'm not involved in all that, really."

"And just as well," Willie proclaimed roguishly. "It's a dog-eat-dog world. You wouldn't want to get entangled in all that, would you?"

"I don't think so," she said. "I mean I guess it might be a good thing, but somehow I've never really tried. One time I was working for Merrill Lynch over in New Orleans, as a secretary, and the manager said he'd put in a recommendation for me to become a broker, and I'd go to New York and be trained and everything, but, well, I just never got around to doing it. I suppose I didn't want to. You're right, I guess. That's a man's world. I'd feel out of place."

Her big brown eyes were wonderfully benign. Willie had always reckoned there were women like Tallulah around, though he hadn't known any of them. All the women he knew, if they weren't housewives, had jobs someplace and were damned glad to have them, but here was a girl—woman—who'd been offered a good professional position and turned it down flat. Daddy had the money, he figured, and in time a husband would support her, and she'd join the legion of motherhood and drive a station wagon and have three or four kids and a couple of servants and a membership at the country club and begin to throw these kinds of bashes as well as attend them and grow old gracefully in her own little ready-made cocoon—all she would want from life. Bienville, he thought, home of the modern Southern Belle.

Willie glanced at his watch. It was a quarter to twelve.

"How much time have we got?" Tallulah asked.

"Fifteen minutes," he said. "Like to take a walk around?"

"Sure."

They went out onto the wide verandah where the New Year's air was chill but not cold and the moon was a shimmering sliver over head. The giant oaks in the park were black and ominous and the old Iron Deer was silhouetted against the light of a far-off streetlamp.

"Want to take a walk in the park?" Willie asked.

"Okay," she said, "but not for long. I'm not wearing a coat."

He guided her down the steps and across the street with his hand at her waist. She seemed to snuggle close to him, perhaps only for warmth. They got to the Iron Deer and Willie said, "Want to take a ride?" Tallulah turned with a faintly puzzled look, but before she could say anything he seized her by the waist and hoisted, intending to set her down on the back of the deer. In midhoist he realized she was more of a load than he'd reckoned. Being almost Willie's height, Tallulah was not only slim and lithe, she was also a very big girl.

"Arrrrrg," he said, letting her to the ground as gently as he could.

"What was that . . ." she stammered. Then, "Oh, to get up on the deer?" Expertly she placed her palms on the animal's withers and hoisted herself up like a bareback rider, her skirt hitching up at the waist.

"Ooooooh!" she cried. "It's cold!"

He bet it was.

He looked again at his watch. It was only a minute or two till twelve. "Want to go back inside? It's about time," he said. The strains of "Chattanoogie Shoe Shine Boy" wafted gently across the park. The band had not yet begun to play "Auld Lang Syne."

"I'd like to get down off this damned deer," she giggled. As she was dismounting, Willie glanced back at the house. Its windows were brightly lit and figures were visible inside against the golden panes. The large door onto the porch opened and two people—both of whom he recognized immediately—stepped outside. They walked to the far end of the verandah where the light was dim and began to embrace as lovers. Whitsey's arm was heavily around the neck of Emile Montague, her blond hair barely visible above his shoulder as they kissed.

"Let's run," Tallulah said, taking him by the arm and tugging at it heartily.

"No," he said sharply. Then, more softly, drawing her toward him, "Not quite yet." He pulled her close and looked for a brief instant into her eyes, which were level with his own, before kissing her. She offered herself to him, her mouth sweet with lipstick, body pressed against his, warming herself. He ran his hand down her back to her buttocks and pulled her closer—a firm and supple ass, her best feature aside from her face. He could feel her grinding into him at crotch level. The first notes of "Auld Lang Syne" blared out from the house. He broke apart for a moment and saw that Whitsey Loftin and Montague were still entwined. Then he turned his attentions to Tallulah.

"You know," he said, nodding across the park, "my house is right over there. We could go there if you want. Maybe build a fire." The new confidence, which had almost failed him after watching Whitsey and Montague, flickered again, but she looked away demurely.

"Oh, I don't think I'd better do that," she said, then, smiling widely, "but if you want, we could go to my house. Mother and Dad are asleep by now. They never stay up past midnight."

Somewhere in the neighborhood a string of firecrackers exploded. Willie's confidence and his expectations were painfully mixed.

It had surprised him when he had come to pick her up earlier that evening that Tallulah did not live in the elegant, intimidating kind of place he had expected. It was a modern style set off in a pleasant copse of trees with a circular drive, a split-level of red brick and white trim. No maid or butler; Tallulah herself had greeted him at the door.

She had pressed next to him all during the drive home and neither had said very much. After the park they had returned to the party for a while where they said their good-byes and were among the first to leave. Willie's feelings were strained between anticipation and aggravation once they got into the car. He agonized over Whitsey and Montague, but frequently glanced over at Tallulah, which lifted his sagging spirits. He didn't know if Whitsey had seen him or not as he came up the steps, but whatever the case, she had certainly torn it now. . . . He then logically forced himself back to the proposition that there hadn't been much, if anything, to tear in the first place.

Tallulah turned the key in the lock and they stepped quietly inside. The living-room lights had been turned off and the house was dark and still except for the glow of a lamp in the hallway.

"Make yourself a drink," she whispered. "I'll be right back," and disappeared into the other side of the house.

Willie fixed himself a bourbon over ice and deliberately sat on the sofa—a calculation designed to test Tallulah's hand when she returned, for if she seated herself beside him, it would be the go-ahead sign for further exploration; if not, he would be forewarned of her circumspection. As it turned out she plumped herself down on the couch, not at the other end, but right next to him, after fixing herself a Scotch and soda—a worldly act, he thought, for someone her age.

"Ummmmm," she said, kicking off her shoes and placing her feet on a coffee table, "the new year."

"Here's to an interesting one," Willie said, raising his glass, "and to you." They clinked glasses, took sips and then he pulled Tallulah to him. They kissed for what seemed like a long time, pausing only to breathe, and in time he worked his hand up to her breasts and brushed across, feeling a hardening nipple beneath the layers of gown and brassiere. She raised no objection to this, so he slipped one of the straps off her shoulder and gently tugged the dress down. This, too, was received without protest, and so Willie proceeded with a surgical dexterity that surprised even himself. Within minutes—though he had lost any account of time—they were entwined lengthwise on the sofa, her gown pulled down to her waist and up to her hips, and her bra and her panties lying on the carpet beside them.

His own concession was slightly more prudish: somehow during the course of the activity he had managed to remove his jacket, loosen his tie and work off his shoes—about all decorum of the day would accept in this kind of situation. One hand flicked at her firm and rounded breasts while the other stroked frantically at her damp crotch.

He became nearly beside himself with excitement and obsessed with raw, animal-like desire. Simultaneously, his mind began to work on the problem of what to do next. He knew, though his experiences at seduction were painfully few, that any real moment of truth would come if he (a) tried to place her hand on his penis or (b) took his penis out of his trousers and attempted to insert it someplace. All women, regardless of race, creed or social background, were inevitably put to a decision at this point, and he was having such a lustfully dirty time doing what he was already doing that he was reluctant to spoil it by forcing the question. As it developed, the issue was rendered instantaneously moot by a far-off voice in the darkness, calling, even before his sex-filled mind could fully assimilate what was about to happen, "Tallulah? Tal-lulah? Are you in there?"

Her panting and writhing were undisturbed by this shrill intrusion, but Willie's eyes, having adjusted to the faint light, made out a tall, short-haired female figure silhouetted against the hallway lamp. He ceased his strumming and sat bolt upright on the sofa just as every light in the room was thrown on by some devilish central switch and they were confronted by a scandalized face belonging obviously to the senior Mrs. Bledsole.

"Tallulah!"

The word ran around the brightly lit room like a rico-cheted bullet.

Tallulah, who had slowly registered the presence of another person, instinctively wrapped her arms around her mostly naked body and was trying desperately at the same time to shake out her skirt and pull up the top of her disheveled dress.

"Mother!" she cried helplessly. "What are you *doing!*"

It was as bad as any scene Willie might have conjured from his wildest nightmares. He stood as Mrs. Bledsole entered the room tigresslike, and only later he reflected that his countenance at that moment, which was characterized by a shit-eating grin, probably resembled the expression on his face when he was caught red-handed with the bag of stolen kumquats.

"Mother!" Tallulah shrieked again. She was holding her dress against herself, top and bottom, while Willie brushed at his trousers to disguise the erection he had developed.

The woman loomed enormously in the doorway, then took several steps toward them, slowly, as if she had stumbled onto the scene of an unspeakable crime. She was dressed in a flowered bathrobe.

"Young lady! You go to your room this instant!" Mrs. Bledsole ordered. Then, regarding Willie up and down, as though he were some loathsome insect, she cried, "And you, *young man*"—these words rang heavily in Willie's mortified senses, for it seemed that she was refusing to admit that he was actually not so much younger than herself—"had better leave this house at once!"

Stunned, but, being an attorney accustomed to handling occasional curves, Willie made a feeble attempt to salvage the situation.

"Mrs. Bledsole," he said weakly, "I am Willie Croft. I'm terribly sorry if we got you up, but Tallulah and I were just, ah, we were trying to, ah, talk, and . . ."

"I see exactly what you were *trying* to do," Mrs. Bledsole said mockingly.

"Mother!" Tallulah whimpered.

Willie had already reached for his jacket. Tallulah had gathered up her underclothing from the floor and was holding it in her hand.

"You go instantly to your room, young lady!" the older woman again said with the demeanor of a drill sergeant.

"Please, Mrs. Bledsole," Willie said, "if you'll simply let me say something for . . ."

"I don't want you to say anything," Mrs. Bledsole said. "You, you . . ." She regarded him in the light as if for the first time, seeming to notice that he was not a youth, that he was in fact of a whole other generation than her daughter. "You just leave here, right now, or I'll call my husband!"

This remark incensed Willie.

He made a grand gesture of straightening his tie and slipped into his jacket. "Madam," he said in his most polished manner, "thank you for your hospitality. I have a deep respect for your daughter. She obviously has a lot to live up to." Then he turned to Tallulah. "I'm sorry," he said. "I'm really sorry," and stalked past the fearsome figure, out of the room and out of the house into the brand-new year.

Thankful that the old Nash started without difficulty, Willie roared out of the driveway and into the shadowy darkness of the curving streets away from the Bledsole house. He had crossed the main boulevard and turned across town to his apartment, his heart thumping and his mind racing with all the things he might have said, but hadn't. The confidence he'd built up after the episode with Augustus Tompkins had evaporated like steam. I am a grown man, he thought acidly, and something like this *always* happens to me.

There was one final note to the end of that particular year and the beginning of the next so far as Willie, the Obsidian Oil Corporation and its tribulations were concerned. At nine o'clock in the morning of New Year's Day a hurried meeting was convened in the otherwise deserted law offices of Augustus Tompkins, at which Tompkins, Brevard and Percy Holt were present. The three men were dressed casually, Tompkins in slacks and a tweed sport coat, Brevard in pressed gray trousers and a green wool sweater and Percy in rumpled khaki and windbreaker; he alone seemed to be suffering the effects of a debauched New Year's Eve.

"Croft knows," Tompkins said somberly, "about our Mr. Crenshaw and the business up at Creoletown."

This news did not seem to register immediately with Percy Holt, but Brevard's face took on the ghastly pallor of a man about to witness all the things he had built for himself in life crumble to nothing.

"How!" he cried. "How do you know?"

"Told me last night," Tompkins said without visible emotion. "At the Pierces' party."

"He knows what?" Brevard said. His voice seemed ready to crack.

"I'm not certain just how much," Tompkins said, "but I can only assume it's enough. Bad enough, I mean."

"What exactly?" Percy said.

"He mentioned the name of your man Crenshaw, and said he was aware of what he did up there—with respect to the nigger woman and burning her house down."

"God damn!" Brevard Holt shouted. He looked glaringly and accusingly at his brother, but spoke to no one in particular. "I was afraid of something like this."

"Is that all he said?" Percy asked.

"Isn't it enough!" Brevard cried despairingly.

"Now let's hold on here," Tompkins said, "because we have got to deal with this calmly and make no mistakes. In answer to the question, yes, that's pretty much all he said. There was no mention of the other fellow, what's his name, I forget—or of how he knew, or what actual proof he might have—nor was there any mention of how Crenshaw might be connected to us—except that I suppose we can assume he knows he was employed by Holt Stevedoring."

"How do you think he found out?" Brevard asked.

"I have given considerable thought to that," Tompkins said, leaning back, taking out his pipe. "The most obvious answer is that someone up there saw him in the car near the place, copied down the license plate and it went from there."

"Have they gone to the police?" Brevard said hesitantly.

"I doubt it seriously," Tompkins said. "I can check that out tomorrow, I suppose, but I'm sure we would have heard something by now if they had. But for the time being, gentlemen, I believe that we are being blackmailed."

"How?" Percy said. Brevard had got to his feet and was pacing by the window.

"Croft's words to me were circumspect, but he put it that I—we—should 'think about it very carefully' before proceeding in this matter—of the old nigger woman, he meant."

"You didn't let on that you . . ."

"Of course not," Tompkins said.

"So what do we do?" Percy said.

"You're a fine one to ask that!" Brevard snapped. "If it hadn't been for you and your damned thugs this wouldn't have happened."

"All right, Brev," Tompkins intervened. "Look, this presents a problem, and a rather serious one for all of us. Myself included. More than just money is at stake—our own lives, reputations. This is an unfortunate incident. But there are questions to be answered and it falls on the three of us to come up with the solutions." He had finished packing his pipe and took out a match to light it.

"First, it would be desirable to learn how much this

bastard Croft actually knows, and if he can connect us directly to the incident. And, of course, there's the question of who else knows about it. Second, there's the problem of what we're going to do about it. Blackmail, as I'm sure you gentlemen realize, has a way of getting progressively worse, once you submit to it."

"Any suggestions?" Percy Holt said.

"I've also given this some thought," Tompkins said. "Now the crucial link in this sorry chain of events is, at this point, Mr. Crenshaw himself—and his associate, what was his name?"

"The Roller, we called him," Percy said. "I'd have to get a pay voucher to get the real name."

"All right," Tompkins continued, "The Roller—now, assuming that someone actually witnessed what they did, and would be willing to testify about it in court, there is still nothing to link the two of them to any of us except they themselves. I mean, otherwise it would simply be coincidental that they happened to work for Holt Stevedoring, but that's no factual evidence against us."

The two Holts were listening, Brevard rubbing his palms nervously.

"So then, if there were no Mr. Crenshaw and Mr. Roller to be apprehended and hauled into court, that would effectively eliminate any connection here, do you see what I mean?"

"No, Augustus, I don't see what you mean." Brevard Holt had suddenly risen to his feet. "But if you are suggesting what I think you are . . ."

"Now, hold on a minute, Brev," Tompkins said. "I am not suggesting anything. I am merely going over a scenario.

"Now," he continued, "there is also a possibility that Croft knows of this from the horse's mouth, so to speak. That somehow Mr. Crenshaw or his partner got to Mr. Croft and told him the tale and they are all in some kind of cahoots to blackmail us."

"My God," Brevard groaned.

"I am only saying that this is a possibility we cannot afford to overlook," Tompkins said.

"Well, what are we going to do!" Brevard said.

"I think," said the suave lawyer, "that the first step is to accede to Croft's demand. We sit tight on this matter of the nigger property up there for as long as it takes, and keep as many of our options open as possible. He hasn't suggested any final solution yet, so I think we just hold tight.

"Second, I believe we must locate Mr. Crenshaw and Mr. Roller wherever they are and ascertain from them what, if anything, they know about this. If it appears they are ignorant of it, then they might prove useful later."

"What do you mean by that?" Percy said.

"Well," Tompkins said, almost casually, the way a man might suggest going to a ball game, or on a fishing trip, "depending on what we can find out about Croft's knowledge of the affair, and who else might be aware of it, we might have to employ their services again. After all, they are in this even deeper than we."

"Good Christ, Augustus," Brevard said, "do you know what you are saying!"

In one of the rare times Augustus Tompkins showed any emotion, the silver-haired lawyer half rose from his chair and leaned forward with his hands on the desk and his mouth pulled back into a horrible grimacing smile, which was not actually a smile at all, but a reptilian baring of teeth.

"All right you two, now just listen to me!" he hissed. "You have gotten me into this, dragged me into it, I might add. I don't know if you've thought of it or not, but if you haven't, you might as well start right now. We are in trouble. Big trouble. If any of this were to get out we—each of us—would be ruined. Our families, our lives, everything we stand for—we would probably go to jail. And for what? For a couple of cheap murdering thugs, or some shit-heaving third-rate lawyer, or a bunch of niggers who don't know their asses from live steam! Well, I'm not prepared for that! We have got to find out what, exactly, everybody in this affair knows and how much, and then we have got to deal with it in the most expedient manner possible, because I don't intend to go around for the rest of my life with the shadow of a noose hanging over my head. Do you understand that!"

There was a long and awkward silence in the room as Tompkins sank back into his seat. Brevard Holt remained standing, staring out the window, his face half-turned from the others, as if to disassociate himself from these vile and criminal intimations. Percy sat hunched over on the leather sofa, and it was he who spoke first.

"How do we know that Croft hasn't covered himself? I mean, that he hasn't put what he knows down somewhere so that if something happens to him, it would all come out anyway?"

"I don't," Tompkins said flatly, "but I wouldn't think so. I know Croft fairly well, know his kind. He's a pissant. He doesn't think that way. He's in way over his head, and he thinks he's playing a game."

"So what do we do first?" Percy asked.

"Find those two—Crenshaw and the other one. Somebody will have to talk to them, find out what they know."

"Christ," Percy said, "that could take weeks—months. I gave them a couple of thou—told them to get lost. They were supposed to have shipped out on a goddamn banana boat to Honduras. I wouldn't even know where to start looking."

"Well, you'd better," Tompkins said, "and I don't care how long it takes. You'd damned well better find them."

III

The Obsidian Oil Corporation

15

A STRANGER PASSING THROUGH BIENVILLE IN THE SPARKLING days of early spring most likely would not have noticed anything extraordinary to comment about. Business and commerce continued its slow and relentless grind; steamships arrived with cargoes of Jamaican bauxite, Honduran bananas, Chilean copper, Guatemalan woven baskets, Cuban sugarcane, Costa Rican coffee and metals from Nicaragua—then departed, their holds filled with cotton, lumber, cattle, soybeans and peanut products and grain. Shoppers, children in tow, bustled through dry goods stores for spring sale buys and in between lounged on the benches on The Parade. Around noon professional men left their offices for their customary luncheon places. Azaleas blossomed and dogwoods flowered. Winter, what there had been of it, was gone and the weather was balmy. Fishermen unlimbered their tackle, dogs chased cats, schoolboys worked neat's-foot oil into baseball gloves and the days had become noticeably longer.

Business as usual to an outsider, but beneath the surface, Bienville seethed.

A newspaper story a few weeks before had started things off. No one ever found out how it leaked, perhaps a spiteful clerk at the courthouse or a secretary's careless tongue, but somehow word of Willie's insidious accusation against the Holt family got out. In a rare moment of candor the *Bienville Post-Herald* had reported to its readers that the question of alleged miscegenation was to be a central issue in the dispute over the second largest chunk of land in the rich Creoletown oil field.

And as if that wasn't bad enough, the paper (which normally ignored business matters of any sort) subsequently got wind of the horrible rumor that the oil land might actually fall into the hands of the poverty-ridden Negroes who lived on it. This dire news prompted a great flood of outcry, incited a debate in the county commission, elicited denunciation in several Fundamentalist churches and spurred one public official to recommend that the oil fields might somehow be "nationalized" by the state to keep them out of the hands of irresponsible parties.

An old Negro woman with a mop was soaping down dirty tiled floors in the hallway of the offices of the Obsidian Oil Corporation. Daniel Holt sidestepped a wet spot, continued down the empty second-floor corridor of this dingy building in a run-down section of town, then stopped in front of an opaque glass door upon which was taped a sign: P. W. Croft. General Counsel.

He opened the door a crack and saw a slender Negro girl whom he recognized as a recent graduate of his high school whom he had recommended for her job. She stopped her filing and stood upright as Daniel came in.

"I'll tell Mr. Croft you're here," she said nervously.

"It won't be necessary," Daniel said. The door to Willie's private office was slightly ajar and he could hear Willie barking something on the telephone. When he saw Daniel standing there he motioned him inside. Late spring sunshine streamed in through a large, half-open window behind Willie's desk and the full scent of a flowering crepe myrtle tree wafted into the room, sweet and cleansing.

Willie cut the conversation short and put the receiver down.

"Just dropped by to see how we're doing," Daniel said.

Willie thought he seemed uncomfortable in the new surroundings.

"Not bad, I guess," Willie said. "When are you going to come in and take your office?"

"Oh, not until the school year is over, I think," said Daniel. "Wouldn't make much sense until then anyway. I don't know what there is for me to do." It was the way he looked around the room, furtively, as though he might have been a new or prospective employee, and not the president of Obsidian Oil.

"There's a lot for you to do," Willie said, a little aggravated. "I'm trying to run this whole show alone. Maybe you could be in closer touch with your people from Chicago. They ought to be sending us some more money pretty soon. We've run through a lot of what they sent so far, what with Skinner's operation and the salaries and all. The bookkeeper you found is good, but I think we need somebody in control of it all."

"I suppose there isn't any news from Mr. Skinner?" Daniel said wanly.

"Not yet," said Willie; "he's got six or seven drilling rigs working, but nothing's changed since the last time I talked to you about it. He says they've just got to keep on going."

"This is costing a lot of money," Daniel said.

"Well," Willie said, trying to look at the bright side of it, "there's a lot of money to be made. And we're damned lucky nobody stepped in with some kind of injunction to stop us before we started. I suppose you know that?"

"Yes, I do," Daniel said, "but it seems like they'd have found something by now, doesn't it?"

"I don't have any idea," Willie said. "That's Skinner's end of it."

Actually, he was more than a little worried about the drilling operation. Skinner hadn't said it in so many words, but Willie could tell things weren't going as they originally planned. They had gone through clay, bedrock, water, schist—everything but oil. It was possible, Skinner had finally admitted in a moment of extreme candor, that it was all a gigantic mistake. That even though all the signs pointed to it, that all the geologists and petroleum engineers, and testings and calculations of science were simply wrong and there was no oil down there or there was so little of it not to be worthwhile. Despite the sophistications of technology, Skinner observed, a man could not actually see a mile or more beneath the ground, where the oil was, or where it was supposed to be.

Willie walked over to a large map of the Creoletown area and pulled it down. The map was shaded in various colors, the most predominant of which was black, the official color of the Obsidian Oil Corporation.

"As of this morning," Willie said, "we control two thousand two hundred and ten acres if we include your mother's place. There are still eighteen parcels up in the air, but I think we've got at least seven of those, hands down. Four or five of the others are good bets, but the rest are a shot in the dark because of the titles."

"That sounds pretty good," said Daniel, "but it's not going to help much if there's nothing down there."

"We'll just have to leave that end of it to Skinner," Willie said.

"I had some more of those calls last night," Daniel said.

"Same sort of thing?" Willie asked.

"Pretty much." Daniel seemed listless and discouraged.

"Well, you could always get an unlisted number," Willie said. "I think I'm going to. They haven't been bugging me much lately, but there's no reason to think they won't pretty soon. At least it's only calls."

"So far," Daniel said. "They talked pretty mean last night. They got my wife first. Called her a lot of ugly names."

Willie nodded. "They got to Skinner too," he said. "Somebody knocked on his door a couple of days ago and when he answered it, they'd left a shoebox of dog shit there."

"It worries me," Daniel said, "what they might do."

"I don't think they're going to do anything," Willie said unconvincingly. "They'd like to scare us, but they'd have to be crazy to really try something."

Essentially this was correct. What most of Bienville felt about the proceedings at Creoletown ranged from intense curiosity to unfettered horror to stewing hostility. But there was no real call to action.

The more affluent families either had vested interests themselves or knew people who did, or who at any rate claimed they did. Middle-class whites secretly cursed their luck at the prospect that either the rich whites or the poor blacks—but not themselves—would be the ones to profit from all this. Poor whites and poor blacks, almost equally downtrodden, did not much care one way or the other, for they were certain they would not be included no matter what. Inflamed by almost daily headlines in the *Bienville Post-Herald,* it became the topic of conversation at family suppers, seated dinners, cocktail parties, fishing boats, drugstores, diners and businessmen's luncheons. Old ladies sitting on their porches after dark gazed at the fireflies and shooting stars and spoke of little else. Everyone had an opinion.

"It's disgraceful."

"Certainly it's disgraceful."

"They say they might even take over the town."

"The town! The whol' durned state—prob'ly the whol' worl'."

"Got to be the Communisiss behind it."

"You're right. Nigras don't know no better. Somebody else must be runnin' it."

"Might be the Jews."

"It's a disgrace."

"Where'd they get the money?"

"Paper says them nigras in the North, Chicago or someplace, gave it to 'em."

"Won't be a fit place to live."

"Certainly is a disgrace."

"You hear one of 'em's bought a place over by Rashland Square?"

"No!"

"I heard it today at the gros'ry store."

"No!"

"Bought one them big two-story white houses right on the square. Put a damn white jockey out front of it too."

"No!"

"Somebody said they bought the schools."

"Bought the schools! How can they do that! Schools ain't for sale."

"Did it somehow. Bought 'em for more'n a million dollars."

"I don't believe it!"

"Don't matter what you believe. I heard somebody say they buying the bank too."

"Buyin' the bank! Who ever heard of such a thing!"

"That's what they say."

"Well, they're wrong! They ain't even struck no oil yet."

"What about all that with the Holts? Ain't that somethin'?"

"Somethin'! I mean to say it's somethin'!"

"I don't believe a word."

"Well, I knew the old man. Seen him around on the streets a lot. And them boys too, when they was young. I wouldn't put it past'm. Any of 'em."

"That's a awful thing to say!"

"S'truth."

"How's anyone gonna know it's the truth? It's jus' the nigras' word against the Holts—and the ole man's dead anyhow."

"How can they prove it?"

"Beats me. But I tell you one thing. I shore would like to set on that jury. Watch them Holts squirm."

"You oughtn't to say things like that!"

Daniel had picked up the afternoon newspaper from Willie's desk and was looking through it while Willie answered a phone call. When the call ended, Daniel looked up from an inside article about the Obsidian Oil Corporation.

"I see they've added a new one," Willie said casually.

"Which is that?" Daniel asked.

"That we're backed by the Communists. That's what one of the city commissioners said."

"Oh, yes, Mr. Nabbs. I don't quite understand how he reached that conclusion."

"It don't make any difference," Willie said. "I expect they'll be saying a lot worse before it's over. By the way, how's your mother?"

"She's doing good," Daniel said, "but I think she's getting kind of restless having to keep sort of in hiding. I was going to ask when you think she can go back to living a normal life."

Willie thought about this for a moment.

"I'll tell you what I'd like to do," he said, "is keep her under wraps a little longer. I think we've got those damned Holts by the tail, but they're slippery people. If for some reason they come out fighting, she's our ace in the hole, along with Mrs. Loftin."

"Oh, yes," Daniel said, "and what about her?"

"I've got a psychiatrist coming over from New Orleans to look at her in a few days. But the real test'll be in court. She's got to undergo cross-examination in front of a jury. It's a touchy thing, but I might have it figured out."

"How do you mean?"

"Well," Willie said, "under ordinary circumstances she's nutty as a fruitcake, but when she takes a drink her senses seem to come back to her."

"You don't say?" Daniel said.

"Saw it myself. Drinks sherry. Probably can hold a bottleful at a time, but her head just clears right up."

"Sherry," Daniel said. "Sherry wine?"

"That's right," Willie said. "An old ladies' drink, but it's got as much wallop as a pint of moonshine if you drink enough of it. I bet half the little old ladies in the South sit around every other afternoon getting smashed on sherry."

"It might be nice for my mother to try it," Daniel said thoughtfully.

"Couldn't hurt," Willie said, "but there's certainly nothing wrong with her memory."

"No," Daniel said, "but it might be something she'd enjoy."

Willie pored over title and contract books for an hour or so after Daniel left, then gathered his things. He needed to go over to his old office in the seedy, run-down building which he only visited now once or twice a week. He was crossing The Parade when a voice called to him. It was Skinner, wearing tan work clothes, hopelessly stained with grime of the drilling rigs.

"Hey, I was just coming over to see you," he said. "I see you ain't keeping long office hours these days."

"I have to go to my other office," Willie said a little defensively. "And what brings you into town so early?"

"Nothin' much," Skinner said. "Everything's going about like it should. Nothing much I can do so I thought I'd come in to see a movie or something."

"Any signs yet?"

"Nope, 'fraid not."

"Daniel was just in. He's worried. He's been getting a lot of those calls. And he's scared you won't find anything."

"Tell him not to worry," Skinner said.

"About what?"

"About anything," Skinner said. "Don't do any good to worry."

"Well," Willie said, "seems like you can't help it sometimes. Isn't there any way to tell anything up there? I mean about when you might hit something?"

"Nope," Skinner said. "I mean, yeah, just before you do, you'll usually come up with oil sand or something, but not really till then."

"Well, don't you have any idea how long it might take? I mean, you can't just keep drilling forever."

"No, that's right," Skinner said. "I figure three, maybe four weeks. If we don't get something by then we're in pretty bad shape."

"God!" Willie grimaced. "I thought this was a sure thing."

"Ain't nothin' in the world a sure thing but dying," Skinner said piously.

"Well, you certainly sounded like it was a sure thing a few months back," Willie reminded him.

Skinner chuckled good-naturedly. "You've kinda been capitalizing on it too," he said, "what with those fancy socialites you been squiring around."

They were standing beside the bandstand on The Parade. A breeze rustled the branches of the oaks and a pigeon fluttered beside them near the fountain. Willie screwed up his mouth, a gesture of resignation. He had, in fact, for the last several months, believed it was going to happen. The Chicago money had come in, they were acquiring the land or the mineral rights at a faster pace than he'd expected, Skinner had been confident, and so against his better judgment Willie had let himself operate on that free-flowing current of supportive air that sometimes causes a man to use his money and his time carelessly. For instance, with the salary he received from Obsidian he had purchased a brand-new, eighteen-foot Dauber-built boat with a hundred-horsepower engine, and a new, expensive fly rod, and other things.

The socialites to whom Skinner had referred were girls he had met through Tallulah Bledsole, who had moved into her own apartment after the disastrous New Year's Eve incident at her parents' house. These girls, with names like Ashley, Victoria, Lolly, Merriweather and Theresa, were almost wildly attracted to Willie because he had acquired sudden status, if not notoriety, in Bienville. The newspaper stories made him out to be a kind of mystery character, a strange celebrity, associated with possible fortunes to be made up at Creoletown. He found himself invited to parties where his presence scandalized many of the guests; others, however, viewed him as a sort of weird curiosity and flocked around to ask questions about Obsidian's operations and the colored men who owned it. These he would answer as paradoxically as possible, and with a knowing smile, as though he were the ambassador from some obscure kingdom, which, in a way, he was.

Naturally, these things gave Willie a certain satisfaction in the forty-third year of his life. He was working hard, doing, so far as he could tell, a pretty good job. He had stumbled into a position where power was thrust upon him, and he had met the challenge.

But Skinner's reports had been becoming less and less optimistic, and that, of course, was the bottom line. Everything seemed to reel and dart in his head like an insect swarm. Skinner's operation was becoming more extravagant and they were fast running through the money from Chicago. Daniel and his colleagues trusted him; what advice should he give? He was squarely in the middle, a solitary voice, and every day it weighed on him more and more.

And then there was Whitsey Loftin. The last few times he had seen her she had not been with Emile Montague. He had run into her occasionally at parties, where she was always polite and friendly and sometimes, he thought, flirting, but he had not found the opportunity or screwed up the courage to speak with her alone or call her, to see if now, given his somewhat elevated status, she still wanted to be just *friends*. But she continued to occupy a portion of his days, and nights, and he frequently found himself wondering where she might be or what she might be doing at a particular moment. And at least several times each week he managed to walk by the bookstore to see if he could catch her off guard coming or going, where they might be forced to talk without it seeming as though he had caved in and made the first move.

"You're both worrying too much," Skinner said huskily. "Told you. It don't do any good to worry. We've come this far, and I think we've got a shot. Now we just have to wait it out."

"Sweat it out, you mean."

"Ain't nothin' worthwhile ever came without a little sweat," Skinner said, "and most of the time, a lot of it."

"Well, we're going to have some more problems and a lot of them if you don't hit something soon. Those people in Chicago are making noises about their money and I'm going to have trouble making your payroll up there in a week or so.

What the hell am I supposed to do—I'm running this whole operation by myself?"

"Beats me," Skinner said cheerfully, "that's your problem."

Willie crossed the street to his old building. The office itself seemed musty from lack of use and was somehow foreign to him now. A couple of times he had thought about closing it down and moving over to the Obsidian offices but something kept him from it. It was not an easy thing to turn his back on ten years in the same place.

He signed several checks the part-time office girl had left for him, and opened a few pieces of mail, including one that contained a ten-dollar bill from the former numbers operator and a note upon which was scrawled, "Now IOU $60." He put the ten dollars in his pocket and recorded its receipt in the ledger book with a sense of nostalgic depression. This part of his life seemed to be behind him now and slipping further away. No longer did he hear the cries of "Groun'man's here! Groun'man's here." He was no longer the Groundman. He rarely even visited the courthouse. There would be another Groundman to take his place.

The pranks he once loved to play in the courtroom had become a fading part of his past. He had graduated from a world of petty thieves, drunks, malefactors, small-time fences, moonshiners and bootleggers, vagrants, trespassers, poachers and other amusing characters to a life of graphs and charts, interminable legal documents in which there was no innocence or guilt to be proven and so many prevarications masquerading as truth that it was difficult to distinguish one from the other.

He missed his twilight walks in the deer park and the one or two nights a week when he used to drive down to Beaudreux's Place and stuff himself on fresh seafood. He hadn't taken a day off, except an occasional Sunday, in months. He missed his regular fishing expeditions up in the Delta, and the camp and popping flies for big bull bream and reeling in big-mouth bass, drinking beer or sippin' whiskey with Guidre, talking about fishing and complaining about mosquitoes. He'd only had the new boat out twice, both on Sunday afternoons and for just a few hours.

Willie gazed out of the window with a sense of melancholy. His eyes followed a tug plying the river channel in the failing light. The last rays of the sun glinted against a window in a grain storage complex across the river and shimmered on the golden marsh grass in the flat sloughs and rivers beyond.

The phone rang and Willie answered it, recognizing the shrill voice of Judge McCormack's secretary: "Mr. Croft," she said, "the judge will be right with you."

It was a phrase that had irritated Willie for nearly twenty years. It was as though she always assumed he was the one who wanted to speak to the judge, and also that the judge always kept you waiting. Moments later, "Hizzoner" was on the line.

"Well, Willie," the judge said sweetly, "now I've been sitting here most of the afternoon with Augustus Tompkins, and I think we've got something worked out about all this mess that might be fair to your client so we don't have to fool with a goddamn trial. Do you want to come over and talk about it?"

"Well, sir," Willie said, "maybe you can tell me a little about it over the phone. Might save some trouble."

There was an edge in Judge McCormack's voice that told Willie he was not pleased with that answer. "All right, all right. It goes something like this. The Holt family will transfer proper title to that place to the estate of the Backus woman free and clear. But they would like in return forty percent of the mineral rights. How does that sound?"

"Sounds pretty good for the Holts," Willie said.

"Good Lord, man," the judge cried, "what are we talking about here? They're giving those niggers all that land and letting them keep more than half the oil rights. What could be fairer?"

"As I've said before, you can't give somebody something they already own."

"What, if anything, those people own is in sharp dispute,"

the judge snapped. "I'm trying to save something all around."

"I'd like to dispute it, then," Willie said.

"You mean you want to take it to trial?" said Judge McCormack.

"That's what I had in mind," Willie said.

"All right, then." There was harshness in the judge's tone. "Two weeks. Two weeks. But I'm warning you now, Croft, you're not going to bring down the reputation of a fine old Bienville family in this affair in my courtroom. Do you understand me?"

"Perfectly," Willie said.

It was twilight when he left the little office and headed for his car. He had to pass the courthouse to get to the parking lot and as he looked up he saw behind bars a lone figure silhouetted by the harsh overhead lights of the cellblock. The figure seemed to watch him as he passed but did not wave or call out. He had an urge to stop and wave and yell up to the man, but refrained, and as he moved on he saw the figure in the window turn and disappear.

The old Nash wheezed and sputtered painfully as he backed it out of the lot and the transmission strained like a cement mixer as he shifted into first gear. On impulse Willie decided to take a swing by Whitsey Loftin's bookstore and, to his surprise, saw that the lights were on, but as he cruised past he saw no one inside. He slowed, wondering, and then in the rearview mirror he saw her, struggling across the street under the weight of a gigantic box. He leaned out the window.

"Say," he hollered, "you practicing for the strong woman's contest?"

She almost dropped the package on the spot, but staggered up the curb and put it down and walked toward him as he backed up the car.

"Let me give you a hand," he said. "I'm accustomed to heavy burdens."

"Thanks," she gasped. "It's a shipment I picked up today

231

and forgot to bring into the store." She walked in front of him and unlocked the door and he set the box down on the counter and dusted his hands on his jacket.

"In the Army," he said, "this is what they called an 'offensive load.'"

"Well," she said, "thanks again. I didn't realize it was so heavy. Would you like a cup of coffee or something?"

He hesitated a moment, as though he was considering leaving, but no such thought actually entered his mind. "I suppose that'd be nice," he said. "Do you want to go someplace?"

"I've got some coffee here. It'll just take a minute." She went into the back room and returned moments later, beaming. His heart fluttered.

"Now, how have you been? I've been reading and hearing about you—but of course I guess everyone tells you that."

"Not really," he said. "I've been all right. Busy, you know."

"I'll say," she said. She smiled sexily across the counter, resting her heavy breasts on top of it. His heart took another leap and he nonchalantly averted his eyes.

"I haven't seen you in weeks," she said. "I was going to phone you a couple of times, but something always happened."

"Usually does," he said. He moved to a bookshelf and absently plucked a volume off it. Something was drawing him against his will into the role of the wounded suitor. "By the way, how are you and your boyfriend?" Instantly he regretted asking that.

She swept her hand through her hair. "No boyfriends for me." Then her smile faded. "I suppose you mean Emile. I haven't seen him for a while. I guess it was something I needed to get out of my system. Emile and I were, well, a long, long time ago, back when we were both in college, we were a *thing*. Even before that. He was actually my first boyfriend, back in the sixth grade, if you can believe it. There's something about those kinds of things. Sometimes you have to go back for one more look. But he's gone his way, and I've gone mine. We both found that out. He came back into town just about the time I met you." She straightened up. "I think the coffee's hot now," and went to the back room.

This news restored Willie's spirits like an amazing elixir. He soared with it. He had a chance again—or maybe a chance, how much of one he did not know, but he wouldn't let it slip away. For some reason the pessimism of the old days did not immediately rear up and sour those hopes. He was somebody now. He was Willie Croft, vice-president and general counsel of Obsidian Oil.

She put a cup of coffee on the counter in front of him.

"Black, with sugar, right?"

"I'm surprised you remember."

"I never forget," she said. "Now, tell me, how are things with Aunt Hannah?"

"Well," he said, "it's hard to tell, but we might have a chance, if I'm right about something."

"About what?"

"You ever been around her when she takes a drink?"

"A drink. She doesn't drink anything but an occasional sherry."

"Possibly it's more than occasional."

She thought for a moment. "Now that you mention it, I guess she does loosen up some. She doesn't drink much around me. I think she believes it's a bad example. She still thinks of me as a child."

"Well, she doesn't have those inhibitions around me," he said. "I watched her put away the better part of a bottle and her head cleared up till it was as good as mine. Better maybe. I think that's the secret. Just before we go to trial, I'm going to get her to drink three-quarters of a bottle of sherry. If it works, she won't have any problems."

"My God!" Whitsey said. "Do you really think so?"

"Wouldn't say it if I didn't," he said. "Now, let me ask you something. How'd you like to go down to Beaudreux's with me tonight?"

"Oh, gosh, I can't tonight," she said. "I'm on the committee for . . . well, it's just some dumb committee I've joined, but it's meeting tonight and I'm late already."

"I see," he said.

"But I really would love to go some other time," she added quickly. "I've thought about Beaudreux's off and on. Won't you ask me again?"

"Sure," he said cagily, "sometime."

He walked her to her car and just before she got in she took his hand and gave it a squeeze. She looked at him for a long moment, and suddenly thought that he seemed to have changed. She perceived something different from those first times together, a poise, a self-assurance. Or maybe it was her imagination. But somehow he even seemed physically larger.

"We'll be in touch," he said, and shut the door. She backed out, wondering. She felt drawn to him again, in an uneasy way. She knew she wanted to see him again.

She stopped the car in front of the house where the meeting was to be. Another car pulled up behind her and as she got out someone called to her.

"Whitsey dear, how nice to see you. We don't see much of you anymore." She recognized the sickly-sweet voice of her cousin, Marci Holt.

"Hello, Marci," she said, "how have you been?"

"Oh, fine. I've been fine," Marci said. Whitsey could tell she'd been drinking. She could smell it deeply on her breath.

"That's good to hear," she said. "And the rest of the family, how are they?"

"*Our* family?" Marci said curtly. "Our family is fine. How's *your* family?"

"I thought we were all one family," Whitsey said. "Has that changed?"

"Well, what do you think, dear girl? After all, families are supposed to stick together. If they don't, then they aren't a family, are they?"

The two women were standing on the sidewalk in front of the large house. A few others passed them by and went inside.

"I suppose what you mean is that because I happen to

234

agree with Aunt Hannah, I'm no longer considered a member of the family, is that it?"

"Well, dear," Marci snapped, "you really never *were,* you know. I mean, the Holts *have* taken in some new kin over the years and when Aunt Hannah married your uncle we were good enough to consider that that made you sort of a member of the Holts. But if you want to *be* a Holt, you have to *act* like a Holt, and Holts don't sneak around and turn their backs on other Holts. It's as simple as that, my dear."

"Look, Marci," Whitsey said, "I really think I should be getting inside. It's been nice talking to you."

"You little hussy!" Marci hissed. "You ungrateful little whore! You would try to do this to us!"

Whitsey had turned to go, but stopped and faced her cousin. "Listen, Marci, the only thing I've done is not to interfere with an old lady who wants to spend the rest of her years peacefully. If she had wanted to have oil wells dug on her place, then I would have been happy with that too. I tried. I don't have any control over her. She does what she wants to do."

"She doesn't do any such!" Marci spat. "She's as crazy as a loon. She's nuts, and you know it. You're costing us maybe millions of dollars, do you know that!"

"It might surprise you," Whitsey said, "to know that she's not nearly as crazy as you think." She felt her face flush with anger. "Especially not like *you* get when you take a drink. You've been drinking and you're the one who's acting crazy!"

"You're the one who's crazy now!" Marci shouted.

"Really?" Whitsey retorted. "Well, you just wait and see when you take her to court. We'll all see who's crazy then. Willie Croft will show you who's crazy and who isn't!"

"Willie Croft!" Marci cried. "That dirty little low-class no class! He's trying to ruin this family just like he's ruining this town. And you even had the nerve to bring him to the Azalea Ball where he could beat up my brother."

"Percy deserved it. He started it," Whitsey said. She noticed that half a dozen women had gathered on the porch steps and were watching the scene quietly. Marci glanced up and saw them too.

"Well, you're no better than he is," Marci said loudly, making sure everyone could hear. "You're nothing but an ungrateful little whore and you probably sleep with the niggers and I'll tell you something else, when I start something, I finish it myself!" Marci had been leaning forward, her mouth almost in Whitsey's face, but she stepped back and slapped out with her right hand, catching Whitsey on the cheek with a stinging open palm. Whitsey recoiled and put her hand to her cheek. Marci was standing squarely in front of her, feet planted, hands on her hips, waiting for a response.

Whitsey barely thought about it before giving her one. She brought her right hand back, doubled into a fist, and shot it out as hard as she could. Whitsey heard the sound as her fist caught her cousin square in the eye, and Marci went down flat on her back. She didn't move for a few moments, then rolled over and put her hand to her eye, but did not try to get to her feet. Whitsey stood looking over her for a few moments, then stalked to her car and drove away.

Several mornings later some reporter discovered that a trial date had been docketed. The afternoon headline shrieked HOLT MISCEGENATION TRIAL SET.

Tompkins and the Holts raised hell but even they were unable to prevent the paper from covering the case. Too much public interest had built up. The case had three elements of a good news story: race, sex and money, and possibly the fourth, violence. Judge McCormack was equally helpless to hold a closed trial for fear the city wouldn't stand for it. They were stuck and Willie knew it and was pleased as punch at the chance for a public trial in case the thing should go to appeal.

But the day before the trial Willie's spirits sank to their lowest ebb. He had spent the preceding weeks like a crazy man, working eighteen-hour days, preparing his arguments, supporting claims, briefing witnesses. Many nights he slept on the sofa in his office, supported by quarts of coffee and sandwiches, and Moon Pies and Twinkies and cartons of Picayune cigarettes. Putting together a case like this, he had decided, was like trying to lift a three-hundred-pound fat woman—there were a lot of places to hold up at once.

Then came Skinner's disastrous call.

"The news is not so good," Skinner reported in an almost offhand way, as though he had had to render this same opinion many times.

"How not good?" Willie asked, his stomach sinking, heart pounding.

"We've run into granite," Skinner said.

"What's that mean?"

"Problems—time, money. Also don't look too good for the overall prospects. If I'd know'd there was granite down there, I might of had a different opinion to start with."

"Well, for Christ's sake, I thought you did know! You had all those charts from the oil companies."

"They didn't know neither," Skinner said casually. "I s'pose if they had, they'd of put it in the charts."

"Shit," Willie said, it being the only suitable thing he could think of for the occasion.

"What you want me to do?" said Skinner.

"Well, how in hell should I know?" Willie protested. "You're the one who knows all about this, not me. How do you expect me to make a decision?"

"Somebody's got to," Skinner replied merrily.

"Well, for Christ's sake . . ." He paused. "Okay, what are we talking about, in terms of money and time?" Willie said.

"Hard to tell," said Skinner. "Impossible, really. If it's heavily stratified or there's more than one layer, it'll be a lot of time and a lot of money. Got to get more equipment; takes time to drill through granite. Tough as a cob. Means all sorts of extra hours. Could take months. On the other hand, if it's just a thin fold we might bust through it tomorrow. Just can't tell about these things."

"Great," Willie moaned. He saw everything slipping away. He was standing, without speaking, holding the receiver to his ear and looking out at the bright afternoon sunshine.

"What's it gonna be, sport?" Skinner said finally. "I gotta tell people somethin' up here. We can't just sit around."

"Well, we've got some money left, but not much. Those bastards in Chicago ever find out what we're doing with the loan they gave us, we'll all be in big trouble. They still think we're just buying leases. . . . Oh, God, how'd I ever get into this?"

"What's it gonna be?" Skinner repeated.

Willie snorted and mashed a cigarette savagely in an ashtray.

"Drill!" he shouted. "And I don't give a goddamn what you have to do, even if you have to go down in the hole yourself and chip it away!"

"That's the spirit!" Skinner cried. "That's the spirit, podner!"

16

WILLIE HAD BEEN UP MOST OF THE NIGHT BEFORE THE OPENING day of the trial. His eyes were bleary and his face worn and haggard from reading cases. He had never worked so hard on anything in his life and was close to exhaustion. At 5:30 A.M. he fell asleep on the secondhand couch in his office and woke at eight with a severe case of cottonmouth. He went to the rest room down the hall and brushed his teeth and shaved. His stomach was in such turmoil he considered forcing himself to throw up. He felt he had the best case he could present, but in the end it would all come down to who believed whom, not pure law, and most of his proof would be subject to the scrutiny of jurors. They would, of course, be white men. It was barely the dawn of a new decade in the South, but the Southern mind was as prejudiced as it had ever been, and perhaps more so.

Methodically he packed away all the files and books and briefs and notes and memoranda into a scuffed old suitcase, the bulk of it being too voluminous for his briefcase. Then he poured a two-finger glass of bourbon and downed it in a gulp and left the building.

It was a hot and airless morning with an overcast sky and a faint Gulf sun, huge and white, pasted sullenly in the sky. He crossed The Parade, straining against the luggage, worry knotting his stomach and nattering at his bowels as though it were an actual physiological disorder.

When he rounded St. Raymond's Street, he saw clusters of people around the courthouse, on the steps and the walk and on the lawn. He detected their murmurings, but as he approached they fell silent. They were mostly older men, and some women, unsmiling, but not necessarily hostile; merely curious, and with time on their hands. He recognized some of the faces from the benches on The Parade or from various street corners around town where men sometimes congregated. He forced a smile and acknowledged a few by name and nodded to others as he passed through them toward the steps and they nodded or acknowledged him back. He glanced up and saw that every barred window on the second floor was filled with faces silent and wondering. As he mounted the steps a man in a shabby gray suit stepped in front of him and took his picture with a large, professional-looking camera and two alcoholic-faced reporters from the *Bienville Post-Herald* fell in alongside him as he entered the building, asking questions. Willie simply shook his head and smiled and spoke only to Burt, the bailiff, who was wide awake, and who replied with "Mornin', Mr. Croft; big mornin' today," and then Willie walked in by the side entrance into the empty courtroom, in which he had spent so many hours out of the past seventeen years, and he put the suitcase down on the desk and stared alone at the clusters of flags, national, state, city, arrayed on either side of the high judge's bench and prayed silently that justice might be done.

The lock on the door to the courtroom suddenly clicked and the door itself seemed almost to burst open and Augustus Tompkins strode in with the air of some Teutonic knight, followed by a court of lesser lawyers, clerks and his own personal stenographer. As the entourage began to set up at the table across from Willie, Tompkins regarded the battered suitcase which Willie had been carefully unpacking, gave him a sneer, seated himself grandly in the center chair and buried himself in a brief. Slowly the courtroom began to fill. Willie could hear the murmuring in the hallways. A court clerk and a bailiff appeared and began puttering around behind the dock. Willie would face it by himself today. All his potential witnesses, Daniel, Priscilla and the rest, would be sequestered until they were actually called to testify. He had never felt so alone in a courtroom before.

A side door opened and the head bailiff appeared, followed by a dozen men, most of them in their forties and fifties. As each entered, he looked around the courtroom curiously, and then the bailiff seated them in the jury dock. Willie stole a glance at the motley collection. He recognized a couple of faces, but most were new to him. They were hard, deliberate faces, as jurors were in those days, men who, for the most part, were out of work, or retired, or who, for whatever reasons, were unable to make an influential phone call to escape their duty.

At precisely one minute past nine Judge McCormack entered the courtroom, robes flowing, took his seat on the bench and the jury selection began.

Willie had a plan and he stuck by it. It was nearly half an hour and too late for Augustus Tompkins to do anything about it by the time he caught on. The damage had been done.

Tompkins ignored the prospective jurors completely as they came in, then approached them almost ferociously, a tactic which seemed to Willie more designed to impress his clients than anything else. He questioned each juror sternly about whether or not they had ever owned land where mineral rights were in dispute, or if they had ever held property where a title was in question, or whether or not they had ever gained property by "squatter's rights." He also asked them if they had ever had any dealing with the Holt family, and if so, was it satisfactory. By the end of the hour he had used both his peremptory challenges and dismissed several other jurors for cause.

This left seven remaining jurors for Willie to deal with. They were a hard-looking bunch, these remaining seven, but Willie calculated on an old trick he occasionally used. He had decided to try it now.

"I have no questions for the jury, Your Honor," Willie said to the judge. "These men look all right to me."

As he sat down he glanced at Tompkins's face and saw the sudden dismayed recognition that Willie had just gained a leg up with at least seven of the twelve men who would sit in judgment on the case. When the five new prospective jurors entered the dock, Tompkins declined to challenge them as did Willie, and the trial of *Brevard Holt et al.* vs. *The Estate of Mrs. Elvira Backus* began in earnest.

"This is a simple case of eviction," Tompkins told the jury contemptuously. "The Holt family, an old and respected institution in Bienville, was one of a handful of founding families of this great Southern city of ours. The piece of land in question has been passed down through generation to generation in this fine family, with not a single cloud on any title until these *usurpers,*" and he emphasized the word with the utmost contempt, "suddenly come forward now, when there appears to be a great deal of money involved, and attempt to lay claim to it."

The eyes of the jury followed Tompkins as he turned and walked behind his table. Willie studied the men in the jury box. Their faces were intent and inscrutable.

"The *defendants* in this case," Tompkins said, deliberately emphasizing the word defendants as though it were a criminal proceeding, "will tell you that the father of my clients, Mr. Johnathan Holt Second, *gave* the property in question to them. We will prove that no such gift occurred. That at the time of alleged bequest, Mr. Johnathan Holt was an old man, short months away from his deathbed, and not of sound mind or body. And that for all the years hence my clients have scrupulously and legally paid the taxes on this property, and retained legal and binding title which has been on record in this courthouse."

Tompkins sucked in a breath and peered at the jury over his nose, letting them digest the information. Then he pursed his lips and drew himself up in a gesture of righteous indignation.

"It may be," he said angrily, turning directly to Willie, "though I hope it does not occur, that the defendants are going to attempt to lodge a pernicious and outrageous smear upon the good name of my client's father, Mr. Johnathan Holt. This smear has been well publicized in the newspapers, and I am sure that each of you is aware of it—that the elder gentleman, Mr. Johnathan Holt, at some point engaged in an illicit relationship with the mother of the defendants, Mrs. Elvira Backus, daughter of the sharecropper who tended my clients' property, and from this union the defendants themselves were produced."

Willie kept his eyes on the jury. They seemed deeply absorbed by Tompkins's speech.

"Only now, nearly fifty years after this preposterous event was alleged to have transpired, do these defendants come forward with this terrible claim to besmirch the memory of a leading citizen of this community and this state, when he is dead and unable to defend himself. To all of us who knew and respected him, Mr. Johnathan Holt was a man of decent Christian values. A man who dedicated his life to helping this fine town of ours. A man who was happily married for more than thirty years.

"What you must ask yourselves, gentlemen of the jury, is why, after all this time, would these people come forward with this story? Is it because there is suddenly much to be gained from fabricating such a tale? Listen to the evidence carefully. Not hearsay evidence. Not the whimsical stories of people who wish to cash in on a good thing and are willing to stoop to any depth to do it, but to hard, factual evidence, such as who actually has the title to this piece of land. Who has had title to it for nearly three hundred years. Clear legal title. Ownership! You all know what that is! To have something of your own, that nobody can take away from you. Your house, your car, your piece of land. It's yours and it belongs to you! Let nothing cloud your sight! That is what this case is about. My clients have kindly let the defendants and their mother live up there on their piece of land for years; out of the generosity of their hearts they let them build a small shack on it. And suddenly they are threatened not only with loss of their own property, but also the ruination of their own good name.

"Evidence!" Tompkins cried. "Where is the evidence, except in the words of the defendants who want to take something they do not own!"

His bull voice still ringing in everyone's ears, Augustus Tompkins sat down. The courtroom was utterly silent, not a cough, not so much as a shuffling of feet. The jurymen were motionless, their faces masklike. The electricity in the old lawyer's voice had sparked a powerful fusion and Willie sensed it.

"Mr. Croft," the judge said.

Willie heard his name called, but it sounded as though it were from afar. Then he heard it again.

"Mr. Croft, you may proceed now."

Willie got to his feet. In front of him on the table lay the notes for his own opening statement. He suddenly knew it wouldn't work. Tompkins had gotten to them. Property, ownership, moneygrubbing, gold-digging niggers. He hadn't actually said that, but he didn't have to. Everyone had read the newspapers.

"I have no opening statement," Willie said falteringly. "If the plaintiff wishes to prove a case for eviction, let him do so." Then he sat down.

Tompkins spent the rest of the morning introducing into evidence titles and deeds and authenticating documents pertaining to the Creoletown property, some going back as far as the original land grant. He introduced the letter of eviction that he had sent old Mrs. Backus months before. He was not going to put on witnesses at this stage. Apparently his game plan was that he had a prima facie case and he was going to put the burden on Willie to show otherwise. After the luncheon recess he summed up the Holts' position in a single sentence.

"There is an unbroken title to this property dating back to the year sixteen eighty-eight and not one shred of evidence proves otherwise." On the surface it seemed like a pretty clear-cut thing. At last it was Willie's turn.

"Gentlemen of the jury," Willie said softly. He had his hands in his pockets and his jacket was opened. He had loosened his tie and was perspiring around the collar. "What you have just heard from Mr. Tompkins is true to a point. And that point was reached on a rainy afternoon in nineteen forty when Johnathan Holt handed Mrs. Elvira Backus, then a sixty-year-old woman living in a cabin on the Holt property, a piece of paper, signed by Mr. Holt himself, and witnessed by his sister, Mrs. Hannah Holt Loftin. That paper deeding that four hundred and eighty acres to Mrs. Backus is what I am now holding in my hand." Willie saw the disapproval in Augustus Tompkins's face when he held the paper out to the jury. Disapproval coupled with resignation, for Tompkins had not until now been certain that the deed hadn't been destroyed in the fire.

"When a man wants to give something to someone," Willie said, "it is his God-given right to do it. That is what Mr. Holt did that December afternoon almost twenty years ago. He had his reasons, and if necessary, we can show them, but for now this lone piece of paper offers incontrovertible proof that Johnathan Holt made a deliberate, conscious decision to make a gift of his land to Mrs. Backus."

Willie put the deed into evidence and had it passed around to the jury. When they had finished looking it over he continued.

"The laws of this state do not rule out the validity of a written deed transferring land simply because it is not recorded. Mrs. Backus, being unsophisticated about the complicated laws of real estate, kept this deed safeguarded in her home, believing, and rightly so, that it was her proof of ownership. For decades the Holt family allowed her to live there in peace, and when Mr. Tompkins asks you 'why, after all this time,' my clients come forward to lay claim to the land, you must also ask yourselves why, after all this time, do the Holts now come and try to seize property that no longer belongs to them?"

Then he sat down. Willie had decided to match tactics with Tompkins head for head. If he wanted to show a prima facie case, Willie could too. Let him prove the deed wasn't legal. Tompkins was prepared to do just that.

He called to the stand a Dr. Martin Wilfred, a shriveled, bald-headed general practitioner who had been the Holt family physician for forty-five years before he retired.

"Did you, Dr. Wilfred, attend the late Johnathan Holt in the period up to and including his death?" Tompkins asked.

"Yes, I did," the doctor said.

"Could you give the jury an assessment of Mr. Holt's mental condition at that time?"

"At what time?" the doctor asked in a high croaking voice.

"At the time from about a year before he died until his death."

"Wasn't so good, I'd say. Got a lot worse toward the end. Didn't want to die. Nobody does."

"But how about his soundness of mind?" Tompkins asked. "Would you say that everything he did in that period was sound? In the sense that he knew exactly what he was doing?"

"Hard to tell," the old doctor said. "I saw a lot of him. Scared, that's what I'd say. He knew he was going. Had a cancer of the stomach. Not much you can do about that."

"Did he ever do anything that struck you as being strange?"

"Well now, a dying man does a lot of strange things. Sort of changes his life, I guess," Dr. Wilfred said with some relish. "Let's see. There was one thing I remember. He decided to go hunting. To go up to that piece of property of his up to Creoletown. I don't think he was feeling very well at the time. Probably in some pain. I advised him against it. Could have taken sick and there'd be nobody up there to help him. But he was bent on going."

"Yes," Tompkins said, flustered, "but now wasn't there a time when he discussed money with you? Doing some funny things with it?"

"Oh, yeah," the doctor said. "One time he's in the office after an examination and he says, 'You know, Marty, what I think I might do is to take all my money—sell the stevedoring company and everything—and go off to India or someplace.' And I says, 'Why is that, John?' And he says, 'Because it's about as far around the world as I can get from my damned family.'"

There was muffled coughing from the gallery.

"And that struck you as odd, did it not?"

"Nothing strikes me as odd anymore," Dr. Wilfred said testily.

"But did it not indicate to you that Mr. Holt was not quite 'all there'?"

"Well," Wilfred said thoughtfully, "that occurred to me. He was under a great deal of strain. And he was getting old too. Old men sometimes have funny ideas."

"Ideas that might call their judgment into question, correct?" Tompkins pressed.

"Naturally. He was what—sixty-five or sixty-two or so. The thought process sometimes gets muddled up with the emotional process at that age. Their arteries harden. The brain doesn't get enough blood—and that's all mixed in with the fear."

"If I told you Johnathan Holt wanted to give away several hundred valuable acres of land to a black tenant farmer during that period, would you have been surprised?"

"Not particularly then," Wilfred replied.

"How about twenty years before? When he was a younger man. Would it have surprised you then?"

"It would have shocked the hell out of me," Wilfred said. "I never knew Johnathan Holt to just up and give anything to anybody without a good reason."

More coughing and shuffling of feet issued from the spectators.

"So it might be fairly said that if he did give something like that away in those months before he died it was likely that he didn't know what he was doing?"

"I rec'on that'd be a pretty fair guess," Wilfred said. "In his day Johnathan Holt was probably the second stingiest man east of New Orleans."

Tompkins's eyebrows raised in curiosity. "Who was the stingiest?" he asked.

"His father," the doctor replied serenely.

"Your witness," Tompkins said, and sat down.

Willie got to his feet and approached the stand.

"Dr. Wilfred," he said, "how old are you?"

"Me? I'm seventy-nine. Be eighty in September."

"And you consider yourself in sound mind?"

"Of course I do," the doctor said sourly. "What kind of question is that?"

"Well, Doctor, you have just finished stating that Mr. Holt, who was sixty-five, was possibly suffering from an unsound mind."

"In my opinion he might have been."

"Do you think that he knew that? That he realized he might be of unsound mind?"

"I wouldn't think so; people in that state rarely do."

"Then how do you know that you yourself aren't suffering from the same thing?"

"I beg your pardon?"

"I said, if people, old people whose minds are going, don't know it, how do you know your mind isn't going?"

The doctor turned to the judge. "Do I have to take this?"

Judge McCormack scowled at Willie. "Are you insinuating that the doctor is not of sound mind?"

"No, sir," Willie said. "I'm simply asking him if *knows* he isn't."

"Hell, yes, I know I'm not!" Wilfred snapped.

"That's all right, Doctor," Willie said. "I didn't mean to get you upset."

"I'm not upset," the doctor said defensively. His voice was irritatingly high-pitched at this point. "How do you expect me to act when you suggest I'm crazy?"

"I don't think you're crazy," Willie said. "I never said that."

"Yes, you did!" Wilfred roared. "That's exactly what you insinuate. Don't you think I know whether I'm crazy or not?"

"I wouldn't know about that, Doctor," Willie said calmly. "You don't look crazy."

"Goddamnit!" Wilfred shouted. He was standing in the witness chair when Tompkins leaped to his feet with, "Objection! Objection!"

"All right, Mr. Croft. I'm warning you," Judge McCormack said.

Willie walked around to the back of the table and let things settle down. Then he continued.

"All right, Doctor, just one more question. You said you saw Johnathan Holt just before he went up to Creoletown to go hunting. Did he seem crazy to you then?"

"No, he didn't seem crazy!" the doctor snapped. "You're misusing that word. There are clinical terms . . ."

"Yes, I'm sorry," Willie said contritely. "Did he seem in any way disturbed then?"

"He was not disturbed. He was serene."

"But you thought it was strange, that he would be going hunting?"

"The man was dying," the doctor said.

"Why shouldn't a dying man do something that gave him pleasure?"

"Well, certainly he should, but in that case, and I remember it well, it was a cold day, and it was raining. It wasn't prudent."

"But it wasn't crazy then?" Willie said.

"I wish you would quit using that word!" Wilfred screeched. "A man can do strange things and not be crazy!"

"Thank you, Doctor. That's all I wanted to know," Willie said.

Wilfred stepped down and Tompkins approached the bench. Willie followed him. "Your Honor," Tompkins said, "I would like to ask for a recess until tomorrow morning. I have a witness who I'd like to have some more time to prepare with."

"Who is that?" Judge McCormack asked.

"Brevard Holt, Your Honor, the son of Johnathan Holt."

"Very well," McCormack said. He leaned over and said something to the court clerk, who arose and dismissed the court until nine in the morning.

Willie was in the corridor, struggling with the suitcase full of his papers, when he saw Daniel Holt standing just outside the door, waiting for him.

"How did it go?" Daniel asked.

"It's too early to tell," Willie said. "Not as bad as it could have been. You all right?"

"Fine," Daniel said. "That witness room was kind of hot, so I told the man, the, er . . ."

"The bailiff?"

"Yes, the bailiff, that if they wanted me I'd be on the steps out back."

"Listen," Willie said, "I've got something I have to do for a few minutes. Why don't you go over to the offices and I'll see you there?"

Daniel left, and Willie, lugging the suitcase, struggled off toward the side street where Whitsey Loftin's bookshop was. He looked through the door and was relieved to see that she was there, and that she was alone.

"Hi," he said, walking in.

"Why, Willie, you look like you're leaving town." She was wearing a light blue dress, and had her hair pulled back. He hadn't see her since the evening a few weeks before when he helped her with the carton of books.

"I've got something to ask you," he said. He had set the suitcase down on the floor.

"You want me to run away with you," she teased.

"No, this is serious. Do you think you can go up and get your Aunt Hannah and have her at the courthouse at nine tomorrow morning?"

"Aunt Hannah?" Whitsey said. "But why? Is her case . . . ?"

"I don't want to go into it all right now," he said. "Do you think you could do it?"

"Why, yes, I guess so . . . but I wish you'd tell me . . ."

"What I can tell you is," he said, "that there may be a way to kill two birds with one stone if you do what I ask. Can we just leave it like that?"

"Yes, all right," she said hesitantly. "I suppose you wouldn't ask if you didn't know what you were doing."

Willie lurched out into the street with the suitcase and headed for his office. The late-afternoon air was heavy, but filled with the fresh fragrances of spring. He bought the afternoon paper from a newsboy. The trial was the lead story.

HOLTS CHARGE SLANDER the headline screamed. There followed an account of the morning's events as given by Augustus Tompkins. Obviously some deadline had foreclosed any mention of Willie's counterarguments.

When he reached his office he found Daniel and several members of Obsidian's board of directors sitting in his room. The mood was glum. "Mr. Croft," Daniel said, "we've been talking about this among ourselves for a couple of weeks now. Not just because of the trial. But I'll come right to the point. Most of us feel the same way, generally— that we see little hope not only of winning my mother's case in court, but also of finding any oil up there. Everything Mr. Skinner has said recently is negative. We are getting into terrible debt with the Chicago people. We are getting harassed by phone calls and who knows what else might happen."

Daniel paused for a moment and Willie looked at the solemn faces around him. He took off his jacket and rolled up his shirtsleeves and went around behind his desk, but he remained standing.

"There is still a way to make money out of this," Daniel continued. "Not as much, of course, but some. What would you say if we decided to accept the deal the Holts have offered us? My mother gets the property and sixty percent of the mineral rights in case they find any oil. And what if we simply stop drilling and all that and sell the leases we have to a big oil company? We would still be ahead. It would be a sure thing. Very simply, we're afraid of the risks involved if we keep on going. We might wind up with nothing at all."

Willie rubbed his face. It felt grimy and numb. His head ached slightly and he could feel bags under his eyes. "Let me get a drink of water and wash my face," he said. "Let me think about it for a minute." He left the room and walked to the water cooler down the hall. Those were frightened faces in his office. He had seen such faces before in the middle of a trial, scared of losing and tense and worried under the pressure and ready to give up for a deal. Willie would always advise them honestly, depending on how he thought their case was going. Sometimes they took his advice, sometimes not. Usually it was good advice, detached, objective. But this was different. There were things for him at stake here too. He had come this far, and to cave in now . . . In the rest room he scooped up water and threw it to his face. He tried to separate pride from his feelings, but found it impossible. Things were not going well. That was an understatement. He couldn't tell about the trial . . . and Skinner's operation might collapse at any moment. Professionally, it would be prudent to cash in now. He dried his face with a towel. Instinct, he thought to himself. Must go on instinct! Get yourself out of it and make a professional decision. Nearly twenty years a lawyer—twenty years . . . He went back down the hall and entered his office again. They had been talking but looked up and fell silent when he came through the door. He sat down behind his desk and took a breath.

He said boldly, "We've come all this way, let's don't crap out now. This is how fortunes are built."

The men in the room looked at each other and at Daniel, who had fixed his eyes on Willie. No one said anything for long agonizing seconds. It was Daniel who spoke first.

"Well, if Mr. Croft feels like this, I'll go along with him. He's been straight so far."

The others nodded and spoke their agreement.

"Listen," Willie said, "I've got a lot of work to do for tomorrow, so I'd better get to it, and one more thing: Stop calling me 'Mr. Croft'—the name's Willie."

After they had gone he sat alone at the desk, gazing at the last faint rays of sunlight. He stayed that way for a long time, until it was dark, looking out the window at the trees and the empty city street below. Oh, Lord, he thought, let me be right about this.

"Do you recall your father's mental condition during the months prior to his death?" Tompkins asked.

On the witness chair was Brevard Holt, nattily dressed in a gray pinstriped suit, white shirt and blue tie, looking thoughtful. "Yes, I believe I have a rather good notion of it."

"Tell the court what you perceived," said Tompkins.

"Well," Brevard said, "he was not in his right mind. Simple as that. He began doing strange things."

"What strange things?" Tompkins said.

"Let me see, once he sat up all night in front of the fire drinking. He must have drunk a full bottle of whiskey. When we came down in the morning he was just sitting there humming to himself. He acted like he didn't recognize any of us, including Mother."

"And this was not normal behavior, was it?"

"Certainly not," Brevard said emphatically. "Father drank very moderately. He rarely if ever had more than two drinks an evening."

"Did he ever talk about giving property away?"

"No, of course not."

"Did you ever hear him speak of giving over any property to a Mrs. Elvira Backus, the woman who was allowed to live on your land near Creoletown?"

"Not a word."

"Would it have seemed strange to you if he had?" Tompkins asked.

"Of course it would," Brevard said primly. "Father did not give away pieces of his property."

Tompkins continued the interrogation in this vein, eliciting from Brevard Holt a host of incidents that might indicate his father was unsound, and splicing them with Brevard's denials of any gift of the land to Mrs. Backus. When he had finished he turned Brevard over to Willie.

"No questions, Your Honor," Willie said. "But I have a witness of my own to counter Mr. Holt's testimony." He walked over and spoke to the bailiff, who disappeared outside and returned moments later ushering into the courtroom Mrs. Hannah Holt Loftin, escorted by her niece, Whitsey Loftin.

Augustus Tompkins jumped to his feet immediately.

"Your Honor," he said indignantly, "this is clearly out of order! Mrs. Loftin is currently the defendant in a competency suit. How can she possibly come in here and testify to anything when her own sanity is in serious question?"

The old lady's voice as she walked down the aisle crackled sternly across the courtroom, firm and clear.

"Augustus Tompkins, don't you dare talk about me that way! You have done everything you can to take over my place and ruin it, including your silly little lawsuit. But you're not going to get away with it! You sit down. I'm going up here to tell the truth!"

Judge McCormack scowled at Willie in exasperation. "Mr. Croft," he said, "what is going on here? You know that Mrs. Loftin is not . . ."

"Dudley T. McCormack!" the old lady bristled, shaking a finger at the judge. She had reached the little gateway to the dock. "I have known you for fifty-five years. I came all the way down here to say what I know about this case and I'm going to do it!"

"If Your Honor please," Willie interceded, "Mrs. Loftin is merely in receipt of papers involving her in a competency case. That case, as the court knows, has not been tried, nor has anyone, other than the plaintiffs in this case before us now, the Holt family, ever suggested that she is not capable. I submit that until such time as her mental capacity might be legally shown defective, she is perfectly entitled to do anything else that an ordinary citizen would, including serving as a witness in this trial."

McCormack, plainly unhappy with the situation, but powerless to do anything about it, nodded for the bailiff to seat Mrs. Loftin in the witness chair.

Willie approached the old lady and noted that her eyes were clear and intent. He had instructed Whitsey to let her sip on a bottle of sherry on the drive down to Bienville.

"Mrs. Loftin," he said, "do you remember the day in nineteen hundred forty when your brother, Johnathan Holt, came by your home in Creoletown and asked you to witness a document?"

"Very clearly," she said.

"Could you tell the court and the jury about it?"

The old woman drew herself up in the witness chair and cleared her throat. "It was raining that day," she said, "and it was cold. Johnathan came by rather late in the afternoon.

His boots were muddy and he was wet and I made him sit by the fire and I fixed him some tea."

Willie had stepped away from the box and was leaning against a wall as Mrs. Loftin recounted that long-ago afternoon. She spoke thoughtfully and with an eye for detail, looking not at the jury or the courtroom of spectators, but beyond them, back through the years, much as Mrs. Backus had the first time Willie had gone to her little cabin months before. Mrs. Loftin remembered it all so clearly, it was as though Johnathan Holt II were suddenly present himself in the courtroom, the muddy boots, the pipe, the tone of his voice when he told her he was going to give the land to Mrs. Backus, and then had her witness the deed. When she finished there was an almost complete stillness in the room. A puff of breeze from the river wafted gently through the open windows, then died.

Willie moved close to the old woman and asked in the most earnest voice he had, "Did you find anything strange or peculiar about your brother's behavior that day?"

"No," she said. "He seemed tired, that's all. He was ill. I think that made him tired."

"Brevard Holt," Willie said, "his son and your nephew, has testified here that his father was not of sound mind. That he was behaving strangely. Am I correct that you observed no such behavior?"

"I knew my brother considerably longer than Brevard, or any of his other children," the old woman said, "and I believe I would be in a better position to say if he were acting strangely. He was not. He simply wanted to give something to that colored family over there, and he did, and I thought it was a very nice thing to do then, and I still do."

"Thank you, Mrs. Loftin," Willie said. He turned to the judge. "I have nothing more."

"Mr. Tompkins," Judge McCormack said, "would you care to question the witness?"

Tompkins, rising, said, "If Your Honor will bear with me, I have sent one of my assistants to locate Dr. Julius Crumb, a psychiatrist. His offices are just a few blocks from here. This is an extraordinary situation, considering that Mrs.

Loftin is under suit in a mental competency case. Dr. Crumb will assist me in my questioning, if we might have a short recess. . . ."

"Very well," the judge said. "Court will recess for half an hour."

Willie's heart sank as he walked over to help Mrs. Loftin out of the witness stand. This was something he hadn't counted on. Crumb, of all people. That sour little nit. He had seen him in action before. More of a rhetorician than a physician. He seemed to delight in breaking people down, and knew all the tricks to do it. She had held up amazingly well under Willie's questions, but what would happen when Crumb got hold of her? How much sherry would it take? Whitsey had the old woman's arm, leading her out of the courtroom as Willie followed behind.

"There's a room down the hall where she can sit down," he said. "I don't think anybody will be there."

Willie opened the door and Whitsey ushered her aunt to an old leather couch. She sank down, seeming exhausted.

"How did I do?" she asked weakly.

"Fine," he said, "you did just fine."

Whitsey took out a handkerchief from her purse and began to wipe the old lady's brow.

"I'm tired now," Mrs. Loftin said. "I could almost go to sleep."

"No!" Willie heard himself say, almost before he realized he'd said it. Whitsey glanced at him sharply.

"She's an old lady," she said. "This has been an ordeal."

Willie took her aside. "Listen," he said, "don't you think I know it!" He was trying to whisper. "There's more at stake here than just that Backus property. Don't you see, if she can stand up through this they'll probably drop the competency suit too. If we can beat them now, everybody'll win!"

Whitsey rubbed her forehead. "She's exhausted, Willie. That drive, the sherry, then having to get up there in front of all those people. She's got to get some rest."

"She can't," Willie said. "Half an hour, that's all."

"Then what?" Whitsey said. "Put more sherry down her?" She looked back at the old lady on the couch. Her eyes were closed and her mouth was open and she was breathing heavily.

"No!" Willie said conspiratorially. "I don't think sherry's going to do it this time. Let her sleep for about ten minutes, then wake her up. I should be back by then, but even if I'm not, make her get up. Walk her around or something, just keep her awake."

"But, Willie," Whitsey said, "she's . . ."

"Please!" he cried. "Just do what I say. This is important!"

"Where are you going?"

He was out the door, but turned to speak over his shoulder. *"Bourbon!"* he said.

17

Dr. Julius Crumb was one of the most truly unattractive men Willie had ever seen. He looked like a cross between a rat and a snake. He had large, prominent teeth and a nose to match. His mouth seemed frozen in a permanent grinning sneer and his eyes were dark and beady. Willie thought of him as the *ratsnake man*.

Whitsey lead Mrs. Loftin to the dock, where Willie took her arm and helped her to the witness stand. She staggered a little as she stepped inside, and when she sat down and faced the courtroom there was a mischievous gleam in her eyes and a wry smile on her lips. Willie had prescribed a dose of three stiff shots of bourbon and Coca-Cola, and was wondering now if he hadn't overdone it a little.

"If Your Honor please," Tompkins said, "Dr. Crumb is here and I have asked him to question Mrs. Loftin regarding her capacity for accurately recalling the events she has described."

"Very well," the judge said.

Crumb got to his feet and approached Mrs. Loftin ratlike, with tiny steps. He stopped in front of her, then moved to the left, then back to the right, watching her intently all the time, as if to suggest to the jury that he was observing a serious lunatic.

"How old are you?" Crumb finally asked.

Mrs. Loftin jumped perceptibly. "I don't have to tell you that!" she said. Willie was halfway out of the chair with an objection but the doctor continued.

"You don't have to if you don't want to," he said, "but it makes me wonder why you won't. Are you ashamed of your age?"

"Certainly not," the old woman said. "It's just that it isn't anybody's business but mine. I don't want it getting around."

"Then you *are* concerned about it?" said Crumb. He seemed to be more snakelike now.

"You are rude," she said.

"Mrs. Loftin," Judge McCormack said, "please do not make those kinds of statements in this courtroom. Please answer the doctor's question."

"He said it was all right if I didn't," she said.

"Well, don't then, but just don't call him names," the judge said.

"I thought I was here to tell the truth," she said.

"You are, madam," Judge McCormack cried in exasperation, "but only in respect to what you've been asked."

"But they said, 'the whole truth, and nothing . . .'"

"For heaven's sake!" McCormack pleaded.

"Perhaps I can sort this out," the ratsnake man interrupted. "Mrs. Loftin, there has been some question raised about your capacity to remember things and make rational decisions. Can you tell me if you think your memory is still good?"

"Good as yours is," she said.

"And how do you know this?"

"I'll bet you can't tell me what color pants you're wearing," she said.

Crumb instinctively glanced down. "Of course I can, they're blue."

"But you had to look, didn't you? You didn't even remember what pants you put on this morning."

"Well now, madam, just one moment," Crumb said

259

indignantly. "That is a very old trick you just tried. In the medical profession we call it . . ."

"Call it not knowing what pants you're wearing," she cut him off.

"It is not my pants that are on trial here!" Crumb rasped. "It is your memory."

"Your Honor," Willie said, on his feet, "the doctor should be reminded that it is not Mrs. Loftin's memory that is on trial here either. That is only his contention. She merely pointed out that he was unable to remember without looking what color trousers he had on."

"That is not relevant!" Crumb stormed. "I am trying to conduct a preliminary observation of . . ."

"Please, please," the judge said, waving his hands. Willie looked over at the jury. There were twelve bemused faces watching the proceedings.

"All right," Crumb said, "let me ask you this, Mrs. Loftin: have you ever had difficulty remembering things?"

"I don't think so," she said.

"Then perhaps you do; I mean, you're not certain, are you?"

"Your Honor," Willie said, again on his feet, "how could Mrs. Loftin possibly be sure of what she might not remember? She wouldn't remember it. It looks to me like the doctor is trying to confuse the witness."

Judge McCormack thought about this for a moment. "It is kind of confusing," he said finally. "Perhaps you would like to rephrase that question, Dr. Crumb." Crumb shot a ratsnake-like glance at Willie.

"What I'm getting at, Mrs. Loftin, is, have you ever felt that your memory of events was bad?"

"Certainly not," she said.

"Well, then, do you remember a time a few months ago when your nephew Brevard Holt came to visit you to talk about the possibility of oil on your property and you did not even recognize him?"

"Certainly I remember it," the old woman said with a relish. "Brevard and his brother, Percival, are two of the least memorable people in my life, even if they are kin. They were that way ever since they were little boys."

There were chuckles in the courtroom and Judge McCormack banged his gavel.

"But in fact you did not know who he was, when he came to your house?" Crumb persisted.

"Of course I knew who he was," Mrs. Loftin said. "I simply failed to recognize him."

"But you said your memory was good. How could you not recognize your own nephew?"

"Because I didn't want to," she said. "If I had, he would have stayed and argued. This way he left almost immediately—and good riddance too."

Tompkins got to his feet. "Your Honor," he said, "I beg the court's pardon, but I would like to confer with Dr. Crumb for a moment." The judge nodded approval and Crumb sat down next to Augustus Tompkins and the two immediately went into a heated discussion from which issued a series of hissing noises and what Willie thought was an occasional expletive. Mrs. Loftin remained on the witness stand and grinned at the court. Suddenly, Crumb rose to his feet and stalked out of the courtroom. Tompkins, also standing, said to the judge, "Your Honor, given the obviously uncooperative spirit of the witness, we have no further questions at this time."

The judge frowned at Tompkins, then said to Mrs. Loftin, "Madam, you may step down." Willie got up to help the old lady, but she staggered past him, still grinning, down the aisle and out of the courtroom, Whitsey following behind.

"I think it will be a good idea to call it a day," the judge said wearily. "Court is recessed until tomorrow morning, at nine."

Back at the Obsidian offices Willie lay down on the couch and closed his eyes. He couldn't remember ever feeling as tired. He considered getting up and pouring a glass of Early Times but for the moment was too tired even for that and he was just about to drift off to sleep when the phone rang; he let the secretary answer it, but it was for him.

"How you making out, boy?" Skinner's voice boomed over the line.

"It's still hard to tell. I think we're holding our own so far."

"That's good, that's good," Skinner said, but he didn't say anything else so Willie screwed up the courage to ask him the big question. "And how about up there? What's the story?"

"Well, not so good, I'd say. Thought we might be getting through that stuff by now, but it ain't happenin'. Three rigs are down, and one'll probably go tonight or tomorrow. We'll have to wait for spare parts. I'm afraid it might be time for another decision," Skinner said.

"On what?" Willie said, as if he didn't know.

"On whether or not to keep on goin'," said Skinner. "How much money we got?"

"Not much," Willie said. "Not after that last payroll, and we owe everybody from here to kingdom come."

"We got ten thousand?" Skinner asked.

"Hell, no. We probably don't have two or three."

"Then I guess we'd better make another decision," Skinner said.

"Then you make it," Willie said. He hung up the receiver.

Some time ago, he couldn't remember when, Willie had assumed that by this age things would just naturally fall into place for him. He'd never asked for much, not in a long, long time, but he'd sort of believed that one day he'd have a wife and a few kids and a nice little house someplace, but he'd never really aspired to them because he also believed that these things would just naturally happen to him. But it wasn't working out that way.

Forty-two years of it! He remembered his parents; their worries were so basic—getting a proper meal on the table, paying the rent and other bills. When he looked back on it, the big things in their lives seemed to revolve around the infrequent purchase of a new car or a refrigerator. They had been defeated, but they'd accepted it, he decided, because they really didn't know they'd been defeated; they simply moved through their lives quietly, hoping to get by. Well, he thought, that isn't going to happen to me!

Willie hadn't been defeated; he'd been beaten down, maybe, into thinking that there was a specific place in life for him, and that was as far as he'd ever go, but he wasn't defeated! Wasn't defeated because there was still that last tentacle of hope left in him that things might work out all right.

He lighted a Picayune and hypocritically toasted some god with the glass of bourbon he'd poured after his conversation with Skinner: If you'll just grant me one month a year—hell, three weeks even—I will wear the shit helmet for the other eleven, but during that month I would like to have everything go right—just so I can see what it's like!

The following morning broke dark and stormy; rain-filled clouds ringed the horizon layered in varying shades of gray, and every so often a rumble of thunder shook ominously in the distance. The crowd in the courtroom was smaller because of the weather, but there were still several dozen spectators. Augustus Tompkins, fresh and crisp in a handsomely tailored blue suit, spoke up immediately after the judge had seated everyone.

"Your Honor, at this point the plaintiff in this case would like to request summary judgment from the bench." It was what Willie had feared. This was the crucial hurdle: Tompkins's attempt at an end run around the jury, asking the judge himself to find that Willie's case was so weak that it did not warrant continuing the trial.

"Very well, Mr. Tompkins, you may state your case," the judge said.

"Your Honor," Tompkins boomed, "it is obvious at this point that there are really no issues of fact here for a jury to decide—only issues of law, which the court is quite capable of dealing with. This case is very simple. My clients have introduced verifiable deeds and titles to the property in question dating back two hundred and seventy-two years. The defendants, on the other hand, have produced nothing but a handwritten scrap of paper which both expert and familiar witnesses for my clients have testified was obviously the work of a dying and mentally incapacitated old man. The defendants have only been able to counter this with the testimony of a feeble and mentally ill old woman who was so obviously uncooperative that we declined to question her fully. I ask the court to dismiss the jury and find in favor of my clients."

Judge McCormack stared down at Tompkins, nodding, as though he agreed fully with what he had said. Then he turned to Willie.

"Mr. Croft," he said. Willie got to his feet.

"Your Honor, the lawyer for the plaintiff has spoken prematurely. We do, in fact, have additional evidence and witnesses to present in this case, and I am prepared to go forward at this time."

"What sort of evidence?" the judge asked suspiciously.

"Your Honor," Willie said, addressing the judge, but clearly intending his upcoming remarks for the jury, "the plaintiffs have asserted that Mr. Johnathan Holt was somehow deranged or not of clear mind when he drew up the deed giving the property to Mrs. Elvira Backus. I am now prepared to show that he was not only of sound mind, but that in fact he had a very specific purpose, which was to provide a legacy to his own two children, which he had in a union with Mrs. Backus. These children . . ."

"I object *most* strongly to this!" Tompkins said indignantly. He had come out of his chair like a shot. "As I have stated before, the defendants' effort to introduce this kind of scurrilous slander at this time is merely an attempt to discredit and bring grief to my clients. I would ask Your Honor to examine this 'evidence' very carefully in private before allowing it to be brought into this trial and stain the name of a fine old Southern family."

The judge pulled at his chin for a moment, thinking.

"Very well," he said. "Court is recessed for fifteen minutes." He looked at Willie disapprovingly. "Mr. Croft, please meet me in my chambers and be prepared to inform me what your additional evidence is."

The reporters hopped up from their seats to get to the phone booths and the spectators milled around with a louder than usual buzzing. Tompkins and his entourage went out into the hallway and Willie went back through the entrance next to the judge's bench for his conference. Fifteen minutes later everyone was assembled again and Judge McCormack rendered his decision.

"Based on what Mr. Croft has told me," the judge said, "I think I had best not render summary judgment at this time. Mr. Croft, you may proceed."

"Your Honor, gentlemen of the jury," Willie said, "I would like to call Mr. Sol Holberg." The bailiff returned momentarily with a sharply dressed man, balding and bespectacled, in his mid-forties.

"Mr. Holberg," Willie said, "what is your occupation?" Except for the court record it was an unnecessary question. Everyone knew that Sol Holberg was the proprietor of Holberg Jewelers, the oldest and also the best in town.

"I am a jeweler," Holberg said.

Willie picked up a small white envelope from his table, opened it and took out two thin gold pieces, about the size of Army dog tags. Their edges were curled, and they were slightly warped, as if they had been in a fire. He handed them to Holberg.

"Do you recognize these?"

Holberg peered at the two pieces intently, examined them, one side, then the other. He held them at arm's distance, then up close.

"Well, sir," he said, "I don't actually recognize these because I have never seen them before myself, but I believe I can say what they are."

"Before you do," Willie said, "could you read the inscriptions for the court?"

"This one," Holberg said, holding one in the palm of his hand, "says 'To Elvira—with love,' and it is dated May twenty-eighth, nineteen oh nine. And this one, 'To Elvira—with love,' and it is dated September seventh, nineteen eleven."

"Now," Willie said, "I have asked you to bring to the

265

court documents pertaining to these two items. Have you brought them?"

"I have the information," Holberg said, pulling a packet of papers from his pocket.

"What are those documents you have?" Willie said.

"These are the engraver's tickets and receipts. They were written up by my father, personally. He is now deceased," Holberg said. "They are June eighth, nineteen oh nine, and September twenty-first, nineteen eleven. They show the orders and engraving instructions for these two pieces of jewelry."

"Do they also show who ordered them?" Willie said.

"Mr. Johnathan Holt Second," Holberg said.

"Now," Willie said, handing Holberg two other pieces of paper from his table, "would you tell the court what these are?"

Holberg examined the papers. "They are birth certificates," he said.

"What are the names on them?" Willie asked.

"Daniel Holt is this one, and Priscilla Holt is the other."

"And what are the dates?"

"For Daniel Holt, it says he was born May twenty-eighth, nineteen oh nine, and for Priscilla Holt, September seventh, nineteen eleven."

"The same dates that Mr. Johnathan Holt had your father inscribe on the two gold pieces?"

"That is correct," Holberg said, "the same dates."

Tompkins was scowling. "Your Honor, I don't see what . . ."

"I will tell you what," Willie cut in. "Johnathan Holt, the father of your clients, had these two eighteen-karat gold pendants inscribed to my clients' mother, Mrs. Elvira Backus, as mementos, with the dates of birth of her two children because he was the father of those children, that's what!"

"That's a slander!" Tompkins shouted. "He may have given them as a gift or something, but it doesn't prove anything. He might have just been nice, assuming in the first place that these *things,* whatever they are, are authentic."

"They are authentic, all right, Your Honor," Willie said. "They were salvaged from a fire which burned down the home of Mrs. Backus several months ago. And since Mr. Tompkins has brought up the question of authenticity, I think my next witness can straighten that out!" Willie strode over and spoke to the bailiff, who disappeared out of the room, then returned with a diminutive Negro woman, and ushered her into the dock and onto the witness stand.

Her dark eyes shone brightly as she shifted them around the courtroom, trying to take in these strange new surroundings, then they lifted, and she looked out the open window, across the tops of the low, tile-roofed buildings and beyond them, toward the river and the dark, ominous rain clouds that hung over the water, and possibly beyond that too, to the green waters of the Gulf of Mexico, and even beyond that too. . . .

"Will you please state your name?" the clerk said.

"Elvira Backus," the old woman said.

For moments there was a stunned silence in the courtroom. Judge McCormack looked down at Willie with a frown on his face. Then a low murmur emanated from the news reporters' section, and began to spread over the spectators' gallery. Judge McCormack banged his gavel gently as Augustus Tompkins got to his feet unsteadily. He seemed in a state of shock and when he spoke there was disbelief in his voice.

"Your Honor, I . . . er . . . don't quite understand who this witness is," he stammered. "She said her name is Elvira Backus, but Elvira Backus is dead . . . she died in . . ."

"Mr. Croft has explained it to my satisfaction," the judge said. "Perhaps he could explain it best to you and the jury."

Willie got to his feet and looked past Tompkins. "Yes, I believe I can, Your Honor. Gentlemen," he began, "it was indeed reported that Mrs. Backus died in a fire at her home in Creoletown last fall, but in fact she did not, as you can see. . . ."

Willie told the jury about the mistaken body and how the secret of Mrs. Backus's having escaped had been closely guarded because of fear that "some party or parties"—he did not insinuate it was the Holts, or mention the car belonging to Snake Crenshaw—"might still profit if she were dead.

"But she has come forward here today," he continued, "to tell the truth about Johnathan Holt and her private affair with him. She did not want to do it, and would have been content to take the story with her to the grave," Willie said, "had it not been for the persistent attempts by the heirs of Johnathan Holt to take away the property that rightfully belongs to her and her children.

"And," Willie said, almost triumphantly, "unless Mr. Tompkins wishes to challenge the identity of this witness, I will begin."

Tompkins seemed deflated, and shook his head and began studying some papers before him on the table.

"Will you tell us, Mrs. Backus," Willie said, "about the first time you met Johnathan Holt."

The old lady hesitated, as though going back in time, and when she spoke it was in a clear and precise kind of crackle, the way a grandmother might sound telling stories to small children on a hot summer night.

"That's somethin' I do remember," she said. "I was eighteen yers ole, and it was on a cool day, 'Tober or 'Vember I think, and he come up to hunt—I think they was goin' afta quails that day. He wuz a pretty young man then, but older than me, an' he come up to the steps and ask where my daddy is. Well, Daddy wadn't there, he'd gone off somewhere then, and then he say, 'What's yoah name?' an' I tole him, and then they drove off and I didn't see him 'gain for 'bout two weeks, but when he come up 'gain he remember my name, and he call me by it. . . ."

Willie led her through the months and years that followed, building up to the first time they had seen each other intimately.

"I rec'on it was 'bout nineteen oh one or oh two," she said. Her eyes glistened as she looked out the window at the stormy sky. "Wuz a hot day, August, I b'lieve, when he come up w' some peaches and he axe if I wanta go down by the Sawmill Creek and et some a them. And aft' a while, he puts

his arm on my shoulders and say, 'Vira, you the pretties'
thing I seen in a long, long time,' and then he kiss me, and
start to touch me, and then we did it. We did it raght they on
the creekbank; wuz the late aft'noon, and hit was dark 'fo'
we got back to home an' Daddy was mighty mad, b'he
donsay nothin' he jus' sit in his chair an' rock, all nite long,
jus' rockin' back and fo'th, all nite long. . . ."

"Well, how did you feel about it?" Willie asked.

"Oh, I rec'on you couldn't blame 'im none. I never
knowed what he thought 'bout it. He never said."

"No, I don't mean your father, I mean, how did you feel
about Johnathan Holt?"

"Oh, 'bout him," she said. "He was a good man. He
always treated me nice. He used to bring me little things.
Sometimes we'd go down by the Sawmill Creek, or up to the
deer skin'n' station, just sit around and talk. Wouldn't do
nothin'. Jes sit there, maybe hole hands or somethin'.'"

"What kinds of things would you talk about?"

"Oh, 'bouts alls kinds of things, 'bout huntin' and fishin'
stuff, mos'ly. He had a big ole business down to Bienville.
Took things off boats. Said he had over a hun'ered people
workin' for 'im. Sometimes things'ud go wrong or somethin', he'd wanta talk about it. I didn't 'stand much, but I
listened real good."

"Did he ever talk to you about love? About you and him
and your relationship?"

The old woman thought for a long hard time. There were
a few awkward and anticipatory coughs in the gallery. Willie
glanced at the jury, who seemed on the edges of their chairs.
Tompkins's head was down, staring at the table in front of
him, and he was shaking it slowly from side to side.

"No, not much," she said. "What he gonna say? Him
bein' a white man an' all, an' me bein' colored. . . ." She
paused for a moment. "When he got married, I guess that
was 'bout three, four yers after, after the first, then he stop
comin' up. Jes stop, maybe a yer a mo', I can't 'member
'zackly. He tole me 'fo'han', he say, 'Vira, I gotta go now, an'
I ain't be comin' back no mo', 'cause I's gettin' married in
Bienville.' Well, I didn' say nothin'; I knew it gonna happen

someday. But I turn over away from him, and he put his hand on my back, and he rub my back, and he didn' say nothin' either, for a long time, an' then we git up and walk jes walk all over the place, thru all them fiel's—it was springtime then, I 'member it now, all the pretty flow'rs wuz out, an' it wuz late in the aft'noon. An' he pick some for me, an' try to give 'em to me but I didn' want 'em, an' then I start'd to cry. I didn' want to, I hadn', all that time, but I jes couldn't help it, and he say to me, 'Vira, I gotta do this, I jes gotta, I hain't got no choice, you 'stan' that, don' ya?' And I said, 'Yes, I 'stan' it,' but I didn' and I did, you see what I mean? An' then we walk back up to the house, and it'd started to rain, and we walked back all the way in the rain."

Willie looked at the jury; the twelve harsh, wrinkled faces were solemn; nothing outward gave away what they might have been thinking, nothing in their mouths, or brows, or hands—except in their eyes, he saw, or thought he saw, not in each perhaps, but all of them collectively, some tender moment in the long and never-to-be-regained past, of a lost and never-to-be-realized love they might once have had— some brief sense for that strange, solitudinous twinge of feeling that leaped across all the hatred and bigotry and pettiness and arrogance and mean-thinking of a dozen generations to allow one member of the human race to see another with a pure and naked compassion, stripped of money or position or manners or color or education or lack of it—to see them only as fellow travelers in the fifty or sixty or seventy or with luck eighty years in which they shared the joys and heartbreaks of this planet. Yes, he thought he saw that, that they must have felt it, bared away like the skin and bone and sinews, which, once removed, reveal a beating heart.

"But he did come back, didn't he, Mrs. Backus?" Willie asked. "After he was married, Johnathan Holt came back to you, didn't he?"

The old woman's face was placid now, the wrinkled skin serenely chiseled in folds and flaps, almost as though she were not real, but had been sculpted there, or photographed long ago.

"Yes," she said, "he did."

"And when was that?" Willie asked.

"'Bout a yer after. He come up one night. It was late summer, an' the sun was jes 'bout gon' an' he drive inta the yard an' git out the car. I come out on the porch an' he jes stan' there, lookin' at me, an' then he say, 'Where yoah daddy?' and I told him, 'Daddy dead,' an' he say, 'When that happen?' an' I say, ''Bout a year ago,' an' then, I couldn't hep myse'f, I run down to him; an' he hole me, an' I commenced cryin'. . . ." The old woman's voice was shaking, but strong, and the knuckles of her hands were strained where they gripped the arms of the chair. Willie secretly wished the jury could see that.

"What happened then?" he asked.

Mrs. Backus took a deep breath and let it out in a long sad sigh, and she ran her hand over her lips and cheeks and for a moment Willie was worried that she might make a fist and try to cram it into her mouth like a little child. Then she spoke.

"Then, we go on inta the house, an' he say to me how he wanted to come back up befo' but couldn' 'cause of bein' married, an' how he think 'bout me mo' and mo', and finally he jes decide to come up, 'cause he want to see me."

"And what was your reaction to that?" Willie prodded her.

"My whats?"

"I mean, how did you feel about it?"

"Oh," she said, "well, I guess I were happy, and some sad too. I don'ts know really. I were happy to seem him 'gain, but sad 'cause he's still gots a wife, and also, he's gots a baby then too."

"And did you . . . make, ah . . . love that night?" Willie asked. He had found himself hesitant to use that word, rather than something bland like "commit fornication," because the old bugaboo had reared itself in him, the old Southern feeling that Negroes don't make love, they just fornicate—especially with white men, or women, and he had had to fight for the words to come out of his mouth, and as he did he saw the jurors' brows frown almost as one, beetlelike, suspicious, disapproving, perhaps scandalized at the suggestion.

"We did," she said.

And after that, Willie said, "Did he come back again?"

"He come back. 'Bout two, three times a month, I guess for three, fo' years, maybe, 'cept for a while when I's carryin' Daniel."

"He didn't come up then?" Willie said.

"Well, he come up three, fo' times, but we didn' do nothin'. He say he don's want to do nothin' to hurt the baby."

"And after the baby was born, did he come up more often?"

"Yes, he start to come up more then."

"And did he ever bring you a gift, a present, in honor of his child?"

"He did. He give me a little gold thing. The one you got from me. He give me the one after Priscilla too."

"And how long did he keep coming up there to see you?"

"Well," the old lady said, "I guess it was twenty, maybe twenty-five years. But not as much. He had got sick then. An' also, I think he stop comin' up some as the chu'rens get older."

"When was the last time you saw him?" Willie asked.

She closed her eyes for an instant, then gazed again out of the window at the stormy weather.

"It was in nineteen hun'red and forty. It was on Christmas Day. Had been rainin' to beat the band but it stopped an' he drove up in the yard in his big ole new car and get out an' come up on the porch. The chu'rens was down pickin' berries or nuts or somephin', and we was alone for a while, sittin' in front of the fire. He look so tired and he sick. You could see that man sick. But he have that paper to the prop'ty with him, and he say, 'Vira, I want you to have this for you and those chu'rens. You been good to me,' he say, 'an' it's all I can give you.'"

Willie was standing by the table and picked up the deed and took it over to Mrs. Backus.

"Is this the paper you're referring to?" he said.

She looked it over quickly. "Yes," she said, "an I kep' it all these years."

That afternoon Augustus Tompkins made an impassioned hour and a half summation of his case to evict Mrs. Backus and in the process called implicitly on just about every notion of racial animosity ingrained in human spirit. Willie's statement, however, lasted less than a minute.

"Gentlemen of the jury," he said, "the real issues in this case involve love, and deep respect, and generosity and the feelings of one person toward another. These are very difficult things to grapple with and there is very little I can say about them. But you have heard the evidence and seen the truth as it was truthfully told. I have the utmost faith that you will come to a fair and rightful decision." Then he sat down.

Judge McCormack gave the jury instructions which were lengthy and complicated and the storm had settled to a late-afternoon drizzle when he released them for deliberation. The spectators hung around for a while, then began to drift away when it appeared a decision was not imminent. Tompkins and his entourage had departed, Daniel had driven his mother back to Creoletown and Willie was standing in a corridor talking with Burt, the bailiff. He was entertaining the thought of walking over to see Whitsey in her bookstore when the court clerk appeared in the doorway.

"Mr. Croft, we have a verdict," he said.

It was thirty minutes before Tompkins arrived, alone, and only the two of them stood before the court when Judge McCormack impatiently strode into the room and nodded for Burt to show the jury inside. They filed in slowly, and with a great deal of shuffling and bumping in the otherwise empty courtroom. Outside it was dark and cooler and the neon lights of the waterfront dives blinked and winked through the open window.

"Gentlemen, I understand you have reached a verdict," the judge said.

The foreman was a man in his fifties with the hands and

273

arms of a laborer. He stood. "We have, Your Honor, we find . . ."

"Not so fast," McCormack barked. "I'll get around to that in a minute. Now, was your decision unanimous?"

"Yes, it was," the foreman said.

"What is it?" said McCormack. "Do you find for the plaintiff, or the defendant?"

The foreman looked puzzled for a moment, and began to stammer, as though he were thinking.

"The plaintiff is represented by Mr. Tompkins here," the judge said grouchily, pointing to Tompkins, who was fidgeting with his hands. "The defendant is Mr. Croft's client."

"Yessir," said the foreman, his confusion cleared up. "Well, we find for the defendant, then."

It took a long moment for it to sink in for Willie that he had won. He felt the beginnings of a grin at the corners of his mouth and a rush of wonderful relief.

"Very well," said the judge, "this court is *dis*missed," and he rose and left the courtroom.

Lugging the tattered old suitcase full of his papers, Willie almost ran back to his office. When he got there he dropped it in the waiting room, switched on the light and made for the phone to give Daniel Holt the news. He was fumbling through his directory trying to find the number when the phone rang in front of him.

"Where in hell you been!" Skinner's voice demanded. "Been tryin' to call you for hours!"

"In the goddamn courtroom. We won, goddamnit! How do you like that!" He picked up the bottle of bourbon from his desk and began pouring a drink.

"Well," Skinner said in a pleasant drawl, "I rec'on I like it fine. 'Cause now you own an oil well too. Obsidian Number One's been capped a couple of hours, but she'll be pumpin' in a day or so. Probably about fifty or sixty barrels an hour."

Willie slammed the bottle down on the desk hard. "Great God Almighty!" he shouted.

IV

Willie

18

"I WANT TO QUESTION THEM PERSONALLY," AUGUSTUS TOMPKINS said. "Where are they now?" Percy Holt was standing by the window in Tompkins's spacious private office looking out over the sere landscape of a late-August Bienville afternoon. The oaks on The Parade seemed to wilt and weep with the heat and the air was clouded with steamy vapor rising from the streets after a brief thundershower. His brother, Brevard, sat on the couch, fidgeting with his coat buttons.

"I have them put up in a motel about ten miles from here," Percy said. "I told them not to leave the room except to eat. It might be better if we go up there, rather than bring them into town."

"That's fairly obvious," Tompkins growled impatiently. "Where'd you find them?"

"Belize. And it's probably a good thing I ran them down when I did. They'd gone through the money I gave them. Whiskey and women. Lord knows what they'd have done then. . . ."

Brevard buried his head in his hands. "This is brilliant, Percy, really . . ."

"Oh, for Chrissakes, shut up!"

"All right, all right," said Tompkins. "Now, you say you don't think they're in cahoots with Croft?"

"I don't think so. I brought it up kind of gently," Percy said. "They both played kind of dumb."

Tompkins leaned forward in his chair. "This whole business is getting messier by the minute. We've simply got to know what their position is. So we can figure what Croft's up to. We might all be in a world of shit."

"You know what he's up to," Percy snapped. "He's trying to ruin us! And already done a pretty good job. He's . . ."

"I *know* what he's done," Tompkins barked. "That business when I filed the appeal, he's made it plain what he's prepared to do. The question now is what to do about Croft."

"The problem here isn't Croft," Brevard said pathetically. He had gotten to his feet and was pacing around the room. "The problem now is these two bums you hired who've botched things so badly they might get us all sent to jail."

"It's Croft!" Percy screamed. "If it hadn't of been for that nigger-lovin' bastard none of this would have happened. Him trying to say Father fucked that nigger woman and had those children and threatening us with that, and now he's threatening us again if we appeal."

"For Chrissakes, Percy," Brevard said, "do you realize . . ."

"What I realize is that Croft is threatening to go to the sheriff and say we killed that nigger woman, whichever nigger it was, and that he's already made a public laughingstock out of our family by saying we've got nigger brothers and sisters running around. Do you know what's happening to my kids at school! What they're saying to them!" Percy pounded his fist on the table. "And now the bastard's screwed us out of Father's property and Aunt Hannah's property and it's cost us millions of dollars! That's what I realize!" He was breathing heavily, his eyes white and menacing.

"All right, I say," Tompkins cried. "It won't do to squabble among ourselves. I'm in this thing too, distasteful as it is. Now we've got to figure a way to get out of it."

"Well, okay," Brevard said. "If Percy's right and those two aren't involved with Croft, then why don't we just give them some more money and send them back to South America or even someplace farther? Let that be the end of it."

"Because they're not the problem!" Percy shouted. "I'll say it again, Croft's the problem!"

Tompkins intervened. "Let's establish some priorities. First of all, Croft knows what happened to that old nigger woman, correct? Even if it wasn't the Backus woman, a woman is dead. How much he knows, we can't be certain. At least not until such time as he decides to blow the whistle on us. But if he does, it will ruin us. Not only our careers are at stake, but our lives, our families."

"So what do you propose to do?" Brevard asked.

"It is my opinion," Tompkins said coolly, "that we should send our two friends to pay a visit to Mr. Croft."

"And do what!" said Brevard nervously.

"You know what," Percy snapped.

"No, I don't know what!" Brevard shouted, half rising from the couch.

"Listen," Tompkins said, "this man is blackmailing us. It's not a question of your property or lost money anymore. This is the most dangerous situation I have ever encountered, and that includes my war service. He will hold this over us for the rest of our lives, or he might decide to use it tomorrow. Either way, we will have no peace until this is resolved."

"Augustus, I can't believe . . ."

"Let me finish," Tompkins said. Brevard leaned forward and began rubbing his forehead in exasperation.

"There might also be a great deal to be gained from your point of view," Tompkins continued. "If I read this situation correctly, Croft is running the show all by himself. He thinks he is holding the high hand. But if he's out of the picture, it is my opinion that his nigger friends will fold like dominoes, and if we move swiftly, we would be free to pursue our claims in an appellate court."

"Well, for Christ's sake, Augustus," Brevard said weakly, "you know he's stashed some paper away that would blow the whole thing open anyway."

"I seriously doubt it," Tompkins said. "Any such paper would subject him to charges of blackmail, as well as being an accessory himself. He's a lawyer, he'll know that. It's a chance we'd have to take, but I read this bastard pretty well. I don't think he works that way. And with him out of the picture, I believe we can handle your Aunt Hannah and your cousin pretty well," Tompkins said icily.

"This is the most appalling thing I have ever listened to!" Brevard shouted with renewed vigor. "I had nothing to do with that colored woman's death and I'm certainly not going to sit here while you two plot the murder of a man—I don't care how bad he is."

"He's trying to destroy you, goddamnit!" Tompkins growled. "Can't you understand that? Any move you make, he's got you covered. As long as he's alive, he's dangerous as a rattlesnake to each one of us! The longer we wait, the worse it gets. Suppose he gets drunk and lets it slip? Or at some point decides to tell somebody? He's a walking time bomb so far as we're concerned!"

"In the name of God, Augustus, you can't just kill a man!"

"He would meet with an accident," Tompkins said coldly. "Perhaps an automobile wreck, or death by drowning on one of these expeditions Percy tells me he makes up in the Delta."

"And I suppose those two animals Percy found for us would see to that?" Brevard said.

"That is what I have in mind," Tompkins said. "Afterward, we can give them a substantial sum of money, perhaps paid out over a lengthy period through some disguised third party, to keep them happy and out of the country. I am far less concerned that they can hurt us than I am about Croft."

"This is monstrous," Brevard said, "and I won't be a party to it! Anything you and . . ."—he gave his brother a condescending glare—"Percy decide to do, you leave me out of it."

"I'm afraid, Brev," Tompkins said, "that you are already in it."

* * * *

In the month of August nothing moved very fast in Bienville. Not even the flying insects. Dogs dug holes in the soft earth beneath houses to get away from the heat. Cats rested on cool kitchen floors and the pelicans and other seabirds drooped forlornly on the bayside pilings. Every man carried two handkerchiefs to mop his brow and a venture out into the heat required tremendous energy. If it wasn't for the intermittent rain showers every afternoon the place would have been unbearable.

But this August there was an unmistakable hum in the air, an intense and electrified buzzing of interest in the proceedings up in Creoletown. The relationship between the two towns had never been much more than casual. It is probable that many young Bienvilleans had never even heard of the place, which at best enjoyed a position of poor relation in the former's sphere of influence. But the oil had changed all of that.

After Obsidian Number One, there had been Obsidian Number Two and so on up to Obsidian Number Eighteen, which had been pumping away for several days. It had the earmarks of one of the richest oil fields in the country.

The wells were producing upward of thirty thousand barrels of oil every twenty-four hours. At the going price of four dollars a barrel, Obsidian and the small landowners who had thrown in were making between a hundred and a hundred twenty thousand dollars a day, gross. There was an overhead of course, and V. D. Skinner was working like a madman to keep production up: ordering pipe and trucks and drilling equipment and house trailers and earth-moving machinery and measuring flow and dealing with the small refinery in Bayfield, Louisiana, where the oil was going. Obsidian now employed scores of workers and was hiring others daily: roughnecks, truck drivers, tool and die men, office workers, mechanics, telephone personnel, heavy equipment operators, pipe fitters, concrete men, welders and a field kitchen staff, all keenly geared to supporting the immense flow of wealth from Creoletown.

At the beginning, the original hostility of white Bienville

had turned to unfettered horror at the thought of Negroes coming into such sums of money. In Bienville, as elsewhere, wealth was power and power was control. There were moneyed classes, and not so moneyed classes and poor classes, but even the moneyed classes found it hard to conceive of the fortunes being made in the Creoletown fields. Naturally, the reports were vastly exaggerated.

"You heah they bought the hospital?"

"I heard it, don't believe it. What's a nigger gonna do with a hospital?"

"Put niggers in it, tha's what!"

"They got they own hospital, what they want with ours?"

"You know what's gonna happen! You go to the damned hospital, you be in the same room with niggers. They be puttin' the same thermometer in your mouth they put in theirs."

"Goddamn!"

"You know I heard a nigger woman went into Molineux's trying on a dress today."

"No!"

"Certainly did. They say she walked in sassy as you please. Started shufflin' through the racks and asked a salesgirl for the dressin' room"

"Well, what'd the salesgirl do?"

"Heard she jus' pointed her to the dressin' room. Didn't say nothin'." Didn't even call the manager or nothin'."

"Lord Gawd!"

"They say they already own the bank."

"Say they already own the schools too!"

"Heard that myself; don't believe it, though."

"I saw one in town the other day. Dressed fit to kill. Big buck, jus' struttin' down the street."

"Somebody oughta do somethin'."

"Do what, they own all the money in town!"

282

"They don't own the money, they own the awl."

"Well, hell, the awl's worth more than money, ain't it?"

But as the weeks and months passed, this gradually began to soften with the realization that the color of money is neither black nor white but green and if there was money to be made it was necessary to go where the money was to make it.

"I hear they hiring people up there."

"Not me, I ain't about to work for no niggers."

"They say a white man's runnin' it."

"Don't make no difference if the niggers own it."

"Does if you want a job. They pay a good hour's wage."

"Well, maybe so, but still . . ."

"Still, nothin'! I say if you want work, you go on up there."

"I don't know . . . you say a white man's runnin' it?"

"You won't believe this! They want *me* to go over to *their* offices tomorrow. Wouldn't come over here. Made me call up and make a goddamn appointment!"

"And did you do it?"

"Not yet. I can't believe the damn nerve! Said to call *Mister* Holt's secretary for an appointment! I'll be . . ."

"You'll do just that, that's what you'll do. They're talking about buying half a million dollars' worth of machinery from us and if they say for you to get down on your hands and knees and howl like a dog, you will do that too! Just get that contract!"

"But for Chrissa . . ."

"Just do it!"

Willie was sitting in a big leather chair in rolled-up shirtsleeves, his new and expensive silk tie loosened around his neck. In the refurbished office of Daniel Holt, president of Obsidian Oil, V. D. Skinner lounged on a couch wearing khakis and mud-stained boots. On the wall was a blown-up, gilt-framed photograph of Obsidian Number One, pumping away. A map on the opposite wall had black pin flags dotted in a huge swath across the Creoletown area. There was a cut-glass vase of fresh flowers on the table and a fist-sized hunk of obsidian stone rested on a carved marble and mahogany base on the glass top of Daniel's desk.

"Well, Willie," Daniel said thoughtfully, "what do you think about the Bayfield idea?"

"Sounds pretty good to me, but I think that's a bit down the road yet. We haven't got that kind of cash right now."

"Yes, yes, I know," Daniel said, "but it sounds like the kind of project that will take some time."

Skinner scratched himself and wheezed. "The sooner the better, from my point of view," he said. "Can you imagine the kind of money we'd make if we owned the Bayfield refinery instead of just selling to them? It wouldn't take much conversion. Hell, in a few years, we could be producing our own brand of gasoline. Obsidian Gas—how does that sound? Probably set up a chain of filling stations around here too. Maybe all over the South."

"Well, we can't afford it now," Willie said. "And it seems to me we might better lie back a little and see just how much more we've got to expand our operation here before we actually make any overtures."

"Yes, yes. You are correct," said Daniel, "but I think you might want to start looking into it, quietly."

Willie nodded and made himself a note. In the several months since he assumed control of the company, Daniel had proven himself a more than adequate administrator. The leap from high-school principal to head of an oil corporation was not so vast as it might have seemed. He was rarely flappable, and made decisions with a quaint, sort of homespun honesty, as though he were not dealing with hundreds of thousands or even millions of dollars, but a shipment of arithmetic books or the problems of an adolescent schoolgirl.

Nor had he much changed his life-style in the wake of his newfound wealth. He moved his mother into a modest red-brick home in the colored section of town not far from the shotgun house where he continued to live with his wife and children. He paid himself a modest salary and had bought a medium-priced car to travel back and forth to work. But, of course, he had given up his job moonlighting as a cook in a short-order restaurant.

It was therefore surprising to Willie when Daniel told Willie about the country club.

"I want to join the golf club," Daniel said.

"The what?" Willie asked.

"The golf club, out by Cypress Lake. You know."

"That's the country club," Willie said.

"Yes, but it has a golf course. I've seen it from the road. I've always wanted to learn how to play that." Daniel was leaning back with his hands clasped behind his head and the pipe clenched between his teeth. There was a broad smile on his face.

Willie exchanged glances with Skinner, who had taken out a Baby Ruth candy bar and was gnawing on it.

"Well," Willie said, "if you want to try, go ahead, but I wouldn't count on it."

Daniel puffed up a cloud of smoke from the pipe. "I want you to take care of it for me," he said.

"Me?" Willie said. "Hell, I couldn't get into the country club myself."

"I know you can figure something out," Daniel said. "I'd like to play golf next Saturday."

Willie sagged in dismay.

"Hellfire, Daniel," Skinner said merrily, "why don't you just build your own golf course? Then you could have all your friends over to play, and you wouldn't have to fool with that other club."

"I don't want to build my own course. As I've said, I would like to join the other club."

"I'd say the only way to do that would be to buy it," Willie said.

"That may be," said Daniel.

The sun was low in the sky but the heat hung heavily in Willie's apartment, even with the window fan on. He had

285

taken a bath, shaved and dabbed his face and neck with Old Spice cologne, the first cologne he had ever used. It stung his skin, but the sensation was pleasing, and he hoped Whitsey might notice the smell when he picked her up later.

Standing in a bath towel he made himself a Jack Daniel's on the rocks and dressed himself in a new pair of slacks, a fresh, blue-and-white checkered sport shirt, slipped into a pair of brand-new Weejun loafers and walked outside. There was an occasional faint breeze when he got to the deer park. The grass was lush beneath the trees and the ivy and the moss and the brilliant green semitropical plants transformed the park into a strange, almost eerie glade beneath the big oaks. Willie sat down on his usual bench near the old Iron Deer, which was now repainted and patched and plugged and welded, sanded and restored, so that it stood proud again and tall, as it had thirty years before, a big brown stag, neck and head erect, poised to bolt at any moment. He considered the refurbished creature. Not unlike himself, with his new clothes and new position, the new fly rod, the new Purdy double gun he had ordered from England, the new salmon-over-gray Chevrolet convertible sitting in the drive. Even though Willie wasn't making a fortune, he was making good money for the first time in his life and people came to him and made him feel important.

In fact, he had become something of a big shot around Bienville. The owners of companies wishing to do business with Obsidian inevitably approached Willie first. Most of the time he simply transferred these people to the appropriate department, but it seemed to make them feel better talking to a white man. More and more he found himself being wined and dined by Bienville's businessmen, invited to social functions at their homes and elsewhere. Invitations came in the mail. He was even invited once for a weekend on a large fishing boat in the Gulf complete with crew serving food and liquor. The papers and television quoted him. People he had never known before spoke to him on the street. Willingly or unwillingly he had become, in the warning words of Guidre, a Bigass Pete.

Bigass Pete, and never more so, he thought, than this very afternoon when he had phoned Canfield Shambeaux, president of the Bienville Country Club, and informed him that Daniel Holt wished to become a member.

"Christ on the Cross!" Shambeaux cried indignantly. "You ought to know better than even to suggest such a thing!"

Willie had been leaning back in his chair with his feet on the desk, sipping a cup of black coffee laced with a shot of Jack Daniel's from the bottle in his drawer.

"I suppose you know that Obsidian has acquired some interest in the bank," Willie said. "Not a lot perhaps, but some, and we are acquiring more all the time. We are aware that Bienville National holds the mortgage on your club. Does that change the picture any?"

There was a silence at the other end of the line, except for what might have been a gnashing of teeth.

"The idea is preposterous," Shambeaux pleaded. "There are rules in the bylaws. . . ."

"They can be amended," Willie said.

"Who's going to amend them?" Shambeaux said. "The membership of the club? There's no way—be reasonable!"

"You can make an exception," Willie said. "What's it going to hurt? He just wants to play golf."

"His children'll want to come and swim in the pool," Shambeaux argued. "And his wife will want to use the ladies' locker room. They might even want to bring people for dinner."

"You let in a Jew," Willie said. "I know for a fact Howard Nussbaum goes out there. You made an exception in his case."

"That was different," Shambeaux begged. "He's only a Jew. And he got in on a corporate membership because of his company. Anyway he's not really Jewish."

"Like hell he isn't!" Willie said. "But that might be a solution. Give Obsidian Oil a corporate membership."

"My God," Shambeaux cried, "then we'd have to have all of them!"

"Let Daniel Holt join separately, then. He probably won't bring his family—I don't know. He told me he just wants to play golf. And he wants to play this Saturday."

"This Saturday!" Shambeaux screamed. "There's a waiting list of two years just to start with—even if you're white. Perhaps we could put him on the list. Nobody would have to know about it except the membership committee. Maybe by then we could work something out. Do you think that would satisfy him?"

"It would not," Willie said. He took a long, deep drag from the Picayune and decided it wouldn't hurt to throw some fear into Shambeaux. "Listen, Shambeaux," he said, "let me give it to you straight. Daniel Holt is not a man to fool around with. If he wants something, he usually gets it. Now, I hear that loan of yours is due in a year or so. I know for a fact that the bank has just been renewing it each time it comes up, with nothing much paid on the principal. Well, it could be that there'll be some changes made at Bienville National—and that might be one of them. How would you like to see that note called in? You've got what, about five hundred members? How would they like it if they each had to fork over ten thousand in cash in the next few months?"

"Please," Shambeaux implored, "don't do this to us. We'd have to close down the club."

"No, you don't," Willie said. "All you have to do is admit Mr. Daniel Holt so he can play a few rounds of golf."

"It's impossible," Shambeaux said. "We'd close it down first."

"So be it," Willie said. "So be it."

"I'll have to get back to you," Shambeaux said.

Willie lit a Picayune and further studied the Iron Deer. Indeed it was classic, handsome. But somehow it did not really belong here. It wasn't meant for parks and mowed grass and sidewalks and streetlights and marble fountains and children playing on its back. Like me, he thought, like me!

A notion began to root itself in his mind.

What in hell was he doing, where was he going? He was forty-three years old, more than half his life was over and he was a Bigass Pete. He was now invited into homes so sumptuous they were enough to turn you into a Communist. He frequently found himself in the company of people who were even more crass and loud and boorish than the people he had once associated himself with—and these were supposed to be Bienville's finest. Yes, there was a veneer of sophistication, and perhaps more laughter, and they were also more interesting, but in the end, he felt he didn't belong there with them any more than the Iron Deer belonged here in the park. And if it did belong here, rooted immutably in the same spot forever, it wasn't where Willie wanted to be in his life. If that's what it took, the 8:00 A.M. to 8:00 P.M. working hours, the preening social events, the daily pressures of the business, the monstrous decisions involving sums he hadn't dealt with since some long-ago high-school mathematics class, well, he really didn't want it.

And yet he did, of course. He took another swallow of the drink.

He enjoyed it because it was exciting, and also because he thought he should enjoy it. It was what everyone aspired to, wasn't it? And here it was, dumped in his lap. Maybe he was just scared. And also, there was Whitsey Loftin; the doubts again began to pile up like shifting dunes.

What was it with her?

After the trial they had begun to go out again, but it was a baffling and frustrating romance, if that was actually a word for it. Frequently he would call and she'd be busy, but then on other occasions she'd go out with him. She had him off balance. He could always tell, toward the end of the evening, whether she'd decided to go home alone, or go to bed with him. If she'd decided to go home, her mood would turn cold. The laughter would stop and the warmth would go out of her eyes perhaps an hour before it was time to go, and invariably she would say, "Well, I've got a big day tomorrow, I'd better get some sleep," and that would be that.

But there were other times, fewer and farther between, when he could tell she wanted him; she'd snuggle close, or take his hand, and there would be an impish smile on her lips and a look of lust in her eyes, and they would go either to his place or hers and have unbelievable sex. And yet there were none of those lovely weekends he'd conjured in his imagination, lying in bed for long hours or sitting by a fire, or lying on a beach. Mornings after she'd always get up early and leave or putter around in her own place if he were there, dressing for some other engagement, and it would be the signal for him to leave.

Still he was driven by her, and lived for the evenings he could see her, whether or not they went to bed. That she was there at all seemed good enough. Suddenly he thought of the girl on the carnival float years before, blowing a kiss to him, then fading away into the distance as the parade moved on, tantalizing, unattainable, desirable. He was in deep and he knew it, but there was nothing he could do about it. The heart, once smitten, can lead a man lemminglike, even if it is to the edge of a cliff.

It was still daylight when Willie collected Whitsey in his new salmon-over-gray Chevrolet and headed south out of Bienville to Beaudreaux's Place. He kept the convertible top down, and the sweet warm scent from the ripe vegetable fields blew in their faces, and he had the radio tuned to the New Orleans station with comfortable big-band music. Stan Kenton wafted out of the speaker and across the countryside. Whitsey had a scarf tied around her blond hair and was turned in the seat so she leaned on the passenger side door and faced him. The sky overhead was blue and cloudless and the setting sun cast a mellow, burnished hue over the flat landscape.

"I like this car," she said.

"What?" he asked above the noise of the wind.

She leaned closer and shouted, "Your new car—I love it!"

He reached over and took her hand. She squeezed his fingers and giggled, but then drew back, and suddenly he wasn't sure if it was because she couldn't lean on her door and hold his hand at the same time, or for some other reason. The old doubt crept into his mind for an instant, then quickly passed. He wouldn't allow it to stay. Not tonight.

The tires growled along the oystershell drive up to Beaudreux's Place, then settled in the dust. The orange sun was a flattened fiery ball tangent to the waters of the bayou, and as they walked up the rickety steps to the shacklike restaurant, armies of fiddler crabs scuttled along the mud flats at low tide. The nets of shrimp boats were visible across the marshes.

Beaudreux, sweating profusely, wearing a soiled white apron, met them at the screen door.

"Oh, oh, oh," he cried joyfully, "such a long time—too long time—and you bring back dat lovely lady with you." He gave both of them a hug and practically dragged them inside.

They sat on a long screened porch directly above the narrow bayou, at a table with a kerosene lantern unlit. The acrid odor of the marshes mingled with the sweet aroma of cypress and the unmistakable smell of the salty Gulf of a few miles away. Willie uncapped the bottle of Jack Daniel's Black Label sour-mash whiskey he had brought and poured a shot into two glasses of crackling ice Beaudreux had brought them.

"We haven't been here together in months," she said.

"I haven't been here since the last time with you."

"You're kidding?"

"Nope," he said, rolling his eyes with feigned anguish, "couldn't bring myself to come back without you."

She smiled. "Go on."

"Truth, I promise."

"All those pretty girls you've been taking out. I've heard about you. Don't think I don't know," she teased.

"Means nothing. Besides, you haven't exactly been a wallflower, have you?"

"Uhhhmmm," she said, "I guess not."

Beaudreux came to the table. "Today I got sahm s'rimps beeg as a cucomber out t'Gulf, an' we fix 'em in a little sauce of fresh tomat's an' a bell pep. Or I got a beeg ju'cy pompano caught dis mornin' an' I got sahm great fat crab peeked and stuff back in de shell—or a souf-shell crab an' also sahm red snapper thas mighty good."

"That crab in the shell sounds good," Willie said. "How do you fix that?"

"Oh, I take the crabmeat an' turn in a littl' butter, then thro' in sahm chop onion and green pep and a littl' tomat' and som' other thing and—well, Mistair Croff—you try, you like it, eh?"

"I will, I think, thank you."

"An' you, pretty lady, what you have?"

"I'll have the shrimp," Whitsey said. "They sound good."

"Okay, okay," Beaudreux said, "thas fine." He hesitated a moment. "Say, Mistair Croff, I been read about you in the paper. You a big shot now, eh? You runnin' all the oil beezness. You think they is any oil down heah?"

Willie leaned back and grinned. "Well, that'd be hard to say, Beaudreux. Doesn't look like it, though. But you never can tell."

A fallen expression came over Beaudreux's face.

"Don't, huh? Oh, hell! I thought might be. Thought Beaudreux get rich and open me a place in town. Have air condition and all. A nice, beeg restaurant."

"It'd be a lot more convenient for me," Willie said. "I'd come every night."

"Yeah, be real nice, you know? Beaudreux's Place—all lit up with electric lights and a sign in front. Lo's of people come there, eh?"

"It's an idea," Willie said.

Beaudreux returned to his kitchen and the two of them gazed blissfully at the flattening sun.

"Gosh, that's pretty," she said.

"Not as pretty as you are."

She let out an embarrassed giggle. "Stop flattering me." There was a sexy look in her eyes. Willie thought this might be one of the nights, but it was too early to tell yet.

"It's okay," he said. He took her hand across the table. "I'm really glad to see you."

"I'm glad to see you too," she said.

The dinner Beaudreux served surpassed all expectations. It began with a dish of cold backfin crabmeat marinated in vinegar and oil and served over crisp lettuce. There were fresh steaming vegetables along with the main course. Afterward, when the table had been cleared, Beaudreux brought them each a slice of cantaloupe topped with ice cream.

Willie felt ebullient. "Beaudreux," he said, "I've been doing a little thinking. You say you want to open a place in town, huh?"

Beaudreux grimaced. "I wan' to, but thas not possible without the oil. I was hoping oil be down here too."

"I wouldn't say it isn't possible," Willie said. "You know, the people I'm with—Obsidian Oil—well, they've been going into a number of different businesses. Maybe you've heard about it. . . ."

"Heard!" Beaudreux shouted. "I read every day in the papers. A bunch of niggers . . ."

"Well, what would you think if that bunch of niggers lent you enough money to open a place in town?" Willie said.

"Me! Why would they give me money?"

"Because I would tell them they should," Willie said. "Because I would tell them how good your food is, and that if they gave you enough to get started you would begin making enough money to pay them back and also turn a profit. How would you like that?"

Beaudreux thought about this for a moment. His face screwed up into a quizzical frown.

"But niggers," he said. "Why would they give anything to me?"

"Not give," Willie said, "lend. You'd have to pay it back. And besides, I think that in fairness you'd have to let them into your place too."

"Eat there—niggers?" Beaudreux said uncomprehendingly.

"Well, I think so, if they gave you the money—don't you?"

"How much money?" Beaudreux asked suspiciously.

"Whatever it takes to get you going."

"With air condition?" he said.

"Air condition," Willie responded.

"An' a beeg kitchen—an' a sign out front?"

"Whatever you want." Willie smiled.

"I don' know," Beaudreux said. "I have to think it over. Okay?" He disappeared into his kitchen.

Whitsey had remained silent during this exchange. But when Beaudreux had gone, she said, "I remember when you tried to discourage him from all that. When you said it would ruin a part of your life if you didn't have this place to come to anymore."

"I didn't say he had to close this place up," Willie said. "Besides, times have changed. I don't get to come down here much anymore. If the Mountain won't come to Mohammed, then Mohammed must go to the Mountain."

"Sounds like you *are* getting to be a big shot," she said cannily. He couldn't tell if she was serious or joking.

"Not really," he said, "but I guess I do have a little pull over things."

"So I see," she said. She stretched back in her chair and Willie took lustful notice of her big breasts straining against her silk blouse. There was a wicked gleam in her eye when she leaned forward. "I've missed you."

"Have you?"

"Passionately."

With his left toe he eased off his right shoe and lifted his leg until it touched her thigh across the table.

"Oooh," she purred. He felt her spread her legs and she leaned farther forward so that the tips of her breasts touched the edge of the table and she began to rub them against it. He lifted his leg higher and extended his toes until they wedged between her legs, and he could feel the warmth there. She seemed to slide herself toward him and sighed, "Aaahhh." They stayed that way for a long moment, looking at each other intently, and she squirmed against him. He was about to say something when Beaudreux suddenly returned to the table, grinning broadly, showing his two gold-capped teeth.

"Iss a deal," he said. "I go into town and I serve the niggers."

Willie dropped his leg and Whitsey hastily straightened

up. "Well," Willie said, flustered, "ah, first off, it's not a deal till I get back and talk to my people and see if they agree. I'll let you know what happens.

"And second," he said, "you've got to stop calling them niggers."

Willie's instinct had been right; it *was* his night with Whitsey. She was all over him during the drive home, and once he almost wrecked the car; when they got back to her place she rushed him inside and into the bedroom. He excused himself to rinse out his mouth and took a little longer to comb his hair and dab on some of her deodorant that he found on a dressing table and heard her call impatiently, "Where are you?" When he walked back into the bedroom she was lying naked on the bed.

"Come here," she ordered, and she sat up and began undressing him feverishly, practically tearing off his shirt, and when they made love she took the lead, satisfying herself several times without regard for him. At one point he had a strange flash of what it must be like to be raped, but finally he came, too, and afterward they lay on the cooling, sweat-drenched sheets, he smoking a Picayune and she drinking a glass of water she had on the bedside table.

"That was great," Willie said. He leaned over and kissed her on the cheek.

She didn't say anything, so he said, "Didn't you think so?"

"Ummmm."

"That's all?"

"Is what all?"

"I said it was great. All you said was 'Ummmm.'"

"Of course I thought it was," she said, but he detected something in her voice, a coolness, a distance that he had felt before.

He took a sip of her water. "You want to do something this weekend?" he asked. "I've been meaning to get away for a couple of days. Maybe we could go someplace."

"I can't this weekend," she said. "Maybe next weekend."

He crushed out the cigarette in an ashtray. That was the way with her. *"I can't this weekend—maybe next"*—what the hell did she think he was, a yo-yo! He sat up and began to fumble for his pants.

"Next weekend I'm going fishing," he said sourly.

19

In the heat of late afternoon the big inboard engine of the Dauber-built boat throbbed contentedly. Once they turned off the main river channel Willie had eased back the throttle and they were now moving slowly through a narrow, hyacinth-choked slough. The bow of the boat cut a swath through the thick green growth, which quickly closed in behind them once the boat had passed. A family of turtles, catching the last of the sunlight on an overhanging log, began to plop ceremoniously into the water as the boat approached. Green bullfrogs stayed motionless on thick, wide lily pads and darted their tongues at gnats and mosquitoes. A blue heron, startled by the intrusion, flew up from a bank and winged its way gracefully out of sight around a bend. They passed several wallows—muddy flats where the swamp grass had been thrashed down—and saw a water moccasin, then two, then three, as the boat chugged steadily deeper into the swamp.

"Dam'f we hain't trav'lin' in style now," Guidre said. His grizzled, sunburned face cracked in a wide and toothless grin.

The August heat of the swamp was almost inhumanely oppressive. The sun baked down hour after hour and the

bogs and marshes and shallow ponds and rivers absorbed
the heat and retained it, and gave off a steaming dampness
that permeated deeply into anyone or anything that happened to be there. A man could feel the fetid moisture go
down in his lungs as he breathed. Even now, after the sun
had dropped, the heat and the moisture remained, hovering
above the bogs and the slow-moving streams and the
stagnant, mosquito-breeding pools. But this was not a
problem for Willie. The heat, the rank swamp odors, the
insects, all of them were part of the adventure and it would
not have been the same without them.

They came round a bend shortly afterward, and before
them was the long rickety wharf reaching out into the lake.
Willie pushed the throttle forward and the big boat began to
plane across the still water toward the camp. He drew it
parallel to the dock, tied up bow and stern and stepped off.

"Hand some of that gear up," he said to Guidre. "I'll open
up."

Willie walked to the door with a satchel of food and other
odds and ends and lay them on the wharf as he took hold of
the handle of the screen door and pulled it open. In the same
instant his eye caught a glimpse of a lightninglike mass of
writhing black muscle at his feet. He jumped back, stumbling over the gear, a jolt of horror sucking his breath away.

"Jesus!" he screamed.

Guidre was on the dock too, by now, and he rushed over
to Willie.

"What the hell is it?"

Willie, who had backed away even farther, but regained
his voice, pointed at a coiled three-foot knot of thick, black
water moccasin backed against the still-closed wood door to
the camp.

The snake's head was raised six inches high and its
cotton-white mouth was bared wide so they could see the
fangs. They seemed out of striking distance, but weren't
sure. Guidre backed away slowly and Willie followed him.

"Goddamn thing was in between the screen door and the
other one."

"I wish I'd brought a pistol, damnit," Guidre said.

Guidre had stooped and was feeling behind him on the wharf. His fingers closed around the end of a six-foot, three-pronged frog gig. "I'm glad somebody left this thing here," he said. Stealthily he made his way back past Willie toward the snake, which remained poised and motionless, its mouth still vicious, wide and menacing. He ran his hand down the shaft of the gig so that he was holding it about a foot above the top, then with an expert darting thrust he lashed out and the rusty prongs of the weapon speared the moccasin just behind the head. Pounds of silent fury thrashed savagely on the end of the gig. The snake's mouth snapped in deadly rhythm, the body and tail curled spasmodically around the prongs and up around the shaft. Bright-red blood from the wound smeared the black skin of the reptile and spattered onto the weathered wharf. Guidre lifted the snake to waist level and extended the gig over the side of the wharf, lowering it so as to catch the prongs on a board. He pulled up and the writing thing slid off and plopped into the water. It seemed to sink for an instant, showing its light underbelly, floating almost lengthwise, perhaps mortally wounded, but both of them got a glimpse of its recovery; the body suddenly straightened, snapped into an S shape, and they watched it wriggle powerfully just beneath the surface toward the swampy shore.

"Too many of them damn things up here this time a year," Guidre said. He put the gig back on the wharf.

"Like to scared me to death," Willie said. He approached the door of the camp again, cautiously, and opened it. The air inside was stale and smelled of mold.

"Here, I'll take that," Willie said. He received a varnished wood box from Guidre, the new fly rod which hadn't been out of its case, and laid it carefully on a table and looked at it admiringly.

"That's a perdy one," said Guidre. "Shor is."

"Find out in the morning if she works," Willie said.

"I imagine it does," Guidre snorted. "What needs to be found out is whether or not *you* can work it."

"I got five bucks says I get catch of the day."

"Hate to take your money," the old guide said.

"Let's have a drink."

"Allers ready for that."

They sat at the table and Willie unpacked a bottle and set it between them.

"Good Lawd, Willie! When 'ju start buying that?" He picked up the bottle of Jack Daniel's and turned it in his hands reverently.

"Like I said, I've been doing pretty good."

"I should say!" Guidre said. "That boat must'uv set you back. Hell, I don't know what, but thousands of dollars."

Willie poured them each a drink. "Here's t' you," he said. He lifted his glass.

"And all this I been hearin' 'bout you's true, then?" the old man asked. "Yew working for the colored people who got the oil?"

"That's right," Willie said. "We're thick as thieves."

"How they to work for?" Guidre asked curiously.

"Pretty damned good."

"Looks like they payin' yew all right."

"I get by," Willie said. "Matter of fact, I've been thinkin' about doing something with this old place up here."

"What?" Guidre asked. "Fixin' it up?"

"Well, something like that. Actually, I was thinking more like maybe just getting rid of it and starting over. You know, a really nice place. Bigger, and with a lot of screen windows and a good kitchen—and a nice dock."

The old man's eyes narrowed. "I s'pose you gonna tear down you ol' man's wharf, ain't you?"

"Well . . . I don't know exactly," Willie said. "This is all just somethin' I've been thinking about a little."

"That's allers the way with folks when they got some money—tear down, build up somethin' new. Y' get money, y' get too damned good for the things that were good nuf for ya before y' got the money. There ain't a damn thing wrong w' it that couldn't be fixed with a little work. Or maybe y'd want somebody to come up here and fix it up a little bit, if y' don't have time y' self."

Willie felt himself becoming agitated. "C'mon, Guidre, this place is a dump. Look around. Half of it's rotting. It's not even sitting on an even keel—it's four or five degrees off. Don't you think my old man would have built a better place if he could have afforded it?"

"I think he wuz damn happy with this one," Guidre said. "Built it with his two hands—an' mine, an' some of yours, too. It's different when you build a place with your two hands."

"What's the difference? If you can do something better by paying for it, and if you can afford it, what does it matter?"

"I said this before, Willie, and I'll say it agin. You're gettin' to be a Bigass Pete!"

"I don't give a damn," Willie said crossly. "I'm tired of this conversation. I came up here to relax." He took a pair of new binoculars and slipped a strap over his head. "I'm going outside."

Even as he walked out into the twilight stillness the old man was still yelling at him. "I s'pose next you'll wanta stock the lake with fish. And crate in ducks. That's it. Build a duck blind with hot and cole runnin' water. . . ." Willie smiled a little and resisted an urge to go back in and argue. It was comforting to be yelled at once in a while. Everybody needs to be yelled at once in a while, he thought.

He walked to the end of the World's Longest Wharf and lifted the binoculars to his eyes. Even in the dimming light their power was remarkable. He adjusted the ocule on a dark spot near the top of the skeleton of a dead tree and discovered it was an egret's nest. He scanned the far shoreline and noticed a large ripple near a clump of water hyacinth. He trained on the spot for a few moments and a big bass slashed out of the water again. For several minutes, although Willie had not really been aware of it, there had been a steady, distant drone from one of the myriad sloughs, like the sound of a motorboat, but it was somehow different, more high-pitched. It seemed to be drawing closer.

Willie was scanning a tall line of trees looking for anything of interest through his new binoculars when he first became faintly aware of the droning noise. He turned his head to catch a better sound of it. It faded slightly, then resumed again, stronger, as though turning bends in a slough. Still he could see nothing and the light was fading quickly. Then, suddenly, the source of the noise emerged in the distance. Willie threw the binoculars to his eyes and saw that it was an airboat. Two men were perched on a high seat amidship, both wearing rubber eye goggles. The driver of the airboat seemed to see Willie, and he quickly veered off and picked up speed until the boat disappeared around a little point of marshy land. Willie curiously trained the glasses at the spot where he had last seen the boat. Moments later it poked out just at the edge of the marsh, and remained motionless. The men seemed to be straining to look at him. They were almost macabre in their appearance, the two men in goggles sitting side by side in the strange-looking airboat.

Willie watched them for a while, then went back inside.

It was still dark, before sunrise, when Guidre shook him awake. The old man had lighted a kerosene lantern and was hovered over the propane stove frying eggs and bacon. Willie sat on the side of his bunk, foggily, and began lacing his boots while the fat sizzled in the pan. The first rosy pink of dawn gave way to a streaked sky of grays and oranges. The two of them, moving silently, slipped the canoe into the tepid, tea-colored water and set out across the lake toward the thick hyacinth where Willie had seen the bass jump the evening before. There was no wind, not even the faintest breeze, and the surface of the lake was glasslike. And it was still; the only sounds were the dipping of paddles in the water and the shrill cries of a lone swamp bird.

As they neared the shore Willie stopped paddling and began rigging his casting rod with a top surface bass lure. The fly rod remained in its leather case in the bottom of the canoe. Guidre took a last dip with his paddle and let the boat ghost quietly toward the hyacinth patch. At the edge of the growth, a bass gurgled near the top of the water and Willie felt a surge of anticipation. He drew back the rod and made a cast, even before Guidre had rigged his own tackle. The line payed out in a high-pitched hum and the heavily barbed lure, meant to resemble a large minnow, plopped into the water twenty-five or so yards away just at the edge of the hyacinth: a good cast.

Gently, Willie flicked the rod tip and reeled in the slack from the line. Then, working the rod back and forth to simulate a darting, fishlike motion, he began reeling in. Guidre had stopped his rigging and watched as Willie's lure jerked along the edge of the water plants. Many times it was the first cast that told the story. The big fish would be lurking near the surface this time of day, before the sun drove them to cooler pools or beneath rotting swamp logs. Neither man said anything, as talk was thought to scare the fish away, and Willie worked the lure slowly back toward the canoe.

Then it struck. A splash and gurgle of water and the glimpse of a green back as the bass hit the lure sideways and carried it beneath the water, running for the thick hyacinth bed.

Willie's heart raced and he jerked back on the rod to set the hook. The bass dived, then reversed direction and headed back toward the boat. Willie frantically reeled in to take the slack out of the line. He whipped the red tip back again and the big bass broke the surface and leaped nearly two feet into the air; it hit the water again with a loud *pop*, dived, then surfaced again, this time seeming to dance on its tail.

"Damn," Willie said, nothing more. The excitement, the confusion and drama of playing the fish created what seemed to be a roar and din all around him. His energies were devoted totally to bringing in the bass, as those of a bullfighter are devoted to the bull, or a punt returner fixed on a ball dropping toward him. This battle seemed to go on for a long time, but in less than two minutes Willie had brought the bass up to the side of the boat where Guidre was waiting with a landing net. He dipped the net expertly into the water and brought it up under the fish.

"Oh, my, my," the old man said, "look at this." He lifted the net with the fish flopping wildly, the lure protruding from its wide mouth. "Four, five pounds he'll go, maybe. We'll be eatin' good tonight."

Guidre seized the bass expertly by the gills and began working the hook out of its mouth, then he dropped it into a cooler in the bottom of the canoe.

Willie felt exhilarated. It had been months since he felt this relaxed. He remembered suddenly that he hadn't thought about Obsidian a single time since he woke up. Usually, it was the first thing on his mind. He decided not to think about it now, either, except that he couldn't help wondering if Daniel Holt might not like going on a trip such as this. He wondered what Guidre would have thought if he'd brought him along. Probably nothing, Willie decided, probably nothing at all.

Guidre brought in the next two bass, both smaller than Willie's but of good, respectable and eatable size. Willie took one more and then their luck seemed to play out. An hour later, when the morning sun was hot and blood red over the trees, they decided to move on. They paddled the canoe along the edges of the marsh around the rim of the lake until they came to an almost hidden entrance no more than three feet wide. They poled their way beneath low, overhanging branches and briars and gnarled cypress knees into a dark slough that widened into a bayou and was overhung with cypress and water pines; a large blacksnake had layered itself in the crook of a branch overhead, lazing in the early sun as the canoe passed under it.

"Knowed a fellow onct that had one a them things fall into his boat," Guidre said.

"Must of scared him shitless," Willie said nervously, glancing up at the snake.

"Had a forty-five in his tackle box," Guidre said. "He grabbed it and blew hell outta the snake," the old man said. "Trouble was, he'd put four holes in the bottom of his boat doin' it. He can't find anything to plug the holes with, so he sticks his fingers in 'em and tries to steer the boat by putting his feet on the outboard tiller. By this time the boat's fillin' up fast. Well sir, he gets his fingers stuck in the holes and while he's trying to work them free his foot slips off the outboard tiller and the boat goes wild and crashes into a tree on the bank or something. Broke all this poor bastid's fingers. Finally a nigger come along in a rowboat and sees him, and tows him all the way to Bon Ton Bayou. Sonofabitch is hollerin' all the while. They had to take the boat with him still in it. Put it in the back of a flatbed truck and got him to the hospital to cut him loose."

"That's the worst story I ever heard," Willie said.

"Teach that sonofabitch to shoot holes in his boat," Guidre said.

They continued down the bayou, past lily pads and marsh grass. Dragonflies hummed above the tea-colored water, which was clearer, so they could see the bottom in shallower places. Somewhere in the distance Willie heard a faint sound of the airboat he had seen the evening before.

On the bayou the sun was higher now, and hot. There was the slightest tide and the canoe drifted quietly with Guidre's paddle steering it and Willie in the bow, rigging his fly rod. He carefully opened the varnished case and began fitting the four pieces together, admiring the delicate craftsmanship: the octagonal facets of laminated bamboo, the hand-wrapped line eyelets. He slipped on the reel, ran the line up to the tip, then waxed it with paraffin so it would float on top of the water. Next he tied on a four-foot nylon leader, and at the end of this he attached the fly he'd selected—a white-and-red-speckled popping bug. He and Guidre had done this many times before. One would fish from the front of the boat while the other steered and paddled from the back. After a while they would exchange places. They almost always had luck in the hidden bayou. It teemed with big bull bream, which Guidre respectfully called "the fightenist fish I have the pleasure of eatin'."

Willie whipped the rod tip back and forth a few times, paying out about three feet with each motion. The line sang overhead with a sharp whipping sound.

"How's that girl you got fouled up with?" the old man asked.

"Hard to say," Willie said. "I can't figure her out." He tried to sound casual but he felt the knot beginning in his stomach. She had been in and out of his thoughts ever since he got up, but he hadn't really had to confront it until now.

"Try to figger her out!" Guidre hooted. "Hellfire, that's the worse thang you kin do. Ever' time you think you done it, you find out you ain't."

"I think you're probably right," Willie said. The bug had begun to pop off the top of the water now; twenty or thirty yards of line had payed out.

"I dunno, Guidre," he continued. "I mean, when I'm with her, it's great. But then, I'm not with her a lot. She likes dating around, I guess. But I can't figure it out—how she, ah, well, she and I can have something so good when we're together, and then she wants to go out all the time with other people."

"You're screwin' her, I s'pose?" Guidre said. His eyes were hard and keen, watching the popping bug. The question and the offhand way he said it took Willie a little aback.

"Well, yeah, we are," he said.

"And what you cain't figger out is how she kin screw you and still go out with these other people, and maybe screw them?" the old man said.

"Well, I didn't say anything about her screwing anybody else," Willie said defensively. He had been trying hard for months not to imagine it.

"Well, don't you spec that's what she's doin'?"

"For Chrissakes, Guidre. I don't know and I don't care! I certainly don't think so. I'm concerned with her and me, not other people."

"Thas the hardest thing to take, boy. I heared it a hundred times. Nobody wants to admit it to themselves, that somebody they're seein', that they might care 'bout, is screwin' somebody else. But they do, boy, right here in the city of Bienville, they screw. Everybody screws. Holts too, I s'pose."

Willie stopped flagging the rod, and spun around to Guidre. "Well, goddamn it! I don't want to hear about it. I don't want to think about it. Besides, she's not a Holt."

"Same type, I tell ya. Ya never would take my advice 'bout anything. But it sounds to me like you pissin' up a rope, Willie. You been seein' this gal all this time and she still wants to see other fellers. That oughta tell yew sompin'."

"Well, it's more damned complicated than that," Willie said weakly.

"Thas what they all say," the old man said. He spat into the water just as the popping bug, which had been sitting motionless, disappeared beneath the surface with a loud gurgle. The line went taut on the rod and the tip arched toward the bank. Willie suddenly came to life and raised the rod high over his head for leverage. He began to pull in the line, holding the slack between his teeth.

"You got 'im good!" Guidre cried.

The bream sought salvation by veering right and left at the top of the water, then dived, possibly for a log. But with each of its runs Willie took in slack until the fish had been drawn close to the boat. Bream amazed him; much smaller than a bass, they seemed to have ten times the fight. He lifted the rod and the bream came out of the water flapping. Guidre lowered the net and swung the fish into the boat, and gently began removing the hook.

Did she? Willie thought painfully. He couldn't imagine it, but then, yes, he could. Why else would she want to go out with the others? Just to have fun? Hell, no! He wondered how many of them she was screwing. And when they did it. His stomach felt sick. He wondered if she ever thought of him when she screwed them. Probably not, the goddamn bitch! Then why did she see him at all? Because he was a good screw? He certainly wasn't in her "social" class, even if he was a big shot now. Maybe it was for his conversation, he thought bitterly. Yeah, he was a great conversationalist. Guidre's words came back to him.

"Everybody screws."

The canoe drifted gently with the tide, Willie casting far in front of it, and it was quiet except for the zinging of the line overhead and the pop of the fly on the water. They rounded a bend and the bayou widened and there were several inlets that fingered into it. The swamp at this point became an enormous maze; sloughs and tiny creeks and inlets and bayous twisted in oxbows and cuts and bights back and forth into each other so that it became almost

307

impossible to tell where one was going, and difficult to remember where one had been. The sun roared silently in the white August sky.

Willie's arm was cocked for a cast when the bullet struck in front of him, just at the gunnel of the canoe. Wood splinters flew into his face and he made a startled sound, a sort of chirp, and then the report of a rifle, a heavy rifle, echoed down the bayou and reverberated in the swamp. Ahead, several large swamp birds took flight. Both men were too surprised to say anything; they were both stammering. Moments later, a second shot crashed into the side of the canoe just behind Willie and drilled a clean hole through both sides and splattered into the water on the other side.

At once, Guidre cried out, "Goddamn it, somebody's shooting!" And then he yelled at the top of his lungs, "Hey! Hey! Stop shooting!" just as the third shot caught him in the shoulder and lifted him clear out of the boat and into the water, almost as though he had been tugged over by a line. The canoe wobbled and almost capsized.

Willie was stunned for what seemed like minutes, but were actually long, agonizing seconds, and then a fourth shot hit just below the gunnel in front of him and he felt the bullet strike his leg near the calf and rip flesh and he cried out in terror and pain and disbelief, as the old man had cried, still believing they were mistakenly being fired at by some idiot or idiots who couldn't see them. "Hey! Hey! Stop it!" Another shot whined overhead and threw up a geyser of water near the far shore. By this time Willie collected himself long enough to grab a paddle and reverse the canoe back to the spot where Guidre was thrashing in the water. Blood from the hole torn in his shoulder stained the water, and Willie saw the look of horrible bewilderment on the old man's face, the eyes, white and wide, looking at him as he drew nearer. It was then that he became aware of the high-pitched sound of the airboat from the direction in which the fire had come, and as he reached out and seized Guidre by his shirt collar, he glanced over his shoulder and saw the boat with the two men, side by side in the high seat with their strange rubber dust goggles, bearing down on them, and the man on the right side held a rifle in his lap and seemed to be struggling to reload it.

Willie paddled with all his strength, one-armed, still holding Guidre by the collar, dragging him alongside the boat. Because steering was impossible this way, the canoe veered, naturally and providentially, into one of the sloughs. Willie crossed the paddle over, backhanded, and began to dig into the stream. The canoe straightened for a moment and began to veer the other way. The roar of the airboat drew closer. He realized that he had to get the old man back into the boat, so he lay the paddle down and heaved mightily until he had him half in and half out. Guidre had said nothing during all of this. Not a cry nor a statement. The blood spattered the bottom and sides of the canoe. Willie thrust the old man's legs into the boat and grabbed the paddle again. Ahead was a stand of marshy brush where the slough seemed to end. He dug the paddle deep into the water, frantically, and brought the canoe hard aground just as the airboat rounded the point where the slough entered the bayou. The airboat stopped, and as Willie stepped out into knee-deep muck, he saw the man with the rifle raise it to his shoulders and take aim again. Instinctively Willie went to ground, lying in the muck beside the canoe. The shot pinged overhead and tore through the marsh grass behind him. "Hey, you idiots—stop it!" Willie cried desperately. What was happening was far beyond belief.

As the man raised the rifle for another shot, Willie squirmed around to the bow of the canoe and took hold of a mooring ring. The muck was just slushy enough so that he could pull the boat forward. He managed to get his feet under him in a sort of squat and heaved with all his might and the canoe drew into the thick marsh grass. Guidre, lying in the bottom, his head resting on one of the thwarts, was gasping and holding his hand over the gushing shoulder wound. Willie heard the airboat's engine rev again, and it began to move down the slough toward them.

He hauled the canoe deeper and deeper into the swamp. The marsh grass quickly gave way to denser cover. Tall trees and cypress knees and the bog became thigh-deep. The wound in his leg was throbbing. Back at the end of the slough, he heard the airboat's engine idle, and he heard muffled voices.

It was a slip-stumble path between giant cypress trees and rotting logs and branches. He had to heave one of the logs out of the way and he suddenly saw a thick moccasin coiled on top of it, only inches away from his hand. The snake slid calmly into the water and squirmed away, not far from his legs. He managed to get the boat twenty or thirty yards, then collapsed, gasping, holding onto the bow and looking at the eyes of the old guide. He seemed to be asleep; his eyelids were barely open and he had stopped breathing so heavily. His hand was still at the wound. When Willie regained some of his breath he turned around and began to search the growth ahead for some way out. To his right he thought he spotted clear water but he wasn't sure, so he staggered forward, leaving the boat. He thrashed through brambles and saw grass until he saw a wide bayou about forty yards away. From the direction of the slough he heard the airboat's engine suddenly rev again and begin to fade away. He returned to the canoe and, by pushing this time, guided it into the water of the bayou.

Once again in the boat, Willie seized the paddle and began to head down what looked like the widest part of the bayou. He wasn't sure where he was, but he figured that would offer the best chance to get back into the main stream, which would lead to the camp and his own Dauber boat. His heart raced uncontrollably, the sun was white and menacing overhead and the bottom of the canoe was stained with dark red blood and swamp water and coal-black muck from the bogs. Guidre's face had turned a sallow gray, and his breathing seemed painfully slow.

Whitsey Loftin was on her way out of the store to go to lunch when the phone rang. It was Johnathan Holt.

"Hey, Whitsey," he said, "how'ya doin?"

"Fine, John. What's up with you?" The call surprised her. She hadn't seen her cousins in months.

"You know that feller you know, the lawyer against our family, that punched Percy at the Azalea Ball?"

"Willie Croft," she said. "What about him?"

"Well, he might be in some kind of trouble."

"What kind of trouble? What do you mean?"

"Well, I was over to supper at Brev's house last night and Percy was there and after supper they were in the den and I sort of heard them arguing and I went in to see what it was but they shut up. But from what I heard, it was about this guy—Croft—and they were going to have him beaten or something."

"What!" Whitsey cried. "Who was?"

"Well, I think it was Percy, because Brev sounded like he was arguing against it or something. He kept saying, 'You can't do it,' and, 'I won't have anything to do with it,' and he got real mad, and so did Percy. And I heard him say something about the feller was going up to the Delta someplace around Humbar Lake today, and that they had some guys or something who were going up there to . . ."

"My God, he is! He did go up there fishing today," Whitsey cried.

"Well, I came into the room then, and both of them shut up and I asked what was going on and they said it wasn't nothing. And I said I heard some, and Percy said for me to keep out of it, that it was between him and Brev, and then Brev walked out of the room. That's all I know, but I don't like it, whatever it was they were goin' to do."

Whitsey didn't say anything for a moment, trying to think. Percy certainly was mean enough to do something. It wasn't Brevard's style, though. But it sounded bad.

"John," she said, "I don't know what all this is about. I'm going to call Brev."

"No," he said, "please don't do anything like that. He'd get mad as hell at me for telling you. They're kind of mad at you now, you know. Especially after that thing with Marci. I never did get the . . ."

"All right, then, listen. You know that place up there, don't you? And you have a boat. I want you to pick me up as soon as you can and we're going to go up there and tell

Willie Croft what you've heard so he can look out for whoever it is."

"Aw, Whitsey, I can't do that. Brev and . . ."

"John, I don't care a damn about Brev and Percy! They're talking about hurting somebody. You have to."

"I can't, Whitsey," the big man said dejectedly. "I just couldn't do anything like that against Brev and Percy. I don't care what it is, they're my brothers. And this guy . . ."

"Well, then, I'll just have to do it myself," she said fiercely.

"Awe, you can't go up there, Whitsey. That Delta's enormous. Who knows where he'd be? How could you find him? Besides, it's dangerous country around there."

"I'm going to do something, John. I'll tell you that. I'm going to do something!"

Willie had ripped up his shirt and tied it around the wound in his leg. It throbbed painfully but most of the bleeding had stopped, and the bullet apparently had not struck a bone. Guidre lay ashen-faced in the bottom of the canoe. He had gone into what Willie assumed was shock, then revived for a while, and now lapsed back. Willie had been paddling for more than an hour through the tangled waterways. Each time he thought he was on a main artery it petered out to a slough or a dead end or simply returned them where they had been before. Several times he had heard the drone of the airboat, which was obviously searching for them.

Guidre groaned and opened his eyes. He saw Willie and tried to raise his head.

"Don't move," Willie said; "just lie still. I'm going to get the boat and get us back."

The old man lifted himself painfully on an elbow and looked over the gunnels of the canoe, studying the banks. "Where are we?" he asked weakly.

"I'm not quite sure," Willie said. "I think I've been covering a lot of the same ground. I pulled us through that swamp, but I'm not sure I've even been here before. There's got to be a cutback into the lake sometime soon."

"Keep taking lefts," Guidre said. "That's the way the cuts usually work up here. Sooner or later you'll get back in the main stream."

"Do you want some water? Or anything?" Willie said. He noticed the old man's lips looked dry and parched. Guidre shook his head.

"You know who they were, Willie?"

"Yeah, I think so," he said slowly. "Has to do with that business I've gotten in. With the Holts, I think. Something like that."

Guidre nodded knowingly. "They still around?"

"I'm afraid so," Willie said. "I hear the boat every once in a while."

Guidre's eyelids drooped and he let out a heavy breath. Willie steered the canoe left down the first slough he came to, then left again, then he saw a narrow opening through some swamp grass that led to a long, straight stretch of bayou overhung by scrubby trees. He shoved the canoe through the opening, and halfway down the bayou he saw where it reentered the lake. And in the distance, halfway across the wide water, he glimpsed the airboat skimming along.

He guided the canoe skillfully along the edge of the bank so that it wouldn't be seen from the lake and drew up just at the lake edge behind a tall stand of marsh grass. There was a clump of trees behind him and a small patch of low, but fairly solid ground beneath them. He pulled the canoe to the bank and stepped out. From the little hummock beneath the trees he had a good view of most of the lake. They had come back into it well below the bayou they had first entered. The camp was a quarter of the way around to the right, and he could see it clearly. Willie spied a man standing on the wharf. He had a rifle in his hand. The other man was cruising in the airboat, alone.

Already, Willie was formulating a plan.

When he got back to the canoe Guidre was awake again, and had propped himself up on one of the thwarts.

"You think you can get out of the canoe and get over to that little patch of ground?" Willie said.

313

"I reckon," said the old man. The shirt Willie had stuffed into his wound was stained with blood.

"All right, let me help you." He half carried Guidre to the hummock and put him down gently as he could.

"What you gonna do?" Guidre asked.

"You're gonna have to keep still for a little bit," Willie said. "Just let me take care of this."

"What you gonna do?" the old man said again.

"Get us home," Willie said.

He took a paddle from the canoe and held one end of the mooring line in his hand, then, wading in waist-deep water, he guided the canoe to the mouth of the little bayou, past the marsh grass. Crouching in the marsh grass he waited until the man in the airboat was close to the center of the lake, where he thought he would have a good chance of spotting them. Then Willie eased the canoe out into the lake, still holding onto the end of the mooring line.

The airboat continued on its patrol, as Willie crouched for long, agonizing seconds in the marsh grass, using the paddle for support. Suddenly the airboat veered in their direction and Willie eased the canoe back into the slough and out of sight. The airboat was coming straight at them now, and he could see the lone goggled figure perched in the control seat. A rifle rested beside him.

About fifty yards away the man slowed the airboat and craned forward, looking for the canoe. Then he saw the entrance to the slough and gunned the throttle again. He slowed down once more just before the entrance, as Willie knew he would, and he remained at a slow speed as he passed the marsh grass where Willie crouched.

Just as the bow of the airboat came past him Willie sprang up with the paddle and swung. The blade of the paddle caught the man square in the face with a sickening thud. He must have reflexively pulled back on the throttle because the boat seemed to shoot out of the water and spin crazily away from Willie. It took one great jump sideways and flipped completely over; the propeller blade threw up a rainstorm of lake water in the seconds before the engine died. Then a silence rolled back in.

Willie had not anticipated this. The boat had flipped over on the man. He waded toward it, but the water quickly deepened and he had to swim. The boat floated bottom up and the man was not visible. Willie dove beneath the boat and tried to feel around. It was about eight or ten feet deep at that point, but the bottom was a deep muck of rotting logs and thick, kelpy grass. He wanted that rifle. He surfaced and made another dive. He felt along the bottom until his breath was about to give out and as he surfaced again he bumped into a floating object. It was the body of the man in the airboat.

Willie swam back to the shore and hauled himself panting onto higher ground. Guidre was lying with his back propped up against a log. He looked a little better. His eyes were open and he was holding the shirt over the wound.

"The damned airboat's ruined," Willie said. "I gotta get my boat."

The old man seemed to comprehend this. "Shore wish I had my gun," he said faintly.

"Yeah, me too," Willie said. "Listen, I'm going to have to leave you here for a little bit, okay?"

"You goin' after him?"

"I got to. I gotta get that boat back."

"Well, why can't we paddle out?" said Guidre. "No need for it."

"Hell, we can," Willie said. "It'd take two days. You gotta get to a doctor. Besides, that other bastard's gonna know somethin's up before long and come looking for his partner and when he finds out what's happened, he'll run us down in my own damned boat. He ain't gonna be looking for me now. I gotta do it now."

Willie couldn't use the canoe for fear of being spotted, so he set off on foot around the lake edge toward the cabin. He kept as close to the water as he could without being seen—because there was less swampy undergrowth there—but sloughs and creeks kept blocking his way and he would have to swim across these. Finally nearer the camp, he reached a boggy, moccasin-infested stretch with high trees and cypress knees and roots and waist-deep muck. He was making his way through this as best as he could when he saw the big alligator sliding toward him.

He began to back up, trying to get out of the muck. He still had the paddle. The alligator's head was cutting a rippled vee path through the water. It was a big one. Willie nearly backed into a water moccasin resting on a log. The snake plopped into the water and swam away.

Willie felt a panic rising and he fought the urge to turn and run away wildly, knowing that the alligator could overtake him easily. They were ordinarily docile, and kept away from man. What had provoked this one's curiosity, Willie didn't know. As the alligator drew nearer, Willie raised the paddle as a club, then, almost instinctively, he lowered it, swordlike. The creature was suddenly within reach and Willie thrust out the paddle and poked it toward the alligator's snout. It thrashed in the water, then turned smoothly and sped away in the direction from which it had come. Willie took a few moments to collect himself, then went on his way.

It took him nearly another hour to get close to the camp. He could barely make it out through the dense undergrowth. Every muscle in his body ached. God, he thought, I am out of shape. Carefully, he stole closer until he saw the man, walking on the wharf, the rifle in his hand. There could be no mistakes now.

It was afternoon and the sun was just above the tops of the trees. Willie was crouched behind the spread-out roots of a huge cypress tree, panting heavily, watching the man on the wharf. He was waiting for the man to walk closer to the camp itself; Willie didn't dare move until then for fear of being seen. The horror of the morning had barely begun to sink in. It was a weird and peculiar feeling, hiding in the swamp beside his own familiar cabin, about to fight for his life with an armed and vicious stranger. Memories of his father and the times they had come up here kept creeping incongruously into his thoughts. He shoved them out. He had to move soon. He might have to kill a man with his bare hands.

The man seemed to be looking for his friend. He paced to the end of the wharf, then back again, straining for a sight of the airboat. Then he turned his back on Willie and began walking back toward the cabin. Willie crept closer until he was within a few yards of the end of the wharf. He could not see the man now, and he hoped fearfully that the man could not see him either. Again he waited.

Suddenly he heard the starter of his boat come alive and the engine turn over. He had to act fast. Just as it caught and began to idle, he plunged beneath the wharf in waist-deep water, ignoring a fat moccasin lying on a stump. The man had stepped out of the cockpit of the boat, leaving the motor running, and was standing on the covered bow untying the line from the wharf. Willie could see him only from his knees down, but that was enough. He lunged up and grabbed the man at the knees, toppling him into the water. The man gave a startled cry and landed almost on top of him, but Willie seized him around the neck with his arm rolled over so that the man's head was underwater. With his right hand he gouged for the eyes. The man thrashed and strained like a speared fish but he was smaller than Willie and could not break the hold. He clawed at Willie's arm. Then Willie brought him to the surface, so that just the head was above water, and he punched three or four short chopping blows to the man's face. One of them broke the man's nose; Willie could feel it crunch. Blood streamed down and Willie ducked the head under again. The man continued to thrash and kick and his head appeared above water again and he began to scream and beg. Willie punched him again, doing further damage to the nose. The man had taken in a good deal of water and was gagging on it. Willie knew he had the upper hand. He climbed painfully onto the low dock at the base of the wharf and hauled the man up on it. The man began to throw up.

Using some docking line from the boat Willie tied the man's hands behind him, and his feet as well, and left him lying on the wharf. He shut off the boat engine and staggered into the cabin and began to shake uncontrollably. It took him several minutes to settle down, and he poured a stiff drink from the whiskey bottle on the table, then went back outside. The man had recovered somewhat too, although his nose was a horrible mess; a piece of white bone protruded from its bridge. The man stared up pitifully at Willie.

"All right," Willie demanded, "why?" He felt animal-like. The wound in his leg ached badly and his arms and back were clawed from the man's fingernails.

The man did not reply.

Willie kicked him in the shin and he cringed.

"Don't screw with me, you bastard!" Willie snarled. "Who put you up to it? The Holts, wasn't it?"

The man whimpered, but didn't answer. Willie glanced around for the rifle. He saw it lying in the cockpit of the boat and as he stepped down to get it, he saw the water moccasin still lying on the stump, sullenly, oblivious to the drama that had just been played out between the two men. Willie stepped up on the wharf and picked up the frog gig. The snake was not even looking at him when he speared it just behind the head, but it writhed viciously and twisted around the prongs and the shank end of the gig. He lifted it up and put the gig down a few inches from the man's face on the wharf.

"Who was it?" Willie said coldly.

The man's eyes were terror-filled, pleading, but he still said nothing. Willie picked up the gig and moved the snake close to the man's face. The snake's mouth gaped savagely.

"Was it the Holts?" Willie said.

"Yes!" the man cried. "Get it away!"

"Which Holts?" Willie demanded.

"Mr. Percy—please take it away!" The man squirmed back as far as he could.

Willie continued holding the snake only inches from the man's face.

"What's your name?" Willie said.

"Crenshaw," the man replied quickly.

"Yeah, Crenshaw. I know all about you. You set fire to that house up at Creoletown, right?"

The man nodded.

"That the Holts' doing too, right?"

"Yeah."

"How much did they pay you?"

"Four thousand apiece. We're supposed to get more later."

"You're cut off as of now," Willie said.

He went inside the cabin and got the first-aid kit from a drawer and sat in a chair to dress his wound. The bullet had torn through the side of his calf and left a two-inch gash of torn flesh, but it had not found an artery or muscle and it was not bleeding badly. Willie applied some iodine with a cotton swab and gave a forced cry of pain. Tears came to his eyes. He hastily wrapped a gauze bandage around the wound, and went back outside, taking the first-aid kit with him. Snake Crenshaw hadn't moved and gazed at him balefully. Willie stared down at him for a moment, then got into his boat and cranked the engine and released the dock line.

The big Dauber-built planed quickly as he turned it across the lake toward the place he had left Guidre. He saw that the wrecked airboat had drifted away from the mouth of the slough, farther out into open water. He passed it by, slowed, and drove the boat as close to the bank as he could, then got out in thigh-deep water and pulled it the rest of the way. He had to wade through some bog and marsh grass to get to the little hummock. His leg throbbed rhythmically.

The old man was lying just as Willie had left him, with his head propped up against the trunk of the tree. His hand was over the wound, pressing at it with the shred of Willie's shirt. But the cloth was blood-soaked and stiffening, and the ground around it was drenched with the life of the old man. The grizzled face was finally serene; the eyes were half closed, as though he were watching Willie; motionless, like an old Indian.

Willie clenched the helm tightly as the boat skimmed along the glassy-flat river in the fast-descending twilight. Behind him, huddled in a corner of the big open cockpit, was Snake Crenshaw, trussed up hand and foot like a hog. Every once in a while during the past two hours Willie had glanced back at him, but not as much as he might have otherwise, because he could not avoid seeing the body of his old friend, lying faceup, covered with a blanket. Willie felt terrible. That it was his fault, although he could not possibly have known what was going to happen. But the old, barking, grimy-fingered, wrinkle-faced man he'd known since he'd been old enough to know anything was dead. Dead instead of him.

There comes a time in almost everyone's life when he truly knows the loss of innocence, and though some people either cannot or will not recognize it, still they know it somehow. It might be as simple as the loss of virginity, or as dark and wicked as an overwhelming impulse to kill or to see someone dead, but whatever the incident, it is almost inevitable that every human will experience it, and Willie Croft was feeling it now with an intensity he had not believed possible before.

These people were actually willing to murder him. Him! Willie Croft. And had in fact murdered an old man, and an old woman—for money. All for money.

Or was it something else too?

Was it revenge, or pride, or fear of what he knew? Or perhaps a combination of all those. Whatever it was, Willie could scarcely believe it; probably wouldn't have believed it if someone had told him before, and found it difficult to believe even now, except for the incontrovertible proof, lying in the cockpit behind him. He turned the boat around a bend and saw a railroad bridge ahead. In a few minutes he would be at the landing.

"Something terrible's happened, Sam," Willie said to the aged Negro dock tender. "Will you tie her up and keep an eye on that guy there in the back?"

The black man's eyes were wide with fright. "Who under the blanket, Mr. Croft?"

"I've got to call the sheriff," Willie said. "I'll tell you in a few minutes." He went inside and placed the call, then returned to the boat.

"A lady come 'roun' heah lookin' fuh yew, 'bout fo', five hours 'go," Sam said. "She say she want to know where yew wuz, an I tole her yew up the river. She seem upset, an' say she be back."

"What was her name, Sam?"

"Didden say her name."

"What kind of car was she driving?"

"I don' know zactly. I bleeve a white one."

"Okay, thanks, Sam. You mind staying here a few more minutes while I make another call?"

"I don' mind, but who under the blanket?"

"It's Guidre, Sam. This guy and another one shot him."

"He daid?"

"Yeah, Sam, he is," Willie said sadly.

He went back inside and dialed Whitsey's number. She answered the first ring.

"Any reason you were looking for me?" Willie said. There was an iciness in his voice that he hadn't intended.

"Oh, Willie, you're back!" she said. "I was just kind of worried about you. I, ah, I don't know . . . I had heard something—I guess it's not important now. Are you at home?"

"No, I'm not at home. I'm at the landing with a dead man in the back of my boat and a goddamn murderer tied up, waiting for the sheriff." There was a silence at her end of the line.

"A . . . a . . . dead? Who's dead?"

"Guidre. They shot him."

"Who did?" she gasped.

"Two thugs," he said.

He told her what he knew of the story, and she listened without saying anything until he'd finished. "My God," she said, "oh, my God, oh, my God, I . . . I . . . don't . . . I can't believe it. . . ."

"Not very pretty, is it?" he said coolly.

"I'm coming down there now."

"No," he said. "I'll call you later. There're a lot of things I'm going to have to do for a while."

"Oh, Willie," she said, "I want to. I want to be with you. I know how much you loved him."

"I'll call you later," he said. "There's going to be a lot of business with the sheriff. And then I'd just like to be alone for a while."

20

Autumn came to Bienville later than usual, and lasted well into what would be winter farther up north. The days were warm and brilliant and the nights were cool, with football games on green fields with golden autumn leaves and dances in high-school gymnasiums and quail shooting in fields bursting with fiery reds and browns and yellows, goldenrod, broomstraw and the scent of pine. Speckled trout began to run in the rivers and the pastures outside of town resounded with the noise of dove shooters. This had been so for as many years back as anyone cared to remember, for Bienville had never been a place where change was welcome or even had made appreciable inroads.

Until now.

Obsidian Oil was a strong and successful corporation, and the oil and the money continued to flow, and if no single individual connected with it was yet a millionaire, it appeared that would soon change. They were on their way to paying off their debts, purchases of new equipment were nearly complete and the plan to buy the Bayfield refinery was well under way. Because of the money that the company spent in the town and the people it hired, Obsidian was becoming a respectable name to be associated with in the white community, and now even Daniel himself and other Negro officials were being courted. They were, of course, not invited into private homes, or the country club (which had flatly rejected Daniel's application, saying, as Shambeaux predicted, that it would first close its doors). But there had been several occasions when black men and white men wined and dined together in restaurants carefully selected for a noncommittal segregationist policy. Daniel himself met regularly with city and county officials to discuss how the operation could be coordinated to the best interest of all the citizens. While in other parts of the South there were walk-ins, sit-ins, teach-ins, boycotts, eat-ins, wade-ins, police dogs, ax handles and flaring tempers, Bienville found itself discussing the possibility of its first interracial football game, the result of a suggestion Daniel had made to the school board chairman at a meeting of county commissioners.

Meantime, to save his own skin, Snake Crenshaw had talked following his arrest and implicated the Holts, Percy and Brevard, as well as Augustus Tompkins in the killings of the old Negro woman and Guidre. All languished in jail awaiting trial for double murder. The scandal had received enormous publicity in the city and state and even got some national coverage.

One day Willie ran into Daniel in the hallway of Obsidian Oil.

"Hi," Daniel said, "looks like you're in a hurry."

"I've got to be over at the jail in fifteen minutes. Got a meeting set up with the Holt brothers to sign those papers over to us."

"Really," Daniel said. "That's today, is it?"

Working through Tompkins's law firm, Willie had finally hammered out an agreement with the Holt family so that Daniel's mother could take full, legal possession of her property. Rather than fight an appeal, Willie had offered a sum of money to get clear title—twenty-five thousand dollars, ironically, the same amount Brevard Holt had first offered Mrs. Backus to buy her out. The Holts had accepted and Willie needed their signatures on the documents.

"They're bringing them down at three o'clock," Willie said.

"You know," said Daniel, "I'd like to go along if you don't mind."

It was a gloomy November afternoon when the Holt brothers, haggard and ruined men, were led into a small room off the cellblock to meet, formally, and for the first time, their flesh-and-blood half brother. Neither of them recognized Daniel at first, and when they were introduced by Willie there were nods, but no handshakes, and the four men sat down at a table, Willie and Daniel at one side, and Brevard and Percy on the other.

Daniel smoked a pipe himself, but he had thoughtfully bought two packs of cigarettes on the way over to the courthouse and he offered one to each of the men, which they accepted wearily, pride having long since been driven from their spirits.

"I suppose you've been told what this is about," Willie said. "I've got the papers with me, and I'll need your signatures on three copies and we can settle this thing once and for all."

Percy shifted nervously in his seat and kept his eyes fixed on Daniel. Brevard, however, seemed distracted. His gaze wandered around the room and he breathed in a strange, gasping way, haggard and pale.

"You might want to read them first," Willie said. "Take your time if you like. But they're exactly what has been explained to you already." Percy reached for the sheaf of papers and began signing them. Then he put them in front of Brevard and handed him the pen. Brevard seemed to sigh a little, then slowly began to write his name. When he had finished, Willie took the papers back and examined them, and then put them into his briefcase. He started to stand, then looked at Daniel and eased back down in his chair. Daniel obviously had something he wanted to say.

"Whether or not you accept it," Daniel said, "we are flesh and blood. I didn't know our father well, but of what I do recall of him, he was a kind and generous man."

Percy began to say something, then looked at Brevard, who was gazing blankly at the wall, and touched his brother's hand, and patted it gently until Brevard turned and looked at Daniel with his blinking, vacant stare.

"There is some verse in the play *King John*," Daniel said in his most austere voice: " 'Who dares not stir by day must walk by night, / And have is have, however men do catch. / Near or far off, well won is still well shot, / And I am I, howe'er I was begot.' " He paused and looked at the two men, and they in turn looked back at him, silently trying to comprehend what they had heard.

"The speaker is Philip Faulconbridge, bastard son to King Richard the First," said Daniel. "I, too, am a bastard, a fact which is neither pleasant to remember, nor easy to forget, but the world is filled with us, and we come to live with it. I suppose I'm fortunate that it was your father, because it is making me a wealthy man."

"Can you help us?" Brevard suddenly asked. His voice was weak and plaintive. Percy shot him a glance which, for an instant, seemed hostile, then softened, as though it were the question on his mind too.

Daniel thought for a moment. "I don't know," he said softly. "I don't think so, at least for the moment. Not with respect to your case, anyway. And even if I could, I don't know that I should. But," he said, taking a breath and looking keenly at his two half brothers, "there may come a time."

Brevard put his hand to his face and began massaging his cheeks with his fingers, as though trying to reassure himself that he still had feeling there. Percy took a deep drag from the cigarette Daniel had given him.

"If there's anything you need, in the way of personal comforts, I could see to that—but then I suppose your family is doing that too," Daniel said. "I really don't know why I came here. I suppose I've always felt strongly about blood kin . . ." He let the rest of the sentence trail off, and there was a silence in the little room, and then Daniel got up.

"Well, good-bye," he said, and walked to the door, with Willie behind him.

Just as he was about to leave the room, Brevard Holt called after him in a shaky voice, "Good-bye. . . ."

They didn't talk, Willie and Daniel, until they were crossing The Parade, when Daniel said, almost to himself, "I don't know what I was expecting, going along over there."

Willie looked at him. "I guess they brought it on themselves." But Daniel ignored the remark.

"I suppose I expected to feel something. Some kind of heartbeat—something. . . . Something. . . . But I didn't. I didn't feel anything at all."

They walked on until they were about to cross the street.

"That seems strange, doesn't it?" Daniel said.

"Maybe so," said Willie. "I never had brothers or sisters myself. I guess I wouldn't know." But he did feel something, at that particular moment. Looking at the hurt in Daniel's face, he almost could have cried.

A huge harvest moon appeared over the Bay, then arched to the sky, bright and silvery on the night of the grand opening of Beaudreux's new place in town. The restaurant was crowded and seemed even more so reflected in the mirrors on the walls. On Willie's recommendation, Daniel had persuaded the board members of Obsidian to back Beaudreux in his new venture which, whether or not it turned a profit, would provide them with a decent place where they could eat unmolested near the Obsidian offices.

Beaudreux himself was ebullient and glad-handing everyone as they came through the door. It was a peculiar crowd, possibly the vanguard of a new order in Bienville. Mixed with a dozen or so top-ranking officials of Obsidian and their wives was an assortment of city and county officials, businessmen and others looking for associations with the corporation. Buffet tables had been set up at one end of the room with a magnificent seafood feast: platters of boiled crawfish, shrimp, whole red snapper, pompano, oysters on the half shell and fresh lump crabmeat.

There was also a whiskey bar and that was where Willie found Skinner when he shoved past the door crowd with Whitsey Loftin in tow. He had seen more of her in the previous months, and there'd been times when he actually thought it might work out for them, then she would back away. Each time she did he felt himself being sucked in deeper. Recently she had consumed his thoughts so thoroughly, violating his most private feelings and emotions, that he knew he had to do something about it. Perhaps tonight was the time.

"Well, podner, how you doin'?" Skinner lifted his glass. "Evening, Whitsey," he said.

"It's good to see you again." She smiled. "We don't see you often enough." There was a warmth in her voice that Willie felt had been lacking toward him when he picked her up. He wondered if he had just imagined it.

"Well, take a good look," Skinner said. "Gonna see less of me before long."

"What's that mean?" Willie asked.

"Movin' on," he said. "Job's pretty much finished here. Everything's runnin' right. Gotta get on down the line before I start feeling useless."

"For heaven's sake," Willie said, "there's still a thousand things to do. We have to finish that Bayfield business and there's . . ."

Skinner held up his hand and stopped him. "That's all taken care of, or at least it will be," he said. "Besides, I'm getting restless. I told you at the beginning I was just in for limited duty."

"Yeah, I guess you did," Willie said. He tried to hide the disappointment in his voice.

"Where are you going to go?" Whitsey asked.

"Gold!" Skinner cried. "To hell with oil from now on. I'm going after gold. South America maybe. Not as dirty."

"South America?"

"No, gold."

"When are you leaving?" Willie asked.

"Oh, maybe next week sometime. I guess I'd better tell Daniel, huh? There he is; I rec'on I ought to do it now. See y'all." Skinner lurched off, glass in hand, toward Daniel Holt.

"I'll be damned," Willie said.

"It's too bad," Whitsey said, "he's so nice."

Beaudreux suddenly appeared behind them and put a large, meaty hand on Willie's shoulder. "Ah, Mistair Croff, iss real now, eh! With air condition and everythin'." He swept his arm around the room. "I never believe I have such a place of my own. Now I don't have ta cook in no shack—an' all because of you." For a moment Willie thought he was going to be hugged.

"Well, that wasn't a shack, now," Willie said. "I like the other place."

"Ahhhh, but so much better here!" Beaudreux gurgled. "Now you won't have to eat on dos ole wobble tables, and you can jus' order a glass of whiskey—and air condition in summer weather, man, oh, man, I tell you . . ."

"You don't mean you're closing the old place?" Willie asked incredulously.

"Got to," Beaudreux said. "How Beaudreux gonna go back an' forth every day, up here, down dere, and cook for people? Beside, if dem people down dere wan' eat Beaudreux's food, dey can come up here an' eat it. Better place."

"But I thought you were going to have both of them," Willie said. "I mean, that's part of the charm, the old place, being able to go down there and get away from here."

"I don't know 'bout dat," Beaudreux said. "Dis place much easier to get to, you know? An' when I make a little money, I'm gonna move uptown here too. Say, you know I jus' talk to the *Mayor of Bienville!* Dat's him, right over dere, stan' by the wall. In Beaudreux's place, imagine dat!"

"Yeah," Willie said glumly, "must have been a fascinating conversation."

"Oh, oh, heah come some more," Beaudreux said. "I better go say hello, huh?" He moved off toward the door.

"I'll be goddamned," Willie said, shaking his head.

Whitsey patted him gently on the arm. "Looks like things are changing," she said.

"Don't do that, will you?" he snapped.

"Do what?"

"Pat me, or whatever it is; it makes me feel like you're doing it to a child."

"I don't mean to." There was a flash of hurt in her eyes. Then she said, "Do you want to try the food? It looks delicious."

"Sure," he said. They walked around the buffet table, picking a little, and exchanging small talk with people. Willie didn't eat much, but got himself another drink. Goddamn it, he thought as he was waiting, goddamn it! Some fearful curtain of loneliness descended over him as he looked around the room, a swirling sea of faces, the talking and the buzzing blending into a sour noise. For a moment he wanted to be anywhere else in the world but here. He took a deep swallow of the drink when it came and the bourbon slid down his throat and into his stomach, hot, sweet, good. He felt a little better, and then he saw Whitsey, talking with a younger man in a plaid sport jacket. She was laughing at what he said and Willie could see that he was eyeing her up and down with carefully stolen glances, checking her out. He marched over to where they were standing.

"This is Brad Barker," she said. "Brad, this is Willie Croft."

"Oh, I know who you are, Mr. Croft," the young man said. "I s'pose everybody in town does. Pleased to meet you." He stuck out his hand.

Willie shook it in a cursory way. "I'd like to talk to you for a minute," he said to Whitsey. "In there, maybe?" He pointed to a closed door which seemed to have an aura of privacy about it.

Whitsey looked almost startled. "Oh, well, ah, sure," she said. "Excuse us for a minute, Brad."

He let her go first but reached around and opened the mystery door. It was dark inside but as the light fell in he could see they were in a large room. At one end were French doors that led to what appeared to be a courtyard. Moonlight streamed in through the doors, revealing an unfinished wing of the restaurant. There were a few tables and chairs, but carpentry work was still being done and there was a smell of sawdust in the air.

"Let's go over there," he said, leading her toward a table beside the French doors. He brushed some sweepings from her chair and held it while she sat down. The moonlight played gently on her face and he could see her eyes, wondering, perhaps a little frightened.

"Will you marry me?" he said.

She giggled. "Is that what you brought me here for?"

"What's wrong with that?"

"Nothing, nothing," she said. Suddenly her tone became somber. She looked at him, puzzled, then looked down at the table and said nothing.

"Well?" he said.

"You're serious, aren't you?" She didn't look up.

"Hell, yes, I'm serious. I want you to marry me. I want you to be my wife. Isn't that serious?" Of course he already knew what her answer was going to be, but he had to ask the question anyway. Get it out. Get it over. Somehow he felt it would stop the nagging hurt and let him begin to face the rest of his life.

I am not, he thought, as big a fool as I sometimes think I am.

There was another pause.

"I can't, Willie, I thought you'd know that."

At least he had anticipated the reply. "Well," he said, "I suppose I'm entitled to ask you why not, aren't I?"

"I've already told you why not," she said softly.

"Well, tell me again," he said.

She drew in a breath, then let it out. "It's because I just don't love you. I mean, I do love you, but as a friend, and as a lover too, but I'm not *in* love with you."

"You mean there's nothing there?"

She was silent again, and looked out into the moonlight. A tear came to one of her eyes and rolled down her cheek and began to dry there, wet and salty, as though she knew his pain, and was powerless to do anything about it.

"You mean there's nothing there?" he said again.

"No," she said. "Not what's supposed to be, anyway."

"But why not!" he demanded. "I don't understand it! I haven't understood it all along. We've been making love, you've been going out with me all this time. What did it mean?"

"We've been through this before, Willie." Her voice was quiet, even. "I've never led you on, I've always told you the truth. It just isn't there, and it isn't going to be."

"But I love you!" he said.

"And I can't love you. I've thought about it, I think I even tried once, but I couldn't."

"But all of this, what I'm doing, this whole thing—I, I . . ."

"I am sharing it with you," she said. "As a friend."

"Friend," he murmured, "friend. You said that before, didn't you? But friends don't—they don't *screw!*" he stammered.

"It was nice, Willie. I'll always remember it that way."

"Oh, so now you're saying that's the end of it, then?"

"I didn't say that."

"But that's what you mean, isn't it?"

"I don't know. After something like this, it's not easy to go back to the way things were."

"No, I guess it isn't," he said.

"There was something I was going to tell you tonight anyway," she said. "I'm going over to New Orleans Friday. To see a somebody I met a month or so ago. They're having a party and I . . ."

"I don't want to hear about it," he said.

"Well, I thought it wouldn't be right if I didn't say something."

"Yeah," he said, "that makes it right. That makes it fine."

They did not talk much on the way home. Willie clenched the steering wheel fiercely and his heart raced, but he tried not to let it show. He wanted very much to say something, to bring it up again, or for her to bring it up, say it was all a mistake, lean over and touch him; even if she said she wasn't really sure, that maybe she'd like to try again . . . he would have settled for that.

But she didn't and they spoke only one or two times, strained small talk, once about a slow-turning car in front of them and again when she mentioned the cool weather. She was going to buy a new sweater.

"It might turn cold over there," she said. "You *know* how it gets in New Orleans."

As though he might be remotely interested in the weather over there.

That was another practice she'd developed recently: little dropped reminders of other people she was seeing. He wondered, as he had before, if she were merely insensitive, or being purposely cruel. But it didn't really matter anymore.

Everything between them had finally ended; he knew it, and so did she. The trump card he'd played had vanished into the void, unable to penetrate the nothingness to the other side where love waited, or might have waited, unfulfilled.

She had taken him in, held him tightly, loved him for a while in her own way, but he realized now she simply couldn't break out of the mold. She might *step* out of it perhaps, temporarily, but in the end she was so firmly fixed within it that no matter how much she might have wanted to leave it, to be free to love a man like himself—even when her reason and her heart told her to—something else held her back. Convention, uncertainty, perhaps even fear, but whatever it was, Whitsey was one of those women who could actually *convince* herself that she wasn't in love, or couldn't be in love.

At least that's the way he saw it. Bienville was that way—a way of life, not his Bienville, but the *other* Bienville, the one he'd never be a part of, no matter how good, or rich, or decent, or witty he was or might become, because he hadn't been born to it. Ham Bledsole told him once that it didn't matter how far you strayed, sooner or later you came home; that Bienville was a way of life. But not for him. Never for him.

Well, he thought, well, well . . . and suddenly he was struck by the false and temporary elation that causes people to feel good when they shouldn't, and see their lives differently than they have before. He was grateful for it, temporary or not, and when they reached her house he made an effort to get out of the car and go around and open her door. On the front porch he leaned and kissed her lightly on the forehead.

"See you around," he said.

Whitsey shifted awkwardly. "Would you like to come in for a drink or something?" The way she said "something" made him wonder for a moment what the *something* might have been, but he thought better of it.

"Nah," he said, "I'm thinking of giving it up."

But he didn't that particular night. It was medicine then, and he knew how to use it. There was half a case of Jack Daniel's Black Label in his kitchen cabinet bar, but he fumbled behind the bottles and felt around until he found the old half-full Early Times. He poured a glassful, over ice, listened to ice crackle and stirred it with his finger. He draped his new wool sport coat over his shoulders, the way he once had seen a Frenchman do in a movie, and stepped outside. The moon was a ball of brilliance, creeping silently westward. He ambled across the street to the deer park, bathed in the thin moonglow beneath the grotesque and ominous oaks. The marble fountain had been turned off for the night and an eerie silence enveloped the whole neighborhood. Most lights were out and no cars disturbed the quiet. The Iron Deer stood in its place, silent and proud.

Willie sat on the park bench near the deer and sipped his drink. Tomorrow would come in a few hours, and he was only slightly worried at the prospect of waking up to the new and different day. It was as though a small era of his life had ended that night, insignificant perhaps to the rest of the world, but it had, and was made all the more real because he actually felt he could see the passage of time marked from that chill November morning when Priscilla Holt had come to him with her story, and his seeing Mrs. Backus and Mrs. Loftin and Whitsey and the rest, and the fight at the party, and the fire, and meeting Skinner and Tallulah and the others, and the trial, and the murder of old Guidre, and Beaudreux's moving.

A year, he thought, a year.

He had fallen in love, and failed at it, and had put together a company, and was successful at that, and people knew his name and he had some money, but what did it all mean? Why couldn't it have happened earlier in his life?

The shadows and the light of the moon danced on the old Iron Deer and a light breeze sifted through the tops of the oaks. He needed a change.

To what, though?

He was tired of all the paperwork, tired of being a big shot. All his life before had been a series of tiny blips and he had never asked for it any other way. He'd never had to wonder what he'd do on a given night or day. He *knew*.

Willie rattled the ice in his glass and shivered reflexively from the chill. He got up and walked over to the Iron Deer and patted it on the nose. Maybe he would follow Skinner to South America, looking for gold. Or go to New York, or Atlanta. Somewhere.

"Hey, old feller," he said, "you're looking good. You're my buddy, aren't you?" He ran his fingers over the Iron Deer's eyes.

No, he knew what he was going to do. Knew instinctively even before tonight, and had known it from the time he had passed by the window of the old cellblock and saw the solitary silhouette of a prisoner, unwaving, wondering. Once again he would become the Groundman, and they would know him, the ones with cutoff ears from knife fights, or the three-card monte sharks and wife beaters and child molesters and automobile thieves, shoplifters, crap-game sponsors, pickpockets, brawlers, small-time embezzlers and safecrackers—the lower end of the wonderful human race, who, despite their felonious intentions, felt the hurt and rage and loneliness that he was feeling now.

Willie circled the Iron Deer, patted its rump as he had so many times in the past, and again felt the urge to climb up and ride on its back.

And this time he did.

He looked to see who might be watching, then hoisted himself with both hands and swung a leg up, careful not to spill the precious contents of his glass. The metal was cold through his pants legs and he leaned back and took a swallow of bourbon. Maybe the first thing he would do Monday morning was go to the courthouse and reestablish himself with the clerk, then tell Daniel of his decision, and then, well, he would spend the rest of the weekend thinking of a new trick to play on Judge McCormack. That might take a day or so, but it didn't really matter now. He knew what he was going to do. At least, that's how he felt tonight. Tomorrow might be different.

Yes, he grudgingly admitted, tomorrow not only *might* be different, it *would* be different. The image of himself becoming the Groundman again began to seep away, fleeting as the wispy clouds that sailed across the fairybook autumn night.

He knew then, Willie did, that when all was counted and sifted through, he could no more go back to being the Groundman than Whitsey Loftin could bring herself to stop perceiving of him as that and nothing more; for he realized that just as it was her irreversible destiny to return to the cloistered, walled-in order of Bienville, it was likewise an utterly necessary motion in his life to escape it, or at the very least to rise beyond it. And so he smiled, and leaned back on the Iron Deer and looked forward to the things that lay ahead.

A year, he marveled—a year.

He was suddenly overcome with a wonderful sense of accomplishment that he had never before known, or thought he would ever know. He had taken a tiny kernel of a plan and nurtured it, and it had worked, by God! It had worked because of him—him! He looked up in awe at the star-filled sky and thought of Whitsey Loftin, rooted in her own little world as firmly as the Iron Deer he was seated upon was rooted to the grass. Well, he thought, they all deserve one another, and so far as his hurt was concerned, time would take care of that. What was important was that he had finally done something in his life he could really be proud of. Nothing could take it away—not even a bullet in the brain.

"Me!" he said to himself, and not quietly. "I *did* it! By God, I *did* it! I really *did* it!"

When he was a child, Willie's parents had taken him once to a pony ride and he remembered nudging at the flanks through the stirrups. He nudged at the old Iron Deer, and would not have been particularly surprised if it had bolted off through the park. But of course it didn't, so he seized its antlers as if they were reins and tried to jiggle them, forward and backward, kicked harder with his heels, pulling and rocking, and shouted numbly over and over, "C'mon, ole boy! Giddyup! C'mon! Giddyup, go!"

Forrest Gump

The book that started it all.

Winston Groom's #1 *New York Times* bestseller, and the inspiration for the Academy Award®-winning film.

Now the phenomenon continues
with the rollicking sequel

Gump & Co.

Coming in Fall 1995 from Pocket Books Hardcover

Don't miss the following wonderfully delectable
Pocket Books, all by Winston Groom

❑ Better Times Than These............52266-3/$5.99
❑ Forrest Gump............................89445-5/$6.99
❑ Gumpisms................................51763-5/$5.00
❑ As Summers Die.......................52265-5/$5.99

POCKET
BOOKS

"Life is like a box of
chocolates...you never know what
you're going to get."
—Forrest Gump